The Real Mackay

The Real Mackay

Helen Graham

Troubador Publishing Ltd
Unit E2 Airfield Business Park,
Harrison Road, Market Harborough,
Leicestershire. LE16 7UL
Tel: 0116 2792299
Email: books@troubador.co.uk
Web: www.troubador.co.uk

ISBN 978 1805143 192

British Library Cataloguing in Publication Data.
A catalogue record for this book is available from the British Library.

Printed by Printed and bound by CPI Group (UK) Ltd, Croydon, CR0 4YY
Typeset in 11pt Minion Pro by Troubador Publishing Ltd, Leicester, UK

This is for you, Mum

1929 - 2019

The immediate motive of my writing to you, my dearest friend, is to make … you aware that a Scots performer, called Mackay, is going up to London to play Bailie Nicol Jarvie for a single night at Covent Garden, and to beg you of all dear loves to go and see him; for, taking him in that single character, I am not sure I ever saw anything in my life possessing so much truth and comic effect at the same time: he is completely the personage of the drama, the purse-proud consequential magistrate, humane and irritable in the same moment, and the true Scotsman in every turn of thought and action: his variety of feelings towards Rob Roy, whom he likes, and fears, and despises, and admires, and pities all at once, is exceedingly well expressed. In short, I never saw a part better sustained.

Extract from Sir Walter Scott's letter to Joanna Baillie, June 11th, 1821

Part One

1788–1828

ONE

'What the devil is that on your skinny back, you wee rascal? Pinched your faither's jacket again to make a mockery of him is it? Get down aff that table at once and let me gie your bahookie a leathering!' Charles's mam lunged for him, eyes glinting, a lookw of barely concealed glee on her sweat-speckled face. Her cheeks, pink and shiny with the heat of the large kitchen, were plastered with dark curls escaping from her linen cap. Charles squealed with delight, jumped onto the flagstone floor and ran around the room, keeping just out of reach of her grasping hands. Suddenly she had him in her arms, strong fingers tickling his ribs, his breath hard to catch with all the laughter bubbling up inside him, his baby brother Peter yelling in his crib all the while.

When their laughter was spent she sat him down by one of the serving girls at the long, cluttered table in the centre of the kitchen, pushed a few turnips and a glistening fish to one side with her forearm and set a bowl in front of him. Charles plunged his hands into the cold water and began to guddle. His mam fetched some muddy potatoes from the scullery and plopped them in the bowl.

'Gie these tatties a wash, would you Charlie?' The serving

girl, busy slicing a pile of onions, looked up and smiled at Charles shyly, her red eyes streaming under the frill of her cap, while his mam picked up the baby and went to sit by the cooking hearth.

He sloshed the tatties about busily, a constant stream of blethering and mimicry pouring out of his mouth, hoping to make his mam smile so her dimple showed, or better still to make her laugh. More than anything, Charles loved making his mam laugh, long and loud. He looked across at her often, watching the brown knitting moving in her lap like a wriggling cat, the baby's head bobbing up and down at her breast. Sometimes she looked up at him and chuckled, mostly she just smiled to herself. Now and then the serving girl went to stir the steaming pots hanging on thick black chains above the fire, tipping in sliced onions or chopped turnips, filling the room with savoury smells.

She was a great storyteller, his mam, a hard worker, too. The only time she sat down was when she was nursing the baby, as far as Charles could see. In the taproom she was always wielding mops and brooms, hauling benches, spreading fresh straw on the earthen floor, trimming tallow candles, swilling and filling tankards; in the kitchen she made mutton pies, shucked oysters, gutted fish, stirred broth and gravy, fetched water and coal, put out the ashes and slops, kept the fire in. His mam had a friendly word for everyone, always remembered names and had a snippy comment or a ribald remark on the tip of her tongue. She never expected the servants to do anything she wasn't prepared to do herself.

Charles loved the way her eyes sparkled when she told stories. His favourite was the one about how they all came to be living in a tavern in the Lawnmarket. Sometimes she made the tale long and winding and full of surprises, sometimes it was shorter than a back alley, but it always started and ended with the same words, and she always pulled him into a hug when she had finished: *Hugh Mackay took the lease on a tavern down a narrow close on the north side of Edinburgh's High Street one frosty morning and proposed to his sweetheart in the evening … and now here we are with two strong boys and the best tavern in town!*

Charles's father was a stern man, too busy to listen to the prattle of his son, quick to skelp his backside or pull his ears if he was out of line. He had a fine voice on him though, could hold a tune like the best of them with a dram or two inside him – or so his mam said.

'Put that women's work away lad and come wi' me the noo!' Charles dropped the tattie he was holding into the bowl, splashing muddy water onto the scrubbed table. He swiped at it with his dirty sleeve and jumped to his feet, wiping his hands on his breeks, wondering how long his father had been standing in the doorway watching, listening, scratching his dark beard with those black fingernails. 'I need you tae help me roll the barrels down the hill from the drey so we can get 'em in the cellar before dusk. Move yersel' now lad, gie yer mam a bit o' peace!' He turned abruptly and disappeared, leaving eddies of sour sweat, bitter tobacco and the rich animal scent of his worn leather apron in his wake.

Rolling barrels was Charles's favourite chore. He grinned at his mam and ran to catch up with his father who was already striding up the steep cobbled close towards the busy High Street.

'Get yersel' up here then, laddie, and nae dawdlin', ya wee bletherskite!'

When Peter learned to walk further than the end of the close, Charles's mam started taking the boys to St Cuthbert's at the foot of the castle rock every Sunday morning. On the way she would tell them stories of the old days when the stinking Nor' Loch stretched from one end of Princes Street to the other, full of drowned witches and other dead bodies; of how the East End was drained and they started building the North Bridge in a deep sea of mud and folk were killed when it collapsed; of the

Orphan's Hospital that used to stand right where the Theatre Royal now stood; of how she used to run down a steep narrow lane from the High Street to watch the stonemasons, back when she was a girl, wondering why they would build such a huge theatre in the middle of fields when they already had one in the High Street. *Folk said it was the Church chased the theatre oot o' the Canongate, mind. They went an' knocked it doon when the new ane opened! Whit a waste!*

There was no smart Princes Street back then for the belles and beaus to parade up and down, hardly anything of the New Town either, just a few houses spread out among the fields. The only way to go to the new theatre was down Leith Wynd. *Nae wonder it took sae long for it tae catch on wi' folk, eh!*

Charles soon learned all the places that sparked his mam's stories and all the words, gestures and expressions she used to tell them. Sometimes he would run ahead and start telling a story by himself, making her laugh and call him her *grand wee mannie.*

St Cuthbert's was the biggest building Charles had ever been inside. He loved the deep echo of it, the hum and thrum of all the people. The first time they went in she whispered in his ear that there was plenty of room for three thousand people and his mouth fell open. She shut it quick smart with a pinch of her fingers, both of them trying not to laugh.

Church was now the highlight of his week.

The hymn had just begun. Charles stood to his full height, shoulders back, hair combed, fingernails almost clean, pulling in a barrelful of air. He opened his mouth wide and let the words he already knew by heart pour out on long breaths, high, loud, sweet and strong. As his voice rose to join all the others Charles imagined them swooping and swirling together in the rafters like a great flock of birds and wished the singing would never end. He wondered if that was how heaven sounded.

When the hymn was over Charles sat on his hands, trying

with all his might not to fidget or poke Peter while the minister's voice droned on and on. If he was good his mam might let them stay for the last hymn.

He was looking up at the huge, arching roof, wondering what it would be like to climb up to the highest gallery and gaze down on the rest of the congregation – maybe he would break loose from his mam's hand one day and find out for himself – when she hissed in his ear.

'Shut your gawping mouth, Charlie boy, a wee beastie might fly in!' His head spun round. She was smiling at him while she fixed the ribbons of her black bonnet, tucking her hair into it haphazardly with quick, jabbing fingers.

'Oh, Mam! Do we *have* tae go home early again? I wanted tae sing another hymn!'

'Whisht now and dinna whinge. You fairly blasted it out earlier son, surely that's enough for one day! Have some mercy on the other puir folk!' She took Peter by the hand and slid with a rustle of Sunday silk to the end of the box pew, opening the little wooden door and slipping away with the children, quiet as mice.

The last hymn was forgotten by the time the boys had hopped and skipped and chased one another the length of Princes Street in the honey glow of a late October sun. When they reached the Theatre Royal Charles ran under the portico and hid behind one of the pillars.

'Come and find me, Peter!' His voice sounded so strange and echoey he added a ghostly 'whoooooo!'.

'Noooo!' came the answer. Charles ran round the side of the theatre and found his brother squatting on the ground in a warm patch of low sun, scratching shapes in the dirt with a sharp stone, his hair a mass of dark curls like a woolly sheep. Their mam was still a good way off, huffing and puffing her way towards them. Charles started parading up and down in front of Peter, imitating her slow rolling gait, trying to make his brother laugh, leaning backwards, hand in the small of his back, face contorted into a straining grimace. She wagged her finger at him as she drew closer.

'Aw Charlie, ya big tease, makin' a mockery of yer puir mammy! Rub my back now laddie, for your penance – down a bit – just there – ah, that's grand!' After a few more rubs she turned to face him, curving her hands protectively under her round belly. 'I'll have ye know I'm carryin' a heavy load in here, so I am!'

'Sorry Mam!' Charles felt bad for teasing her and scuffed the toe of his boot in the dust. He hated it when she was cross with him.

'Ach, never you mind, Charlie, I'm fine, so I am!' She pulled his chin up with the crook of her finger, smiling brightly, and he gazed up at her adoringly, basking in her renewed approval.

She turned and squinted at the sun, one hand shielding her eyes. 'What a braw day! I'm minded of the day you were born, Charlie, about this time o' year it was, on a day full o' sunshine like this one.' She looked down at them both fondly, then took their hands. 'Let's tak a wee look at the playbills, eh?'

Posters announcing performances were plastered all down the side of the theatre, some old and familiar, growing tatty round the edges, others new and smart and commanding attention. Most of them were covered with lines of fancy writing which Charles had no hope of understanding. The letters at the top were huge, and underneath there were crowds of very small ones, all bunched together. His mam started trailing her fingers over one of the newer playbills carefully, reading the words out slowly.

'See this one, boys, look … *For the Benefit of Mr Henry Erskine Johnston … This present evening, Wednesday, July 23rd 1794, will be performed the celebrated Scottish Drama "Douglas"*.' Charles had hardly noticed how very swollen her belly had become until today; but what had she meant about carrying a load in there?

Suddenly impatient with her slow reading, he skipped across the road to Register House and looked back towards the theatre, craning his neck to see the statues perched high on the roof. What would it be like to climb up there and stand beside one of them? What a fine view they must have!

His mam had stopped reading and was walking slowly along the wall, eyes and fingers searching.

'Come back here and look at this wi' me will you, Charlie! Ach – I'm vexed I didnae tak the time and spare the coin to go and see it for mysel', so I am. Aye, but mebbe I was a wee bittie feart o' the crush o' folk.' Charles wandered back across the dusty road and she began to read, her finger following the letters carefully: '*This present Wednesday … will be performed a comedy called …* The Beggar's Opera … *with esteemed London actors … Mrs Sarah Siddons and Mr John Kemble.*'

Charles noticed the familiar faraway look on her face with delight, knowing she was about to tell a story. He grinned at Peter.

'Did I ever tell you lads I once saw a peep o' the famous Mrs Sarah Siddons from London's Drury Lane Theatre outside this very building?' She had told them before, several times, but they always loved to hear it.

'Tell us again, Mam!' She leaned back against the wall and sighed, closing her eyes as though it would help her remember.

'Well now, I was just wed to your faither and the toon was all astir wi' news o' a famous actress coming up frae London to visit our new theatre. I was never allowed tae go when I was a lass for fear of what the minister would say, but I sometimes used tae sit outside and watch folk goin' in. Back then the ministers said actors and plays were wicked. Some of 'em still say that now! I never knew whit tae think, but I reckon telling stories cannae be all bad, there's plenty stories in the Bible after a', as well as songs and dancin', so I've bin telt!' Suddenly she opened her eyes and twirled around, laughing, her skirts swirling out. She was something, his mam! Charles thought she probably looked like a duchess in her purple Sunday silk and black bonnet. She leaned back against the wall again and took a long, slow breath, her face glowing in the orange sunlight.

'What did the ministers used tae say when you were young, Mam?' Charles knew fine well, but he loved the sound of the awful words, the terrible rage of them. She arranged a stern expression on her face and began to wag her finger at the boys, adopting a pompous manner of speech to recite what she had heard repeated in her father's tavern.

'*Playactors are the most profligate wretches and vilest vermin that hell ever vomited out: they are the filth and garbage of the earth, the scum and stain of human nature, the excrement and refuse of all mankind ...*'

'What does estrement mean, Mammy?' Peter's interruption made her stop and bend over laughing, holding her big, round belly with both arms, until Charles tugged her sleeve and begged her to finish the story.

'Aye, the London actress. Well, after a slow start wi' no' much success, someone ca'ed out, *That's no' bad!,* and it made everyone laugh. Ah, the rage for seein' Sarah Siddons aifter that grew sae big that, in spite o' the ministers' warnings, there were mair than two thousand folk after six hundred tickets on one night alane! They called it "Siddonimania" – a kind o' madness that sent the women intae a frenzy. The manager even put soldiers at the door wi' bayonets, and, oh my, they caused such a rumpus that blood was spilled and he had to send them away!' Charles's mind filled with surging crowds, clashing bayonets and scarlet uniforms as she spoke – all because people wanted to see a famous actress from London!

'What happened next, Mam?'

'Night after night I heard nothing else frae folk comin' intae the tavern. Rich folk even had their porters camp on the street by the theatre to queue at the box office at the crack of dawn for want o' tickets! As for the ministers, well – talk was that the General Assembly had tae change its meeting times, there were that many ministers aff to the theatre!' She shook her head and chuckled again.

'Oh, laddies, they were such times!' Her voice dropped to a whisper. 'One night a sailor came intae the tavern an' I heard him tell how he'd climbed up the front o' the theatre tae try and get in through the windae because he couldnae buy a ticket. Nae sooner was he through whit he called the *porthole* than he was knocked on the heid and tumbled doon the *hatchway* – meanin' the stairs o' course – puir fellow!' Both boys laughed with their mammy this time. Then she sighed and leaned back against the wall again, closing her eyes and slumping slightly as though all her energy had drained away.

Charles was not ready for her to stop yet, though. He was in another world. One that drew him like a moth to a sputtering candle flame on a dark night. He could never hear too many stories of the theatre.

'Tell us aboot when you saw the London actress, Mam!' She opened her eyes again, took their hands and crossed the street to sit on the steps of Register House.

'Ach, I'm needin' a wee seat, laddies, this story-tellin' tires me out, so it does.' It was cooler out of the sun and his mam put an arm round each of them, pulling them in to her side. Charles stared across at the theatre again, wondering which of the three arched windows had been the sailor's *'porthole'*.

'After a week I was that keen to see Sarah Siddons mysel' I hatched a plan. I picked up my basket and told your pa I'd heard there were oranges just arrived in Leith and I was away tae fetch some.'

'Oranges?' Peter's face brightened.

'I told him a wee white lie, Peter, for my sins! Said I would walk there and he was not to expect me home till late!' She tousled his hair and carried on. 'I sat mysel' on a big block o' stone frae the building site right here where these steps are and waited as the light fell that midsummer's night. It was her last show in Edinburgh. I still mind the play was ca'ed *The Grecian Daughter* and the ticket money was tae go to the workhouse. I sat right here till it was late an' the play was over, then I watched a' the grand lords and ladies, a' the servants an' workin' men, a' the drunken riff-raffery an' hures, leavin' the theatre frae their different doors till the street was quiet save for the snorting and stamping of horses.

'Suddenly there she was, the famous Sarah Siddons hersel', comin' down the side o' the theatre, a wee crowd of friends millin' round her, everyone talkin' and laughin' and proud as roosters to be in her circle. Ah, she looked sae fine! Her dress was yellow and shiny as buttercups in the summer sun. Curls from her silver wig were burstin' oot frae her bonnie black hat with its long, inky feathers and its big, floppy satin bow. How anyone could think she was *vile vermin* was beyond the understandin' o' my simple brain.

'Her voice though – ahhhh! It rose above the rest, clear as a bell. And, like a tune played by a fine fiddler, it pulled at my heart strings till I almost swooned! What it would be like tae hear her sing inside the theatre I cannae imagine!' Charles could contain himself no longer.

'That big high roof would mak it sae loud it would surely blaw yer ears aff, Mam!' She smiled widely so her dimple showed, then swept his hair out of his eyes with cool fingers.

'It surely would, Charlie, it surely would! But imagine seein' her in the theatre on the stage, though, that fine lady all dressed up and actin', wi' an orchestra and dancin' and everything!'

'But what about the oranges, Mam?'

'Och, Peter ...' She pinched the wee lad's cheek, smiling fondly, but Charles grabbed her arm.

'Mam! – If Mrs Siddons comes back frae London again I'll find some work and earn half a crown and tak you to the theatre mysel' to sit in a fancy box and watch her!'

Her face lit up, as he had hoped it would. She hugged him

tight, kissing the top of his head, his heart full to bursting that he had thought of such a fine thing to say.

Charles was hovering pleasantly on the edge of sleep, dreaming about the promise he had made a few weeks ago to take his mammy to the theatre. His imagination had conjured a glittering hall – even bigger than St Cuthbert's – full of people dressed in their colourful best clothes. Music was spiralling into the rafters, all the galleries were decorated in swirling gold lit by hundreds of flickering candles, and there were long, thick, red curtains on either side of the stage. He was just watching the first actor step out to roars of applause when his brother's bony knees poked him in the back and broke the spell. Charles pushed him away, irritably, and turned on his side again, eager to find his way back into his favourite dream.

He had almost drifted off to sleep when a scream tore through the normal rumblings of the night and Charles sat up, trembling. *Mam?* He jumped out of bed and ran barefoot to his parents' room, nightshirt flapping round his knees, heart knocking against his ribs like an angry rap at the window. Unsure what to do, he hovered in the dark landing listening to women's voices, low and urgent, and the clatter of a bucket.

Another moan began, swelling into a scream, and he flung the door open. There was blood everywhere: on the bed, on his mammy's nightdress, on her bare splayed legs.

'Get *out* Charles!' Her face was red, wet and angry. *But I want to help!* A woman he had never seen before came and stood in front of him, a tallow candle in her hand, blocking his view of the bed with her broad frame and dazzling him with the stinking, sputtering flame. There was blood on her apron.

'This is no place for the likes of you, lad, this is women's work. Yer faither's away for the howdie. Since you're awake, though, you might as well get your brother up. The pair of you had best make yourselves scarce before Mr Mackay's back – unless you want a row and a skelpin'.' She bundled him out of the room and pulled the door shut behind her. 'I'll cut you some scran and leave it on the table wi' a cup o' milk. It'll soon be mornin'. You lads'll have tae roam about till dusk though, so be sure and keep out o' trouble, and look after yer wee brother, mind. Oh, an' watch yer step! I doubt the scaffies hae been doon our close yet to clear the filth. Ye dinnae want tae be slippin' an' slidin' aboot in all they peelings and shit and fish guts, laddie, or ye'll pong like the flooers o' Edinburgh, so ye will!' The woman smiled and ruffled his hair with her stubby fingers, looking at him kindly with her small dark eyes, like currants pushed deep into a squashy bun. Then she turned and clumped down the narrow staircase to the kitchen, leaving Charles shivering in the dark.

The watery winter sun had long set by the time the boys arrived home wet, cold and ravenously hungry. Charles pushed the heavy studded street door open and sidled through the tavern to the kitchen, pulling Peter by the hand. Normally invisible in the smoky taproom, he felt shy of the eyes on him, unsettled by the murmuring behind hands. Something bad must have happened.

In the kitchen another strange woman was sitting by the cooking hearth, holding an infant wrapped tightly in a cloth. One of her paps was bare for all to see, pale and swollen and strange. She nodded at the boys as if nothing unusual was happening and turned her dull eyes back to the fussing bairn. Charles felt his heart sinking into his dirty boots like a stone in the Nor' Loch. Where was his mam?

Two cups of milk and two plates of porridge had been left out for them. Charles steered his brother to the table and they shovelled the cold, salty oats down greedily. When he had finished gulping his milk, Charles wiped his mouth with the back of his hand and led Peter outside. They ran to the end of the close and pissed against the wall, steam rising from the cobbles all around them, rats scattering into the night.

He could think of nothing to say to his brother as he helped him into bed that night, but Peter went to sleep at once without a murmur. He was a good handful of years younger than Charles, not much more than a baby in some ways. Charles was still awake after the noises of the tavern had settled down. Outside he could hear the muffled rattle of wheels on cobbles in the High Street; the running feet of chairmen carrying late-night revellers in sedans; the lighter tread of link-boys lighting their way; a scrap of shouting, a burst of laughter, someone whistling and some thumps he could not identify. Inside, the clock was ticking downstairs, wooden beams were creaking under their heavy loads and mice were skittering behind the wainscot. Empty. That was the word. Lying in the dark, for once letting his brother curl round him, he realised the tavern was empty of his mam. He thought of her angry face when she had shouted at him to get out and felt his own face grow wet with tears.

Much later a door slammed downstairs and Charles heard his father knock a bucket over and curse. He must have been out drinking hard. Charles knew he never drank more than a 'wee drappie' in his own tavern, enough to loosen his voice for a tune or two. He lay there, ears pinned back as slow, heavy footsteps came up the stairs. His parents' bedroom door creaked open. Silence. Then a sound he had never heard before, a sound that filled him with horror. His father was sobbing like a child.

'Jeannie! Oh, my Jeannie!'

Charles and Peter were sent to Leith to stay with an aunt they barely knew for a fortnight. When they came back all trace of their mam had gone: her long red apron no longer hung on its hook on the back of the door, her knitting basket was not by the hearth and all the flowery plates on the dresser had vanished.

It was impossible to sleep that first night back home. When Peter finally settled Charles got up and crept to his parents' room. His father was downstairs in the tavern, but the moment he opened the bedroom door Charles could smell him: his bitter tobacco, his stale sweat. The shutters were still open and he saw by the moon's peck of light there was only a rough grey blanket on the bed. The colourful patchwork quilt his mam had made was nowhere to be seen. The shelf by the window was empty of her knick-knacks too. Wherever his mam had gone she was not coming back, that much was clear.

In the days that followed no one mentioned her or explained why there was often a woman sitting at the hearth suckling a baby. Charles longed for someone to tell him, to put what he already knew into words so it would be real and he could weep for her. There were two serving girls and a kitchen maid at the tavern and between them they kept the boys fed and clothed, after a fashion. Charles pestered them about his mam, hoping to wear one of them down or catch them off guard, but he never really expected a reply. It was just something he needed to do, like scratching an itchy scab even though he knew the scratching would make it bleed again.

It came as a shock when the worst of the winter was over and he finally had his answer.

'Sit doon, lad, and I'll tell you what you're sae desperate tae know – I canna stand another minute of your whingein'!' Charles was sitting in the kitchen with the youngest of the servants, watching her pound a lump of dough on the table, sleeves rolled up to her skinny elbows. Suddenly she stopped,.

'Y'ken how baby kittens slip oot o' their mammies into the world, Charlie?' He blinked in surprise. 'All in a tangle and mess o' blood lad, that's how. You've seen it yersel', so you have. I saw you watching them behind the ash bin!' She pushed a stray wisp of red hair out of her eyes with the back of her floury arm, leaving a faint trail of flour on her bony white cheek, then began to pound the dough again. 'Well, and so it is with people, Charlie, so it is with us. Our mammies grow us in their bellies and push us out intae the world in a mess of blood, so they do – d'ye ken that, laddie?' He nodded, dread squeezing his stomach, making it hurt. The girl hesitated for a moment, her pale eyes darting around, then looked him in the eye. He clutched his stool with both hands.

'So, and all, Charlie, your mammy – God rest her soul – was pushing wee William oot on that terrible caud day in November when he got himself stuck and the howdie couldnae do a thing to budge him. The doctor came and pulled the bairn out wi' his tongs, but he couldnae stop the bleeding. So.'

'She died, didn't she? She died because of William!' Charles jumped up, balling his hands into fists, looking around for something to punch, but the lass was strong and caught him by his forearms, pulling him into her waist. She wiped the snot and tears from his face with her apron and held him tightly for a moment, her chin resting on the top of his head.

'It's a sad, sad story, Charlie, but you mustnae blame your wee brother.' Then she held him at arms' length, and there was a sharper edge to her voice. 'Now then, you'd best run along and be brave and never say a word to a soul or I'll be losing my job and have nowhere tae sleep!' Charles looked up at her, blinking away his tears, and nodded again. Then he sniffed, swiped his arm across his wet face and left the room.

He never told a soul, not even his brothers.

When William was weaned, Charles's father moved the family to Glasgow.

TWO

A volley of rapid drumbeats ricocheted off the high stone walls, waking the soldiers of the Argyllshire Militia to a sky full of dark clouds, heavy with the promise of rain. Charles Mackay had all the military drum rolls down to a fine art. He had been a drummer and fifer in the regiment for more than five years now, since shortly after he was recruited as a young lad in Glasgow, a few years into the new century. He was making his own way; his brothers had been too young for the army. War was raging overseas and militia regiments across the land were preparing to defend the British Isles. Charles was proud to be playing his part and hardly thought of his family these days. Their father had apprenticed William to a weaver in Glasgow, he knew that much. He had no idea where Peter was or what he was doing.

The regiment was like family to him now. It had given him a decent education too. He had developed a neat, sloping copperplate and gained a firm grip on spelling and grammar, not to mention having a good idea of the impressive extent of the British Empire. Charles had also learned to read sheet music and considered this to be one of his finest accomplishments.

A drummer's pay was better than a regular private's and

Charles's duties were less onerous too: practising and performing, playing reveilles, retreats and tattoos for the regiment every day, playing for the soldiers marching to church on Sundays. He was often asked to sing with the military band too, at civilian concerts, barrack-room dances and evenings of entertainment for the officers. Charles had always enjoyed belting out a stirring song and he quickly earned a reputation for it. More than the money and the privileges, he loved the music.

He finished the sequence with a flourish and stowed his sticks in their leather pouch. The handsome brass snare drum, with its wooden rims and catgut tensioners, was slung on a long strap round his neck. He pushed it to one side and strode over to the mess as a few fat raindrops began to fall, hoping for an early breakfast. A fillet of fresh fish perhaps, now they were billeted by the coast again. They always had plenty of fish in Aberdeen and he wondered if it would be the same here in Ayr, a town on the south-west coast of Scotland where the infantry barracks had been set up in the disused Sugar House near the harbour.

Another singer, John Sinclair, had recently bought himself out of their regiment to pursue a career on the London stage – *and the best o' luck to him, he has a grand voice on him, for sure!* Charles was happy to step in. He enjoyed the banter of introducing tunes and goading officers too and always made sure he had a few conundrums up his sleeve to tell between songs.

The military band had been asked to put on an entertainment for the officers that evening and Charles was going to join them, playing the fife and singing a few songs. They gathered in the usual place after dinner and made a dash for the officers' mess through pelting rain – collars up, bonnets tipped forward – laughing like children as they splashed through puddles, soaking their pantaloons. Something more ambitious than conundrums had been scratching at the back of his mind all week and he was wondering whether he would risk trying it that night.

The officers' mess-room was large and well-lit, with candles on all the tables. An iron stove was pumping out a good heat too, and evidence of excessive feasting littered the tables. Across the room steam rose like mist from red jackets slung over the backs of chairs while lively conversations, punctuated by gales of bawdy laughter, indicated most of the officers were already well-lubricated.

The band struck up some lively reels and strathspeys and the evening's entertainment was soon off to a good start. Then Charles led everyone in a few rousing songs, followed by a song from a popular comic opera. His powerful bass voice and melodramatic expressions and gestures gained the attention of most of the room, and after taking his bow, Charles asked the band to begin the opening strains of one of John Sinclair's signature pieces.

One of the officers called out, 'Sinclair's gone to London to make his fortune on the stage – or have you forgotten?' Laughter broke out across the room, but the band played on and Charles took everyone by surprise by blasting out the opening line of the song in a tenor voice that sounded exactly like Sinclair's. He had transformed his whole demeanour too, and was swaggering and bowing, smiling coyly, and exaggerating all his friend's little mannerisms to the point of buffoonery.

The officers loved it and showed their appreciation effusively, so Charles surged straight into another of Sinclair's songs while they were still cheering the first. When he had finished he bowed deeply, relishing the enthusiasm of the applause and gathering his courage.

Suddenly, with no warning, he started shouting orders in perfect imitation of their commander-in-chief, the 7th Duke of Argyll, Colonel John Campbell. It was so unexpected that a few officers jumped to their feet and saluted, before being pulled back to their seats by their friends amidst helpless laughter. Charles began to march up and down between the tables. He picked up a cane and used it to prod people, chastising them for various ridiculous and imagined misdemeanours. Two officers sneaked from their chairs and followed him around like naughty schoolboys, pulling his jacket and running away. The place was soon in uproar.

The response to his little ruse was so overwhelming that Charles felt obliged to bring it to a conclusion before it turned into a riot. He returned to the band, took a huge gulp of air, mopped his brow and transformed himself back into John Sinclair to sing another of his favourite songs, a Burns poem about auld acquaintances he had come across that had been set to music a few years ago. The song was greeted by more shouting and cheering, hands banging tables, feet stamping, and all over the room shouts of 'Mackay!'

Six weeks later the main hall in Ayr's Assembly Rooms was filling fast and Charles was backstage, listening to the gathering crowd, shivering like a leaf about to fall from a tree. What on earth had possessed him to hire this huge venue and put on a concert with himself billed as the star? True, he had been a hit in the officers' mess-room over a dozen times now and his repertoire had greatly expanded, but why on God's earth had he taken literally the casual suggestion of a drunken officer – *you should put on an entertainment in town, Mackay, you really are the funniest man I've ever seen!* Now his vanity had landed him in this intolerable situation and he was filled with dread.

The band had agreed to support him, for which he was deeply grateful. Already they were quietening the lively audience and introducing the opening song. *Oh Lord, there's no turning back now!* Charles took a last glance in the looking-glass and saw fear written all over his pale face. He pushed a hand through his dark, wavy hair, pulled his shoulders back, assumed the familiar countenance of John Sinclair, and strode onto the stage.

The evening was a disaster from beginning to end. Most of his efforts at mimicry were met by blank stares and Charles quickly realised he had failed to consider whether the good citizens of Ayr would be familiar with John Sinclair's little ways, or Colonel Campbell's for that matter. There were a few laughs when he wrapped a plaid round his waist and mimicked the Duchess of Argyll mincing along to the accompaniment of the well-known tune named after her, but a sudden memory of himself as a little boy prancing on the kitchen table with a cloth wrapped round his waist made him feel utterly foolish.

He performed a few more songs as himself, which were acknowledged by smatterings of polite applause, but people began to leave before he had finished.

Charles brought the proceedings to a close twenty minutes earlier than he had planned with an impromptu speech thanking everyone for their indulgence and apologising for his incompetence. Then he bowed deeply and retreated backstage where he shut himself in the broom cupboard, sat on the floor and hugged his knees tightly to his chest, screwing up his pricking eyes and wishing he had never woken up that morning.

Persistent knocking eventually forced Charles to his feet. He opened the door cautiously, fully expecting to see someone from the band come to winkle him out of his shell. Instead, he found himself face to face with a tall, smart gentleman in a dark grey frock coat with a square chin and a determined look in his deep-set grey eyes. He held out his hand and Charles shook it.

'Good evening, Mr Mackay. My name is Robert Mackay – no relation as far as I know! I would like to congratulate you for your lively entertainment this evening, and more than that, for taking such a personal risk to try something new. Bravo!' Charles could not meet his eye; he was lost for words. The last thing he wanted was pity.

'That's very kind of you, Mr Mackay, but I believe I am nothing but a fool for putting on such a vanity show and now I am also a fool who is out of pocket.' Charles could not resist assuming a clown's grimace and turning his pockets inside out to illustrate his point. Robert Mackay laughed, his eyes lighting up with genuine amusement, then put his hand in his own pocket and drew out a small leather pouch.

'Well now, if you will allow me, Mr Mackay, a few of us – including a banker in this town called Mr James Morris who is a great lover of the theatre – have made a collection in appreciation of your considerable talent as an entertainer and entrepreneur and your admirable modesty as a performer. We hope you will accept it with our good wishes.' Robert Mackay dropped the pouch into Charles's hand and doffed his black top hat. 'I very much look forward to watching your next performance.' Then he turned abruptly and left before Charles could think what to say.

The dream did not die after that disastrous night. Quite the opposite. It gathered momentum, grew stronger, more tenacious, more considered.

There were theatres in many of the towns and cities where the regiment was stationed, lively entertainments in assembly rooms and trade halls presented by strolling players and touring companies. Charles went to see them whenever he could. Halfway through the evening, when tickets were half-price, he could often be found pushing his way through rowdy crowds in the pit to squeeze onto a bench as near the front as possible.

People came and went throughout these performances, eating, drinking, laughing, shouting and generally ignoring the players, while footpads threaded their way amongst the crowds, watching for moments to slice pockets from belts and filch watches from pockets. Prostitutes looked out for eyes filled with longing or tears during moments of romance and tragedy and slipped alongside their prey, far more skilled at acting than most of the players on the stage.

Charles discovered that storytelling on a stage, catching and holding the attention of an audience, mesmerising, delighting and entertaining them, was an immensely challenging task, but far from being discouraged, he was inspired. He learned tricks to grab attention, recognised the power of dramatic gestures, noticed what made people laugh, shout, heckle, cheer, cry or even start a fight. He made mental notes about common mistakes and felt his confidence growing month by month. Meanwhile he continued to develop his own material and use it in the officers' mess, putting into practise all he was learning and earning quite a reputation.

The regiment were stationed in Dunbar when a letter from his recently wed brother, William, found Charles there. He took himself to Glasgow for the baptism of his first nephew, Hugh, on November the 8th, 1813, and was delighted to find Peter there too. Sadly, their father had died just days before, so the brothers mourned his passing together before celebrating the new life of his namesake. William had married the moment he finished his weaving apprenticeship, and this was the first time Charles had met his wife, Jean. Peter had taken the lease on an inn and was hoping to follow in their father's footsteps, perhaps even to move to London. Charles surprised himself, as well as his brothers, by telling them he planned to become an actor when he left the militia.

Out of the blue, another letter arrived for him one morning shortly after his return from Glasgow, postage paid. Charles slit it open carefully.

Dear Charles,

I am writing to advise you that, far from forgetting you and your inimitable acting skills and talents, which I was privileged to witness in the Ayr Assembly Rooms several years ago, you have been much on my mind. I believe you may have a fine future in the theatre.

I have taken it upon myself to write to a good friend of mine on your behalf, the well-known Edinburgh-born actor Mr Henry Erskine Johnston. I have given him my highest recommendation of you, both as an actor and a singer, and as an Edinburgh-born man of excellent character.

You may have heard of Henry. You may even have seen him acting on the stage. I believe he has made quite a name for himself in London and Dublin as well as in Edinburgh and Glasgow and many of the provincial theatres.

He has been managing the Ayr Theatre Royal recently and is currently managing theatres in Aberdeen and Greenock. He is planning to take over the management of the Glasgow Theatre Royal shortly and has written back to me to say he would be happy to meet you on my recommendation alone, and to give you such employment as you can make yourself free to accept considering you are, for the time being, still in the employ of the Argyll and Bute militia.

I hope you will forgive me for interfering in your life, should you not wish to pursue this opportunity. But should you wish to take it up, may I suggest you get up to Glasgow's Theatre Royal at the first opportunity and present yourself to him with this letter as provenance of your identity.

I wish you every success with your forthcoming career.

Your friend and admirer,

Robert Mackay.

THREE

Her heart was beating like a wooden spoon in a bowl of batter: *me next!* Charlotte could hear the honeyed voice of the great Henry Erskine Johnston breaking Betsy's heart in the most charming manner, telling her she should, perhaps, have spoken up more, that her song had been pretty, but that she should hurry along now and go back to work. Betsy ran off-stage, holding her skirts with both hands and almost colliding into Charlotte. Her pink, shiny face was streaming with tears.

'Next!'

This is it, I'm on! Give it yer all, girl, it's now or never!

Charlotte walked hesitantly onto the stage, the red damask gown she had stitched and embroidered with such care mostly hidden by a long white apron, her fair curls swept up under a maid's cap. She adopted the look of an innocent who had lost her way, feigning complete oblivion to the presence of anyone else in the barn-like vastness of London's Drury Lane Theatre. When she reached the middle of the stage she turned slowly to the front and looked up in wonder at the familiar ceiling as though she had never seen it before.

'Gawblimy, lawks a' mercy, what kind of a place is this? It's bloomin' marvellous!' Charlotte stared at the intricately designed plaster on the ceiling so high above, then let her eyes drop slowly, ranging along the rows of extravagantly decorated balconies, until they fell on a group of gentlemen sitting in the pit just in front of the stage. She gave a little scream, dropped a curtsey and hung her head in shame for an awkward second. Then she began to brush down her apron, muttering apologetically and tucking her hair into her cap as though gathering the courage to look up. She lifted her head slowly until she caught the eye of the tall, rather striking gentleman seated in the centre of the little group: Henry Erskine Johnston.

'Oh deary me and beggin' yer pardon, sirs, I never saw you there!' Charlotte noted the confusion on the gentlemen's faces with satisfaction. One of them was scribbling in a notebook. *Just you wait, mister!*

'I'm just an 'umble servin' wench from a tavern in the East End, sir. Lord knows 'ow I found meself in 'ere. Is it one o' them theatres for playactin'?' Dropping the act for a split second she winked at the man with the notebook and his pencil fell on the floor with a satisfying clatter. She had them now! 'Nice to meet you an' all, but I'd best be off, 'fore the mistress misses me. Sorry to disturb yer important busyness.'

Charlotte gave another curtsey and smiled cheekily over her shoulder as she turned to go off-stage. Behind the crimson swags she pulled a fan from her pocket, whipped off the apron and cap and straightened her shoulders. Slowly, imperiously, she walked back on-stage, stopping in the centre to fix her eyes on Mr Johnston. She was almost distracted by his extraordinary good looks, his deep, dark eyes regarding her with such close attention, such evident amusement, and that famous face, so beautiful. She lifted her chin.

'Aha, there you are, you young scoundrel! Make no mistake, I have heard *all* about you and your capering, both on-stage and off!' Her voice had dropped to a low, powerful, melodiously rolling cadence and her diction was perfect. Her golden hair, swept up in a glorious pile on top of her head, was decorated with a red silk rose and some colourful dyed feathers she had borrowed; her full-skirted red gown shone in the gas lights, the tight bodice with its boned front panel flattering her full figure and small waist. Charlotte knew she looked gorgeous and stood very still. She felt completely composed as she held Mr Johnston's gaze, aware that all the men were equally transfixed. Then she lifted an imperious eyebrow, flicked out her fan and cooled her face with it gently. One gentleman nudged another and they both sat back, grinning, settling into the entertainment. Henry Johnston seemed unable – or unwilling – to drag his eyes from her.

'I thought I might find you here in this den of iniquity, Henry! I have come to tell you that we are, none of us, either amused or impressed by your scandalous behaviour towards the Prince Regent.' Her fanning became slightly agitated as she continued. 'Least of all my dear friend Arthur, so fresh from his victory at Waterloo. I must say, he is particularly disappointed in you.' She waited a beat for them to catch up with her, to connect the name, Arthur, with the duke who had so recently brought the interminable Napoleonic wars to such a decisive end.

'Really, Henry, to horsewhip Prinny in your own dressing room – whatever his intentions were towards your wife – was simply inexcusable. You may well smirk, young man, but it is nothing to be proud of!' Charlotte was enjoying herself immensely. 'I imagine you feel yourself beyond the law, now, having escaped from gaol and disguised yourself as an old soldier to limp your way to North Britain. Hah! We know all about you, young man, thundering onto the Edinburgh stage as a Highland chieftain in all your tartan glory when you were hardly more than a child. However, your success on the stage does *not* elevate you above the laws of decency, and I am here to tell you that a scoundrel such as yourself is no longer welcome in Polite Society. Good day to you, sir!' She flounced off-stage to the gratifying sound of the gentlemen clapping and laughing heartily.

Charlotte had not finished yet, though. She pulled her hair loose, stowed the flower and feathers in her apron pocket, then grabbed the large grey blanket she had left behind the drapes. She quickly covered her head and most of the dress with it, holding it together tightly beneath her chin, then limped back onto the stage, hunched over, reaching out her hand to the small audience like a beggar.

'Forgive me, gentlemen. I'm but a puir wee colleen fresh off the boat from Ireland and I've nothin' tae eat, sure I haven't. Same goes for ma wee brothers – nine o' them there are – an' not a crust for us to share since our mammy an' pappy died o' the fever. Can ye no' spare a coin?' She fell to her knees, stretched her hand out again and felt her pleading eyes brim. When a tear trickled down her face she knew she could really do it, this acting business. Her shoulders slumped and she turned away, crumpling into a heap on the floor.

Under the blanket Charlotte ran her fingers through her long, loose honey-coloured curls, then jumped up, whirling round to face the auditioning panel, her red skirts flaring out and her face beaming. She dropped a deep curtsey, then stood to her full height – which was all of five feet – shoulders back, ambition burning brightly in her eyes.

'Charlotte O'Keefe's the name, gentlemen!' One more push and she would be over the finishing line. What happened next was out of her hands – she had done her best. 'I've given you three good reasons why you should choose me for your new Scottish company, Mr Johnston. Here are three more: Firstly, I'm the best actor you'll see in here today by a country mile!' She flashed her biggest smile to show she was making fun of herself, while meaning every word. 'Secondly, I can sing like a lark.' She drew in a breath and launched into a rousing two-octave arpeggio, holding the top C for considerably longer than would normally be expected, then adding an exaggerated vibrato and pulling an anxious grimace. Her little audience began to laugh and one of them shouted *Bravo!*

'And thirdly, Mr Johnston, because my uncle, the famous playwright Mr John O'Keefe, is sitting right behind you, ready to persuade you with his fist should you need further encouragement!' Everyone burst out laughing and turned to look at her uncle, slapping him on the back and shouting: *jolly good show!* She could feel sweat breaking out on her face and on the back of her neck. Her hands were growing slick with it too, but she retained her poise, kept her breathing calm and steady, waited for Mr Johnston's response.

'Well now, young lady – Miss O'Keefe – I must confess you've made quite the impression – hasn't she gentlemen?' He stretched his arm along the back of the chair beside him, oozing confidence and superiority. 'You've certainly proved yourself to be a competent little actress today; someone who researches their subjects and is prepared to take risks, too, have a bit of fun. And that voice!' Mr Johnston turned to face his colleagues. 'Her face and figure are quite presentable too, don't you think gentlemen?!' His full lips curled in a sardonic smile, then he boomed at the playwright sitting directly behind him. 'O'Keefe – you're a dark horse keeping this one under your hat! No need to raise a fist to me though, John, my mind is made up already!'

Henry Erskine Johnston stood and stretched languidly.

'I think we can call it a day now, Chambers. Can you run backstage and let the other girls know they won't be required, there's a good chap.' He looked directly at Charlotte, still holding her pose and her half smile centre stage, watching his every move. 'Can you have a trunk packed and be waiting at the White Horse Inn, Fetter Lane, first thing Thursday morning, Miss O'Keefe?' She nodded, holding her face in a neutral expression while fireworks exploded in the pit of her stomach. 'The coach for Edinburgh leaves at 8 o'clock sharp. From there you will travel by coach to Glasgow, then to Greenock and on down to Ayr. You'll be travelling with Mr and Mrs Bromby. He will be the keeper of tickets and money and such like for the entirety of your journey – your chaperone, as it were. I look forward to renewing our acquaintance at the new Theatre Royal, Ayr, in due course. Farewell, Miss O'Keefe – and well done!'

He patted his pockets, pulled out a clay pipe, lifted a hand to Charlotte, then turned on his heel to lead the others out in search of food or drink or perhaps somewhere to go and smoke. Her uncle smiled at her, mouthing 'well done!' as he followed them out.

Two weeks and several tediously buffeting carriage journeys later Charlotte was standing in front of a cheval glass admiring herself in a lilac taffeta dress, pinning her plaited hair on top of her head, fixing a sparkling tiara and adjusting stray locks. The newly formed stock company in Ayr's Theatre Royal comprised eleven men and eleven women, many of whom had travelled from London, Newcastle and Edinburgh, and some of whom had already worked with Mr Johnston in other Scottish theatres. The actors had been learning their parts for two days and it was late morning on the first day of rehearsals, with the opening night only three days away.

'I saw *The Honeymoon* in Drury Lane ten years ago with Henry Siddons as the Duke of Aranza. Did you see it, Charlotte?' Mrs Bromby was full of airs and graces and usually viewed the world down her splendidly long nose, but her wicked sense of humour made her highly entertaining and Charlotte had grown fond of her over the course of their interminable journey.

'I was only twelve in 1805, Mrs Bromby, but I've seen the play and I like it well enough. I can't believe I've been chosen to be

Juliana, though! I shall have such fun! She's a prickly character who speaks her mind, isn't she?'

'She certainly speaks up for herself in the first half, my dear, but she is tamed eventually, as most women usually are.' Mrs Bromby was sitting at a table applying makeup, peering into her hand glass, spectacles perched at half-mast. Charlotte watched the older woman dab a little rouge on her fingertip and apply it carefully to her cheeks, blending it into the white foundation she had already spread evenly over her face. Then she scooped a tiny amount of bright red lip salve onto her finger and applied it carefully and precisely to her thin lips.

'Watch and learn, Charlotte, watch and learn, dear girl!' Mrs Bromby smacked her lips together loudly and rubbed them sideways against each other, like a sheep grinding its teeth. The result was startlingly effective. Next, she picked up a feathery puff and applied powder to her nose and cheeks with the lightest of touches.

Charlotte pulled up a chair beside her and began copying the application of makeup, dipping her fingers into the various pots and lotions and peering into the little hand glass.

'You're right, I suppose. The fight goes out of Juliana by the end, which seems inevitable, but such a shame.' Mrs Bromby nodded, scraping her thin grey hair into a net, then pulling on an extravagantly tall curled and coiffed grey wig.

'That said, you must never forget that the life of an actress, my dear, is one of the few professions in which a lady can develop her talents and live an independent, respectable life in this society.' Mrs Bromby put down her brush and looked at Charlotte with a new intensity. 'You only have to think of the inimitable Mrs Siddons to see that even a married woman, even a mother, can make a grand life for herself on the stage!'

Mrs Bromby stood abruptly and assumed the whining voice and subservient pose of Juliana's handwringing, man-pleasing sister in the play they were about to perform:

'Heav'ns preserve me ever from that dull blessing – an obedient husband!'

Charlotte jumped to her feet, adopting a confident carelessness in her demeanour, and replied, *'And make you an obedient wife! – a thing for lordly man to vent his humours on; a dull domestic drudge, to be abus'd or fondled as the fit may work upon him: "If you think so my dear", and "As you please", and "You know best" – even when he nothing knows!'*

'It's good to hear you running your lines, ladies – I see you're ready to rehearse on-stage!' Mr Johnston had entered the ladies' dressing room unannounced and was leaning on the doorframe grinning at them in their various states of disarray.

'We will be starting the run-through in five minutes, hurry along now and get yourselves to the green room as soon as you can!'

Charlotte had met the other actors briefly, at an introductory supper. The man who was to play the Duke to her Duchess was called Mr Charles Mackay. He was of medium height and build with thick, dark, wavy hair, strong, expressive features and a great twinkle in his deep-set blue eyes. He was quick to smile and joke as well and had a marvellous energy about him. She was confident they would get along well. Like her, Charles had smoothed away his regional manner of speaking, transforming it into that neutral English so beloved of actors, although now and then a Scots word or phrase slipped through, which she found quite charming. At the supper he mentioned he had worked with Mr Johnston now and then over the past two years in various theatres but had only recently left the militia. This was his first appointment as a full-time actor.

A flutter of butterflies was hatching in her belly as Charlotte waited backstage for her cue. She felt hot and sticky under her arms, even though it was October and she was so far north. She put a cool hand to her neck, wondering if her skin was turning blotchy. It was hard to believe she was standing in the wings and about to go on-stage at last, after so many years of scrubbing laundry with her mother and sisters, dreams of acting swirling in her head like billowing steam.

Sometimes her uncle used to take her to watch a famous actor perform in Drury Lane or Covent Garden, and her heart would be near to breaking with yearning. Once he even arranged for her to join the chorus on-stage and her mother had let her off work for a whole week so she could go to the costume fitting, the rehearsals, the performance. What a night it had been! Yet her heart was bruised by it, standing there at the back of the stage in a line of swaying girls while the actors strode about in front of them, the attention of thousands fixed on them as they wove a magical story. Charlotte *knew* she could do it as well as any of them if only she were given the chance.

She had saved her coin, bought some gorgeous red silk and sewn an elegant gown, so she would be ready when her opportunity came. All those hours of stitching by candlelight helped her hold onto the dream, helped her feel she was doing something to achieve it. One evening, soon after the gown was completed, Uncle John came calling to tell her he had signed her up for an audition. She had jumped up and hugged him without thinking twice and her father had scolded her for being so forward.

'*But – she comes!*' It was her cue! Charlotte pinched her cheeks, pulled her stomach in, pushed her shoulders back and walked onto the stage, carrying herself as she imagined a duchess might.

At the beginning of the second act Mr Mackay took Charlotte's hand to lead her on-stage and a shiver shot up her arm. His hand was large and warm and dry, his fingers strong and supple. Throughout the scene he was either holding her hand, placing a hand in the small of her back or taking her arm, staring passionately into her eyes as he spoke his lines, his kisses as gentle as a feather brushing her lips. Thankfully her well-rehearsed lines tripped out on cue even though her whole body was tingling and her breath was shallow. They argued and bantered as if their conversation was real, and when, at last, she pulled her hand from his and shouted at him she felt a genuine swell of emotion.

'*You shall know me for a right woman, full of her own sex; who, when she suffers wrong will speak her wrongs; who feels her own prerogative – and scorns, by the proud reason of superior man, to be taught patience, when her swelling heart cries out: revenge!*'

Charlotte flounced off-stage to the enthusiastic applause of her fellow players and realised she was drenched in sweat.

'A good start, my dear, a very good start! Come over here and sit down, you must be tired!'

She sank gratefully into the seat beside Mrs Bromby and began pulling her hair free and combing it through with fidgety fingers. She was both exhausted and exhilarated as her mind jumped all over what had just happened. Suddenly she began to tremble. Mrs Bromby wrapped a shawl round her shoulders and rubbed her upper arms briskly.

'That may have been a rehearsal, Charlotte dear, but I believe it was your first real performance, so it's quite normal to be shivering. You'll soon warm up.' She offered her a bottle of rose water and a cloth. 'Here, this will soothe you.'

Charlotte wiped her cheeks and eyes with the deliciously scented water, then scooped some cold cream from Mrs Bromby's proffered pot and spread it generously on her face, smoothing it into her skin, enjoying the coolness of it, the faint scent of honey. The trembling soon began to dissipate and she smiled gratefully at Mrs Bromby.

Suitably cleansed and restored, Charlotte changed back into her grey linen day dress, hung up the lilac gown and wondered what to do next. Mrs Bromby had attached herself to a mother and daughter by then and they were all laughing at something. Several other little groups of chattering women had formed but she was too shy to join them and decided to go back to the green room to see if there was any talk of dinner. She was suddenly ravenously hungry.

The opening night was a great success. There was a full house of about six hundred people who all showed their appreciation energetically throughout the evening. Mr Johnston was delighted and decided to run the programme for a few more days, then another week. Charlotte was in her element, growing in confidence with every performance, lapping up the enthusiastic applause of the audiences and relishing every moment she spent with Charles Mackay. The way he looked at her on the stage, touched her, embraced her, kissed her tenderly, seemed so convincing that she had to keep reminding herself he was only acting.

'Would you care to accompany me for a short stroll, Miss O'Keefe?' Charlotte was so taken aback by Mr Mackay's suggestion after yet another rehearsal that she dropped her glove on the floor. He bent at once to retrieve it, then put his hand under her elbow as he returned it to her, sending tingles to her fingertips. 'I believe a breezy stroll would do wonders to clear our heads before tonight's performance, don't you agree Miss O'Keefe? And then, perhaps a bite of supper?' The mischief in his eyes was in such contrast with his polite words that her shyness evaporated and she burst out laughing.

'Well, Mr Mackay, I do believe you're right!' She swirled her cloak round her shoulders, tied her bonnet under her chin, then slipped her arm through his as though it were the most natural thing in the world.

The extended run of *The Honeymoon* turned into six weeks, taking them almost to the end of the year and soon Charles and

Charlotte's handholding and kissing were no longer confined to the stage or subject to the scrutiny and directions of the stage manager and the ogling of the audience. During those halcyon days they went for long walks and told each other about their lives, making much of little and little of much.

One evening, after rehearsals, they left the theatre and walked hand in hand through Wellington Square towards the sea front, where a sharp December wind was whisking creamy spume from the roiling grey water. She was wrapped in the green plaid he had presented to her after their performance the previous night, folding it gently round her in the moonlight. Already she adored it. They both had woollen mufflers round their necks, and brown woollen bunnets pulled down against the cold.

'Only three more nights of *The Honeymoon*. I shall miss it, Charles!'

'Aye! A pantomime of Robinson Crusoe won't be quite the same, will it?'

'Ha – no, but surely we'll both have a part in *The Merchant of Venice*?'

'Some small role perhaps.'

'Ah well, no doubt we'll find out in due course.' Charlotte tucked her arm under his and leaned her head into his shoulder. 'Charles,' she wheedled, skipping an extra step to keep up with his stride, 'when are you going to show me that review you took out of my hands, three weeks ago or more?' He pulled a long face, pursing his lips together in defiance. 'I really want to read it Charles. Please! Do you have it here in your pocket?'

Quick as a seagull stealing a herring from a creel she had her hand inside his waistcoat and fished it out. 'I knew you'd have it on you!'

'Oh, come now, Charlotte, don't torture me with the truth of my dreadful playacting!' She stopped walking and turned to face him, looking up into his face with genuine concern.

'You, Charles Mackay, are a very fine actor and a great comedian, not to mention your musical talents and your marvellous singing voice. You have a wonderful career in front of you, I have no doubt of that whatsoever.' She reached a hand up to touch the face that had already become so dear to her, his cheek as cold as her fingertips. 'Perhaps you sometimes trip over your own feet by being so enthusiastic though, Charles, and don't always know when to stop.' His shoulders slumped and she guided him to a low wall where they sat down together. A snappy little breeze tried to snatch the paper from her hand but she held it tightly, and though the light was failing there was still enough for her to read: '*Mr Mackay, in the mock Duke, made us laugh exceedingly; but he seems to have a habit of raising then lowering his voice a full octave in the same sentence, which though comical …*' Charles grabbed the paper from her hand and stuffed it back inside his pocket, trying not to laugh.

'Enough, Charlotte! Enough!'

'See! You made everyone laugh *exceedingly*. That's the thing to remember, Charles. As for the raising and lowering of your voice, well – that can easily be fixed. I'll just tell you every time you do it – on-stage and off– and we'll soon cure you of it!' He grinned and nodded, then kissed her into silence. They sat quietly on the wall for a while, holding hands, as the rhythm of the whispering waves washed over them. When at last he spoke it was in a low voice charged with emotion.

'Charlotte O'Keefe, I do believe I love you!' Charlotte wondered if she was dreaming. She turned to him and smiled brightly, telling him the same with her eyes, squeezing his hand. Her heart was so full she could not speak, so she rested her head on his shoulder and they watched the sky grow dark, drawing warmth from each other's bodies. Gradually the wind dropped and the moon climbed out of the sea, scattering scraps of light across the black water like snippets of white satin. The song they sang together in *The Honeymoon* every night was playing over and over in Charlotte's mind, but she had substituted Charles's name for the Duke's:

'But when she look'd up, and her lover espy'd
Ah! What was the maiden's surprise!
She blushed as he woo'd her and called her his bride,
And answered him only with sighs
The bells rung,
And she sung,
Ding, dong, dell,
It is well!
They shall ring for dear Charles and me!'

FOUR

'What the blazes d'you mean, Mr Johnston's gone to London? What's to become of the Ayr Theatre Company now? Some of us have travelled a great distance to be here and expected to be employed a good deal longer than two seasons, y'know!' Mr Bromby was upset. Half a head shorter than his imposing wife, he was a red-faced man with unruly ginger and white-flecked sideburns and not a single hair on his shining pate.

'Mr Bromby, I do apologise, but this is often the way with Mr Johnston and his theatrical enterprises. Indeed, he has quite a history in that regard. He was offered a lead role in Covent Garden – his first in twelve years – and was anxious to go at once.' Mr James Morris had gathered everyone in the green room first thing in the morning to impart this important news. As a part owner of the theatre he had been thrust into an untenable position through no fault of his own. A dignified gentleman, a banker by trade, he had neat white hair and was wearing a grey coat and a cream linen cravat, his lined face bearing witness to his many, weighty responsibilities. Charlotte was the first to speak.

'What role could that be I wonder, Mr Morris? It must be a very important one for Henry to abandon us in such a hasty manner without a by your leave.' Charles looked round, surprised to hear her speaking as though Henry Johnston were her friend.

'Yes, Miss O'Keefe, you're right.' Mr Morris seemed relieved, grateful even, for Charlotte's intervention. He dabbed his brow with a white, folded handkerchief. 'It is the leading role of Archy MacSarcasm in *Love à la Mode*. Henry was extremely pleased to receive such an offer – which came with the promise of more – and asked me to be sure to extend his sincere apologies to you all and wish you the best of luck in your careers.' Muttering broke out amongst the gathered actors.

'Well! The blasted cheek of the man – don't you think?' Mr Bromby's voice was the by far the loudest, but Mr Morris continued, raising his voice considerably.

'Rest assured I shall do my best to hold the tiller steady here until we can find another suitable manager, and for now at least, your salaries will continue to be paid.'

Charles smiled gratefully at Mr Morris and attempted to restore the peace.

'Now then, everyone, I assure you Mr Morris is a fine, honest gentleman and we can take him at his word. Indeed, he was most supportive to me at the outset of my career, and I count him among my friends. I'm sure he will do all he can for us.' Mr Morris nodded gratefully and Charles continued. 'Meanwhile we must undertake not to be an undue burden on him at this trying time.' His mind was whirring with ideas as he spoke: he would form a small troupe of travelling actors! He had met the managers of several provincial theatres over the past few years and could hardly wait to put pen to paper.

Mr and Mrs Bromby and Charlotte O'Keefe were the only ones to join Charles's group of strolling players, as it turned out. It was not the best of times to set out on such a risky venture – there had been no summer to speak of and food was short everywhere due to bad harvests – but Charles was fizzing with optimism.

Mr Morris sent the little troupe off in a carriage one dreich September morning with his blessing and two tin trunks full of props, costumes, wigs, drapes, candles and cushions, as well as a month's salary of five shillings jingling in all their pockets. The Brombys came initially as Charlotte's chaperones, but before long they seemed to be enjoying their adventures immensely, despite the privations of the itinerant lifestyle. The first letter to catch up with them on their travels was from Charles's brother, William, announcing the birth of his second son, Lauchlan, and inviting Charles to attend his baptism.

Other letters followed, mostly invitations to perform, and throughout the autumn of 1816 Charles and his troupe performed in Greenock, Kilmarnock, Irvine and many other towns in the southwest, travelling in carriages and open carts, improvising sets and costumes with what they had, invitations following them from one theatre to the next, making sure they were in Glasgow for the baptism on October the 16th. They quickly gathered quite a reputation, particularly for comedy and lively songs. Where there was a royal patent for legitimate theatre, they presented scenes from well-known plays. Where there was not, they entertained with songs and mimicry, tricks and skits, bowdlerised versions of Shakespeare scenes and melodramas as illegitimate and joyful as a penny geggie.

'It's all very well, the life of a travelling player, when one undertakes such challenges during the milder months of the year and confines oneself to civilised towns connected by road, don't you think, dearest? It can be fearfully wet on the west coast, and I do not find open carts on bumpy tracks, or boats on turbulent seas, at all commodious.' Mrs Bromby was gripping her shawl tightly at her neck with one hand and her seat with the other, bracing herself against the alarmingly large waves buffeting the steamboat relentlessly. Charles nodded in sympathy, wondering how he could help them.

'Quite so, my dear, quite so.' Mr Bromby seemed equally

uncomfortable. His habitually ruddy face had turned an alarming shade of pale green. They were sailing from Glasgow to Campbeltown in the newly launched *Waterloo* – a miracle of engineering that had reduced a week's journey to a mere fourteen hours – but the poor Brombys were quite distressed already and there were twelve more hours to go.

'Mr and Mrs Bromby, I do apologise for this difficult situation. I was assured it would be a pleasant journey, but clearly that is not the case today.' Charles smiled ruefully and fetched a leather bucket for them, then returned to the deck to enjoy the exhilaration of the wind and spray with Charlotte.

She was standing at the bow, the wind in her face, hair streaming out behind her like strands of liquid honey. He stood watching her for a moment, his heart full to bursting that such an exquisite creature had come into his life and seemed so very fond of him. The first time he saw her she was wearing a snugly fitting tartan dress, her blue eyes bright and full of fun, and he had known she was someone special. He strode across to the bow, leaning into the swell as the deck tipped, then stood behind her and wrapped his arms round her waist, kissing her neck, inhaling her gorgeous lavender scent – lavender with a hint of something altogether sharper that he had not yet identified.

'Charles!' She whirled round, laughing, the wind whipping her hair into a tangle around her face. Her eyes shone as she pulled the wayward curls from her mouth and tucked them behind her ear with her slim fingers. He grinned like a fool, then kissed her again, savouring the salt on her lips.

There was a disappointingly low turnout for their performance at the playhouse in Campbeltown the following night. The supper they were offered in the kitchen of the inn was dismal too: a quarter of toasted oatbread each with a few slivers of cheese and some slippery pickled onions. They were obliged to share a little parlour room for the night, as they often did, grateful in this instance not to have strangers sharing it with them too. The landlady assured them the two iron bedsteads were *well-aired*, despite a distinct smell of mildew, but, most importantly, there was a fireplace and a bucket of coal. Charles ordered whisky and they stayed up into the wee small hours telling stories and playing cards, building up the fire till flames leapt round the room, throwing long shadows on the dank walls.

In the morning Charles was woken by a sharp rap at the door. He jumped out of bed in his long, striped nightgown and opened the door to find a letter on the floor.

'What on earth is going on, Mackay? You woke me from a deep sleep, flinging the blanket off like that!'

'Sorry, Bromby – I think you'll find it was the rap at the door that woke you, though.' Charles opened the shutters, but dawn had hardly broken so he lit a tallow candle instead, sending a slim spiral of black smoke curling up towards the low ceiling.

'Aha! It appears another invitation has arrived! It must have travelled with us on the boat!' Charles was smiling mischievously at his fellow thespians, all of whom were now awake, waiting for their full attention, drawing out the suspense.

'Mr Mackay, ever the optimist!' Mrs Bromby was sitting up in bed, swathed in a voluminous pink silk peignoir. She pulled off her frilly pink nightcap and fussed with her thin grey hair. Charlotte sat beside her, rubbing her eyes, and Charles thought how beautiful she looked when she was half asleep. He pulled at the tab and began to read.

'Well now, I fear you will have to save your mockery for another day, dear Mrs Bromby. I have in my hand an invitation to join Mr Corbett Ryder at the Theatre Royal, Aberdeen, this coming new year. He is about to take on the lease and make it a base for what he is calling his northern circuit, and he's putting together a stock company.' Charles felt his eyes grow wide as he thought of the implications. He looked at Charlotte, who was sitting on the edge of the bed, her long white, lace-trimmed nightgown demurely buttoned up to her neck. Her feet, not quite touching the floor, were dangling daintily in pink-striped stockings. She clapped her hands like a little girl, her eyes sparkling back at him.

'My dear Charles,' Mr Bromby began, scratching a field of white stubble that had sprung up overnight on his chin. 'Am I right in surmising this invitation is for yourself, rather than for this little troupe of strolling players?' Charles glanced down at the letter again, then looked up apologetically. Mr Bromby was an astute man and had guessed the time had come for a parting of the ways. Charles sat beside him, holding the candle up to show him the letter and wondering how to deal with the awkwardness of the situation.

Mrs Bromby pulled her spectacles from her reticule, perched them on the end of her magnificent nose, then went to read over her husband's shoulder. Charlotte wrapped her plaid round her shoulders and stood beside her. Charles could feel her watchful eyes on him and looked up, his wry smile and raised eyebrow posing a question. She grinned and nodded.

'Well, my dears, it seems fate has dealt you young people a most excellent hand today!' Mrs Bromby had read the signs as well and was taking charge. 'Clearly you must make haste and marry your beloved, Charles, and the two of you must go to Aberdeen and follow your thespian dreams!' She was patting Mr Bromby's hand as she spoke. 'Mr Bromby and I were thinking of going back to London soon in any case, weren't we, dearest?' He covered her hand with his own, looking relieved. 'We have been finding the life of travelling players rather onerous for our advanced years of late, especially with the winter coming on. I do believe this is the perfect solution! We will buy tickets for the stagecoach directly after the wedding. I, for one, have had my fill of travelling by sea!'

Charles jumped to his feet, dropping the letter on the bed, and the Brombys clapped and cheered as he swept Charlotte off her feet. She fell back into his arms, laughing helplessly as he cavorted around the room, singing their song from *The Honeymoon* at the top of his voice.

FIVE

'His Majesty's Servants of the Theatre', as Mr Ryder called his Aberdeen company, were in Perth again, relaunching the newly decorated St Anne's Lane Theatre in its second season under his management. All the takings were to be donated to the relief of the local labouring poor and the house was packed. It was May 1818 and the Mackays had spent over a year touring the northern circuit. Charlotte was extremely proud of her husband, who had begun to make quite a name for himself as a comedian.

The play was *The School for Scandal*, and Charles gave the delightfully pompous Sir Peter Teazle a marvellous outing while Charlotte had a small part as the maid. Henry Johnston had arrived in the Fair City the previous week, unannounced, and had availed himself of a part at the last minute. He greeted the Mackays like old friends, complimenting Charlotte until she felt confused and flustered, and never once apologising for leaving his company in the lurch in Ayr.

The actors took their final curtain call and filed off into the wings. Shouts for more grew louder and more persistent, and suddenly Charles ran back on-stage. The audience went into a frenzy. Charlotte watched him quietening them with his hands, looking supremely confident, and wondered what on earth he was planning to do. He began strutting up and down, performing some of his most recently developed mimicry, making fun of some of the most well-known actors in British theatre with his perfectly pitched accents and gestures. Shrieks of laughter soon filled the auditorium again. Charlotte put her hand over her mouth in disbelief when he gave his impression of Henry Johnston playing the part of Sir Archy MacSarcasm. Henry was standing near her in the wings and Charlotte was mortified until she realised he was laughing as much as everyone else.

'Gie us a wag o' your lufe lad! Why, ye are as diligent in the service o' your mistress as in the service o' your looking-glass, for your een.' A standing ovation was followed by stamping feet, whistling and shouts for even more. Charles looked round and caught Charlotte's eye, an expression of panic on his sweat-drenched face, and she knew at once what he should do. She waved her arms like a conductor, smiling brightly to reassure him, and he grinned back at her, wiping the sweat from his forehead with his sleeve. Then Charles turned confidently to face the rowdy audience again.

'And now, ladies and gentlemen, Mr Conductor, let's gie it all we've got for "Auld Lang Syne"!' The orchestra took his cue and Charles winked at Charlotte as the opening bars of the song – which was now quite popular – soared up into the rafters. He transformed himself into the famous operatic singer and darling of Covent Garden, his old friend John Sinclair, and began to sing. The audience joined in with gusto and the whole troupe came back onto the stage again for a final finale. *What a night!*

Charlotte slipped her hand into Charles's as they walked along the banks of the broad River Tay the following day, the blue midsummer sky stretching out high above them like a length of freshly pressed silk. A visiting actor was going to play the Duke to young Mrs Ryder's Juliana in the forthcoming production of

The Honeymoon and Charlotte had been asked to play Juliana's sister, Volante.

'Charles.'

'Hhmm?'

'Don't you think it's strange, you and I not taking the lead roles in *The Honeymoon*, not singing our song together, like we always did in Ayr?' He stopped and picked up her other hand.

'It *will* seem strange, I agree, but this is how it will be for us, now we're professional actors, Charlotte. We must play any part we're given to the best of our ability, whether it's large or small, and learn from every experience, don't you think? Anyway, you'll make a marvellous Volante! And I'll be sure to bring the house down with my Lampedo!' He gave his broadest grin, rolled his eyes and pulled such a ridiculous face that she laughed despite her disappointment.

'Ladies and Gentlemen, as you know, we have almost run through our entire repertoire here in Perth, so I've decided it is time to put on a brand-new production.' Mr Ryder, a dapper little man with a thin nose and a loud voice, had gathered his company in the green room first thing in the morning to make an announcement. 'I have something rather special in mind. As you know, the stage version of *Guy Mannering* has always been a great success for us, so there's a good chance an adaptation of another *Waverley* novel will prove equally popular.' Ryder held up a script and pointed to the title. '*Rob Roy McGregor – or Auld Lang Syne* – Isaac Pocock's version, which I think is by far the best of several currently in circulation.' Ryder took a pile of scripts from his pretty young wife, who was standing beside him, and held them up. 'I would encourage each of you to familiarise yourselves with your parts with all speed. Rehearsals start on Monday and we open the following Saturday!' He handed the scripts back to his wife to distribute and departed swiftly, leaving a hubbub of excited chatter in his wake.

Charlotte was sitting curled up on a chair by the window in their lodgings with volume three of the novel, *Rob Roy*, open on her knee, catching the last of the daylight to read. She had been given the non-speaking role of a hostess in a tavern in the opening scene, while Charles had been given the main comedic role of a self-important Glasgow magistrate called Bailie Nicol Jarvie. Charlotte had been hoping for the more interesting part of Mattie, the Bailie's faithful servant, but she was excited to see what Charles would make of the Bailie.

'Why do you think John Sinclair's song has been added to the title of the opera, Charles? I can see Pocock has inserted several songs into the play to make it an opera, but the inclusion of that one seems rather forced, don't you think? Or am I missing something? And it's even become part of the title!'

Charles looked up from his perusal of the script. 'It's not actually Sinclair's song, of course, Charlotte, although he's made it very popular. I think Pocock was simply trying to entice Sinclair to perform in the play, hoping thereby to guarantee packed audiences at Covent Garden.'

'Hhmm, you're probably right.' A cool breeze came through the opening at the top of the window, billowing the thin blue cotton curtain like a twirling skirt, and Charlotte stood to close it.

'I know this man, Charlotte. I recognise him as a type I've often come across in guid auld Glasgae toon! I feel a great deal of sympathy for his blundering good intentions too, I must confess.' Charlotte turned and smiled at his enthusiasm as he waved the script in the air. She loved his energy when he was inspired.

'I'm so happy for you, Charles. There's a glint in your eye that tells me you feel this play is going to be something special.'

'Quite so!' Charles put the script down and began pacing the room, raking one hand through his hair and gesturing with the other. 'I find myself unaccountably drawn to the Bailie, to his concerns – even to his pomposity and vanity. I'm not necessarily in agreement with all his Unionist politics, of course, but I must say he puts his ideas across in a most genial manner. And he's a weaver, like my brother William. Ha!' Charlotte sat down again and put her book on a side table, giving him her full attention. 'As far as politics go, of course, Rob Roy and his wife speak so passionately of the national cause that everyone in the audience will be bound to feel fairly represented whatever their politics.' He stopped beside her to look out into the darkening street and she stood up again, slipping an arm round his waist. 'Being set in the past somehow makes it seem safer to tackle these thorny issues, don't you think Charlotte?'

'Absolutely, Charles. A very clever tactic!' She could see, even in the half-light, that his eyes were puffy and tired – a little bloodshot, even.

'It's as though this part were made for me, Charlotte! Bailie Nicol Jarvie – it has quite a ring to it, don't you think?' He rubbed his eyes and she reached up to stroke his eyelids gently with her thumbs, then took his face in her hands.

'Charles, dearest, you really must try to give your mind a rest tonight. You've spent so long reading the novel as well as the script, you need to stop now and allow yourself to process everything.' He put his arms around her and she felt his shoulders slump as he spoke quietly into her hair.

'You're right, as usual, my darling.' He stepped back and looked into her eyes, as if he were trying to read her thoughts. 'I hope you're not too discouraged with your own small part, though.' *He knows me too well!* 'Mr Ryder really had no choice but to give you a role he could quickly fill with an understudy after your dreadful bouts of sickness these past few weeks. Remember, there was almost a disaster the last time you played Volante? I don't know how you held your vomit down till you could run off-stage!' Charles made a silly face and she smiled and sighed, looking at him with her head on one side.

'I know. But I feel so much better now! Still.' Charlotte bent to pick up her book and carried it over to the bookshelf, where she stowed it beside its companion volumes. 'I understand it's a case of better safe than sorry for Mr Ryder. He has a great deal to supervise on his northern circuit. The last thing he needs is me making a spectacle of myself on-stage!' She stared at the three gold-trimmed black leather books for a moment, trailing her hand over them to hide her disappointment from Charles. They contained a story Charlotte was beginning to feel might change the course of both their lives. She would need to return them to the circulating library soon.

Charlotte walked into the green room the next morning to the sound of raised voices.

'But I absolutely insist, Mr Ryder! I've been at this game far longer than Mackay! It's only right I should have the Senior Comedy role.' She could hardly believe what Mr Williams was demanding, with the play opening in just four days' time. Mr Ryder squeezed his eyes shut, pinched the top of his narrow nose with his fingers and muttered under his breath. Mr Williams planted his large red hands defiantly on his broad hips, one foot tapping the floor impatiently. Charlotte noticed Charles was clenching and unclenching his fists as if he wanted to punch the man. Ryder began flicking through the script.

'Let me see, yes.' He looked up sharply. 'Mr Williams, Mr Mackay, we must endeavour to sort this out amicably.' Ryder addressed Charles first. 'The part of Rashleigh is an excellent part, Mr Mackay, and as you have studied the play so thoroughly I'm confident you would be more than capable of turning your hand to it most effectively. What do you say?' Charles looked aghast. Charlotte's heart sank and she began twisting her kerchief tightly round her fingers, hoping and praying for a good outcome. When Charles spoke she felt her face flush.

'Mr Ryder – with the greatest of respect – I must object! I've put a great deal of preparation into the character of the Bailie. I have a very strong affinity with him. In fact, I'm confident I can make him come alive better than *anyone else* in this company, and I'm simply not prepared to compromise!' Charles folded his arms resolutely and Mr Ryder ran his hand through his scant brown hair, sighing. Suddenly, Mr Williams grabbed Charles by the elbow and spun him round, shoving him in the chest with the flat of his hand and pushing his big florid face close to Charles's as he spat out his words.

'How *dare* you Mackay! The part should be *mine* and there's an *end* to it!' Charlotte could hardly breathe. Her kerchief fell to the floor and she bit her lip, willing Charles to stand up for himself.

'That's *enough*, Williams!' Ryder boomed, pulling the men apart with surprising strength. '*Neithe*r of you shall be the Bailie! I shall scrap the whole performance! I never liked the play anyway. And now, with all this infernal jockeying for position, I want *nothing* more to do with it! I hope you are both satisfied!' There was a shocked silence in the room. Mr Ryder was usually such a self-possessed man.

'What on earth is the matter? Why the ominous silence and glum faces? What have I missed?' Charlotte looked round to see Ryder's young wife, Jessie, coming through the door with a quizzical smile on her neat, pretty features, her two little daughters in tow.

Hardly old enough to be a mother, Jessie was petite, with long dark hair worn in ringlets, and the kind of bold self-assurance that fills a room. She was also a spirited actress and seemed to Charlotte quite determined and fearless. Jessie had married the newly widowed Ryder when she was only fifteen, and now – at just twenty – she had four-year-old twins of her own and was stepmother to Ryder's two older children. She took her husband to one side for a few minutes, soothing him with her mellow voice and effortless charm, then turned towards the waiting actors to make an announcement herself.

'I'm sure you'll be delighted to hear the disaster has been averted and the play will go ahead! Mr Mackay will play the Bailie and I will play Diana.' Then she turned to Mr Williams and dismissed him with perfect confidence, wishing him all the best for his future endeavours as he stormed out of the room.

Corbett Ryder advertised *Rob Roy* for a run of three nights and gave the leading role of Rob Roy to a visiting actor. The opening night sold out, the play received rapturous applause, and after three such nights Ryder admitted defeat and allowed the production to run its course. Tickets at three shillings for boxes, two shillings for the pit and one shilling for the gallery sold out night after night. The moment the doors opened at six o'clock, people piled in at least an hour early, filling the theatre with their excited chatter. It was the first time the Mackays had experienced such a phenomenon.

'Listen to this, Charlotte!' Charles had a broadsheet open on his knee and could hardly speak for laughing. 'I thought the Saturday crowd were a bit lively!'

'Read it out then, why don't you?' It was Monday morning, the beginning of the second week of the extended run, and Charlotte was lying on the bed kneading a sore stomach. She was relieved not to have been plagued by any more sickness and proud of the way she had conducted herself in the opening scene each night, taking her little moment of attention, expanding it with her gestures and expressions and usually receiving a smattering of applause as she left the stage.

'*... Rob Roy would have appeared to better advantage had he been a little more conversant with the Scottish dialect.*'

'Ah well,' Charlotte chipped in, 'perhaps that's why Mr Ryder has taken the lead role away from that poor fellow whose name I've already forgotten!'

'I heard Ryder's father made him take it, Charlotte. Apparently, he couldn't bear to hear all the cheering night after night from his desk in the foyer where he was taking tickets. He was steaming with rage out there because the applause wasn't for his son!'

'But the cheering was mostly for *you*, Charles – for the Bailie – not for Rob Roy!' Charles fluttered his eyelashes at Charlotte until she laughed. 'So tell me, then, what did the reviewer say about *you*, Bailie Nicol Jarvie.'

'Oh, not much.' Charles lounged back in his chair, feigning ennui, then leaned forward, his eyes lighting up. 'Only that I *possess talent of a very superior cast*.' She threw a pillow at him and he caught it with glee.

'Ach – away an' bile yer heid, ye big daftie! Now, read me the part about the lively audience you mentioned earlier.'

'That's a bonnie Scots accent you're developing by the way lassie – nae bad for a Bow-bell Cockney!' Charlotte smiled, hugging his praise to herself like a gift. He continued to read.

'Ah yes – apparently some of them *returned home next morning roaring out like madmen, Rob Roy for ever"!* It seems the play is touching a Scots nerve, reminding folk to be proud of our great nation. Ah, I forgot – you Cockneys wouldnae ken!'

'Proud o' me Cockney blood, though, ain't I!' They were both laughing when Charlotte suddenly remembered something she had been meaning to ask him for a while.

'But seriously, Charles, who wrote these *Waverley* novels, and why do you think they want to stay anonymous?'

'I've heard they call him "*The Great Unknown*". Folk say it might be an advocate called Walter Scott. He probably doesn't want to risk his reputation by owning up to writing popular novels. He seems proud enough of his poetry, though.' Charles flopped down onto the bed next to Charlotte, drawing her to his side. She curled into him, closed her eyes, and decided not to mention her stomach pains.

The last notes of a short overture were echoing round the auditorium as the red velvet drapes opened to reveal the interior of a small tavern. Tables and benches were scattered across the stage and the back plate was painted with a large window, displaying a sweeping landscape with a grand country house in the distance. A group of travellers were enjoying their drinks, singing a merry song about the outlaw Rob Roy, setting the scene for the story.

The innkeeper commended them, picked up on the political theme with his comments, then told his wife to fetch them a last drink.

Charlotte gave her full attention to the moment, ignoring the stabbing pain in her belly, controlling it with her breathing as she placed the drinks on the tables. When it was time to leave the stage she was determined not to run off clutching her stomach. She realised it was too late to avoid a catastrophe when she felt warm liquid trickling down her leg. Moving carefully towards the wings she turned to the audience, dipped the slightest hint of a curtsey, and smiled graciously at their applause. Then she walked sedately off-stage, turning once to survey the drips of blood she had left in her wake.

There was uproar in the green room when Charlotte hobbled in, bent double. She begged everyone not to tell Charles until he had finished the play then collapsed in a pool of blood.

'Please don't worry about me, Charles, it'll give me a chance to recover my strength.' The Mackays were sitting on a wrought-iron bench beside the River Tay, just a short walk from their lodging house. The water was flowing fast after a week of rain, and the power of its dark, swirling depths was mesmerising. Ryder's company were about to go on tour again, visiting Montrose for a few weeks, then alternating between the Theatre Royal in Dundee and the Trades Hall in Arbroath. They would be returning to Aberdeen in September and Charlotte had decided to stay in Perth for the summer until Charles returned and they could go back to Aberdeen together. She was still feeling very weak.

Charlotte put a hand to Charles's cheek. 'Something special is happening for you with this Rob Roy play and I want you to enjoy every moment of it!'

'Are you quite sure, my darling girl? Won't it be insufferably boring for you?' Charles pulled one of his lopsided grins and Charlotte smiled, as she always did.

'Of course not! I shall borrow some of the *Waverley* novels from the circulating library. I certainly won't be bored. When you come back I'll be blossoming with health.' He kissed her softly, wrapping her gently in his arms as though afraid of her fragility, and Charlotte had to summon all her resolve not to cry.

Charlotte had read all the *Waverley* novels by late September, and all four volumes of a recent addition called *The Heart of Mid-Lothian*. The librarian had recommended the new publication to her enthusiastically, explaining in hushed tones that, although it was part of a series called *Tales of My Landlord*, written under the pen name of Jedediah Cleishbotham, the author was widely thought to be the anonymous author of the *Waverley* novels.

She had also sewn two new day dresses with puffed sleeves in pretty cotton prints, a silk chemise and two pairs of linen drawstring underdrawers, and befriended the landlady at their lodgings. The two of them had boiled and scrubbed their laundry every week, side by side, spreading it to dry on the riverbank or in the drying green behind the house, running out laughing in sudden showers of rain to gather it in. Charlotte had not been idle.

She was sitting on her favourite bench on the North Inch one afternoon, the flat green racecourse stretching out behind her, the wide brown river flowing sedately in front of her and the low, orange sunshine draping her shoulders like a warm shawl.

A swan dipped its head gracefully into the dark water, creating circles that spread wider and wider and faded into nothing. Then it drifted downstream to join three large grey signets and her eyes filled. She pressed her hand on her belly, where the grief of losing her first child sat like a stone. Charles would be home in the morning and she was not ready. She had not grieved.

Charlotte pulled her green plaid round her face and allowed herself to sob quietly into the warm, bunched wool, hoping no one was watching, not really caring if they were. It was such a relief to cry. Soon her shoulders were heaving and the great pain inside her came out in a long moan. If only she could be weeping into her mother's soft linen apron, inhaling the lavender and rosemary scent of her, sinking into the comfort and safety of her strong embrace. Suddenly she felt so far from her mother she could hardly breathe.

When the sobbing subsided and her breathing calmed, tears continued to roll down her face like raindrops on a windowpane. Charlotte's thoughts turned to her four sisters in London, her two brothers, her darling father who always told her she was his rosebud. It dawned on her for the first time since she had left London that she missed her noisy, hectic family more than she had ever dreamed she would. Closest in age to her was Ann, who occasionally wrote with family news. Her letters were short and stilted, but infinitely precious. She had the most recent one in her pocket and took it out, holding it to her lips.

She had missed Charles terribly, but she would never mention it and make him feel guilty. She put her hand to her neck and fingered the heart-shaped gold pendant he had given her as a wedding gift. Charlotte had given him a gold pocket watch in return and she pictured it, safely secreted in his waistcoat pocket. It had been a comfort throughout these long summer days, being linked by their golden gifts. She sat back and closed her eyes, allowing the sun to dry the last few tears still slipping down her cheeks. Charles was such a warm and wonderful man and he loved her more than she had ever thought anyone would. She loved him dearly too. All would be well for them both. This summer had been a setback for her, but better days would surely follow. She remembered Mrs Bromby's parting words: 'If you ever need inspiration to persevere as an actress, my dear, just think of that great tragedian, Sarah Siddons. She has lost so much throughout her long life, but she has never once given up. She even gave birth to her second child on-stage, halfway through a performance!' *What an extraordinary woman!*

Charlotte took a deep breath and stood up, smoothing the skirts of her printed cotton dress and pulling her plaid round her shoulders. It was time to go back to their lodgings and prepare for Charles's triumphant homecoming. The newspapers had begun to refer to him as 'The Great Mackay' and she was determined to give him the hero's welcome he deserved.

SIX

A coach and four thundered along Princes Street in thick, dark fog, appearing and disappearing between pencils of light drawn by the thinly spaced streetlamps. It clattered into the bright blaze of the Theatre Royal and came to a halt, steam rising from the snorting horses' flanks. A young man in a long grey cloak and black stovepipe hat jumped out and turned to hand the ladies onto the icy surface of the packed snow. Three ladies and four gentlemen, all clad in cloaks with hats and bonnets low on their brows, whisked into the theatre, the oldest gentleman making good use of a walking stick.

Charles and Charlotte were sitting opposite the theatre on the steps of Register House, watching. It was a cold December night and they had just arrived in Edinburgh after a long journey from Aberdeen by carriage, ferry boat and cab. Shortly after his return to Perth Charles had received a letter from Mr William Murray, manager of the Theatre Royal in Edinburgh, inviting them to join his company, offering them both a salaried contract. They had accepted at once and travelled down as soon as the autumn season in Aberdeen was over.

'I wonder who those latecomers could be!' Charlotte huddled into Charles and he wrapped his arm around her protectively.

'I've a hunch it might be Walter Scott and his family, Charlotte – I know he walks with a limp at any rate, and I've heard he loves the theatre.'

'You're probably right. They were ushered in by the steward like important folk.' Charlotte pulled her plaid over her mouth and Charles turned up the collar of his great coat. He was cold to the bone. It had been his idea to come and sit on these steps to remember old times, maybe even to tell Charlotte about his mother, but it turned out the words were buried too deep. He stood and pulled her to her feet with both hands.

'Come on – let's go and find some supper and retire to bed early, it's been a long day and we've work to do in the morning.'

They breakfasted on freshly baked rolls and smoked kippers with strong coffee, then strolled across Shakespeare Square to the stage door at the back of the theatre, where they had been told to report for duty in good time for ten o'clock. A grim little man in a fur cap opened the door a crack and looked at them suspiciously, jangling the large bunch of keys hanging on his wide leather belt. Charles smiled politely.

'Good morning, sir. Mr and Mrs Mackay, reporting for duty.' The man grunted and looked them up and down.

'Aye. Himself is expectin' yous.' He stepped to one side and pulled the door open. Charles was sorely tempted to laugh but concealed his glee, making a mental note: *this carnaptious Cerberus will no doubt be perfect for some character I need to develop before long. Best keep on the right side of him though, he's the man with all the keys!* They followed him past his cramped little watch-box down a dim corridor.

'Ye'll need tae gie notice of yer arrival tae the prompter, yer place o' abode an' that. He'll gie ye a copy o' The Rules and tak ye to the manager's office up the stair – or more likely straight to the green room, seein' you've no' left much time.'

'Thankin' ye kindly, guid sir.' Charles gave a slight bow and they were left standing outside a closed door behind the stage, trying not to laugh, presuming the prompter was within.

'Ach, Charlie, there's nae need tae mock the wee mannie wi' yer faux Scots brogue!'

'Faux it isnae, my London lassie, unlike your own! D'ye no' ken I'm a true Edinburgh gutter-bluid mysel', born and bred? This is me comin' hame!' The door swung open and a red-faced man with a broad smile and a shock of white hair like a full head of thistledown appeared.

'Ah, it's yerselves blethering away outside my door! Come away in!'

'Mr and Mrs Mackay, sir, arrived last night from Perth. We're staying at the Red Lion behind the theatre till we can find lodgings.'

The man shook Charles's hand enthusiastically, like a man pumping water from a well.

'O' course you are. Sandy's the name – Alexander Bell – but everyone knows me as Sandy. So! Mr Murray is expecting you in the green room at ten o'clock sharp, same as everyone else.' They stood near Sandy's desk, surreptitiously holding hands while he rummaged through a precariously balanced pile of papers.

'Ah, here it is – a copy of The Rules!' He opened the pamphlet, smiling broadly, and began to read. '*Regulations to be Observed by the Company of the Theatre Royal, Edinburgh. Section One: General Regulations, first item: accommodation*.' Sandy looked up, his ruddy cheeks bunching into a broad smile, his fine hair a fluffy white halo. 'You've given me notice of your arrival, where yer staying and all that, but remember this,' he tapped the page with his forefinger, 'when you find lodgings you must be sure they're less than half a mile from the theatre, so they'll be inside the limits of "*The Call*".' He handed the pamphlet to Charles. 'Best read it carefully, we're very strict about the fines!' Sandy's smile seemed at odds with his words and Charles tickled Charlotte's palm with his thumb, knowing it would make her want to laugh. Sandy pulled a silver pocket watch from his green brocade waistcoat, glanced down at it, pushed his chair back and stood. 'Right then, follow me tae the green room, guid people, if you will!'

The spacious green room, with its long windows, high ceilings and sea-green walls, was crackling with energy. Actors and dancers chatted in groups, lounged on sofas and peered at themselves in large looking-glasses; voices trilled and the air was filled with a cornucopia of smells, from greasepaint and leather to powder and perfume. No one paid the Mackays much attention.

On the far side of the room, deep in conversation, a neat gentleman in a black frock coat with a charcoal-grey cravat tied over his white wing collar looked up, raised a hand and made his way towards them.

'Good morning – you must be Mr and Mrs Mackay!' He was a very self-possessed man with an air of authority that belied his modest stature. There could be no mistaking his identity.

'A pleasure to meet you, Mr Murray.' Charles shook the manager's hand and was pleased when Mr Murray shook Charlotte's hand too. He had a high forehead, thin dark hair, large, lively eyes and a small, round chin. His droll little sideways smile lit up his otherwise rather austere countenance delightfully.

'The pleasure is all mine, I assure you. Welcome to "Playbills", as some of us call our good old theatre. I trust you slept well and are raring to go – rehearsals are about to begin, but there's still time to introduce you to the company.' He clapped his hands and a hush fell at once.

'Ladies and gentleman, I present to you Mr and Mrs Mackay, freshly poached from Corbett Ryder's northern circuit.' There were one or two chuckles. 'I'm expecting great things of "The Great Mackay", as they already refer to Charles in the north. He specialises in Comedy and Old Man roles, but I'm sure he's more than capable of turning his hand to anything, aren't you Mackay?' Charles suddenly felt rather warm under the scrutiny of the company, unsure if it was entirely welcoming. Mr Murray continued regardless.

'Mrs Mackay will also be taking to the stage, so please, all of you, make them both welcome and show them the ropes.' He turned to Charles, lowering his voice, 'Your debut will be in *The Jealous Wife*. D'you know it?' Charles nodded. 'You'll have the part of Mr Russell – Old Russet. Miss Nicol here will get you a copy of the script.' He beckoned an elegant young lady, considerably taller than himself, to join them. 'She will be in the production too, won't you, Miss Nicol?' Not pausing for her to reply Mr Murray pulled a small notebook from his pocket. 'The performance is on December the 26th, rehearsals begin tomorrow morning, ten o'clock sharp.' He looked up and Charles felt the full intensity of his new employer's gaze for a few seconds before his eyes dropped back to his pocketbook, his forefinger leafing through the pages. 'Next up will be *The Wandering Boys* with you in the part of Lubin, Mackay. I assume you're familiar with it?' Again, Mr Murray flicked a quick glance at him and Charles nodded, not wishing to interrupt. 'Take him to fetch the scripts from Sandy, if you would Miss Nicol. Better include *Henry IV*, *Merry Wives* and *The Navigators*, too – oh, and *The Wanderer*. We'll be straight into all those in the new year. I hope you've a good head for lines, Mackay! Thankfully Miss Nicol's memory is second to none, so she won't forget my list of scripts for you, will you my dear! Ha! Wait just a moment though.' After another look at his pocketbook Mr Murray turned his attention to Charlotte, softening his expression and his voice slightly.

'Now then, Mrs Mackay, I trust you are in the best of health these days?' She nodded and smiled. 'We shall be easing you in rather more gently than your husband, you'll be glad to know! I have you down for *The Wanderer* in January. Miss Nicol can tell you all about it – you'll be joining her and some of the other girls as attendants.' Mr Murray slipped his book back into his pocket, straightened his shoulders and changed the subject again.

'I hope you two have no plans for supper tonight? My sister and I would very much like you to join us at York Place. Would five o'clock suit?' They barely had time to nod before their new employer was striding across the room, plunging into a discussion about scenery, pulleys, trapdoors and substage machinery with someone Charles imagined must be a carpenter. Miss Nicol's warm, leisurely voice came as a welcome relief.

'I hope you're both ready for the whirlwind that is the Theatre Royal! Mr Murray is a wonderful manager – quite the disciplinarian at times too – but he runs a good ship. Some go so far as to call him the Napoleon of Managers, but I can assure you he has a heart of gold!' Miss Nicol had strong, expressive features that Charles would not have described as pretty, but he found her strikingly attractive and wondered if it was her confidence and poise that made her so.

'I've heard Mr Murray's an accomplished actor himself, is that true Miss Nicol?'

'Oh yes, he's magnificent on-stage, as is his sister, Harriet. Did you know she's been the lessee of this theatre and effectively his employer since her husband Henry died several years ago? Henry was Sarah Siddon's son – you may have heard of her, she's a famous actress.'

Charlotte's eyes grew wide. 'Oh, how thrilling! I've seen Sarah Siddons on-stage in London, as it happens. It'll be lovely to meet Harriet for supper, there'll be so much to talk about!' Charles nodded, unable to speak for a moment, overwhelmed by memories of his dear mother, who would have been so proud to know her son was going for supper with Sarah Siddons' daughter-in-law.

'Ah, here's Mr Calcraft! He was in the military, like yourself, Mr Mackay.' A tall, straight-backed gentleman with a hawklike nose and hooded eyes, somewhat on the northside of friendly, shook his hand and excused himself at once. Miss Nicol ushered several more actors over to greet them: Jones, tall and wiry; Hamerton, bluff and ruddy; Chippendale, Duff, Alexander, Shaw – and finally her three delightful sisters and their charming mother. Charles was politeness itself throughout the introductions, although he was longing for Miss Nicol – Emma, he had heard her sister call her – to hurry up so they could go and fetch the scripts from Sandy, trying to remember all the parts he had been given, longing to begin.

SEVEN

On the night of Charlotte's first performance in Edinburgh's Theatre Royal she played one of three attendants. The other two were Emma Nicol, who had quickly become a good friend, and Mrs Shaw, who had not. Charlotte was given a fusty pale blue gown with a frayed hem from the bottom of a trunk, and an extravagantly tall grey horsehair wig which smelt of greasepaint and sweat and reminded her of Mrs Bromby. It was good to be back on-stage.

Ten days later she took part in a lavish production of *The Tempest* and the indomitable Mrs Garbutt, who ran the costume department like a major general, gave her a delicate silver silk dress to wear for her brief and silent appearance as Venus. Charlotte took great care with every detail of her costume, her makeup, her hair, and made the most of every moment she was on-stage, reminding herself that gestures and expressions often speak louder than words.

On the first Monday of February 1819 the company gathered in the green room in the morning to hear about the month's programme. Mr Murray strode in on the stroke of ten, followed by Sandy carrying an armful of scripts, raking a hand through his puff of white hair, his red face wreathed in smiles.

'Alright everyone, your attention please.' Silence prevailed at once. 'I have decided to present a lavish production of *Rob Roy Macgregor* this month. Some of you may have seen it, and several of you have acted in it already.' He glanced over at Charlotte and Charles, giving them a brief nod. Several members of the troupe turned to look. 'I have invited Mr Grieve from Covent Garden to design the scenery, which will comprise no fewer than fourteen panels.' Appreciative mutterings fluttered round the room. 'No expense shall be spared. I believe it will be a huge success and one we may well repeat more than once. Sandy here has your scripts, so I suggest you get to work learning your parts as soon as this morning's rehearsal has finished.'

There was an immediate rush towards Sandy, but Charlotte hung back.

'Look, Charlotte – I'm to play Martha! It's so exciting!' Emma Nicol was making a beeline for her, her face shining, waving her script in the air. Charlotte was swept up in her new friend's joy until another voice cut across their happy chatter.

'Aha! It seems I have been given the part of the Hostess, Charlotte – a part I believe you are familiar with.' Mrs Shaw smiled triumphantly. 'How interesting that this updated version has dispensed entirely with the Host and given all his lines to the Hostess! It seems I shall, effectively, be setting the scene for the entire play. I wonder why Mr Murray gave the part to me and not to you, my dear.' Mrs Shaw tipped her head to one side as though in pity, then flounced away to tell her husband her good fortune.

Charlotte stood perfectly still amongst all the comings and goings. When Sandy finally left the room it was clear she had not been given a part and she felt utterly humiliated. Was it because she was still regarded as new to the company? If so, then what about Charles? She looked around the crowded room for him, hoping for the best. He had almost come to blows over the role of the Bailie in Perth and there were bound to be actors in

Edinburgh who would want such a choice role for themselves. What if he had been bypassed too? When she spotted him talking to Mr Murray by the door, looking at his script with that familiar enthusiasm on his face, she breathed a sigh of relief. She was about to go and join him when someone behind her began speaking in a low voice, and she froze.

'I can't believe how that Mackay fellow has wormed his way into Murray's favour. Just look at him! If Mason hadn't gone to Glasgow on some daft business scheme he would definitely have been given the part of the Bailie.'

'Absolutely, old boy. Murray seems blind to Mackay's lack of height and his rather homely visage, neither of which are at all suitable for the job of an actor in my opinion. In fact it downright annoys me that a fellow with his lack of gentleman's breeding and education can muscle into our company and be given leading roles at once. Quite frankly, it's ridiculous!'

'I quite agree. What can Murray be thinking? It'll end badly, you mark my words, Mackay will fail miserably.' Charlotte was furious. *What utter rubbish! They're green with envy!* Charles had played the Bailie many times with great success already; he had not become known as The Great Mackay for nothing! She turned to face the two gossiping gentlemen, giving them a broad smile and thoroughly enjoying their embarrassment, then she strode across the room to congratulate her husband, beaming at him proudly.

Although she had no part in the production, Charlotte went to the theatre on the first night of *Rob Roy.* She wanted to watch Charles from the wings, to be able to smile at him or touch his hand as he passed her, to whisper to him how well he was doing.

At seven o'clock she risked a discreet peep at the audience, keeping well back in the shadows. The theatre was full. She watched the conductor raise his baton, but a shout from the pit made him turn round. Suddenly there was a great commotion.

The audience were on their feet, turning to face the boxes. Applause rolled across the auditorium like thunder and chants of 'Scott, Scott, Scott!' rose above the cacophony as a distinguished older gentleman stood to take the ovation, smiling benevolently down from his box. After a few moments he indicated to the conductor to strike up the overture, flicked his coat tails under him, and took his seat. Charlotte ran upstairs at once to tell Charles, who was still in his dressing room.

'He's here again tonight, Charles, that famous poet advocate, Walter Scott! You'd better give it more than your best!'

'Do I ever give less, my dearest?' he replied, raising an eyebrow and smirking. She grabbed the collar of his red jacket and planted a kiss on his lips. Then she pushed his cocked hat even further back off his high forehead and began to fuss with his cream silk cravat.

'Get yourself down to the green room then, ya big lump, you don't want to miss your cue!'

The performance brought the house down, as she had known it would, especially the antics of the Bailie. Tickets for the following night were sold out by early afternoon the next day, lively queues pushing and shoving and upsetting Mr Garbutt at the box office. Crowds had piled up outside by late afternoon, ready to surge into the pit and galleries the moment the doors opened. Three nights of *Rob Roy* had been advertised, but on day two William Murray decided to extend the run indefinitely.

Charlotte was sitting on the wooden settle close to the window in their new lodgings in Broughton Street, her sewing on her lap, thinking how satisfying it was that her husband had been so thoroughly vindicated in front of his critics. In no time at all he had become very popular – famous even – in Scotland's capital city. She picked up the length of striped silk she was sewing, peered at it, then jabbed the needle expertly back and forth a few more times, finishing the hem of her new dress almost invisibly and snipping the thread with her bone-handled tailor's scissors. *Now I just need Mr Murray to give* me *another role soon.*

Familiar footsteps on the stairs propelled her to her feet and she hung the pot of broth on the chain near the centre of the fire, giving the red coals a poke that sent sparks spitting up the chimney. Charles burst through the door, out of breath and glistening with sweat. She straightened her back and quoted the words of *Rob Roy*'s Hostess she had been practising: '*Sir, ye'll be for a dram, na doubt, till we can tass ye up something hot for your late dinner!*'

His eyes lit up and he laughed, taking her in his arms. They stood entwined for a long moment and she felt the hammering of his heart slow down until it beat in time with her own. When he pulled away and swept her hair from her brow tenderly she knew by the glint in his eye he had news.

'A mysterious letter arrived at the stage door for me this morning, Charlotte – I can hardly believe what it says!' She took his hand and led him to the fireside to sit on the settle, patting the space beside her.

'So, who's it from?'

He was grinning like a mischievous boy. 'The Wizard of the North!'

'What on earth do you mean – let me see!' She tried to take the letter, but he held it high above his head.

'Ha! I think it's from Walter Scott, my darling – incognito of course! It's about *Rob Roy*. Remember he was there on the first night?'

'How could I forget?'

'Well – this letter came via Ballantyne's office, according to old Cerberus at the stage door. Ballantyne is Scott's printer.' Charles took a deep breath. 'It's signed by Jedediah Cleishbotham, the so-called author of those *Tales of My Landlord* – you know the ones. People say they're written by the same person as the *Waverley* novels, though, which everyone thinks is Walter Scott– you said as much on our very first day here, remember? That means the writer of *Rob Roy* has just written to me!'

'Oh, my goodness!' Charlotte managed to whip the letter from his hand.

'*Friend Mackay* – that's nice, a good start.' She followed the slanting, scribbled hand carefully with her finger as she read. '*I was enamoured of the very lively representation of Bailie Nicol Jarvie* – that's a great compliment if it's from the man who wrote the book! Oh look, Charles, he's sent you a promissory note for five pounds for your first benefit night!' She looked up. 'Is Mr Murray putting on a benefit for you already, Charles? When's it to be?'

'I don't know yet, but I suppose he'll arrange one if Scott mentions it to him.' Charles was grinning from ear to ear. 'Calcraft says Murray gives all his leading actors benefit nights every year so he can keep their salaries low and conserve the theatre's funds. He even has them for himself!' He stood up suddenly and pulled Charlotte to her feet.

'Come and have dinner with me somewhere grand, will you Charlotte? We've a great deal to celebrate, not least this review I have in my pocket – which I shan't let you snatch!'

'What? Let me see it, Charles – is it good?' She followed him across the room but he held the cutting well out of her reach, teasing her with his eyes.

'Do you want to hear it?'

'Of *course* I do! Which publication is it?'

'It's that new rag, the one the Radicals are so fond of. They're calling it the *Scotsman*. Now, let me read you a wee excerpt, listen to this: *He who is at once a man and a Scotsman must be delighted with Rob Roy. Why should we not be proud of our national genius, humour, music, kindness and fidelity? Why not be National? ... The manner in which the different parts were cast and supported not only preserved it to the last, but made it grow upon us, so as to become absolutely intoxicating ...!*'

Rob Roy ran for forty-one consecutive nights at the Theatre Royal, and when William Murray finally announced the last night at the end of March everyone knew it was not for lack of ticket sales. Charlotte watched Charles take his final bow from the wings to the roar of the over-excited crowd and longed to embrace him, to tell him how proud she was of him. He was swamped by well-wishers the moment he came off-stage though. It was impossible even to catch his eye so she decided to go home and wait up for him, however late that may be.

Waiting up proved impossible, though. The fire was low when the click of the door woke her. She lay quietly, feigning sleep, watching Charles creep into the room and undress in the low glimmer of the last few coals. Then he slipped into bed and enveloped her in his arms, the chill of the night air on his skin, the smell of whisky on his breath. She shivered slightly as he buried his face in the loose curls of her hair, inhaling deeply.

'Are you awake, Charlotte?' She turned and stroked the bristles on his *homely visage* with her forefinger, chuckling.

'I am now!'

'Ah yes, forgive me!'

'I'm only fooling – I've been waiting for you. Tell me everything!' Charlotte propped herself up on her elbow and he began to talk.

'Now it's over, Charlotte, I can hardly believe we've had such an incredible run – six weeks in Scotland's capital city! The Theatre Royal is second only to the London theatres you know – so it's truly amazing!'

'Absolutely!'

'Murray sought me out in the green room to thank me for my *excellent work* and asked if I would join him for a late supper at the Red Lion. That's why I'm so late and have the smell of whisky on me, which I know fine you've already detected!' She buried her nose in his hair and sniffed him back until he laughed and pushed her away.

'Listen, Charlotte – Murray wanted to talk to me about the Edinburgh Theatrical Fund his sister Harriet has founded. I heard Chippendale crowing about being the chairman last month, Jones and Hamerton are in on it too. Anyway, Murray told me they now have five dukes, seven earls, three lords and four knights of the realm, as well as Walter Scott and his good friend, William Erskine, all willing to put their names to the fund.'

'Oh goodness, Charles, what a PRO-DI-GI-OUS company of people!' She knew Charles would appreciate her reference to the Dominie character he had been playing in *Guy Mannering* since their Perth days. He smiled and continued in a perfect imitation of Murray's precise English, using the slightly higher pitch of his manager's voice: '*The thing is, Mackay, dear fellow, those of us on the Theatre Royal Committee feel it would be right for you to join us. After all, it's almost entirely because of your extraordinary popularity as the Bailie that the crushing financial burden, under which I have been labouring since my brother-in-law died four years ago, has been lifted from my shoulders and I can finally see my way ahead.*

'I tell you, Charlotte, I was *clean bombaised*! Murray was quite *emotional*, he even mopped his brow with his napkin. I assured him I would be honoured to join him in such a worthy venture, and that there was no need to attribute such an outcome to my singular efforts. *We're a company of players under the Managerial Sheet Anchor that is your good self*, I said, *and as such, each of us depends on the other*. Well – Murray was temporarily lost for words, if you can believe such a phenomenon! I ordered us whisky and we raised a toast to Harriet's Theatrical Fund, and to all who will benefit from it down the years!'

'*Hout tout Mackay*! It seems you're moving up in the world! But I forgot to mention something when you came in so full of news.'

'And what might that be, dearest?' She could tell he was grinning, even though it was almost dark in the room now.

'The night soil man will be round soon and that stinking

bucket by the door won't take itself outside!' He jumped up, laughing, stirred the ashes with the poker to light a candle, then went to pick up the cloth-covered pail.

'Ha! I wondered why there was such a stink in the place! Thank you kindly, madam, for saving it for me. How very thoughtful!' He opened the door and the draught made Charlotte shiver again.

'You're welcome, good sir, but dinna tarry, there's a cauld wind blawin'!'

'When I was a lad we waited for the Town Drum to announce ten o'clock, then we chucked our slops "oot the windae" and pity help anyone who got in the way!' He slammed the door behind him and she listened to his running footsteps, hoping he would not spill the slops in the stairwell in his haste. *What a man!*

Charles grew in confidence as winter gave way to spring, and Charlotte was thrilled for him. He worked his way through any number of new parts, making them his own, and his fame and popularity continued to grow. A benefit night was arranged for him at the end of May and he chose to reprise his role as Dominie Sampson in *Guy Mannering.*

Charlotte crept into the wings to peep at the audience when the orchestra began the overture that night, feeling unaccountably nervous for him. The theatre was packed. She slipped back into the green room and waited for Charles to come down from his dressing room. The moment he appeared she ran over and took his arm, trying to keep up with his energetic stride.

'The audience is going to love you, you're such a funny Dominie!' She was rewarded with a quick grin and the hint of a wink before he whisked through the curtains and the audience erupted.

Although Charlotte was delighted with her husband's burgeoning success, she had not been on-stage herself since *The Tempest* in February three months ago. She was beginning to wonder why. Perhaps Murray thought she would let him down with another episode like the one in Perth. He had even had the gall to suggest she might usefully fill her time helping Mrs Garbutt in the wardrobe department. Still, she had been feeling exceptionally tired recently and found the work of cutting and stitching in the bright sewing room on the top floor of the theatre strangely soothing. Perhaps she was with child again.

As the days grew hotter Charlotte became more certain of her condition. Her figure was still slim, her stomach firm, but she had missed her courses twice. Charles had recently been over to Glasgow for the baptism of his third nephew, who was named after him, and she was longing to tell him he was to become a father himself. But he was always so busy, coming and going to the theatre, pacing up and down rehearsing new lines, trying out new characters, more inspired than she had ever seen him. She was usually asleep when he came home at night.

On midsummer's night Charlotte was sitting by the window later than usual, enjoying the golden light of the long evening, when she felt a sharp pain in her abdomen. *No! Surely this can't be happening again!* She pressed her hands hard on her belly as if to make the child to stay inside her. Then a wave of dizziness swept over her and she fell to the floor, another pain slicing across her stomach. *Oh God! What did I do wrong?* Charlotte dragged herself across to the bed and climbed onto it, curling up with a sheet stuffed between her legs as she felt the blood start pulsing out of her, weeping in great heaving gasps into her pillow. It was nearly dark before she had the strength to move. She bundled up the sheet and put it by the door to deal with in the morning then lay back down, exhausted. Charles could make of it what he would.

She had fallen into a light doze when a sharp intake of breath alerted her that Charles was home. She kept her eyes closed, unwilling to catch his eye in the soft light of the early sunrise. He slipped into bed and put his arms around her. Then he whispered,

'Dearest Charlotte, I didn't know you were with child, forgive me. I'm so sorry this has happened to you again my love, my darling girl, so very sorry.' He held her close all that night, comforting her with whispered dreams of a brighter future, and she loved him for it.

A fortnight later Charlotte felt well enough to return to the theatre in the afternoons to help Mrs Garbutt in the costume department. Before long Mr Murray handed her a small part in a comedy. She only had two short lines, but it meant she was back onstage, and it felt good. A few days later she was in another production, playing one of two ladies at a dinner party, the other lady being played by Mrs Shaw. They both had very little to say, but they were on-stage for the duration of their scene, wearing very elegant gowns. His Royal Highness Prince Leopold of Saxe-Coburg attended one of these performances, and the excitement of the royal visit did much to thaw the frosty atmosphere between the two women.

In late August Charlotte was given her best role of the summer, that of Mrs Lenient in a comedy called *Gentlemen, We Can Do Without You*. Mrs Lenient was a humorous character with plenty to say, which gave Charlotte a real chance to act at last. As if to emphasise the theme of the play, Charles had gone to Perth for a few days, with Murray's blessing, to perform in one of Corbett and Jessie Ryder's productions in Perth.

She was adjusting her costume in front of one of the cheval glasses in the green room halfway through the performance when Henry Johnston suddenly appeared behind her. She gave a little gasp and whirled round.

'Well, well! Miss Charlotte O' Keefe! How marvellous to see you are still thrilling audiences with you own special blend of humour and hauter!' He slipped a hand around her waist and she quickly pushed it away, adopting the character of Mrs Lenient, which was easier than being herself.

'Don't for one moment think you can take liberties with me, young man! You may be known as the Scottish Roscius, with your *sweet, melting voice* and your *boyish good looks*, but I see you for what you are!'

'And what, pray, is that?' He was playing along with her, running his fingers up and down her bare arm, archly confident of his powers of seduction. She shook him off angrily.

'Leave me alone, Henry, I'm due back on-stage any moment.' A flash of anger darkened his eyes. He took a firm grip of her wrist and lowered his voice.

'You thought yourself so clever mentioning my contretemps with the Prince Regent all those years ago, didn't you? But you clearly didn't know my wife was in the process of divorcing me at the time of your audition, making your mockery rather cruel, don't you think?' His breath smelt of stale tobacco and his grip on her wrist was growing tighter. 'No matter. I found it amusing. I believe I gave you the contract in Ayr for the fun of seeing you again, Charlotte, of acting with you, perhaps. You might go as far as to say that Charles Mackay whisked you out from under my nose, and I haven't quite forgiven him!'

'Let *go* of me at once!' she shouted. The room went quiet and everyone turned to see what was going on. 'I think you mistake me for one of the hures Mr Murray lets into the theatre at half-price!' He dropped her hand at once and she wrapped her fingers round her gold pendant, staring at him defiantly. He had not finished.

'I've a mind to tell Murray to put on *The Honeymoon* instead of *Man of the World* this week, to cast me as the Duke and you as Juliana. Then I can have my fill of kisses for all the world to see!'

Charlotte was suddenly furious. 'I would refuse the part!'

'Then you would be fined a guinea, according to Murray's Marvellous Rules!'

She could see the Call Boy beckoning her and pulled herself to her full height, which was more than a head shorter than Henry.

'In that case, Mr Johnston, I would consider it a guinea well spent!' Charlotte flounced into the wings, delighted with the line she had just delivered. The line she was about to deliver on-stage was already fizzing on the tip of her tongue and seemed rather appropriate: *Oh, I am better now!*

The players took their bows and Charlotte watched from the wings, Henry's moment of madness the previous week all but forgotten now that Charles was home. It was Henry's last night in Edinburgh and designated as a benefit for him. They had just finished a performance of *Macbeth* in which he had played the lead role and made an excellent job of it. Charles had played the First Witch, with Chippendale and Mrs Nicol playing the other two, their scenes causing gasps of horror and gales of laughter.

The actors came streaming back into the green room as the applause continued in the auditorium and Charlotte watched Charles run to the overmantel glass and swipe most of the green paint from his face with a cloth. Then he threw off his witch's cloak and gown, pulled on the breeks being held out for him by his dresser and shrugged his arms into his red Bailie jacket, whipping a cream cravat around his neck. His hair was standing on end and still full of green powder, but he stuffed his cocked hat over it, pushing it back to a jaunty angle, and grabbed the proffered poker from the Property Man.

In less than two minutes Charles had transformed himself from a medieval witch to a Glasgow magistrate and was back on-stage standing in front of the red drop curtain. Charlotte returned to the discreet place she had found and watched from the wings. Admittedly, he looked somewhat dishevelled, but his dishevelment seemed to add to the comedy of the moment and pockets of laughter began to bubble up across the theatre in anticipation of what might happen next.

The orchestra struck up a well-known air – 'The Quaker's Wife' – and Charles began to sing. Some clever wag had written a song for him and called it 'Bailie Nicol Jarvie's Journey To Aberfoyle'. Charles had been practising it at home all week. He had made the Bailie his own in a way he had never done with any other part. People came back time after time to watch him, as though they could never have enough of him in that role. His powerful bass voice rolled out across the auditorium, rising above the orchestra, above the laughter and cheering of the adoring crowds, and Charlotte felt so proud she thought she might burst.

'*You may talk o' your Wallace and talk o' your Bruce,*
And talk o' your fechting Red Reiver;
But whar will you find a great man o' sic use
As a thorough-bred Saut-Market weaver?

Let ance Nicol Jarvie come under your view,
At hame whar the people adore me;
Whar they made me a bailie, and counsellor too,
Like my faither, the deacon, before me.'

EIGHT

'You remember that novel, *The Heart of Mid-Lothian*, Charlotte?' Charles was standing by the window watching snow falling softly onto the wide incline of Broughton Street while Charlotte sat at the hearth sewing. A length of soft pink fabric was draped across her knee like a blanket and the concentration on her face made Charles want to compete with the cloth for her attention.

'Yes, of course. Why do you ask?' Her hands continued to jab and pull the needle and he wished she would look up.

'A *Terry-fication* of it has been playing in Covent Garden recently, but apparently it isn't nearly as good as Daniel Terry's play of *Guy Mannering*. In fact the Pantheon has just advertised a better version of it by Dibdin for this coming weekend, and Murray's steaming!'

'Why?' He watched Charlotte tie off her thread, pull out another length from the spool, cut it with her bone-handled sewing scissors and hold her needle up to the white light pouring through the window to thread it. She still had not looked at him and Charles wondered if he had said or done something wrong. He ploughed on regardless.

'Murray has been planning for some time to put Dibdin's

version on himself in the new year. Now he's in two minds, apparently. Old Bannister at the Pantheon is a tricky fellow, the way he ducks and weaves around his lack of a royal patent. He's started calling the Pantheon Edinburgh's second theatre now, even boasting of its superior position at the top of Leith Walk. No doubt Murray will sort it out. I shouldn't put it past him to write his own version while juggling the role of Gulliver in the New Year pantomime and dealing with his wife's illness.'

Charlotte laid her sewing on her lap and finally looked up at Charles, her head on one side, her face full of concern. 'Oh dear, what's the matter with Ann?'

'Nothing too serious, as far as I understand. Women's problems, I imagine.'

She sighed and picked up her sewing again. 'These problems of ours are not something to be dismissed lightly, Charles, they can be a matter of life and death – and they often are.'

As I know only too well and try to forget, dearest, or I wouldn't allow myself to touch you for fear you might die like my mother! Charles left the snowy window and sat down opposite Charlotte.

'I'm sorry my darling, that was flippant of me, especially considering the trials you've had to bear yourself. Flippant!'

She pinned him with a sharp look and he punched himself on the cheek to make her laugh.

'Yes, it was. You need to remember, I am not a wife who says: *"If you think so my dear", and "As you please", and "You know best" when you nothing know!'* Her eyes flashed at him darkly as she spoke the familiar lines from *The Honeymoon* with passion, holding his gaze fiercely for a moment. Then she burst out laughing and took up her sewing again.

'*Touché*, my dearest, *touché*!' Charles chuckled and picked up the poker to jab the fire into life, relief flooding him warmly like a dram of whisky. He sometimes felt such a clumsy oaf when it came to Charlotte's feelings. In many ways she was still a complete mystery to him. He placed a few coals carefully on the fire with the tongs. 'Will you tell me the story of *The Heart of Mid-Lothian*, Charlotte, please? A short version, of course! I think Murray has me down for the Laird o' Dumbiedykes!'

Charlotte put her sewing away in her basket, folded her hands in her lap and gave Charles her full attention.

'To begin with, it's unusual for being a story about women of a lower class. There's an honest, Protestant girl, Jeanie Deans, who walks to London to beg for a pardon for her sister, Effie – a fun-loving rascal accused of killing her illegitimate baby. Effie is languishing in the Tolbooth, sentenced to be hanged. Jeanie encounters a gang of ruffians on her way, obtains a pardon from the king and queen and comes home. Then she marries her beloved. Effie marries the father of her baby, who is subsequently found to be alive. Her son has become a criminal in the same gang of ruffians Jeanie met earlier, who had kidnapped him as a baby. He ends up shooting his father. The widowed Effie goes to France and becomes a Catholic nun and Jeanie is perplexed that her sister could change her religion. The end!'

'Ah – how very succinct, Charlotte! Now then, I have two questions – when and where is it set, and how does the Laird o' Dumbiedykes come into the story?'

'It's set in old Edinburgh at the time of the Porteous Riots, and Dumbiedykes is the young landlord of Jeanie's father. He's a gawky-looking boy who's hopelessly in love with Jeanie.' Charles pulled a face and Charlotte shook her head, smiling to herself.

'Alright. So, it's a gawky lad I'm to be – unless Murray writes the part differently, of course.' Charles went to look out of the window again. Snow had already drawn a thick white blanket over the dirty cobbles.

'I wonder if there'll be a part for in it for me, Charles. I should like to have another speaking role in a good Scotch play. I think I did rather well with my accent as the Hostess in *Rob Roy* recently. I'm still pinching myself that Mr Murray gave it to me. It was like a Christmas present!' Charles turned to face her, smiling his most encouraging smile, but his mind was tripping over itself as it ran back and forth over the new story.

'Aye – you certainly did a grand job, my darling!' He turned back to the window. 'There must be about three inches of snow lying out there now. You'll need your pattens the next time you venture out!'

Almost five years had passed since the end of the war with France and, in the aftermath, many had sunk into terrible economic hardship. Newspapers fanned the flames of discontent with talk of a possible uprising, but in the Theatre Royal what happened on-stage was what mattered most. In the middle of a freezing February, the green room was fizzing with excitement: the curtain was about to go up on the first performance of *The Heart of Mid-Lothian.*

As Charles predicted, Murray had reworked the Dibdin script and produced a five-act play of his own from it. In addition, Alexander Nasmyth had painted twenty glorious scenery panels, the opening one a sublime depiction of Edinburgh at sunrise from the foot of the Salisbury Crags. Murray had cast his sister, Harriet Siddons, as Jeanie Deans, and his wife, Ann, as her sister Effie. Charlotte was playing Lady Suffolk, a lady-in-waiting to the Queen of England, who was to be played by Jane Renaud, the company's leading lady. It was a small part with no dialogue, but still quite a prominent role.

Charles adjusted his cocked hat over his wig in front of the cheval, pulled an empty pipe out of one pocket, an empty pocket flask out of another, and began to think himself into the character of the well-meaning, lovelorn, tongue-tied young gentleman he was about to depict. The overture finished, the play began, and he could hear the sisters on-stage, bickering about Effie staying out so late. When their father intervened Charles stuffed his props back into his pockets and stood ready. Jeanie and Effie ran off-stage, leaving their father talking to himself about marriage options for his daughters, and when Jeanie returned to the stage Charles strode after her, causing her father to say: '*Eh, here's Dumbiedykes!*'

'*Jean, I say, Jeanie, woman, it's a braw day out bye!*' The audience hooted with laughter the moment Charles opened his mouth. *This is going to work!* They laughed at the awkward way he walked, the gawky turn of his head, the confusion he arranged on his face, the way he simply stood there, looking helpless. He had developed a silly voice for the part, too, and a few other little tics and mannerisms, and the audience lapped it all up. When he came to the line, *I hate a playhouse, for I never saw one in my life*, it brought the house down, as he had known it would, and it was a full minute before the audience was quiet enough for the play to continue.

The performance was going even better than Charles had expected, but, as Charlotte's moment on-stage approached, he was surprised to find himself feeling slightly nervous for her. Charlotte and Jane looked regal in their glorious dresses, their sparkling jewellery, their tall powdered grey wigs. He could feel the tension radiating from Charlotte as she passed him and caught her hand briefly. She had always been shy around Jane, and now they had been thrown together he wondered how she would cope.

Queen Caroline and Lady Suffolk walked imperiously onto the stage to a decent ovation and Charles watched his dear wife make as much of her part as she possibly could. When she came off-stage he could not resist pulling her into his arms and planting a kiss on the little black beauty spot she had stuck on her powdered cheek. Jane Renaud looked down her nose at them, but he ignored her. The next moment he was Dumbiedykes again, ready to bustle back on-stage.

The new play garnered rave reviews. It ran for twenty-eight consecutive nights and Charlotte made it through the whole run without a mishap, even though she had mentioned more than once to Charles she was feeling rather tired and thought she might be with child again. By the end of March he had managed to persuade her to take some time off to rest, although she took small parts now and then, if they were offered. After reprising the role of Lady Suffolk at a grand benefit for the Edinburgh Theatrical Society in early June she bowed out gracefully for the rest of her confinement, much to his relief.

That summer the Mackays moved to larger lodgings further down Broughton Street where there was a bedroom as well as a room with a cooking hearth. Charles let it be known among the seamstresses and dressers at the theatre that they were looking for someone to help Charlotte at home when the baby was born, and that they could provide a kitchen bed and would pay a fair wage. One of the older seamstresses took up the offer. Dorothy was at least ten years older than Charles, short, stocky and strong, with a round face and dark brown hair that she kept tied up and tucked away under her old-fashioned mutch cap. She had a lovely quality of gentleness about her blue-grey eyes. A quiet soul from a big family, she assured him she was grateful to have her own bed and promised to work hard.

Charlotte had grown huge by this time, and often laughed at her awkward waddling gait, clearly proud of her enormous round belly. Although he was excited, Charles was also filled with dread.

'I do wish you'd stop pacing up and down, Charles. You've been like a bear with a sore head since the theatre closed! Why don't you go for one of your long rambles on Arthur's Seat like you normally do between seasons? It'll be open again in a fortnight, then you'll be wishing you had more time to yourself. You really should go to that dinner Mr Murray invited you to attend tonight. Dorothy's here, so I'll be fine if the baby starts to come.'

'Well – if you're quite sure you'll be alright, my dear.'

'I'm certain of it. Noo aff ye go frae under ma feet, I cannae thole ye sae fidgety!' She smiled brightly, her face plump and pink and pretty, and Charles tried not to think of his mother.

The door swung open and Dorothy came in with two buckets of water, nodding shyly at him. Charles was more grateful than he could say for her calming presence in their new home. She had transformed it in a host of little ways, making Charles feel steady and safe. He grinned broadly at her, kissed his wife, picked up his hat and cloak and bade the women good evening.

Charles Graham Mackay was born with a minimum of fuss on September the 30th, 1820. When Dorothy came out of the bedroom and beckoned Charles with a smile on her face he could have hugged her. He strode across the room and sat on the bed. Relief at the sight of Charlotte sitting up, looking fit and well and holding out their son to him was stinging his eyes and blurring his vision.

'He wants to meet his father!' Charles took the child in his arms, overawed by his fragility. Mesmerised by his son's knowing eyes, his own began to stream and he suddenly felt a fool. He handed the little boy back to his mammy with a sigh of relief, pulled out a handkerchief to dry his face, then kissed them both on their warm noses and left them in peace.

A month later, on a golden October morning, Charlie was baptised in St Cuthbert's. His Uncle William, the weaver, made the trip over from Glasgow by coach to join their little gathering, bringing a cold blast from the outside world with reports of the uprisings earlier in the year and tales of his friend who had been tried and transported for his part in it.

The early morning air felt fresh as newly drawn water and the midsummer sun was already bright as the Mackay family walked down Broughton Street towards Bonnington Toll, where a coach would take Charles to Newhaven. He had been invited to perform in *Rob Roy* at the Theatre Royal, Covent

Garden, on the recommendation of the recently knighted Sir Walter Scott, and had a three-guinea ticket in his pocket for the *James Watt* steam packet to London. Charlotte had tied little Charlie on her chest with her green plaid and Charles had slung his canvas travelling satchel over his shoulder so he could hold her hand. Charlie had become such an interesting wee character already, though not yet a year old. He was going to miss them both enormously.

'Be sure and ask Dorothy to carry out the ashes and slops and bring up the coal and water, won't you – she can fetch provisions, too, to save you carrying them now Charlie's so heavy – or you could leave him with her when you go shopping.' He could see Charlotte was trying not to laugh at him.

'Don't forget, young man, *We Ladies Can Do Without You!*'

'Of course you can, Mrs Lenient!' Charles grinned and took his son in his arms for a moment, less fearful of holding him now he was so much bigger. He kissed Charlie's cheek and Charlie grabbed a handful of his hair, chortling happily. A few minutes later a coach appeared and the driver reigned in the horses to pay the toll and pick up his passenger.

'Be good for your mammy now, wee mannie!' Charles untangled his son's hand from his hair and handed him back to Charlotte, folding them both into an embrace for a long moment. Then he hitched his bag back onto his shoulder, tipped his hat and climbed into the coach. 'Wish me luck!'

'Oh we do, Charles, we do! And safe journey. Have a wonderful time, we're so proud of you, aren't we, Charlie?' The driver flicked his whip, the coach set off and Charles watched his little family slowly shrinking to nothing as the distance between them grew. *I shall miss them sorely!*

It was going to be quite an adventure. The *James Watt* was the first steam packet to go between Edinburgh and London, cutting the travelling time down to a mere sixty hours, and it was leaving soon from the new Chain Pier in Newhaven.

Three days and five hundred nautical miles later Charles arrived in central London in a lighter that had taken him up the River Thames from Blackwell. He had heard so much about this great metropolis, seen pictures of it even, yet nothing had prepared him for the reality of its vast sprawl, the density and intensity of it, the incessant noises and smells, the constant activity. The sheer pressing weight of so many people living and trading and breeding in one city felt like a physical force.

Charles slept deeply and woke feeling ravenously hungry. After a hearty breakfast at his inn he arrived at the theatre in good time for ten o'clock. It was magnificent. Vast. It had five tiers of balconies and could accommodate over three thousand people, at least double anything Charles had previously experienced.

The thought of rehearsing with a company of actors he had never met before almost robbed him of his courage at first, but he soon relaxed, and a group of them went out for dinner before the performance.

Charles was standing in the wings, preparing himself to change the mood completely, as the last sad notes of lovelorn Frank and Diana's song faded to appreciative applause. The stagehands whisked the curtains closed and shifted the scenery panels so that the library at Osbaldistone Hall quickly became an apartment in an old Glasgow house. When the curtains parted again he was ready. He blustered fussily onto the stage, trailed by the anxious messenger, Saunders Wylie, then he stopped, centre stage, to take a good look around at the huge audience, his posture and features perfectly arranged into the persona of the pompous Bailie Nicol Jarvie. Titters and snorts began to echo round the cavernous auditorium. He opened his mouth and the Bailie's ridiculous voice bellowed forth: '*I tell you Saunders, you're daft!*' Laughter erupted. Soon there was no vast theatre, no London even, just the story unfolding on-stage with all the familiar moments of hilarity, and the audience in the palm of his hand.

There was plenty of drink on offer afterwards, and food to go with it – rather than the other way around, which Charles thought might have been a wiser approach. Lively congratulations and celebrations went on well into the small hours and Charles was swept off his feet by all the praise.

When he finally ventured out into the cool night air he was relieved to discover he still had enough of his wits about him to steer clear of the bawdy wenches offering themselves to him on every street corner. Thankfully he remembered his way back to the inn, too.

The next morning brought a persistent banging in his head and a summons to the neighbouring theatre at Drury Lane where the manager engaged him for another performance of *Rob Roy*. This one was for the benefit of good old Henry Johnston, who had turned up again. One performance became several and soon Charles found himself detained in London much longer than he had first anticipated.

NINE

A letter arrived from Charles a week after he had left. Charlotte was not surprised to learn he would be staying in London for a whole month. It did come as a surprise that he had been performing at the Theatre Royal in Drury Lane and they had asked him to consider joining their company. Charlotte was very tempted by the idea. How incredible it would be to act on that stage after watching so many plays there with her uncle, not to mention her audition for the Ayr Theatre. She would be so close to her family if they moved to London, too. But the decision was not hers to make. Charles would probably prefer to stay in Scotland.

She also read that Henry Johnston had turned up again and had been acting with Charles, playing the role of Douglas in *Rob Roy* and wearing a ridiculous red wig. Charles was hoping to acquire the wig and bring it home to make Charlie laugh. He finished by saying he was going to be in London for the coronation of King George IV and was looking forward to seeing all the celebrations and pageantry, especially the hot air balloon that was going to carry people up into the sky. He sent all his love to her and Charlie, hoped they were well and told her he was missing them very much.

Charlotte put the letter down on the table and looked out of the window, wondering whether to take Charlie for another walk up Calton Hill while the sun was still shining. She was happy for Charles, although a little homesick thinking of him so near her family in London. She had written to her sister to say he was in London. Ann had replied on the family's behalf, saying how much they would love to meet him, that he was always welcome to come and stay with them. Still, London was a vast city. She thought it unlikely he would have time.

Charlotte heard Charles's familiar footsteps running up the stair one morning at the end of July and scooped Charlie into her arms, sweeping her hair out of her eyes, her heart tripping over itself in excitement. Dorothy, discreet as ever, bustled off into the bedroom with a broom just as the door burst open.

'I'm home my darlings!' He stood there, grinning at them, taller and brighter and more handsome than she remembered him. He dropped his bags on the floor and opened his arms wide. 'How I've missed you both!' Charlie squealed with delight as Charlotte fell into Charles's embrace, a huge wave of relief washing over her.

'I have something for you, wee man!' Charles chucked his son under his chin and crouched down to fish about in his canvas bag. 'Aha! Here it is!' He pulled something out that looked more like a dead cat than a wig and put it on his head as he stood up, pulling a silly face at Charlie, who hid his own face in his mother's neck.

'Oh Charles, it's quite revolting! Is that Henry's dreadful wig? No wonder Charlie's afraid of it!' Charles was prancing around the room like a satyr by this time, pulling the tufty red hair in all directions and singing a daft song. Soon they were all laughing. Dorothy came back into the room, nodding a shy welcome to Charles, who blew her a kiss. She quickly picked up an empty bucket and went out, blushing like a rose.

Charlotte sat down on the settle with Charlie on her lap, and Charles joined her. He put his hand inside his jacket and pulled out a small brown paper parcel.

'I've not forgotten you, Charlotte. I've brought something for you that I think you'll like better than Henry's Horrible Hairpiece.' She tore the paper open to reveal a white handkerchief with initials and flowers delicately embroidered on each corner and a large 'M' in the centre, surrounded by rosebuds.

'Where did you get this, Charles? It's exquisite!'

'Take a good look at the initials in each corner, I think they'll provide a helpful clue.' Charlotte put Charlie on his father's knee and spread the handkerchief on her lap, turning it round and reading the letters. Her eyes filled as realisation dawned: A for Ann, J for Jane, M for Maria and a slightly clumsy G for Georgiana, who was only eleven. All her sisters! And in the centre an 'M' for Mam with rosebuds signifying Pa. She put the handkerchief to her face and inhaled deeply, unable to speak.

'Your brothers and your pa sent their love and apologised for their lack of sewing skills!' Her face crumpled. Charles set Charlie on the floor and held her close.

'You went to see them! Thank you! It means the world to me!'

Another production of *Rob Roy* began at the Theatre Royal at once, running throughout the month of August. To Charlotte's delight she was cast as Hostess for the whole season.

On the morning of the final performance she was woken early by Charles's hacking cough. She sat up in bed, rubbing her eyes. Charlie started to whimper in the wooden cot on the floor beside the bed and she shook Charles awake.

'What time is it, Charles – is it early? You've woken the lad as well as me!' Instead of reaching for his pocket watch as she expected, he continued coughing and Charlotte began to feel alarmed. 'Are you ill, Charles? Do you want me to fetch a toddy?

A medic, even? I have some honey on the shelf that would soothe your throat.' His voice, when it came, was hoarse and strange, but he still had a twinkle in his eye.

'Ach, dinnae fash yersel', wummun! It's nae but a wee bit hauchin'!'

'D'you want something to eat, or a cup of your Earl's tea?'

'I'll mebbe tak a wee bit parritch in a while.' He sank back under the blankets, groaning, and Charlotte put a hand on his forehead. It was hot and damp. She got up, wrapped her plaid round her shoulders, slipped her feet into her red leather slippers and went into the kitchen. Dorothy was already up with the fire on and water heating. The buckets were full too.

'Dorothy – you're a saint!' The maid smiled shyly.

'Jes' doin' ma job, Mrs Mackay, it's nae bother at all.'

After breakfast Charlotte took Charlie with her to the theatre for ten o'clock rehearsals leaving Charles to sleep, hoping he would be well enough for the performance. The last night of a run of *Rob Roy* was always sold out. The moment she saw Mr Murray she explained the situation.

'He's in great spirits, Mr Murray, just a little feverish with a nasty cough. He's asked me to send his apologies for the rehearsal and to assure you he will be in tonight, even if it means he takes a day or two to rest afterwards.' Mr Murray looked slightly alarmed and pulled his notebook from his pocket.

'Hm, Perhaps I'll warn Mr Douglas to have a look over the part, just in case. We'd better have Mr Rutherford ready as an understudy for Mr Douglas, too.' A deep frown line that Charlotte had never noticed before appeared on his forehead.

'I'm sure he'll be along, Mr Murray. Nothing can keep Charles from the stage, as you know!'

But when Charlotte was ready to go back to the theatre that evening, Charles was still coughing. He had taken two hot toddies but she could feel his brow was still hot. Although he had insisted on getting up and dressed, it seemed to have exhausted him and he had gone to sit down again. Anxiously, she picked up Charles's gold pocket watch as she went to wrap her plaid round her shoulders.

'Charles, it's after six o'clock. You know what happens if we don't leave on time.'

'I'll just be another moment, Charlotte. Can you not wait for me and we'll go up together?'

'I think I should go now, Charles, or they'll be sending the Call Boy for us! If you're not feeling well we should give Mr Murray time to tell the audience, give Mr Douglas time to prepare as well.'

'I said I'll go, and I will!' There was an angry edge to his husky voice which was not like him at all, so Charlotte waited a little longer, trying to suppress a rising sense of panic. Sure enough, a few minutes later there was a rapping at the door. She opened it quickly. As she had expected, it was the Call Boy – whose name had been lost in the mists of time and who had not been a boy for many years but had remained in his job because he could run fast and was reliable. He stood there, arms akimbo, frowning.

'Are yous comin' or no', Mr and Mrs Mackay?' He was a stocky, thickset man, considerably shorter than Charlotte, with a jutting chin and an air of determination that could not be ignored. It was the first time he had been sent to find them. The tension in the room felt like a thread being pulled so tightly it was bound to snap at any moment. Dorothy stirred the fire and Charlotte waited. Charles was suddenly seized by another fit of coughing.

'I'll tak that as a no then, will I, Mr Mackay?' Charles finally conceded, his shoulders slumping as he tried to speak.

'I'm so terribly sorry to let everyone down – I should have decided this morning – I just assumed I could …' His coughing interrupted him again and Charlotte looked at Dorothy.

'I'll tak care o' him, Mrs Mackay. Mak a poultice, I'm thinkin'. Never you worry, you jes' tak yerself up there the noo an' gie it yer best. An' wee Charlie here'll be fine too.' Dorothy ruffled Charlie's hair. When he smiled up at her Charlotte noticed a new sprinkle of freckles on his little snub nose and wondered when they had appeared. Then she turned and whisked out of the door to catch up with the Call Boy.

There was a great commotion in the green room when Charlotte came running in, breathless and sweating. Mr Murray was pacing up and down, his pocket watch in his hand, the orchestra already playing the overture. Mr Douglas was dressed as Bailie Nicol Jarvie and looked extremely uncomfortable. He was holding a script in his hand, his face white as a sheet, the script shivering like a leaf in a breeze.

'So that's it! He's not coming!' Charlotte had never seen Mr Murray so cross.

'He's terribly sorry – he really intended to come.'

'He should have decided earlier. Now it's too late to announce his understudy to the packed house. There will be uproar!' Mr Murray turned to Mr Douglas. 'Just do your best, man, I can't ask more of you than that. I'll go and tell Mr Rutherford he's to take your part as Lancie.' He strode across the room, bristling with fury. Charlotte was engulfed by a wave of guilt and dressed more quickly than she had ever done before. Somehow she had composed herself enough to go on-stage as the overture faded.

The play proceeded with the usual enthusiastic applause and sense of anticipation. She could hardly bear it, but decided to stay in the wings and see how it turned out. Mr Douglas and Mr Powell were quite near her, waiting for their cue. She could see Mr Douglas's hands trembling, his face paler than the moon. *One thing is certain, it'll be a busy night tonight for Mr Sandy in the Prompt Box!*

There was a hush in the audience and the two actors came on-stage as though entering a lion's den. Charlotte had her hands over her mouth. She could hardly breathe.

'I tell you Saunders, you're daft!' There was a small ripple of laughter. Mr Douglas struggled bravely on, often glancing over at Mr Sandy in the Prompt Box who was glowing pink with pleasure, his back straight, his eyes sharpened like a pencil so he would miss nothing, even his fluffy white hair was standing to attention.

The audience grew restless. Charlotte could hear their whispered complaints growing louder and tried to make out what was being said. Soon, what had begun *sotto voce* picked up momentum, and before long the whole theatre had taken up a chant, adding the stamping of boots for emphasis.

'It's no' The Real Mackay! It's no' The Real Mackay! It's no' The Real Mackay!' She put her hands over her ears and sank to the floor. *Oh, Good Lord! What a disaster! Mr Murray will be furious!* He strode past her onto the stage, brought the play to a halt and called for silence.

'Ladies and gentlemen, I apologise profusely for the unannounced changes that have been made in the cast for tonight's performance, due to the unforeseen ill health of Mr Mackay. I beg your patient support for Mr Douglas, who has been called upon at the last minute. I also ask for your good wishes for a speedy recovery for Mr Mackay.' His last comment was met by cheers and whistles. Then he thanked the audience for their kind indulgence and signalled for the play to continue.

Charlotte stayed to the end of the performance to sing 'God Save The King' and take her bow, fearful of offending Mr Murray further by going home too early, or worse, incurring a hefty fine. She held Mr Douglas's hand and squeezed it as they bowed, giving him a sympathetic smile. All evening she had been unsure whether to laugh or cry, fervently hoping Charles would be feeling better by the time she arrived home. She could hardly wait to see his face when she told him what had happened.

TEN

Charles woke to the sound of Charlotte flinging the shutters open.

'Back to yourself again, I see!' His fever had broken overnight, and he was feeling much better. He sat up and stretched, then caught her nightdress as she passed and pulled her, tumbling and laughing, onto the bed. He buried his nose in the crook of her neck to inhale the delicious scent of her, holding her firmly while she yelped and giggled and struggled to sit up. When little Charlie let out a shriek from his cot he let her pick him up and push her dishevelled hair out of her eyes.

'Ach, I let them all down royally last night – didn't I? I can hardly bear to think of poor old Douglas, thrust into my shoes with less than five minutes' warning!'

'The dear man was trembling and sweating all through the performance, Charles. And I've never seen Mr Murray so cross. But the audience were very understanding, so I think you got away with it!'

Charles beamed his biggest smile and opened his arms. 'Come here you two, and gie The Real Mackay a hug!' They rolled about and tickled each other until the smell of freshly baked bannock drew them into the kitchen for a hearty breakfast.

Charles sipped his morning tea, watching his wife and son over the rim of his cup, and realised he had never felt so happy.

Later that week he decided to turn down the offer from Drury Lane, even though it was very flattering and tempting. His success in Scotland would be hard to replicate south of the border, and, far from being a disaster, his last-minute absence from the theatre seemed only to have added to his popularity. It was almost as though the adoring public had given him a new name so he could belong to them even more. The broadsheets picked it up quickly and within days The Real Mackay was being bandied as if it had always been his name. Charles was rather fond of it. He much preferred it to The Great Mackay, which had always seemed rather pretentious.

'Last night Murray told me Sir Walter wants me to join the two of them at his home in Castle Street for an informal *"dinner without silver dishes"* this Sunday evening, Charlotte.' Charles was standing by the window shaving, his small looking-glass propped on the frame.

'Apparently, it's to do with the potential visit of King George this summer. I can't imagine why they should want to talk to *me* about it, but – hey ho!' He rinsed his razor in a scummy bowl of soapy water on the washstand beside him and patted his face with a pink towel. He would have to leave shortly to make it to the theatre for ten o'clock.

'How exciting! You must tell me every single detail about his enormous house, what the ladies are wearing, what you have for supper!' Charlotte was sitting at the table peeling and chopping turnips, her honey-coloured hair piled on top of her head, a white apron covering her blue cotton print dress. Charlie was sitting in a shaft of sunlight on the floor beside her, absorbed in a pile of wooden bricks that tumbled down every time he stacked them more than three high. Dorothy had gone to the washhouse with the laundry.

'What will you wear, though, Charles?' Charles crossed the room in two strides, pulled Charlotte to her feet, wet hands and all, and waltzed her round the room, making Charlie laugh at them both.

'I, my dearest, shall wear something *tartan*! I hear Scott is very keen on it.' He twirled her round, dipped a mock bow then picked up the slop bucket on his way out of the door, grinning a lopsided grin and rolling his eyes to make Charlie laugh even more.

Rumours of a visit from King George IV had been gathering momentum for months, ever since the monarch visited Ireland shortly after his coronation the previous August. All manner of improvements had already been made to roads and buildings across Edinburgh, and extensive renovations were underway at the palace of Holyrood. The City Council was investing vast amounts of money to ensure Auld Reekie would look her best for the monarch, should he agree to come, and the sense of excitement in the city was mounting daily. Charles wanted to find out as much as he could on Sunday. Everyone knew Sir Walter was on friendly terms with the king.

He set off up the hill to York Place on Sunday afternoon at half past four, turning right and walking along Queen Street. It was a mild midsummer day and he was wearing his best blue coat, with its puffed shoulders and cinched waist, a red tartan waistcoat, a green Paisley silk cravat, tartan trews and his best black stovepipe hat. Quite the dandy, as Charlotte had sweetly remarked when he went out of the door.

Charles called at Murray's house in Thistle Court, as arranged, and they walked to North Castle Street together. He had to employ his best acting skills to cover his jitters as they strolled along, sauntering with his best saunter, hooking his thumb into his jaunty waistcoat pocket and nodding at Murray's comments in what he hoped passed for casual agreement.

Murray rapped at the door of the impressive three-storey house and it opened almost at once. A large hound lurched towards them, tongue lolling sideways, and Charles took a step backwards, barely suppressing a yelp. The dog's chuckling master appeared next, with several smaller dogs milling about his feet, and the old hound went straight to heel.

'Ah! The Napoleon of Managers and The Inimitable Bailie – welcome, gentlemen – please do come in. We have a little supper ready and much to discuss.' Sir Walter's face was bright and gleesome and he rubbed his hands together as though in anticipation of a marvellous evening. They handed their hats to the maid in the brightly gas-lit front hall then followed their host's limping gait into a spacious candlelit parlour which smelt delightfully of beeswax and lilies. Sir Walter's gracious wife greeted them warmly in her charming French accent.

''Allo, and good evening to you both, Monsieur Murray and Monsieur Mackay. I 'ope you will enjoy our petit soirée!' Three of Scott's four children were there too, though they were hardly children anymore but young adults somewhere around the age of twenty. Charles glanced round the room, making a mental note of all the details Charlotte was bound to ask him for later. Several large portraits hung on the walls, one of Scott's wife, another of himself with the large hound that had greeted them so enthusiastically. There were wax candles in silver holders on all the side tables, shedding a warm glow on the crimson walls; dark green velvet drapes framed the long windows, and the artfully arranged chintz-covered chairs and settles looked most inviting.

Murray and Charles were the only guests to join the Scott family at their generous table that evening. Claret and champagne were soon flowing as generously as the rich and sparkling conversation, which was far less high-falutin' than Charles had expected.

'Now then, as today is the Sabbath I'm afraid there will be no musical interlude after supper to aid our digestion. My daughter, Ann here, is a charming singer and plays the harp as beautifully as her older sister, don't you my dear?' Scott's youngest daughter beamed in the glow of his attention. 'You must come again another night, gentlemen, and we can enjoy some songs together. I always enjoy hearing you sing the auld Scots songs on-stage in that rich voice of yours, Mackay!' Charles dipped his head and smiled, unsure what would be an appropriate comment.

When Sir Walter rose from the table his family took their cue to retire to the parlour.

'Come along now, gentlemen, follow me. We shall discuss the matter in hand in my little den.' Charles and Murray followed their genial host into a small, square room behind the parlour, dimly lit by a few candles and one Venetian window. Around the walls from floor to lofty ceiling shelves of books were set out in neat rows and, sprawled on the top step of the library ladder, a large, striped cat regarded Charles sleepily with one eye. Charles stared at the books. His mind was reeling to think a person could read so many in one lifetime. He and Charlotte paid their subscription to a circulating library, as most people did, and the idea of collecting his own books had never occurred to him until then.

'I see you're a man who appreciates books, Mackay! Excellent! Now then, do take a seat and make yourselves comfortable, we have much to discuss.' In the centre of the room was a large table with an elbow chair beside it. On the table sat a richly carved wooden box, lined with crimson velvet, containing ink bottles and a silver taper stand. *So this is where he writes!* There was no other furniture in the room except two occasional chairs, upon which Sir Walter indicated his guests should take their seats.

'There's no question the king will come, you know, it's simply a case of when – and we should know that very soon.' Charles learned that it would be the first time a reigning monarch had visited Scotland for nearly two centuries. Scott was hoping it would bring about a renewed sense of national pride, as well as support for the Union. There would be military processions and dinners, levees, grand balls and banquets, pomp and ceremony, extravagance and romance, the presenting of colours and saltires and regalia, the firing of cannons, even an enormous bonfire and fireworks on top of Arthur's Seat. Scott had already begun to invite the Highland chieftains to come down to the capital and meet the monarch in all their tartan splendour. He wanted to popularise the wearing of tartan again in all of Scotland. Although it had not been illegal for some years it was still, for the most part, only worn by Highlanders. Kilts would be obligatory for those attending grand balls and reams of tartan cloth would be used to decorate the venues. No one would be able to forget they were in Scotland – even the king himself.

Walter Scott's hands were never still while he talked. Charles found it mesmerising watching him fold letter covers, twist paper into spills, and snap his fingers so that his noble dog, Maida, came and lay his head across his lap to be fondled.

'The best of both worlds, then. Fully Scottish and fully British! I see your thinking, Walter, very astute!' Murray commented. Charles had never asked Murray about his politics but had always assumed he was not much of a Unionist, judging by the productions he put on at the Theatre Royal. A new phrase, National Drama, had been coined recently to describe the emphasis on Scottish history and culture Murray was promoting and a huge appetite for it was growing across the nation. How strange that Scott, supposedly the writer of so many of those national stories, was such a Unionist himself. Perhaps it was possible to be both? Charles found it quite a conundrum.

Murray's eyes were shining as he agreed to take charge of dressing the venues where all the magnificent events were to take place. He would commandeer the help of his set designer to create grand theatrical spectacles, like theatre sets on a massive scale. No expense would be spared. Charles was overwhelmed by the ambition of their plans. The thousands of yards of tartan cloth alone that would have to be woven was enough to leave his mouth hanging open. What his brother William would make of it he had no idea. He had even less idea why he had been invited to the meeting and his mind began to drift in and out of their lively conversation, his eyes continually drawn towards the books.

'As a fitting finale to the proceedings, Murray, I want you to put on a performance of *Rob Roy* at the Theatre Royal for His Majesty's entertainment.' *What?* Charles sat up a little straighter. They had his attention now! 'It's a special request from the monarch himself. He's heard such great reports of my play. You'll need to revamp the old place of course, make it fit for a king – ha!'

So that was why he had been invited! *King George has asked for* Rob Roy *– so I am commanded to entertain the king! Whatever next!*

'What do you say, Mackay? It will be a sensation!' Murray put his hand on Charles's arm and Charles blinked as though blinded by a bright light.

'It certainly will, Murray!' He was scrabbling about for something fitting to say when he remembered a few pertinent lines from the play in question. 'But, Sir Walter, as for all this tartan – *Lord help you, think what a figure I should cut with my poor bare thighs in a kilt, and gartered below the knee – my conscience!*'

Sir Walter laughed at the well-placed quote and countered it. '*Why, Mister Jarvie, unless you keep your opinions to yourself, I shall resort to unpleasant measures!*'

Not to be outdone, Murray drew the evening to a close by reciting the first line of the glee song that opened the play: '*Soon the sun will gae to rest, let's awa' together!*'

The moment the sun peeped over the horizon on August the 15th, 1822, Charles, Charlotte, Charlie and Dorothy ate a little porridge together. Although it was a Thursday, they were all dressed in their Sunday clothes. As requested by Sir Walter in his widely distributed pamphlets, Charles was wearing his blue jacket and white trews, which were still slightly damp from a soaking in the rain the previous day. He had added his tartan waistcoat for fun. Charlotte looked radiant in the tartan dress she had worn when he first set eyes on her, and wee Charlie had a tartan bunnet perched on top of his golden curls.

'Come here and let me pin this heather on your lapel, Charles.' A jug of heather stood on the table and Charlotte had already fixed a sprig to her breast and one on Charlie's hat. He bent forward obediently and she pinned it on. 'There!' Then she picked Charlie up, tying him deftly on her back with her plaid, and handed Charles his canvas satchel. He peered inside and saw she had packed a rug, a leather flagon of small beer and some barley bannocks and cheese. *Isn't she grand?*

Dorothy was going to walk down to Leith to join her sisters and their children to welcome the king when he took his first steps on Scottish soil.

'Here, Dorothy, take some heather, and some for your family, too.'

'Thank ye, Mrs Mackay. Have a braw day, noo, the three of yous! I'll be back on the morrow in guid time to make scones for breakfast!' Charles hitched his satchel onto his shoulder and they all traipsed down the stair, parting ways at the Pantheon Theatre.

The Mackays crossed Leith Walk and went down a narrow street crowded with clusters of little cottages and tiny gardens. From there the path led steeply up Calton Hill towards the summit.

'The weather's fairly changed since yesterday, Charlotte. Look how bright and clear it is!'

'Isn't it glorious! Dorothy and I were so glad we didn't join you yesterday, though – that rain was relentless.' Charlotte plucked at his sleeve, laughing. 'Look how your jacket's steaming in the sunshine even now from that drenching you had!'

'Aye, and the thick haar yesterday hid the Firth completely. There were thousands of us up here all day though, getting soaked in case the king decided to come ashore. No one complained, though – people shared their food and their umbrellas – it made me proud to be a Scot! Widow Kerr did a roaring trade from her wee restaurant under Nelson's Monument, too. It was like a fair, all the wee barefoot bairns and their trays of pies, all the barrows of apples! I might have stayed up there longer, despite the rain, if I hadn't been needed at the theatre last night. No doubt they'll all be up there again today.'

'I don't know how you can talk so much, when you're climbing such a steep path Charles – maybe you should try carrying Charlie on *your* back!'

They stopped for a moment to catch their breath. Hundreds of people were on the hill already, claiming spaces for the day. Some of them had set up makeshift camps and stayed overnight to be sure of a good place to watch the processions. Charles found a grand spot just below the summit on the north side of the hill with a wide view of the Firth. He pulled the rug from his satchel and set it down for Charlie. Charlotte sank down gratefully, lying flat on her back beside their son, while Charles remained standing, shielding his eyes with his hand, peering into the distance. It was so clear. He could see for miles. The Firth was teeming with boats and vessels, all decked out colourfully. He even fancied he could hear the strains of a piper floating up from one of them, wild and pensive, full of yearning.

For days Calton Hill had thronged with people hoping to be the first to catch sight of the *Royal George*. Now there it was, floating in all its glory. Charles gazed around the city spread below him and saw people sitting on every rooftop, hanging out of windows in New Town mansions, crammed together on wooden scaffolding. Behind him smoke still billowed from the previous night's enormous bonfire on Arthur's Seat.

Edinburgh was saturated with people. Both theatres had been doing a roaring trade for weeks, as had all the hotels, taverns and coffee houses by all accounts. None of the gentry had gone to the country for the summer, according to the broadsheets; instead it seemed the whole of Scotland had come to Edinburgh. Every spare room, corridor and outhouse was full of makeshift beds, and people were paying a fortune to stable their horses. Visitors from the Highlands and Islands strode about the streets in full Highland garb and buildings everywhere were decorated with flowers and branches and flags and coloured glass light displays. It was as though a kind of intoxicating madness had gripped the entire city. *Daft. Completely daft – but wonderful all the same.*

Calton Hill was so thick with people by late morning it was impossible for the Mackays to move from the place they had chosen. Charles was relieved they had come so early and found a good vantage point. It was a day that would go down in history, and he wanted to be able to tell his son he had been there and seen it all too.

At twelve o'clock an innocent little puff of smoke rose silently from the royal yacht, closely followed by the boom of a gun. It was the signal that the king had entered his barge. Everyone knew what it meant because pamphlets and newspapers had been doling out information every day for the past three weeks. An almighty cheer went up far below and ships and forts along the Firth thundered their salutes in reply.

Cheering broke out on the hillside and Charles hoisted Charlie onto his shoulders. Charlotte stood up and slipped an arm round his waist. About ten minutes later more cheers from below announced that the monarch had entered the port of Leith. Then a lone piper struck up a national air.

'D'you hear that, Charles? Isn't it strange to think of Dorothy down there, cheering with her family and all the other folk!'

'Aye. Everything about today is strange, Charlotte! I think the High Street must be empty with all the folk up here and on Leith Walk. Indeed, I think all of Scotland must be empty – just look at them all!'

The distant cheering grew frantic and Charles imagined the king must have stepped onto Scottish soil. Dignitaries would be kneeling in obeisance, everyone beside themselves with joy to see their monarch. Faint strains of 'God Save The King' wafted up the hill. *How can this be happening in Scotland? Why are we all so wildly joyful to be visited by this self-indulgent, overweight and slightly ridiculous monarch who has had so little to do with our nation?* Despite his reservations Charles was surprised to find himself overwhelmed with joy. He burst out laughing.

'What is it, Charles? Did I miss something?'

'No, Charlotte. I'm just imagining Henry Johnston horse-whipping this very monarch we're welcoming here today, for going after his pretty wife in her dressing room all those years ago! We're all mad aren't we! But somehow, it's glorious as well!'

Another wild cheer went up far below, somehow audible above all the yelling and singing on the hill. *The royal procession must be underway.* Soon, mounted soldiers and pipers and heralds appeared at the far end of Leith Walk, then wave after wave of them came into view. Charles was blessed with good eyesight, but they were still so far away he could only make out moving colours. The cavalcade kept coming, the sound of cheering below grew louder and excitement mounted on the hill. The procession was so long it was still coming into view at the bottom of Leith Walk by the time the cavalry at the front were appearing through gaps in the trees and buildings right below where the Mackays were standing.

'Oh look, Charles – can you see the king? Just there. Watch, he'll appear again soon – there, look! Oh, he's in a landau, with eight beautiful bays! Look at his uniform! He's standing up! Oh Charles, listen to the cheering! Look, Charlie, wave at the king!'

Behind the sovereign the procession continued streaming up the hill, squadrons of soldiers, many in full Highland dress, followed by scores of plain carriages, no doubt carrying noblemen and women.

'That procession must be at least a mile long, Charles!' Charlotte's face was bright with excitement, like a child's.

'Listen!' Charles cupped his ear with his hand as the roar of cheering rolled up the hill and engulfed them like a mighty wave.

Twelve days later the king's extraordinary visit was almost over and the Theatre Royal was gathering itself for the final night of glorious pageant. Charles and Charlotte left Charlie with Dorothy all day and told her they did not expect to be home until very late. They arrived at the stage door shortly after eight o'clock in the morning to find workmen and seamstresses had been labouring all night – ever since the end of the previous night's performance. The transformation was already stunning, but there was more to be done.

'Ah, here you both are – excellent – all hands on deck today, Mackay! Rehearsals at ten as usual, then back to work!' Murray sounded remarkably composed considering the responsibilities he had been carrying for weeks. Like the conductor of a great orchestra bringing a symphony to its climax, he seemed swept up in the momentum and excitement.

'Have no fear, Murray, we shall make ourselves useful!' Charles watched Charlotte disappear upstairs to help the seamstresses, then he went outside to help the workmen erect an enormous portico at the front of the theatre. It had to be finished before the crowds began gathering at lunchtime, so the pressure was intense. Huge cast-iron pillars were being lowered into sockets that had been sunk into the street, while under the shelter of the portico a platform had already been built. Two seamstresses arrived with a bolt of crimson cloth to cover it and

Charles held the weight as they unrolled it, the carpenters fixing it in place with nails.

'This is where the king will step out of his carriage to be greeted and led through to the royal box, Mackay – what do you think?' Murray was everywhere, supervising, encouraging, urging people to do their very best.

At ten o'clock Charles went inside through the main door for rehearsals and was completely disorientated by the changed layout. Huge folding doors covered in crimson cloth now led to the old box office, which had been transformed with lamps and girandoles. On the walls were a series of immense pier glasses, reflecting everything around them to marvellous effect. He stopped to stare. Never had he seen such enormous looking-glasses. The effect when all the lights were lit would be stunning. He walked through the revamped old fruit saloon and was confronted with a reflection of himself in a gigantic glass placed directly opposite the entrance. *What an impressive way to greet the king!*

He noticed Charlotte helping carry heavy crimson drapes down the stairs and called out to her.

'Murray has created a palace, a wonderland, Charlotte! I'm lost for words!' She smiled and lifted her hand, miming a pinching movement to suggest he should close his gawping mouth.

Throughout the afternoon the Call Boy came and went from the green room, reporting a massive build-up of crowds outside the building. He told them people were pressing and heaving at each other to try and get near the doors, even climbing over each other in their desperation.

'It's the chance of a lifetime for ordinary folk to spend an evening with their king, that'll be why they're going mad out there!' Emma Nicol was sitting by Charlotte finishing off the hem on another crimson drape, the two friends chattering comfortably together. Charles stood quietly where he was and began to breathe slowly, preparing himself for the performance, while conversations eddied round him like water.

'I heard Murray wouldn't sell tickets to people who'd already been to an event with the king – he wanted to give ordinary folk a chance. But there's just too many of them out there. It's a shame so many'll be disappointed.'

'How many can the theatre hold? A thousand, mebbe? I think there'll be double let in tonight, though – let's hope there isn't a fire!'

'Ooh – don't even say such a thing!'

'There'll be an almighty stramash when the doors open!'

'Let's go upstairs and look out of the window, I want to see for mysel' – it's sure to be a sight to remember!' Charles came out of his reverie to see half the actors were running out of the room. Charlotte slipped her hand into his.

'Come on, Charles, we're all going to have a look at the crowds from the upstairs windows. History is being made today, and I, for one, don't want to miss anything!'

The fine weather had been short-lived and it was pouring with rain again. The unfortunate people gathered below were wedged so closely a piece of paper could not have been slid between them. Steam rose in thick clouds from the jostling, swirling, multitudes and here and there desperate measures were being employed to move nearer to the doors. Charles watched open-mouthed as a big man in full Highland dress climbed onto someone's shoulders and began to crawl over the crowd towards the doors. *Pity help the door johnnies when they open up at six!*

ELEVEN

Charlotte had a secret. She had told no one except Dorothy and Emma and was confident the careful alterations Dorothy had made to her red dress would not be detected. She felt well and strong and was determined to be on-stage at the Royal Command Performance. The tiredness had not been so bad this time. Charlotte had not yet mentioned her condition to Charles, but she had missed her courses twice and was quite sure she was with child. Tonight she would play the part of Hostess again – opening the play, setting the tone of it, speaking her lines loudly and clearly to King George – and nothing would stop her. She remembered the boldness of young Jessie Ryder and straightened her shoulders.

The sound of a huge, excitable audience amusing themselves by singing ragged but joyous versions of 'Auld Lang Syne' and other old Scots songs swirled round the crowded green room where actors in costume were competing for space with members of the orchestra. The Call Boy had been rushing in and out, breathlessly updating everyone, as they had all been confined in there since just before the doors opened at six.

'That's yon Duff, Earl of Fife, arrived in his box wi' all his folk! Ach, you should see them in all their feathers and finery!'

It was seven o'clock now, and the monarch was due to arrive at eight. He would probably be a few minutes late, and then there would be all the bowing and ceremony in the portico. Mr Murray expected the entertainment to begin at half past eight at the earliest and, for Charlotte, the minutes were dragging their feet like reluctant children.

When the orchestra filed through to the pit as eight o'clock approached Charlotte checked her makeup in a looking-glass and found a seat near the wings, where she sat with her eyes closed. Charles was standing nearby, but he too had retreated inside himself in preparation for the performance.

A huge roar from the multitudes out in the street announced the arrival of the royal carriage and, without thinking, Charlotte stood, almost as though it would be wrong to stay seated in such close proximity to the monarch. Under her linen apron she stroked her belly, as if to tell the little scrap of a daughter she believed she was carrying they were taking part in a historic moment.

Several minutes later, silence gripped the boisterous audience for a moment, like a held breath, then deep, heartfelt yelling and shouting erupted, resonating round the auditorium for more than a minute. The Call Boy called out from his position in the wings.

'Himself is standing in his fancy box up there, dressed as a field marshal, wavin' and smilin' tae folk like some friendly, fat soldier ye micht ken! There's a bunch o' dukes and that beside him, too!' He disappeared again for a moment but was soon back. 'Aw, ye should see a' they bunnets and plumes and kerchiefs and tartan scarves, wavin' like trees in a hurricane – sic a bonnie sight!'

The musicians began to play and the whole company filed on-stage in front of the red velvet drop curtain for the national anthem. The entire audience rose to its feet, hundreds of faces shining brightly in the light of the glorious chandeliers. The actors began to sing the first verse, their voices almost drowned by the professional singers Mr Murray had added to their number. It was magnificent. When the massed voices of the audience joined in for the chorus it was even more thrilling. Charlotte gazed up at the king in his royal box, hardly believing it was really him. She could hear Charles's deep booming voice behind her and imagined how wonderful it was going to be to talk to him about it all later, when it was over. But there was acting to be done first.

After the anthem the company left the stage as friendly shouts and halloos resounded round the auditorium. Charlotte and several other the actors took their places behind the curtain. Then it was time. She felt as though she was floating when the overture began. Slowly, ever so slowly, the curtain rose, and there they all were again, that bright multitude, all looking at her as she moved around the stage, filling tankards and wiping tables. After the overture the travellers sang their unaccompanied glee song with its delightful layers of harmony, then Charlotte stood facing the singers as they finished the song and waited for the applause to fade.

'*Brawly sung, my maisters, brawly sung!*' The applause soon resumed, this time for her, and she paused for a moment to receive it, dipping a slight curtsey to the royal box. Then she turned back to the travellers and continued, projecting her voice and enjoying the feel of it bouncing from the walls and the lofty ceiling.

'*I wish ye safe hame, for yer ain sakes, an' quick return for mine!*' Laughter rippled all around and Charlotte looked directly up at the king, who smiled broadly in return. She continued serenely, feeling she had been born for this moment. When the travellers left the inn she had the stage completely to herself and she turned to the king again, cupping her ear as if listening to something. She addressed her words to him alone.

'*Odd! There are twa mair travellers just alighting. Wha'd hae thought o' mair company at the Thistle and Bagpipes sae late in the day. But, what wi' Whigs and Tories, Jacobites an' Rob Roy, we in the North here drive a bonny trade o't!'* She grinned widely at King George and he nodded, smiling and clapping his big hands slowly three times. Then Rob Roy and his man appeared on-stage, in disguise, and the audience erupted. Charlotte graciously offered her guest supper, feigning ignorance as to his identity, then curtseyed to the monarch again and disappeared off-stage to warm applause. She had done it!

After a few sips of small beer Charlotte had recovered sufficiently to creep into the wings and settle herself at the back, well concealed, in readiness to watch Charles. The Call Boy saw her and nodded. He would not send her away tonight. He seemed to know she must witness this moment for herself. It was the most important performance of Charles's life, too, and she had no doubt whatsoever that he would make the king roar with laughter more than once.

Even though she was so familiar with every word and gesture, Charlotte was mesmerised by her husband's acting, and by the particular attention the king paid to it. The overwhelming enthusiasm of the crowds whenever Charles made an appearance or spoke made Charlotte wonder if he might be becoming the Darling of Scotland. *He may lack a little in height, a little in fineness of feature, in education, too, but no one can deny those lacks are more than compensated for by the electrifying attraction of his stage presence.* Charlotte was surprised to find herself feeling slightly jealous of her dear friend Emma Nicol, who was playing Mattie and shared several affectionate moments with him.

The king laughed a hearty and sonorous laugh at the ridiculous scene when the Bailie defended himself with a hot poker, not having a sword, and singed his opponent's plaid. The royal face expressed childlike delight on many other occasions, too. As she watched, Charlotte often whispered to the tiny flame of life inside her how proud she would be of her father when she met him, how much he would love her and make her laugh.

'*When you cast a look towards poor old Scotland, do not forget Rob Roy.*' Calcraft, as Rob Roy, uttered his final words, looking directly at the king, then bowed deeply as the orchestra began the final song. A storm of cheering, stamping, whistling and applause was unleashed while the actors sang the finale. Charles was standing quite near Charlotte in her hiding place – she could almost have reached out her hand and touched him. She slipped back into the green room and waited with the rest of the company for the final bow.

'Let your hands and hearts agree, set the Highland laddie free;
Mak us sing wi' muckle glee, Rob Roy Macgregor, Oh!'

It was over! Charlotte and the rest of the company filed back on-stage, and she contrived, as always, to stand beside her husband for the thunderous curtain call.

'God Save the King' was loudly called for again by the audience, who stood – the men bareheaded – and lustily joined the singing of the chorus. This was followed by hearty acclamations shouted by members of the audience across the theatre for several minutes, all directed towards the monarch. His Majesty looked very moved by such demonstrations of loyalty, bowing to his subjects repeatedly, and the sounds of shouting and cheering continued long after he had left the box.

The actors draped themselves over chairs and chaise longues in the green room in various states of dress and undress, exhausted and bemused, gazing at one another and laughing in disbelief at what has just happened. Mr Murray walked among them, congratulating everyone individually, his face shining like a polished apple, his hands clenching and unclenching at his side. Charlotte wondered if he would collapse with exhaustion soon, or if he would just keep going like a tightly wound carriage clock.

TWELVE

Charles spread a copy of the *Edinburgh Dramatic Review* on the breakfast table and began combing through it for comments about himself. Launched a couple of months after the royal visit, the sole purpose of the daily four-page publication was to shed a bright light on the Theatre Royal. It had been packing a punch from the first edition. Reviews were sharp and witty, information about forthcoming plays full of detail. Before long it began to include readers' letters too. Charlotte was balancing Charlie on her knee, spooning porridge into his mouth, the clink of the spoon and the murmurings of mother and son washing over Charles very pleasantly that late autumn morning.

'I'm not sure it's a good idea to read those reviews, Charles. Who gave them the authority to judge us anyway?'

'Hmm?' Charles tore his eyes away from the page, keeping his place with his index finger and raising a quizzical eyebrow. 'Am I mistaken in thinking you are the lady who has always grabbed reviews out of my hands in her eagerness to read them!' He smiled at her indulgently then continued reading, thinking how bonnie she looked when she was with child. She had not finished.

'Maybe I've changed my mind.'

'Ah, I see!' he replied, without looking up. After a moment he grew suspicious of Charlotte's silence and found she was staring at him, her pretty features drawn into a frown, her mouth a tight line as she waited for his attention.

'I heard Mr Murray gives those pesky critics free entry in exchange for publicity – I hope he doesn't rue the day.'

'Have you read this already, Charlotte? What have I missed?' Instead of answering, she made a fuss of wiping Charlie's mouth. Charles turned the page over and saw his name at once. He began to read.

'What? The cheek of it! *Mr Mackay was more appropriately dressed last night than on Monday; we suppose Solomon had a letter from Tom Twist upon the subject.* I have no idea what this is supposed to mean!' He pushed the paper away. 'Perhaps you're right, Charlotte, I shouldn't waste my time reading this rubbish.' She smiled a satisfied little smile and began to wipe Charlie's sticky fingers.

'Did you see yesterday's copy?'

'Aha – always at least one step ahead of me, Charlotte! No, I did not. I hope they had something better to say?' She sat Charlie on the floor with his bricks and fetched a copy of the review from the bookshelf. Charles put his hand out for it, but she stood by the window and began to read, a smile twitching at the side of her mouth.

'*Mr Mackay played Robin. It is a character he cannot do justice to. He was not at all a careless tar; but he would have improved it much had he not worn that everlasting red wig.*' Charles jumped up and snatched the rag from her. She burst out laughing. 'At *last* someone has told you how ridiculous you look in Henry Johnston's horrible old wig! It's high time you ditched it for good, you know, it was never meant for you anyway!' He shook his head and sat down with his hands over his ears, determined to read the rest of the review himself. Charlotte came to the table and leaned over him, her voice low and threatening, her face full of mischief.

'Give the wig to Charlie, as you first intended, Charles. Either that or it's going in the midden!'

'Wait a moment. It says here that I was *very amusing as the gouty old justice* in *Love in a Village*.'

'I mean it, Charles!' She was standing beside him, hands on her hips, a glint of mischief in her eyes.

'Ha! You're just jealous of the way the lovely Miss Stephens from London looked at me when she sang "Charlie is My Darling"!'

'What nonsense! She's no competition to me at all!' Charlotte ran her hands over the curves of her blossoming body seductively and gave a little curtsey. He pushed his chair back and jumped up.

'How can I resist such a marvellous example of womanhood?' Then he took her in his arms and began waltzing round the room with her, singing at the top of his voice:

'I shall fetch that wig at once,
and put it in the midden,
I shall fetch that wig at once,
and do just what I'm bidden!'

Charlie put his arms up, crying out to be included in the fun, and soon all three were whirling round the room. When Dorothy opened the door she almost dropped her mop.

Charles announced he was going for a hike up Calton Hill with Charlie the following Sunday morning and Charlotte said she would prefer to stay in bed. She was still there when they returned. It was most unlike her. Dorothy was sitting at the table peeling potatoes, so he put his two-year-old son on the floor beside her with his box of wooden bricks and went to see what was wrong with his wife.

'Charlotte, dearest, are you ill, is it the bairn?' She had told him her secret when they lay awake into the early hours, still buzzing with excitement, after the Royal Command Performance. It had hit him like a pail of cold water. He had curled his body round her and muttered into her hair *be safe, my darling girl, be well and safe*. Yet, so far, she seemed well and strong, and last week she had told him she could feel the child move and was convinced she was carrying a girl. *A daughter would be grand!*

She shook her head and sat up, rearranging her pillows behind her back.

'I'm perfectly well, thank you. You must know what's upsetting me, Charles. I told you about it yesterday.' *His heart sank – not this again!* 'You must promise to talk to Mr Murray about it soon, Charles. It's not long before the opening night, which everyone is saying will be a disaster unless he casts me as Kitty, not Julia! I know the Nicol sisters are popular, but they're all too tall and slim – even Emma wouldn't do in that role.'

'What do you want me to say?'

'It's obvious, isn't it? *The Belle's Stratagem* is a play about people pretending to be who they are not. If the actress playing Kitty looks nothing like Lady Touchwood – Mrs Cummins – then the joke about her impersonation will fall flat. Everyone knows I look more like Mrs Cummins than Julia does. Julia as Kitty would be ridiculous – the audience would never believe in the dupe! You must tell Mr Murray I should have the part. He's bound to listen to his *pride and joy*!' Charlotte climbed out of bed and went to stand by the window, her hair swinging in a golden plait down her back, the swell of her belly clearly visible under her long white nightgown. Charles felt ambushed.

'I understand what you're saying, Charlotte, but I don't want to put Murray in an awkward position. He must have his reasons.'

She turned abruptly. 'He doesn't trust me not to collapse, like I did in Perth! It seems I will *never* shake that off, Charles!'

'What makes you think that, Charlotte?'

She narrowed her eyes. 'Because Julia Nicol herself suggested to Mr Murray that I would be better as Kitty and he told her my health was too unreliable for such a strategic part!' Charlotte sank back onto the bed, her body slumping. 'I don't know why I bother, Charles – Mr Murray seems determined to block me, however hard I work to prove myself! A silent maid – that's what he's given me – *again*!' Charles sat beside her, stroking her arm, not knowing what to say. When Dorothy put her head round the door and said she was going to take Charlie with her to visit her family in Leith for lunch he almost wept with gratitude.

Audiences at the Theatre Royal had been neither as full nor as enthusiastic in the second half of the year as they had been in the first. Murray had not put on a single national drama since the king's visit and Charles was beginning to wonder if his friend was losing his way as a manager. It came as a great relief to all the actors when they heard that *Guy Mannering* was next on the programme.

Emma Nicol and her sisters Julia and Maria were with Charlotte in the green room, all of them dressed in gypsy outfits and peering into looking-glasses to apply last-minute adjustments to their makeup. They seemed oblivious that their chatter was loud enough for all to hear. Charles was sitting nearby, pleased to see his wife so happy again and surrounded by friends. Maria Nicol usually danced her famous *Pas de Seul* in the interval between items, sometimes with a skipping rope, occasionally accompanied by their shy youngest sister, Caroline. It would be good to see these three sisters on-stage together for a change. Their mother had an Old Lady role as well. *What a family of marvellous women they are.*

'Thank goodness Murray has put his Manager's Hat back on his head!'

'I know, Emma! I was beginning to wonder if he'd mislaid it! All these bland farces, and our audiences shrinking by the day!' Julia and Maria giggled at Charlotte's expression of distaste. Charlotte stood up and smoothed her wide skirts, turning round to look at her side view in the cheval.

'Would you guess I'm with child?'

'Does it matter? You're a gypsy girl!'

'Maria!'

'Well, it's true, that's what people think, isn't it?' The sisters continued chattering to each other and Charlotte looked over at Charles, smiling coyly with her rouged cheeks and lips, her flouncy tartan skirt and revealing bodice. Then she put the flat of her hand on her rounded belly suddenly and smiled. Charles wondered if it was their child moving, or just her nerves.

To everyone's relief, the season ended with a full house. Murray declared on-stage that he was going to redecorate the theatre and bring all the variety of the London theatres the following season, which would open in less than a fortnight. Charles listened from the wings, admiring the scale and bravado of Murray's vision, given the short length of time he had for the refurbishment and the limitations of the troupe. Charlotte had been right about the part of Kitty, though. The miscasting was so obvious it was even mentioned in the *Dramatic Review*: *Could the manager find no person to represent Kitty Willis who could look more like Mrs Cummins than Miss J Nicol? Why not Mrs Mackay? The great contrast destroyed the illusion of the scene.*

An early frost nipped at their ears and fingertips as Charles and Charlotte wandered up the road to the theatre twelve days later, leaving Charlie tucked up asleep and Dorothy knitting by the fire. It was the night before the grand opening and Murray had invited his company to come and see what he had done to the old place. The intervening days had passed more quickly than usual for Charles in the company of his growing son. Charlie loved nothing more than being hoisted onto his father's shoulders and taken out in all weathers to walk the streets and hills, and it seemed to suit the women fine as well.

'Oh look at the lights, Charles, they're magical!' They had stopped opposite the theatre to enjoy the new illuminations, so beautiful against the ink black sky. They crossed the road and went to see what transformations had taken place inside. The auditorium was freshly painted with diamonds of gold beading on the front of all the boxes and gold thistles, shamrocks or roses painted in their centres on a white ground. *Murray has certainly delivered on his promise regarding the theatre itself. Let's see how he intends to stage his London-style productions!*

'Are those the crimson drapes you helped sew for the royal visit, d'you think Charlotte?'

'Oh yes, so they are! It's good to see them have another outing after all that work!' She held his arm tightly as they walked slowly round, not venturing any more comments, even when they met some of their fellow actors. After a while she murmured in his ear.

'Can we go home now, Charles? I'm not feeling well.' They set off at once, walking slowly through a light scattering of soft snowflakes, but before they had reached the main door of their lodgings she stopped and gasped.

'Oh no! We need to send for a doctor, Charles. *Right now*!'

'Charlotte! My darling! What is it?' His heart was thumping with fear and he looked wildly around for help. There were no cabs anywhere to be seen. The street was empty.

'I fell, Charles. Two days ago, after our walk. I was tired. I slipped on the stair and landed hard on my rump, nearly passed out with the pain of it. Then I stood up and went inside and Dorothy made me tea and I thought I would be alright …' She buried her face in his chest. 'I'm going to lose our daughter, Charles, and it's my fault. I'm so *stupid*!' He stroked her hair gently, his mind jumping around like a demented rabbit, trying to think what to do.

'Shh, now, my darling, shh. It's not your fault. Let's get you up the stair and into bed. Then I'll fetch the medic and we'll see. You're a strong woman, Charlotte, you'll be alright. You'll both be alright.'

He ran through the dark streets in a dream, unable to believe what was happening, mesmerised by the snow that was now falling thickly. What had he been thinking, dragging her up Calton Hill in her condition? How had he not picked up the signs sooner, made her rest? *What a fool! I can't lose her!* Thankfully the doctor was at home and had a cab at his disposal. They were back at Broughton Street within the hour.

Dorothy was sitting by the hearth with Charlie on her lap when he opened the door. She looked up, her face pale and drawn. There were bright spots of blood on her apron.

'She's resting through bye the now, Mr Mackay, but it's no' over. She'll need the medic tae help. She'll need me too. I've water on the boil and clean clouts ready, but ye'll need tae tak the bairn away and come back on the morrow. Ye cannae let him hear it, Mr Mackay, it'll no' be guid for yersel' either. Here – tak the laddie, he's all wrapped and ready tae go.' Charles took his sleepy son in his arms and stood, paralysed. When he made to go and say goodbye to Charlotte Dorothy blocked his way.

'Ye can see her on the morrow. She'll be braw. Noo – aff ye go, the both o' ye!' A low moan began to rise into a scream and he closed the door, clamping his hand over Charlie's ears, kissing his eyes, carrying him carefully down the stairwell gripping the banister tightly with his other hand. When he found himself standing on Murray's doorstep in the pitch dark, shaking and covered in snow, he could not remember walking there. The Murrays welcomed them warmly and he slept deeply that night, despite all that had happened.

Charlie woke in a good mood early the next day and seemed delighted to be allowed to play with the Murrays' little boy – another Charles – who was about his age.

'You must leave Charlie with us today, Mr Mackay. He's most welcome and will be no trouble. You need to go home to Charlotte now.' Ann Murray was one of the kindest women Charles knew. An actress when Murray first met her, she had given up the stage to run her gracious home and care for their child. He thanked her quietly and left.

Snow had fallen in the night and Charles set off in the half-light, leaving a trail of black footprints behind him, steeling himself to face whatever had happened in his absence.

Dorothy was stoking the fire when he walked in. She looked up wearily and he knew by her bloodshot eyes she had not slept.

'What happened – is she ...?'

'Charlotte's asleep, Mr Mackay. The medic says she's needin' plenty rest, but she'll be braw.' Charles sank onto his chair and felt the breath he had been holding go out of him. He glanced at Dorothy again, a question in his eyes he could not bring himself to ask. Her tight mouth and the slight shake of her head told him what he suspected. He gulped and dashed the back of his hand across his wet cheeks.

'Was it a girl, Dorothy? Did we lose a daughter?'

'I cannae say and I wilnae say – it's no' for us to be givin' they wee lost bairnies names. They were no' for this world, is all. The bairn's in heav'n the noo wi' all the other lost ones – and there's an end tae it, Mr Mackay. Yer lucky tae have yer wife still, if ye'll pardon me sayin'.'

'Thank you, Dorothy. Dear Dorothy. I'm more than grateful for your help. I've left Charlie with the Murrays for the day. May I go and see Charlotte now?' She nodded and he rose wearily. *Thank the Lord we still have each other, and Charlie.*

Charles sent a note to Murray asking for a few days' leave while the family recovered from their calamity. When he returned to the theatre a week later Charlotte asked him to tell Murray she was ready to go back on-stage too. He did so with a heavy heart. Murray was kind enough to offer her a good part, that of Margery in *The Spoil'd Child*, but they both knew she would not be ready. An apology was made for her shortly before the performance and the part was played by her understudy. Charles decided not to read the review.

The very next morning Charlotte surprised everyone, including Charles, by turning up at the theatre and asking if she could play the Hostess in *Rob Roy* that night. Mrs Shaw stepped graciously aside and Charlotte gave an excellent rendition of her favourite role. Charles was so anxious about her he lost concentration more than once. He even committed the cardinal sin of interrupting one of his fellow actors in the middle of a song to correct his pronunciation. *Of all things, Mackay! A man of your experience should know better!*

Although the redecorated theatre looked most impressive, no fabulous new London-style productions had materialised by Christmas and audiences were often thin. Then the new year began with an almighty row, stirred up by the meddling critics of the *Dramatic Review*, who had decided to investigate the salaries of the actors. Murray had been so furious about the rag interfering in the financial concerns of his theatre he had rescinded his offer of free entry to the critics.

'It's thoroughly scurrilous, implying, as they do, that the Theatre Royal gives such paltry salaries it is only able to employ mediocre actors. I tell you, it makes my blood boil!' Calcraft was pacing the green room as he spoke, his hands clasped behind his back. He stopped beside Charles and lowered his voice. 'There is also a particularly unpleasant piece of correspondence about your good self, Mackay, I'm sorry to say. Might I advise you to keep it from Charlotte until she is quite well again, old fellow? I'm afraid it's extremely harsh.'

'What on earth d'you mean?' Charles took the two copies of the *Review* Calcraft was holding and read the relevant sections. 'Good Lord, Calcraft! It's a blatant attempt to destroy my entire reputation, to tear the very foundation of my career to pieces! What the devil?' He sat down and scanned two long letters that had been printed in full, amazed to see himself the object of such personal, vitriolic criticisms, by an anonymous writer calling himself 'Crito'.

'It's outrageous!' Charles could hardly speak. 'Listen to this: *Mr Mackay is a mere child of fortune, for had not those National Tales been dramatized Mr M would never have been eminent and must, obviously, have been known as an actor possessing powers a few degrees beneath mediocrity.* And that's not the worst of it ... *always monotonous; no natural force in his acting!*' Calcraft put a sympathetic hand on his shoulder.

'Try not to take it to heart, Mackay. It's part of our job to take such knocks. As I said, best not to let Charlotte see it just yet, though. I understand she is most sensitive of your reputation and is still quite frail.' Calcraft was usually so buttoned-up, with his military moustache and ramrod-straight back, Charles wondered why he was being so considerate of Charlotte's sensitivities. Perhaps her bravery after her recent calamity had endeared her to the whole company.

'Oh, and Charles – turns out it's that old fox Henry Johnston behind all those renovations at the Pantheon. Planning to open it with a host of talent from London next week. Murray had better be ready for some healthy competition! Holding the royal patent won't be enough to keep his audiences if Johnston puts on some good spectacles.'

'Well, I'll be blowed, Calcraft! It seems we've sailed into something of a storm these past few weeks, after such a long stretch of fair weather.'

THIRTEEN

Charlotte could feel herself breathing more deeply than she had done for weeks. Charles's rich, bass voice was soaring high into the rafters of St Cuthbert's, mingling with hundreds, even thousands of others, in glorious harmonies that sent shivers down her spine. The loss of the child she had expected to carry to full term had affected her deeply. Today, at last, the weight of it was beginning to lift.

'I love listening to your voice in here, Charles, even more than in the theatre, somehow,' she whispered as they sat down after the hymn.

He whispered back, tickling her ear with his soft breath. 'We must bring Charlie with us soon. Peter must've been about his age when our mam first started bringing us here.'

Charlotte held her breath, hoping for more. It was the first time he had talked about his childhood, apart from answering her questions as briefly as possible. She longed to know more but knew she had to tread carefully.

'Was it far to walk here from your home? Charlie would want to be carried part of the way from ours at least, I should think.'

'It was far enough, but we managed.' He squeezed her hand as if to end the conversation and she squeezed it back. She knew he found it painful remembering his mother and preferred not to talk about her. But maybe Charlie would help him remember some of the good times he must have had. He and his brother William wrote to each other occasionally and Charles would read out snippets about his three nephews, but Peter seemed to have disappeared to London. Charlotte could hardly imagine not knowing where one of her siblings was. She wrote to her family often, wondered if she might visit them one day. It was good to have dreams.

They were walking along Princes Street on their way home from church, both lost in their thoughts, when the sound of workmen reached their ears. There had been complaints, recently, about Mr Murray putting painters, carpenters and tailors to work on Sundays, breaking the Sabbath whenever a new piece was about to be produced.

'It seems Murray's at it again, Charles.'

'It's for the launch of *Coriolanus* tomorrow. Murray's showcasing that new leading male tragedian he's employed for the season. Apparently, Mr Vandenhoffe is a truly *classical* actor. We shall see!'

Charlotte detected a sour note in Charles's comment and tucked her arm through his, leaning into him as they walked. 'You must feel awful about the remarks of that "Crito", Charles, but …'

He stopped walking and turned to her. 'How d'you know about that?'

'Oh Charles, Emma's mother has the *Edinburgh Dramatic Review* delivered every morning and Emma keeps me well informed. Did you think I didn't know?' She smiled up at him from under the brim of her blue bonnet. 'Everyone's talking about it, but no one likes to mention it to you. That awful man's tirades were so terribly unfair and untrue. I do hope you can brush it all aside, think of his words as nothing more than annoying flies buzzing round your head. You're such a popular and talented actor,

Charles, not to mention the funniest and dearest man I've ever met!' She beamed at him and he kissed her smile. Moments later Charles strode on past the end of Leith Street, instead of heading down the hill towards home, and Charlotte pulled at his hand.

'Where are we going? I'm not quite ready for another hike up Calton Hill yet. Besides, Charlie will be wanting his lunch soon, and Dorothy will want to go to her family for the afternoon as usual ...'

'Whisht wi' yer bletherin', lassie, an' come away wi' me. I've something bonnie tae show ye that's no' sae far frae here!' It seemed Charles had quickly found his sparkle again and she was curious to know what he had up his sleeve.

They turned left at the new Regent Bridge, walked a few steps down Calton Street and turned right. Charlotte was convinced he was taking her up to the summit, but instead, he stopped and surveyed the scene, gesturing at the rows of cottages and houses crowded together on either side of the narrow street.

'You can tell this wee street used to be a village, with its cottagey houses and wee pecks o' gardens. It's homely, don't you think?'

Charlotte caught on at once and her heart started racing.

'So it is, guid sir. A bonnie place for a wee family tae coorie in and grow a few tatties and flooers.'

His face lit up. 'You're far too canny, Mrs Mackay!' He pulled a paper from his waistcoat pocket with a flourish. 'I have here a five-year lease on a wee house at No. 12, Calton Hill.'

She gasped. 'Oh, my Lord! Can we go and see it now?' She felt like a child asking for a treat.

'Of course! Why d'you think I brought you here? Neither of us are acting tomorrow night, so I thought we could move in tomorrow morning!' Charlotte was so surprised by his audacity she burst out laughing.

He led her through a street door into a small courtyard with six little cottages crammed round it.

'There's a privy out back, and a washhouse too, come and see!' It was nothing like their lodgings, nothing like Charlotte's home in London, either. Inside, the cottage was dark and cold and smelt of old smoke. The windows were small and dirty and the ceiling was very low compared with their Broughton Street lodgings. There was a wide hearth with black chains and pots, a box bed in the corner, and a table with four wooden chairs. On the wall were three shelves and several hooks.

'Oh look, Charles, there's a scullery that leads outside!' Charlotte pushed another door open. 'And there's a room here with a bed and a trunk for our clothes!' She clapped her hands in delight. 'Oh, it'll be perfect when I clean the windows and put pretty curtains on them and scrub the floor!'

'And, there are *no stairs*!'

Her face fell. 'Oh, Charles, please don't.'

'I'm sorry.' He cupped her chin gently in his hand and kissed her nose. 'D'you think we can make a new start, Charlotte, after all our sadness? D'you think you and I could be happy here, with Charlie?'

'I think we could.' She sat on one of the chairs and closed her eyes. How had he known this was what she needed most of all right now? She had not even known it herself until that moment. *What a way to start the year! I will make a home here – there will be more children.*

Charlotte stood in the light of the kitchen window, reading a review of Henry Johnston's New Caledonian Theatre. She was consumed with curiosity to see what he had done with the old Pantheon. His opening speech – reproduced in full – covered two pages with self-serving doggerel and she laughed out loud.

'What's so funny, Charlotte?' Emma Nicol had come to see the new cottage and had brought several copies of the *Edinburgh Dramatic Review* with her, as well as some pretty blue and white china cups and plates.

'Have you seen the speech Henry Johnston gave on his first night, Emma? His vanity is unbelievable! Listen to this: *Years have rolled on since, with aspiring aim,/Here, I essayed the rugged path of fame!*'

Charlotte's finger moved down the page, her smiling lips moving silently over the words. 'And this: *The travell'd bird returns, no more to roam,/To find his native grove, his latest home.*'

'What doggerel! Do you think people laughed out loud at him, Emma?'

'I have no idea. I don't really know the man.' Emma was draped on a chair by the fire supping her tea, her strong face glowing warmly in the light of the flames. Charlie sat on the floor beside her stacking his blocks and Dorothy was pottering in the scullery. Charlotte surveyed the scene and sighed contentedly. *Home.*

The next day she set off to buy fish in the High Street but instead found herself outside the newly named Caledonian Theatre, wondering if Henry was inside. Charlotte knew he was despicable, yet she was fascinated by him.

'Well, if it isn't Miss O'Keefe! How nice of you to come by!' Charlotte whipped round to find the very man standing behind her, glowing with pride and confidence, tall and broad and still rakishly handsome.

'Mr Johnston. I was simply passing on my way to do some errands and thought I would have a look at your new theatre.' She was a good enough actress to keep her jitters under control but felt torn between the urge to flee and her eagerness to see inside.

'So, you've heard about my little venture?' She nodded curtly. 'Would you like to see what I've done with the old place? I could give you a guided tour!' His eagerness set alarm bells ringing.

'I'm sure you have better things to do with your time, Mr Johnston. You must be a busy man, setting up in competition with the Theatre Royal. I must say, I don't know how you plan to get around your lack of a licence.' She gave him no time to reply. 'I see you've put on *Gilderoy* for your first week – is it your intention to produce many of these national dramas? The critics don't like them at all, you'll find.' *Why was she doing this?* It was like playing with fire, yet she seemed unable to resist pitting her wits against his towering ego.

'Well now, let me see.' Henry looked at her with his infuriating air of mild amusement. 'I plan to put on mostly so-called illegitimate productions and farces, but, unlike Murray, I will reinstate the tradition of offering the good working people of Edinburgh half-price entry for the second half of the programme, leaving the toffs to pay full price for the whole evening. I have no doubt every night will be sold out!'

'Well, you make it sound so easy! I shall follow your progress with great interest, Mr Johnston.'

'As for your other question, Charlotte, I've heard critics refer to these great Scottish plays as melodramas, but I think they're simply displaying their ignorance. The viewing public of Scotland know the difference. Healthy ticket sales are worth far more than the approval of critics, don't you think?'

'I suppose you're going to tell me what the difference is?' *Why am I encouraging him?*

'Well now, let me see. National drama is utterly Scottish, for one thing. Its characters are more down-to-earth than those in a melodrama, wouldn't you say? Then there are all those guid auld Scots songs.' He was holding forth as though to a full theatre and Charlotte was suddenly desperate to leave. 'I think it's fair to say melodramas usually attempt to draw a moral, too, don't you agree? Whereas national dramas are content simply to tell stories.' She conceded with a dip of her head, wrapped her green plaid more tightly round her shoulders against the chill wind and began fingering her gold pendant underneath it. Henry pulled his pipe out of his pocket and continued his lecture while stuffing it with tobacco from a little leather pouch. The smell reminded her of the unfortunate incident in the green room and she began to panic.

'I really must …' Her throat felt tight, her voice came out in a hoarse whisper and Henry talked on, oblivious of her polite attempt to leave.

'Of course, when I first trod the boards in our dear Athens of the North I was still a lad. As you know, I launched myself on-stage in full Highland costume in what is widely acknowledged to be the first of our national dramas – the tragedy of *Douglas*. The impression I made has reverberated through the decades.' She felt as though she was drowning in the stream of self-love pouring endlessly from his full, red lips, but she was powerless to stop him. Perhaps she should just walk away while he was talking. 'One member of the audience famously shouted, *Whaur's yer Wullie Shakespeare noo?*, knowing the writer of the play to be a true Scot.' Her head snapped up and she countered him, confidently.

'Henry Johnston, you are such a fraud! Even *I* know that remark was made when the play was first performed in 1756 – you *cannot* claim it for yourself!'

His eyes became slits and his full mouth curled into a smirk.

'Ah, but Charlotte, that's just it, *I can!* No one cares about the accuracy of my rhetoric. They just enjoy being swept up in the emotion of it. You should know, being such a fine actress yourself!' She turned to leave, but he continued talking.

'*All the world's a stage*, Charlotte, *and all the men and women merely players*.'

'Balderdash, Henry Johnston. I wish you good day.' Charlotte strode off towards Leith Street, her face burning with a mixture of fury and embarrassment, his mocking laughter resounding behind her. *There is simply no stopping that despicable, insufferable man! He won't last long with his new theatre, though. People will soon see him for the fraud he is.*

As Charlotte had predicted, Henry Johnston gave up after only one season. Then, to everyone's amazement, Corbett and Jessie Ryder arrived in Edinburgh and took on the lease of the New Caledonian, adding it to their northern circuit. The first thing they did was blatantly ignore the constraints of the royal patent by putting on *Rob Roy* in competition with the Theatre Royal. The green room was awash with gossip about it.

Murray let it be known he regarded it an act of aggression and battle lines were drawn. His sister Harriet, owner of the exclusive royal patent in Edinburgh, for which she had paid heftily, was furious with their cavalier attitude and instructed her lawyer to write to them. However, there was a new energy in the Theatre Royal throughout that summer season, and Charlotte wondered if it might be the result of such robust competition.

The winter season opened with a comedy called *The Poor Gentleman* and Charlotte was given the first major role she had ever had in Edinburgh, that of Dame Harrowby. The Harrowby family all spoke with a humorous Cotswold burr, which Charlotte thoroughly enjoyed mastering, and Mrs Garbutt's team of seamstresses made her a dark chintz gown, a red petticoat and a checked apron. She added her own colourful neckerchief, white cap and black shoes to complete the outfit. Although she was not mentioned by name in the reviews, which she could not resist reading, Charlotte took heart that one critic wrote, *the performance was creditable to the company.*

If Mr Murray decided to bring her forward more often next year, he might, at last, begin to trust her as a Walking Lady, like dear Emma Nicol.

FOURTEEN

Charles was standing by a gas lamp in the green room, a script in his hand, allowing his mind to wander. Tonight he was playing Launcelot Gobbo in *The Merchant of Venice*, which would be followed by the hugely popular melodramatic extravaganza, *Tom and Jerry*. He had no part in the ridiculous farce and was hoping to go home early, if he could clear it with Murray. The year had begun well for Charles and Charlotte. Already they had acted together in *Macbeth*, *George Heriot*, *Rob Roy* and *Hamlet*, and it was only the middle of January. Although Charlotte was still playing utility parts, her confidence was growing. Murray had not yet produced anything to rival the London stage, but Vandenhoffe had turned out to be a good sort. He had a tall, imposing figure and a fine voice. His Coriolanus was perfectly adequate and critics and audience alike seemed to enjoy his performances. But everyone knew Charles was still by far the biggest draw.

It was just past ten o'clock in the morning and rehearsals were not yet underway. A group of women with small, frivolous parts in the farce were sitting together gossiping and knitting. Whenever he raised his eyes he noticed them glancing in his direction.

'I'm curious to know, dear ladies, what it is you find so fascinating about me this morning? You seem unable to drag your eyes from me!' He smiled his most ingratiating smile. 'Pray tell!' Emma's sister Julia smiled back, carefully draping her shawl over the *Dramatic Review* on the seat beside her. It was too late. He had seen it.

'Oh Charles, you're not going to like it. You must make sure Charlotte doesn't see. She'll be broken!'

'Thank you, Julia. Please hand it to me, if you would be so kind.' It was the second annual review of salaries at the Theatre Royal and Charles was horrified to see the Mackays had been singled out for criticism.

'*Look at Mr and Mrs Mackay's salary, which must be considered as the salary of Mackay alone, since Mrs Mackay is not of more value than a common supernumerary ...* No! The perfidious creature! How dare he say such a thing about my wife!' Charles threw the paper on the floor and stamped on it. Then he bent to pick it up, feeling rather foolish, and sat down beside Julia, straightening the offending publication and handing it back to her.

'Oh Charles, isn't it awfully unfair! Emma saw it at breakfast today. She said she would go and keep Charlotte company in case she hears about it and is upset. She won't tell her, of course.' Julia put a hand on his arm and looked at him with great concern. 'Try not to worry, Charles, Charlotte will weather the storm. She's strong and determined. You must go home after the rehearsal, though, put your mind at rest before tonight's performance.' He thanked her for her kindness and retreated to the relative privacy of his dressing room until someone came to tell him the rehearsal had started.

That afternoon Charles entered the courtyard of No. 12 with trepidation. The moment he pushed the front door open he knew something was wrong. Charlotte was sitting with her head in her hands by a fire that had nearly gone out. There was no sign of dinner cooking, nor of Charlie or Dorothy. She looked up, her eyes red from weeping.

'Oh Charlotte.' He knelt beside her, taking her face between his hands. 'Talk to me, darling girl.' He needed to know if she was crying because she had read the review, or if her tears were about some other horror. She removed his hands from her face and held them tightly in her lap.

'I went to see Jessie Ryder this morning, Charles.' This was not what he had been expecting. She must have been out when Emma came to see her. 'I wanted to know what she's up to at the Caledonian Theatre, to find out if I'm right in thinking she's behind all the conflict with Harriet Siddons and the royal patent. I should've known not to meddle, but I was curious to see her again. She's always seemed such a confident, successful woman – acting major roles, managing a theatre company, caring for all those children – somehow she does it all!' Charlotte pulled her pretty London handkerchief from her apron pocket and wiped her nose.

'What did Jessie say?'

'I thought we were friends, Charles, that we could have a conversation about it. But it turns out she is an ambitious, single-minded woman who cares only about expanding Ryder's theatre company, with no regard for those who might be hurt along the way.'

'But how could she hurt you, Charlotte? Surely it's for Murray and his sister to sort this out?'

'Of *course* it is, Charles. But Jessie made it clear she resented my interference, and, as a parting shot, she gave me a copy of today's *Dramatic Review*, folded open at page two. Oh Charles! I am *not* merely a common supernumerary taking walk-on parts worth only sixpence! It's such a dreadfully *cruel* thing to say! I thought I was going to be given more substantial parts this year, like Dame Harrowby,' she sniffed and wiped her face on her sleeve, 'but Mr Murray has started giving me small, silent parts again. I need to know if I'm doing something wrong. Please will you ask him, Charles?' She looked so desperate that Charles could not say no to her. Neither could he say yes, though. Although Murray was a friend, he was also his employer and a force of nature – the Napoleon of the Theatre. *No one* questioned his casting. He held her close until her grief subsided, hoping things would improve for her in time without the need for his intervention.

Murray asked Charles to join him at the Red Lion for a stoup of brandy after the evening performance later that week and Charles wondered if he might, after all, find an appropriate moment to mention Charlotte. It made him jittery as they walked across Shakespeare Square together. Once they had their drinks in front of them, however, Murray drew a script from his satchel, dropped it on the table and smiled his droll little sideways smile. Charles relaxed. *Another time, perhaps.*

'*St Ronan's Well.* It's going to be a huge success, Charles. I can feel it in my bones.' It was the stage adaptation of the latest novel from the prolific author of the *Waverley* novels. 'It's just been performed to great acclaim in London's Adelphi Theatre and I'm thinking of putting it on for my summer benefit, Mackay. What d'you think?' Charles picked it up and began flicking through the pages.

'I must confess I haven't read it yet. Perhaps you could fill me in on the story?'

'Absolutely.' Murray sat forward in his chair, both hands wrapped round the wide bowl of his glass, eyes gleaming. When Murray had his sights set on something new and ambitious it was best just to listen to him, to nod, to go along with it. 'The story is set in the fashionable spa town of Innerleithen in the present day – quite a risky departure for Sir Walter – or should I say, "the anonymous writer of *Waverley*".' Murray smiled his tight little lopsided smile, tapping the side of his nose. Charles tapped his own nose in return, smiling conspiratorially. 'Essentially, it's a love story, Charles. A story of rival suitors, a tragedy, even. There's an element of humour too, of course, which is what holds the play together. There's only one problem I foresee.'

'Oh? And what might that be?'

'The thing is, there's no obvious part in it for *you*, Charles. And as you are, without question, the Theatre Royal's major asset, I consider it essential that you have a significant role in all major new productions, or ticket sales will suffer.'

Charles smiled modestly, raising an eyebrow for more information.

'I'm wondering, Charles, in consideration of your inimitable comedic skills, and your ability to transform yourself so convincingly into an old hag whenever we put on a production of *Macbeth*, might it not be rather original if you were to play the principal comedic role of Meg Dodds, the landlady of the Cleikum Inn? What do you think?' Playing the part of a woman in a role like that was such an unexpected idea it took Charles all of two seconds to agree.

'Good Lord! You've quite taken me by surprise, Murray, I must say. But I believe you're right, it could be a triumph, a sensation, even! It would certainly be something new, something that has not yet been attempted.' Already Charles could hardly wait to take up the challenge.

Murray continued, 'Of course, it goes without saying you would also give the address – in character!' Charles burst out laughing at the audacity of the idea, at the same time confident he would be more than able to pull it off. He was delighted to hear Murray had also suggested it to Sir Walter Scott, who was very much in favour and had agreed to write the address in rhyming couplets.

'Sir Walter based Meg Dodds on the landlady of his local inn in Peebles, you know. I should very much like to take you down there to meet her next week, if you have the time. I think it would help enormously towards your understanding of her character. What d'you say?'

'It's a splendid idea, Murray, I shall look forward to it.'

Charles was bursting to tell Charlotte all about the new play when he arrived home, but she was already asleep. He slipped quietly into bed beside her and lay wide awake for most of the night, imagining how it would all turn out. He had not felt so excited about acting a new character since he first encountered the Bailie in Perth.

His excitement about the part only grew when Murray took him to meet Scott's inspiration for the role a few weeks later. The moment Miss Ritchie entered the tap room of The Cross Keys and bustled over to their table Charles was transported back to his childhood. She looked exactly as he imagined his mother would look now, had she lived. He hardly heard a word she said that evening, but the tone of her voice, her mannerisms, her exaggerated expressions, the heft of her hands on her ample hips, her smile, her quick wit and sharp tongue, were all as familiar to him as the hands on his arms. Suddenly he knew exactly how he would embody the character of Meg Dodds: he would become the woman his mother should have become, and it would be a joy. The rest of the night passed in a blur as the cogs of his mind rattled and whirred, putting flesh on the bones of the words and gestures he had already begun committing to memory. Rehearsals were to begin immediately after his benefit night in May.

'A strange situation has developed concerning my benefit next Monday, Charlotte. I'm at a loss as to how to deal with it.' Charles and Charlotte were enjoying a ten-day break between seasons in early spring, along with the whole theatre. It was late morning. The day was mild for the time of year and they were sitting outside with Charlie in the little courtyard of No. 12 taking their meridian. The wooden bench by their front door was a pleasant place to sit sipping tea, exchanging pleasantries with neighbours in the other cottages as they came and went and watching Charlie filling his little buckets with mud, stirring them with sticks. Sometimes the smell from the privy was slightly distracting, depending on the direction of the wind, but it was good to feel the sun on their faces.

'What do you mean?' Charlotte had not mentioned her request for Charles to talk to Murray again, much to his relief. She seemed more content these days, too. There was a serenity about her, a new bloom to her skin. It struck Charles she might be with child again. If so, she would tell him when she was ready.

'Well, you know Jones is having his benefit on Saturday night – and he's had some personal difficulties recently, so we're all very supportive of him?'

'Yes, I know about that. You're to be a character called Bonus in the comedy, aren't you?' Charlotte was crocheting a shawl in pale mint green and her shepherd's hook flicked and flacked with such speed Charles found it mesmerising.

'The thing is, there was also to be a benefit for the Deaf and Dumb Institute on Saturday night at the Assembly Rooms with the popular ventriloquist, Monsieur Alexandre. Well, I have just heard that Jones wrote to the French Consul and asked them to persuade him to move his performance to Monday night, so he would not suffer from a lack of an audience!' Charlotte put her knitting down.

'Oh no, Charles, that's most unfair of him! Now your benefit will have to compete with the great Alexandre – on a weekday evening, too!' Charles scuffed the toes of his brown boots in the dry dust.

'Exactly so. But what am I to do? Jones is a good friend – or has been until now – and he needs as much support as he can muster. The man is panicking. I feel sorry for him. I shall give my performance in his comedy all I've got, Charlotte, and then we shall just have to hope we fill the theatre on Monday evening.'

Charles was surprised, and hugely relieved, to find the house was packed well before the performance began on Monday night.

'It was a full house, my darling, after all!' he whispered as he climbed into bed with Charlotte later that night. 'And the audience have been very generous. Our bank balance is boosted beyond belief!' She rolled over to face him.

'Well done, my darling – everyone loves you, and that is a proven fact!' He wrapped his arms around her, kissing her softly.

'So long as *you* love me, Charlotte, that's all I need.'

'Is that a proven fact, too, you old rascal?'

Charles assembled his costume for his role as Meg Dodds with great care and plenty of help from Charlotte. He was determined there would be nothing ridiculous about it and they spent several evenings trying out different ideas in their bedroom, leaving Dorothy in peace in the kitchen, and whispering so as not to wake Charlie, who slept beside them on a truckle bed.

'I think you should tie some padding round your middle, Charles, to thicken your waistline. It would make all the difference.' Charlotte held up a blanket and Charles lifted his arms so she could wrap it round him. She tied it tightly with cord, then slipped the shapeless grey linen dress he had chosen over his head again and stepped back to survey the effect.

'Oh yes, that's much better! You look just like a middle-aged innkeeper's wife now – all you need is your apron and cap, a wee touch of rouge and a smack of lip balm.' Charles tied a dirty white apron round his thickened waist and pulled on his linen mutch, leaving its ribbons dangling untied, as though he had dressed in a hurry. Then he puckered his lips and closed his eyes.

'Ooh, my darling! How can I resist you?' Charlotte was trying not to laugh. 'Those little frills round the edge of your cap frame your face so sweetly.' Her kiss was firm and inviting, and before long his grey dress and the blanket beneath were discarded on the floor beside her skirts and petticoats.

There was a full house for Murray's benefit on June the 5th, 1824, and the play was extremely well received. Charles kept his voice believable rather than adopting the easy comedy of falsetto. He kept his mannerisms understated, too, choosing not to exaggerate them for laughs. He soon had the audience in his apron pocket, as though they were customers in his tavern.

The story ended sadly, and the ovation was heartfelt rather than raucous. Sir Walter's poetic address had to be given straight afterwards, which meant Charles had to lead the audience through a complete change of mood without causing offence.

When the applause faded Charles left a respectful pause, then ran onto the stage with several boys chasing and tormenting him, including Murray, dressed as a boy and acting the part with gusto. The audience began to titter again. A town officer came to chase the boys away and Charles turned to face the crowds, smoothing his apron and adjusting his frilly mutch, bringing his breathing back under control, looking for their sympathy.

Gesturing towards Murray he suggested the officer should *Lend yon muckle ane a whack*, which brought gales of laughter at once. Then, hands on hips and lips pursed, he ranted on in rhyme about the *Embrugh bairns* and bemoaned the recent changes that had come to Edinburgh. Sir Walter had inserted a dig at himself and his cronies about the controversial demolition of the old Butter Tron, which had been pulled down to tidy up the High Street for the king's visit.

Charles had assumed the identity of Meg so completely by this time he felt as though he was just having a grand old gossip and moan with his customers. He delivered the rest of the address to shouts of agreement. The compliments for William Murray and his sister at the end of the piece brought the audience to their feet and the applause was deafening.

When Charles left the stage Charlotte was there in the wings. She caught him in her arms and kissed him all over his face until he had to beg for mercy. They stumbled back into the green room together, laughing and breathless, to be greeted by the rest of the company with great enthusiasm and hearty slaps on the back.

'Another triumph, Mackay! Bravo!'

'What a marvellous woman you make, old man, I would never have guessed!'

'That tops it all, I think, Charles – well done indeed sir!'

'Thank you, Mackay, you did a magnificent job – as I knew you would. I have a feeling the coffers will be full tonight!' Murray put a proprietorial arm around Charles's shoulders and steered him out of earshot of the others.

'Sir Walter was here tonight, of course. He sent me a message saying how well he thought the play had gone. He said he thought you had kept your gestures far more within the verge of female decorum than he had expected, too. Quite a compliment, coming from the Wizard of the North himself, eh, Charles?' Charles smiled and nodded. He could think of nothing to say. He was utterly drained, completely thrilled, exhausted, exhilarated, inspired and overwhelmed. It would be a long time before he could join Charlotte at home, there was still the second half of the programme to endure, then he would be expected to join Murray and the others for a wee toddie at the Shakespeare, no doubt. He hoped she would still be awake when he finally collapsed into bed. If not, he might just have to wake her.

When Charles came through for breakfast the next morning there was a pile of newspapers on the table.

'I knew you wouldn't be able to resist, Charles, so I got up early and went to buy these for you. The reviews are quite good!' Charlotte's face was glowing, almost as if she were blushing at the memory of how she had greeted him late the previous night. He winked at her and picked up the *Dramatic Review*.

'Thank you, my darling, how very thoughtful.' Charles took a bite of toast and skimmed through to find that the reviewer had praised his *cool and composed irony* even though he pulled the script itself to pieces. Charlotte poured him a cup of the aromatic tea he liked.

'I think you'll find the *Edinburgh Weekly Journal* has the best review, Charles.'

'Have you read them all, my dear?' She nodded, looking rather pleased with herself, and he began to read the article she had pushed towards him.

'... *We hardly thought it possible that any performer of the masculine gender could have got through it without extravagance and burlesque. But Mr Mackay's steady good sense kept him safe. He dressed the character with the most careful propriety and acted it without conveying any impression of a ludicrous sort beyond that which properly attached to the part.*'

After a rocky start, 1824 had turned into a good year, all in all. Several etchings of Charles as the Bailie had started appearing as frontispieces to the play *Rob Roy*, none of which bore much resemblance to him, but Charles found them quite flattering and amusing. Then up-and-coming artist, William Allen, wrote to ask if he might paint Charles's portrait for an exhibition depicting scenes from Scottish history suggested by the *Waverley* novels and Charles agreed at once. As expected, he would be portrayed as the Bailie, wielding his poker. He was rather proud of the result, especially as the painting was given to Sir Walter after the exhibition, to hang at his beloved Abbotsford.

The *Dramatic Review* continued to publish critical reviews about Charles's acting but he no longer took offence. He simply did not care. They criticised his eccentric jumping and capering on-stage; his frisking and leaping like the god Pan leading a band of satyrs; the exercising of his lungs and limbs with a vigour not the youngest porter in Edinburgh could be bribed to do for love nor money; and he did not care two hoots. Nor was he worried in the slightest to hear that he exercised his jaws incessantly as a waterfowl uses its mandibles; that he aimed at emphasis either by cocking up his chin and grunting, or by forming his mouth into a truncated cone and protruding his words through it in a most elaborate manner – not to speak of the hitching of his right arm and his left leg and other unnatural contortions.

Charles could not care less what anyone thought of him anymore. He was happy. His popularity with audiences was going from strength to strength, Charlie was growing bigger and more fascinating every day and Charlotte was blossoming beautifully with their next child, who was due in October, all being well.

FIFTEEN

'I'm going to London soon, Charlotte. I've been trying to find the right moment to tell you.' Charlotte and Emma Nicol were strolling arm in arm along Princes Street, a midsummer sun stroking their bare forearms from high in the clear blue sky.

'What d'you mean? Are you planning to stay there?' Charlotte stopped walking and turned to face her dear friend.

'I've had an invitation to join the company at Drury Lane. If I turn it down I'll never know if I could have made more of my career. I'm torn, I must confess – and I'll miss you all so much – but, well …'

'Oh my goodness!'

'I know – I'm sorry to spring it on you like this!' It was a terrible blow and Charlotte could think of nothing to say. They continued walking in silence for a while. Drury Lane was *her* theatre – the place where she had fallen in love with the stage – the first stage she had trodden – the place she had auditioned with Henry Erskine Johnston. At the same time, it was a wonderful opportunity for Emma, and she really deserved it. *After all, I have dear Charles and little Charlie – and this child I'm carrying, too – Emma only has her mother and sisters.* Charlotte pasted a smile over her distress.

'You've been a true friend to me, and I'll miss you sorely, Emma, and that's the truth of the matter. But I'm so proud of you – excited for you, too. You must promise to write often and tell me everything that's happening – all the parts you play, who you meet, what the critics say – everything!' When they reached the North Bridge they embraced in the sweet sadness of the moment.

'Perhaps you might find the time to visit my family, Emma. I should like that. I could give you letters, some playbills with my name on them – do you think you might have time?'

'My darling friend, nothing would give me greater pleasure!'

It had been raining relentlessly for two weeks and the courtyard was covered in sludgy brown leaves. Charlotte knew her time was near so she decided to send Charlie, four years old and full of curiosity about everything, to stay with Dorothy's sister and mother for a few days. She could not risk him witnessing a calamity should the birth be difficult, or if, God forbid, something should happen to her. When the day came for him to leave he seemed to sense there was something afoot and tried to cling to Charlotte's hand by the cottage door. Dorothy pulled him firmly towards her and distracted him with comforting chatter as they squelched across the leafy courtyard cobbles together, turning to reassure Charlotte before going out through the street door.

'I'll be right back, Mrs Mackay, once he's settled.' Dorothy had three sisters. The youngest, Morag, and her husband lived at home in the family's small tenement in Leith. They had a little girl a year older than Charlie called Izzie. Dorothy had taken him there several times before and Charlie had always enjoyed playing with her niece. *He'll be fine. It's just for a few days.*

Charles was reading by the fire and Charlotte was sitting opposite him, adding finishing touches to some embroidery on a tiny white nightdress she had made, when the first pain swept over her. She held her breath for a moment, then let it out slowly. He was not performing that night and had arranged to stay at home for the morning so Dorothy could go and buy some food. Neither of them wanted to leave Charlotte alone for a moment.

'It's begun, Charles.' He looked up, a bemused expression on his face as though reluctant to pull his mind out of the story he was reading.

'Hmm?'

'The baby, Charles. It's coming!' He froze for a moment, as realisation dawned, then he dropped his book on the floor and jumped to his feet, looking more like a frightened boy than a husband and father.

'Charlotte, my darling girl! Are you alright?'

'I'm alright, but I'll need the howdie to come as soon as she can, Charles. I'm not as confident as I might have been, after what happened last year.'

'Of course, of course. I'll fetch her at once.' He was standing in the middle of the room dithering, his face such a picture of panic she almost laughed. 'But I can't leave you here alone! When will Dorothy be home?'

'She's sure to be back with the messages any time now. I'll be alright, Charles. Now, put on your greatcoat and hat and off you go, its freezing outside and there's a driving rain.' He nodded and took his coat off the peg on the back of the door. 'Once you've sent the howdie, Charles, it's best if you don't come back here till tomorrow. This is women's work!' Charlotte pushed herself awkwardly to her feet, handed him his hat and ushered him outside. 'Tell her to hurry, please.'

She shut the door and leaned against it, another spasm sweeping through her body. Charlotte clamped her hands over her mouth to stifle a shout which would have brought him running straight back in.

When Dorothy came bustling in with a basket full of eggs

and vegetables, Charlotte was lying on the bed in her day dress, shivering in a scramble of sheets.

'Thank God you're here, Dorothy! Will you help me put on my nightdress and straighten the bed, please? And a cup of tea would be wonderful.' It was such a relief knowing Dorothy would take charge now.

A few minutes later Charlotte lay propped on pillows sipping tea in a clean nightdress with clean sheets and two warm blankets over her, listening to the comforting sounds of everything being tidied and mopped. After a few sips Charlotte fell into a doze, drifting from one pain to the next, hardly aware of time passing between contractions. When the pain grew so bad that she had to scream she opened her eyes and there was a stranger at her side.

'Ah, you're awake at last! Had a nice wee rest, have you?' The sharp-chinned woman pulled back the covers, shoved her nightdress up and felt all over her stomach, pressing hard with cold, calloused hands. Then her hands moved down below and she began to peer between Charlotte's legs while Dorothy held a candle for her.

'The bairn's stuck fast, lassie – face up instead o' down. I'll have to help a wee bit but it'll no' be for long.' The midwife rolled up her sleeves and Dorothy pulled her elbow, indicating the bowl of hot water she had set down beside her, handing her a bar of soap. Charlotte watched the woman scrub her hands with a sour expression on her face and smiled gratefully at Dorothy. Without warning the midwife hoiked her nightdress up again and pushed her bony fingers inside Charlotte's body. The pain was so blindingly intense Charlotte thrust her hips in the air as if to buck her off. Dorothy gave her a rolled cloth to bite on and stroked her brow with a cool hand. She clamped her teeth on the rag, yelling muffled cries into the fabric and soaking it with her saliva, wishing she were dead. The midwife persisted, ignoring Charlotte's shrieking and squirming. She was longing for the oblivion of unconsciousness by now, but Dorothy kept holding smelling salts under her nose and pinching her arm.

'That's it, lass. The bairn's turned and doing fine.' The woman pulled her fingers out roughly at last and plunged her bloody hands back into the basin of water. 'When the next pain comes, ye'll need tae push for all ye're worth, mind.' Charlotte felt so weak she could hardly open her eyes, let alone summon the strength to push.

Suddenly the next pain roared into her belly and her eyes flew open. The urge to push was overwhelming. She heard herself yelling and swearing like a sailor as she strained and gasped and pushed and strained again. At last, there was a hot gush between her legs and she knew the worst was over. She was so relieved she began to cry.

'Dinnae greet, lass. Jes one mair michty push, then you're done!' Charlotte moaned and whimpered, begging for mercy, only managing a few feeble pushes, but the child slipped out quickly, closely followed by the warm, wet placenta.

Charlotte lay still, spread out empty on the bed like a gutted fish, the tiny, waxy infant limp and warm on her stomach. She cupped its buttocks in her palm and watched the cord that still joined them pulse almost imperceptibly. The midwife pulled a knife from her apron pocket and Dorothy put her hand over it.

'I've fresh hot water ready for ye to wash yer knife, ma'am, if ye'd oblige.' The old woman muttered about interference but Dorothy insisted, so she plunged her knife in the freshly boiled water before tying the cord in two places with string and slicing through it.

Dorothy picked up the child tenderly and swaddled it in a white cloth, tapping and clucking until juddering little mewling cries filled the air. Then she handed the tiny bundle back to Charlotte.

'A wee lassie, Mrs Mackay, a delicate wee lassie.'

Charles adored his daughter. He often came clattering across the courtyard to their cottage after rehearsals, eyes shining in anticipation, arms stretched out for his little girl as he burst through the door with a blast of cold air.

Charlie was less sure of her. Sometimes he hid under the table when Charlotte was feeding her, or tried to clamber up onto her knee and nudge his way into her embrace. Once he even kicked his father on the shin when Charles walked straight past him to see the baby without stopping to ruffle his hair and kiss him.

Dorothy was a marvel during those early weeks, keeping the wheels of the household running smoothly, allowing Charlotte to heal and regain her strength. Charles brought her flowers, kissed her softly on her nose to make her laugh, promised to restrain his passion until she was completely healed.

The days passed slowly and dreamily: she napped in bed whenever she felt tired; nursed her daughter and handed her to Dorothy to be cleaned; read stories to Charlie; ate the deliciously nourishing broth which magically appeared at lunchtimes and was hardly aware of all the other work Dorothy was doing. She felt like a princess.

One morning Charlotte woke early to find Charles lying next to her, his face smudged with soot, the smell of smoke in his hair. She shook him awake.

'Charles – what on earth has happened, you look like a chimney sweep!' He opened his bleary eyes and rubbed them with black fingers.

'Oh, Charlotte, there's a terrible fire raging in the High Street! I went up to look and got covered in ash!'

'What d'you mean?' The baby started whimpering and Charlotte leaned over to lift her from her crib.

'I was reading by the hearth late last night when a strange, flickering light appeared in the sky. I went to the window and saw what I thought were thousands of insects flying past, like black snow. Suddenly the truth dawned on me and I had to find out where the fire was at once, in case I needed to move you all to safety.'

Charlie woke with a little cry and climbed sleepily into bed beside them, blinking in confusion at the sight of his father's soot-streaked face. Charles put an arm round him and pulled him in to his side, continuing his account without a pause.

'It must've been close to midnight. I grabbed my cloak and hat and ran up the hill faster than ever before. Ash was flying all about, getting into my nose and eyes. I could hear the fire crackling. There was quite a gathering just past the gaol on Regent Road – there's a good view of the High Street from there. Flames were raging towards the Cowgate by then. I could see men from that new fire brigade struggling to hold the fire back with their hoses, poor souls. There was nothing any of us could do but watch. Oh, Charlotte, I think people may have died last night. Hundreds of families must have lost their homes and all their possessions!'

The fire, which had begun on a Monday, raged all week, dampening down when it rained, then flaring up again. Charles often ran up the hill to see what was happening, then paced about in the flat complaining of feeling useless. It was a great relief to Charlotte when he came home for dinner on Wednesday night and told her Mr Murray was putting on a three-day run of the comedy *She Stoops To Conquer* – *'in aid of the poor victims of the calamitous fire'*. At last there was something he could do to help.

On Friday evening the fire was declared officially out from the stage of the Theatre Royal. The packed audience cheered and gave generously. Charles went straight to sleep after telling Charlotte all about it, but she lay awake for a long time, wondering what it must be like for those who had lost their homes, or worse, their loved ones. The thought of losing one of her precious children, or her dear husband, was too awful to contemplate.

Little Charlotte was a quiet, sleepy baby. Charlotte loved

stroking her soft, fuzzy head, watching her curl and uncurl her slender fingers while she fed. She learned to divide her attention between her children by telling Charlie stories in funny voices while she nursed his sister, giving him helpful jobs to do and telling him he was her *grand wee mannie*. Soon it was as if they had always been a family of four.

The baby never complained when Charlotte handed her to Dorothy for a while, or even to her elderly neighbour, Mrs Maclehose at No. 14, who sometimes came by in search of a cup of tea and some company, an audience for her fascinating stories. So, about three weeks after the fire, Charlotte decided to risk going back on-stage.

There was a showcase for a visiting child prodigy called Clara Fisher on Charlotte's first night back at the theatre in early December. It was her second visit to Edinburgh. Mr Murray had chosen the opera *The Spoil'd Child* for the second half of the programme and, once again, he had offered Charlotte the part of Margery. This time she was able to do it. She brought her six-week-old daughter with her to the first rehearsal and was swamped by dancing girls the moment she entered the green room, all clamouring to hold the baby.

Margery was quite a character to play. She had an important speaking role in the story, although her time on-stage was short. Charlotte knew she had made an impact on the audience that night; their enthusiasm was extremely gratifying.

The next morning Maria Nicol, Emma's younger sister, knocked tentatively on the door at No. 12. When Charlotte opened it, her swaddled baby in the crook of her arm and Charlie hiding behind her skirts, Maria handed her a copy of the *Dramatic Review*.

'Mother bade me come down here with this, Charlotte. We read it at breakfast and agreed you should see it. We're very proud of you!' Maria declined Charlotte's offer of tea with a shy smile and slipped away quickly. Charlotte sat down and spread the *Review* on the table, little Charlotte asleep in her arms, her heart hammering against her ribs.

It was only one word, but it was a wonderful word, and it was for her alone: *excellent.*

Mrs Mackay's Margery was excellent.

She could not stop smiling all day.

SIXTEEN

Every spring William Murray held a benefit for Charles, and 1825 was no different. The year had begun well, with Charlotte joining Charles on-stage in January as one of a chorus of witches in *Macbeth* – he always played the First Witch himself. They had laughed a good deal together over their costumes and Charles was delighted to hear her talking so positively about her developing career. She had been on-stage every month for at least one production so far since then, and to add to his joy, both the children were thriving as well. Harriet Siddons gave one of her rare performances at Charles's benefit, and the play was *St Ronan's Well*. The theatre was packed, the audience were enthusiastic and the coffers overflowed.

'Come on, old boy, let's go and have a drink – you deserve it after such a successful benefit night, especially considering how slack audiences have been of late. I'll wager old Garbutt took plenty at the box office tonight– no doubt he'll be up late counting the money! Everyone loves you, Mackay, they simply can't get enough of you! Ha!' Charles and his fellow actor, Jones, whom he had long since forgiven for his pernicious trick over last year's benefit, were crossing the North Bridge before Charles realised what was happening. He had been so focused on reviewing his performance in his mind that he had hardly noticed his lanky friend steering him out of the stage door. Charlotte would probably be asleep by now – and anyway, he hardly ever went out with his friends. Jones was right, he deserved to celebrate his success. Charles was riding high and did not want the night to end.

Jones took him to an oyster bar deep inside the South Bridge, and before long Charles was frolicking with the best of them. The next thing he knew he had been deposited outside the door to No. 12 and a dog cart was clattering away into the dark. He stood in the cold white moonlight, swaying on his feet, and began to sing 'Green Grow the Rashes!' at the top of his voice. Charlotte came into the street to fetch him inside, shushing him and scolding him, taking him straight to bed.

She was so lovely. The scent of her, the warmth of her skin, the feel of her breath whispering on his neck. He began to kiss her before they were inside the cottage. She pulled him through the kitchen, warning him in sharp whispers not to wake Dorothy, and they tumbled into bed together, trying not to laugh and waken the children.

'I've been given a most generous offer in London, gentlemen, and I wanted you to know in good time that I'm seriously considering taking it. It would be extremely difficult to leave my dear sister Harriet without a manager, of course, so I am in something of a quandary.' Murray had asked a few of the actors he trusted most to come to his office after rehearsals. Charles caught Jones's eye, wondering if he was having the same idea. He winked back and the two of them nodded in agreement.

A few days later Murray had a proposal on his desk from Jones and Mackay, outlining how they would take on the management of the theatre should he choose to go to London. Charles was beside himself with excitement while he waited for a response, but decided not to tell Charlotte about it, in case it came to nothing. Although Murray decided against the London opportunity, the seed of an idea had germinated in both men, so when news came that Corbett Ryder was closing the ailing Perth Theatre Royal, having bitten off more than he could chew with the Caledonian in Edinburgh, Jones suggested they could ask Murray to let them have a longer summer break and take on the lease in Perth for a short season. Charles agreed at once, as did Murray.

'I don't know why you think running a theatre will be easy for a pair of actors – it requires an entirely different set of skills, you know, Charles.' Charlotte was pacing up and down in the courtyard of No. 12, patting the baby's back in an agitated fashion, while Charles sat on the bench beside Charlie and his mudpies. 'Besides – how can you trust Jones after he played that despicable trick on you when your benefit nights clashed?' Charles nodded glumly, knowing it was best not to comment at this stage. 'I just hope you don't lose all our savings, Charles, that's all I can say!'

The two actors went up to Perth at the end of July 1825 with high hopes, great enthusiasm, and healthy bank accounts. They invested in new gas lighting and spruced up the theatre with fresh paint and hours of dedication and Charles was supremely confident his national fame and his ongoing popularity in Perth would ensure good ticket sales. Most theatre managers he knew were actors too – how difficult could it be? Word that financial disaster was rocking the very foundation of the British financial system reached Perth midway through their preparations and added another layer of risk to what was already a risky project. They held their nerve.

'There are rumours that even Sir Walter's publisher is floundering, Charles! It must be a serious situation to knock someone as successful as him so hard.' Jones was up a ladder adding the finishing touches of gold paint to the plaster work in front of one of the boxes, his long arm just able to reach, eyes screwed almost closed in concentration, splashes of gold paint speckling his shirt.

'I don't believe Sir Walter himself will be affected, though, if I know anything about him. He'll just write another best-selling book or two.' Charles was standing precariously on top of a step ladder, fiddling with the glass covers on their new lamps. 'Anyway, it shouldn't affect the pennies in the pockets of the ordinary folk who are going to pour through our doors tomorrow night to watch us in *Laugh When You Can*. People need to laugh in a time of crisis, remember!'

The opening night was a great success, partly because most of the other players were from Perth and already had a good following. Charles and Jones revived the old half-time half-price arrangement, too, which proved extremely popular. They put together a production of *Mary Stuart* next, giving Charles a chance to sing many of his guid auld songs, but their version of *Waverley* failed to draw crowds and the two-month season ended rather dismally. They returned to Edinburgh in the autumn with their hopes dashed and their bank balances somewhat compromised.

Charlotte was furious. She would hardly look at Charles for the first few days he was back, let alone hold a decent conversation. He was perplexed. Normally she would reprimand him then quickly forgive him, begging for all the gossip and supplying some of her own. He knew he must have done something else wrong, but had no idea what.

'It's a beautiful day, Charlotte. Why don't we leave the children with Dorothy and go for a walk? We could visit the new Botanical Gardens, perhaps. What do you say?'

'That would be a nice change, Charles. It would give us a chance to talk, as well.' Her voice was brittle, her bright smile false. He was right. There was definitely something amiss. He fetched her plaid and wrapped it gently round her shoulders like an embrace, willing to face anything to clear the air and make peace between them.

They had walked no further than the bottom of the road when she turned to face him, her brow crease into a frown.

'I'm with child again, Charles!'

'What?' A wave of nausea surged up from the pit of his stomach. Their daughter was still a babe in arms, still nursing at her mother's breast – *how could it have happened?* Charlotte began to walk again, briskly, refusing to take his proffered arm or look at him.

'Didn't you notice a change in me when you came home?' He knew he should say something, but the right words kept slipping out of his grasp like eels. He placed a hand in the small of her back as they walked and she did not slough it off.

The night of his benefit. That must have been when it happened! *Oh God!* Now he thought of it he had a vague idea Charlotte might have tried to stop his advances that night, but he must have assumed she was teasing. Shame washed over him as the scene replayed in his mind and he watched himself being such a fool. They walked in silence all the way down Broughton Street and stopped under the trees at Bellevue Crescent. He looked down at her hands, taking one of them in both of his and holding it gently.

'Charlotte, I've been so foolish, so selfish. Please forgive me. I don't know what I would do without you. We must make sure you're safe. That's the most important thing in the world right now.' She allowed him to hold her hand but still would not look at him.

'It's too soon for me to have another child, Charles. Especially after the struggle I had last time. But this child is strong and determined. I've felt him kicking already.' They leaned into each other for a few moments, both their faces wet with tears. There was nothing more to say.

The Mackays took on another maid to see to the washing and cleaning and fetch the messages, allowing Dorothy to concentrate on looking after the children. She took over most of little Charlotte's care at once, comforting her with cow's milk and soothing lullabies, especially at night. Charlie was already used to being with Dorothy most of the time and quickly learned not to clamber on his mother's knee anymore, to treat her very gently. Now and then the Mackays went for a stroll together after lunch, but Charlotte usually slept in the afternoons.

When the theatre closed for a fortnight between seasons again time hung heavily on Charles's hands. He sometimes took invitations from provincial theatres to fill these short pauses, but the last thing he wanted to do was leave his family again. So he took Charlie for walks when the weather was fine and started browsing in bookshops on wet days, finding solace in the distraction of new stories. Sometimes he bought a book to add to his growing collection. It would be a relief to start working again.

The winter season opened with Rossini's comic opera, *The Barber of Seville*. Charles played the part of Rosina's comical guardian, Doctor Bartolo, and worked his usual magic, losing himself in the unfolding tale, singing his heart out and thoroughly enjoying being swept up in the emotion of it all.

When the cast assembled on-stage for the closing anthem, the audience began to stand and turn away from the stage, shouting, whistling and clapping at one of the boxes. Sir Walter had arrived in time for the second half, accompanied by his friend, the famous Irish bard, Thomas Moore. Such tremendous shouts went up that the orchestra stopped playing and all the musicians rose to their feet to join in the salute to the bards. Charles lifted a hand to his friend Sir Walter. Thomas Moore was on his feet by this time, bowing repeatedly to all sides of the house. The moment he sat down he was obliged to stand again and repeat his acknowledgements until, to everyone's delight, the orchestra began playing some Scottish songs, alternating them with songs from the Emerald Isle. It was all very jolly and spontaneous and continued until the interval was announced.

The second item on the programme required a good deal of singing from Charles. He belted out his lively rendition of an old Scots song he had recently discovered in one of his books, called 'Byde Ye Yet', and when he took his bow for it, Thomas Moore stood up and applauded him loudly. Charles bowed deeply and went home that night bathed in a warm glow.

He stumbled on through the winter season, lurching from excellent performances to bad reviews, from full houses to thin audiences. Sometimes he gave too much energy to a part, sometimes not enough, always he was distracted by the dangers of the battle Charlotte would be facing in the new year. Murray put on *Rob Roy* yet again in mid-November and Charlotte wanted to play the Hostess. She promised to be very careful, to go home and lie down the moment she came off-stage, and Charles agreed reluctantly. Both galleries were full, even though the weather was atrocious, and Charlotte seemed like her old self for a few days.

A rowdy bunch of young wags started frequenting the theatre and, more than once, Charles had to stop and speak firmly to them. There was even a scuffle in one of the boxes involving Murray, who had taken it upon himself to defend Charles and exact some revenge. It really was not good enough.

One night Charles was pelted with oranges. He stooped and picked some of them up, thanking the hooligans for their generosity, which the audience found hilarious. But it left a bitter taste in his mouth. Later that night he sat quietly beside Charlotte, peeling the oranges and sharing segments with her as he told her all about it.

When another performance of *Rob Roy* was announced, for the benefit of a visiting actor, Charlotte made a show of dressing for breakfast and eating heartily.

'It seems I'm feeling quite well again, Charles. Isn't it wonderful?' She was huge with child and had a lovely glow about her, an energy Charles had not seen for weeks. He took her hand across the table, smiling, going along with her little ruse.

'You're positively blossoming, my darling. How marvellous! Perhaps we could take a little stroll together later on?'

That afternoon she wasted no time.

'Charles, I'm sure you've already guessed that I would very much like to play the Hostess again to end the season. It's a role I've made my own and I know it would give me such a boost. I would be very careful, and go straight home to rest afterwards, like I did last time.'

'I'm uncomfortable about it, Charlotte, but I won't forbid it. It must be your decision, just as it's your body that must cope with such a great challenge in a few weeks' time.' Charlotte promised Charles she would do nothing but rest and conserve her energy during the remaining weeks of her confinement if she could only do this one performance.

The theatre was packed. Charles watched the opening of the play from the wings. When Charlotte delivered her lines it seemed to him she was transformed. He was mesmerised. She glowed with passion, her face was glorious, her voice deep, low and powerful. Although it was such a trifling role, with so few lines to deliver, she was extraordinary. Suddenly he could imagine her swathed in tartan as Rob Roy's wife, delivering the most passionate and powerful lines of the play. He had always known she could act, even that she could act well, and he had always assumed she would develop her skills further when the children were older. But it had never occurred to him until that moment that she was exceptionally gifted and could easily have been a leading lady if only she had been given the chance. How could he have been so blind? He must tell Murray to give her a more prominent role the moment she recovered from her confinement.

When she came off-stage he kissed her and held her close, whispering into her hair, 'You were magnificent my darling, truly magnificent!'

'I understand your predicament, Charles, believe me, I do. But I cannot take unnecessary risks with my main asset – who is, of course, your good self.' Murray tone was ingratiatingly patronising. Charles stirred more sugar into his coffee vigorously, focusing on the spoon. 'If Charlotte were to start acting in more demanding roles now, you see, she might quickly become distracted and your children would soon be fretful. Besides, there is always the risk she might have another episode at any time.' The two men were taking morning coffee in an alcove at Mr Muir's Refreshment Rooms in the Lawnmarket.

'But Murray,' Charles began. Murray held up his hand.

'Allow me to finish, Mackay. Even if Charlotte *did* manage to balance all the various demands of her life and made a decent job of more prominent roles – which I've no doubt she would, as we all know she has the talent for it – if just one of the elements she was balancing were to tumble down … Well – you see my predicament, don't you?' Charles was furious, but Murray droned on, oblivious.

'My own dear wife, Ann, is a case in point, Mackay. As you know, she was an actress when I married her, and continued taking acting roles after the birth of our son. However, she has had a few mishaps over the years and we can no longer rely on her good health. It was far better for her, for our son and for my own peace of mind when she retired from the stage altogether to concentrate on keeping a good home for us all.' Murray sipped his coffee, a self-satisfied little smile on his face, and Charles suddenly felt the urge to slap him. It was as though Murray's Genial Gentleman mask had slipped to reveal a ruthlessly selfish businessman. Charles had never questioned him about anything, never even queried their consistently low salaries over the years. Perhaps he had been taken for a fool.

'I understand very well what you've said, Murray. Thank you for being so candid with me.' He took a sip of coffee, cleared his throat, and forged on. 'But you must understand that I do not consider it my purpose in life to be the *Main Asset of the Theatre Royal.*' Murray looked up with surprise. 'You see, Murray, I believe my main purpose in life is to entertain people to the best of my abilities while ensuring the wellbeing of my wife and family, whatever that might involve. Hmm. So, I believe it is *you* who must understand *my* position.'

'What on earth d'you mean, Mackay?'

'What I mean, Murray, is that I will withdraw my services from the Theatre Royal entirely if you continue to deny Charlotte the opportunities she deserves, contract or no contract!' Murray's eyebrows shot up. 'There. I've said my piece, and it has cost me a great deal to do so. I hope you will give my proposal serious consideration.' Charles could not bear to sit beside Murray for another second, nor to hear his reply. He stood, gave a curt nod and went to pay the bill.

Charles's challenge was never put to the test. Charlotte survived the birth of their second son, Hector, but only just. She was so badly damaged she could hardly walk. The doctor's assessment of her condition was not good. In addition to the damage from the birth, he had found a growth inside her womb the size of an orange and there was nothing he could do to prevent it from growing bigger. She was going to die. It was just a matter of time.

SEVENTEEN

Charlotte was stoical. After a month of lying-in she began to get up every day, heaving her sore, swollen body around until she was forced to sit down. Charles could hardly bear to watch her but knew better than to fuss. She insisted on feeding their screaming, colicky new baby herself, refusing to employ a wet nurse, but allowed Dorothy to change his clouts, to bring him to her and to settle him in his crib.

The rest of her time was spent taking naps or sitting with Charlie and young Charlotte: reading to them, singing snippets of songs together, brushing their hair, holding their hands, extracting every drop from each moment she still had with them. When he came home at night she was often still awake and would recount all the mundane little details of her day to him softly. It broke his heart.

The five-year lease on the cottage in Calton Hill was coming to an end and Charles decided it would be a good idea to change the scenery for Charlotte's last act.

He moved the family into a spacious, airy flat back in Broughton Street. There was a large, sunny corner window in the parlour where Charlotte was able to sit on a chair filled with cushions and watch the activity in the busy street below. He placed an occasional table beside her so she could take her meals there too. Although she asked to have her sewing basket nearby and a few books, she hardly ever picked up her embroidery and never once opened a novel. It was a peaceful place to nurse little Hector, though, to spend a few moments with the children now and then, to doze and dream.

Neither of them had slept well since Hector was born. Soon after they moved house Charles reluctantly conceded Charlotte needed her own bed and transformed the parlour into a grand bedroom for her.

He bought a beautiful mahogany bed and wardrobe at Mr Lyon's new auction room in George Street and had them delivered. Inspired by her smiling response he brought all Charlotte's costumes home from the theatre the following day and collected her clothes and shoes and scarves and hats from their bedroom. Then he asked her to supervise him while he folded and hung and stacked it all into the wardrobe.

'Could you hang the scarves on the inside of the door d'you think, Charles?' He pulled the doors wide open and made a silly sad face at her. One of the doors was covered by a large looking-glass, the other was smooth, polished wood, with not a hook in sight. He began hanging scarves on nothing and picking them up off the floor again until they were both laughing.

'I'm sure you could bang a few nails in, don't you think?' She laughed at the shock on his face, so he strode off to the scullery and returned with nails and a hammer, bowing as he entered the room.

'Your wish is my command, dear lady!' Soon there was a slightly uneven row of brightly coloured scarves and necklaces hanging on the back of the wardrobe door. Charles saw Charlotte's smiling face in the looking-glass and smiled back.

'I said it would work, didn't I Charles!'

Throughout that afternoon she told him exactly how she wanted everything to be organised, exclaiming at some of the gowns, sharing memories with him, both of them pretending she might wear them again on-stage one day. It was the happiest time they had spent together since Hector was born.

Once everything was shipshape Charlotte suddenly looked exhausted and asked him to help her into bed.

'I wonder if you might move the bed to the window tomorrow, Charles. I've been finding it painful sitting in my chair recently, even with all those squashy cushions, but I do love watching the comings and goings in the street. Perhaps it can be your chair from now on. You can sit beside my bed and read to me!'

She struggled bravely on through another year, turning more and more to the night nurse Charles had employed for help with her personal needs. Charles started buying laudanum from Butler's Medical Hall in Waterloo Place and soon she was taking it every day, sometimes more than once.

Dorothy became like a mother to the younger two children, but Charlie began to keep her at a distance, refusing cuddles and stories from her and insisting on dressing himself. Charles hated dishing out false hopes to his son, but the urge to tell him his mammy would be better soon was often too strong to resist. *How can you tell a child the mother he adores is dying?* He had not been much older than Charlie when his own mother died, and Charlie's distress pressed hard on that old, deep bruise, over and over again.

Charles spent whatever time he could with his son when he was at home, but the theatre was busy, and he was still in great demand. Besides, Charlotte insisted he should continue to perform.

When Charlie was seven he began attending a small school round the corner from the flat in the parlour of a doddery old dominie. He was growing into quite a serious boy who enjoyed looking at books and practising his letters, quite unlike his father, who could never sit still and was always looking for attention.

Charles had heard the dominie was kind – unlike the whisky-soaked, tawse-inflicting tyrant who had attempted to introduce him to his letters in Glasgow so many years ago. It was good for the boy to go out and be distracted.

Young Charlotte was a tottering bundle of sweetness. Just two and a half, she trailed happily after Dorothy all day, hanging onto her apron strings, chattering her nonsense, playing with soap bubbles and dolls, oblivious of the sadness all around her. Hector was another matter, though, and Charles began to wonder how long Dorothy would be strong enough to keep him under control.

In the evenings Dorothy or Charles brought the children one by one to see their mother, urging them to be careful, not to climb on her or even to lean on her. She had long since stopped nursing Hector, who could run around and climb and needed to be restrained in her presence. Charles sometimes allowed Charlie to sit quietly beside her for a while, though, trusting his eldest son to be careful. It was the least he could do for the poor lad.

Edinburgh was covered in snow, white as fresh sheets and soft as a woollen blanket. Charles was sitting in his chair talking quietly with Charlotte after everyone had retired for the night. He had finished his nightly ablutions and pulled out his truckle bed, and they were both deferring the moment of saying good night. The shutters had been left open and the light of a nearby streetlamp was illuminating flurries of falling snow, bringing a dream-like quality to the darkened room, lifting them, for fleeting moments, out of the despair that clung to them like heavy clods of earth.

It was the middle of February and Charles was still acting at the Theatre Royal, although he had to steel himself to perform these days, longing instead to run home and weep at her bedside. His most recent performance had been less than two weeks ago, when he'd performed with Murray in *A Comedy of Errors*.

Singing and strutting and playing the fool to make people laugh seemed so futile and meaningless when Charlotte was lying there, suffering so terribly.

'You must promise me you will continue acting, Charles, when I'm gone.' She squeezed his hand weakly, the corner of her beloved London handkerchief protruding from the cuff of her nightgown. 'What good would you be to the children drooping around at home miserably?' Her words drifted quietly, like the snowflakes, and his broken heart ached as though it was being squeezed. She was so brave, so unselfish, so fragile. He stroked a stray lock of hair from her brow and smiled.

'You must go to the Theatrical Fund dinner tomorrow night too, Charles. I wouldn't want you to miss it for the world! Remember, I depend on your stories – I *need* to hear all the latest gossip. It's so much more interesting than these books from the library which I haven't the will to read.' Charlotte's eyes seemed to have grown bigger now her face was so gaunt. Charles picked up her delicate, creamy hand and kissed it.

'I'll go if you insist, my darling, but I would far rather be here with you!'

The steam of his breath rose like yellow clouds in the sharp cold air each time he passed the halo of a streetlamp. At the Assembly Room he handed over his greatcoat and hat and was ushered up the sweeping staircase. Huge sparkling chandeliers hung from the high ceiling, illuminating hundreds of gentlemen of influence milling about in the vast, elegant banquet hall, all dressed to the nines and full of their own importance. Enthusiastic conversations, bursts of braying laughter and the scraping of chair legs on the floor bounced off the walls, assaulting his ears, making him want to clamp his hands over them. *What on earth was he doing here?*

He took his allotted seat at one of the lavishly set tables and noticed Murray sitting nearby. They nodded across at each other. Then Sir Walter came limping slowly across the room in their direction, looking pale and weary, and Charles wondered how he had found the strength to attend the dinner when he had been so recently widowed. Scott took his seat at the head of their table, nodded genially at everyone, and was soon deep in conversation with Murray. Charles was relieved they were sitting too far away for him to join them.

Somehow, he survived the inane conversation over dinner, picking at each new dish of rich food that arrived and hardly touching his wine. The glasses were chinking and the chairman, Sir Walter, was rising to his feet for the opening speech. Charles mopped his brow, knowing it fell to him to reply.

He sank into his chair with the greatest relief once he had delivered a suitably eloquent response, wondering if he could make his excuses and go home early without causing offence. But Lord Meadowbank was standing again, tapping his glass for quiet with a mischievous look on his face.

'Hhmm. I would beg leave to propose a toast – the health of one of the Patrons, a great and distinguished individual, whose name must always stand by itself, and which, in an assembly such as this, or in any other assembly of Scotsmen, must ever be received, I will not say with ordinary feelings of pleasure or of delight, but with those of rapture and enthusiasm.'

Enthusiastic 'ayes' peppered the air around him and suddenly Charles knew exactly what was about to happen. Lord Meadowbank was going to announce that Sir Walter Scott was, indeed, the Wizard of the North, writer of the *Waverley* novels. It would cause a sensation up and down the country and beyond. The Scottish broadsheets would be full of it in the morning, the London publications soon after. Although it had long been suspected by many, Charles knew the announcement was a truly historic moment and was glad he was there to witness it. Murray caught his eye across the table and winked as Meadowbank called for silence.

'The clouds have been dispelled – the darkness visible has been cleared away – and The Great Unknown – the minstrel of our native land – the mighty magician who has rolled back the current of time and conjured up before our living senses the men and manners of days which have long passed away, stands revealed to the eyes and hearts of his affectionate and admiring countrymen.' The worthy judge soldiered on towards his great unveiling despite the growing hubbub of excitement. 'He it is who has conferred a new reputation on our national character and bestowed on Scotland an imperishable name, were it only by her having given birth to himself. I propose the health of Sir Walter Scott!' Everyone was on their feet by this time, some even standing on chairs and tables. The storm of applause was deafening. Charles stood and clapped until his hands hurt, watching the play of emotions of Sir Walter's features, blushing when Scott caught his eye and smiled. Charles had experienced considerable fame himself, deafening, sustained applause on numerous occasions, but this was different. He wondered what it must be like for a man to be treated thus, almost as a god.

As the ovation showed signs of abating the bard himself rose to his feet and begged silence. His response was modest, measured, witty and precise.

'I certainly did not think, in coming here today, that I should have the task of acknowledging before three hundred gentlemen a secret which, considering that it was communicated to more than twenty people, has been remarkably well kept.' Charles was deeply impressed by the composure of the man on his first foray into public society since his beloved Charlotte had died. He wondered if he would be able to find a fraction of that strength in himself when his own Charlotte was gone. The room was respectfully quiet as Scott's voice rang out strong and true.

'The wand is now broken, and the book buried. You will allow me further to say, with Prospero, it is your breath that has filled my sails – and to crave one single toast in the capacity of the author of these novels.' There was a profound moment of silence while the collective breath was held. 'I would fain dedicate a bumper to the health of one who has represented several of those characters, of which I had endeavoured to give a skeleton, with a truth and liveliness for which I may well be grateful. I beg leave to propose the health of my friend Bailie Nicol Jarvie – and I am sure that when the author of *Waverley* and *Rob Roy* drinks to Nicol Jarvie it will be received with the just applause to which that gentleman has always been accustomed – nay, that you will take care that on the present occasion it shall be PRO-DI-GI-OUS!'

Charles was stunned. The room erupted in gratifyingly prodigious and thunderous applause and every eye turned towards him. He gathered himself and stood, fixing a wry and modest smile to his face, dipping his head in acknowledgement and preparing to assume the ridiculous voice of the pompous Bailie, as everyone expected him to.

'My conscience!' he squeaked, and laughter erupted across the vast banquet hall. He waited a moment, then continued. 'My worthy *faither, the deacon*, could never have believed that his son would hae sic a compliment paid to him by The Great Unknown!'

Quick as a flash the 'King of Scottish Society' gave the perfect retort. 'The "small known" now, Mr Bailie!'

Applause rose to an even higher crescendo and Charles looked across at his esteemed friend, catching his eye again. They were two grieving men, standing under a golden shower of praise and affirmation the like of which most people would never dream of receiving. It was as though an unspoken agreement passed between them in that moment: they would both soldier on beyond their sadness, they would continue to be the storytellers and entertainers they were born to be and live out the rest of their lives in honour of those they had lost.

But it was Murray who suffered the next bereavement. Charles did not have the heart to tell Charlotte when Murray's wife, Ann, died giving birth to their second son later that year. The tiny child died shortly afterwards, too. Murray's awful loss terrified Charles. He could hardly look at him, let alone think what to say. Somehow the theatre continued to operate, though, and Charles continued to perform.

Charlotte grew weaker, until she was barely a shadow of her former self. By April the following year she was mercifully beyond everyone and everything. Her terrible pain had been brought into abeyance by an unconscionable amount of laudanum, its metallic smell heavy on her breath. After the final performance of the season, Murray told Charles to take as much leave as he needed.

He sat beside Charlotte for hours every day, staring at her face, holding her hand, willing her to move a finger or lift her lashes a fraction, dropping tiny drops of water on her parched lips, wiping her eyes with the precious handkerchief she had kept in her pinnie pocket or up her sleeve since he had brought it to her from London.

She lay on her back all the time now, her damp hair spread on the pillow like seaweed, her skin yellow with jaundice, hardly moving except for her shallow breaths and the flickering of her eyes under eyelids as pale and fragile as the wings of a moth. Charles only left the room when the nurse came to wash and change her in the mornings and evenings.

On a grey day in the second week of May, 1828, the doctor came for his weekly visit. After a brief examination he sighed deeply and rested a hand on Charles's shoulder.

'It won't be long now, Charles, old fellow. I'm so sorry.'

Charles replied without looking up, afraid he would cry in front of the medic. 'I know. Thank you.'

The doctor left the room quietly, closing the door with a soft click, and Charles allowed himself a few tears.

After a while, he became aware of a new and unpleasant

smell which he knew at once to be the sweet, sickly odour of Charlotte's impending death. He could not bear to have it in his nostrils and flung the sash window open, only to be assaulted by a din of clattering hooves, screaming seagulls and shouting people. He pulled it shut at once and sat down.

The rhythm of her breath was mesmerising. Her chest moved up and down almost imperceptibly, her white cotton nightgown failing to disguise a pitifully skeletal frame. *At least she will have no more pain soon.* His breathing fell in step with hers for a while, until he began to feel light-headed from taking such short, shallow breaths.

The church clock struck four o'clock, rousing him from a light doze. He rubbed his eyes.

Charlotte was perfectly still.

She was icy cold.

A searing pain scorched his heart and he cried out, clutching at his chest.

She had gone.

Part Two

1852–1857

EIGHTEEN

Charles stared at the wilting flowers until they dissolved into a pink blur, then wiped the back of his hand across his damp eyes. Sharp points of sunlight flickered and darted between the leaves of overhanging trees, creating shifting patterns on the fresh mound of turf. He sighed, his shoulders slumping under the weight of everything.

It was the third time he had visited her grave since the funeral last week, unable to settle to anything else with her lying there, alone, under the cold, dark, pressing earth. He knew it was foolish, that he must accept what had happened and look after the child. His daughter had joined his wife now, and he was left behind with his granddaughter.

Lottie.

Charles was uncomfortably aware of Lottie's need for his attention and affection. The child was devasted. A small breeze brushed his face, and it came to him that she, too, had been crushed by the loss of hope.

Every morning for months she had run from her bed the moment she woke to try and wake her mother, prancing and dancing and twirling, singing little snippets of nonsense in her piping soprano, leaning over the bed to cover her mother's face with kisses until she had been banned by the nurse a few weeks ago. Watching her, knowing it was hopeless, had twisted his heart into a hard tight knot.

There had been times when Charles was tempted to take his daughter by the shoulders and shake her, to shout: *try harder, won't you, if only for Lottie's sake!* She had always been such a delicate creature, especially since her childhood brush with cholera, often succumbing to long bouts of illness over the years that followed. When she had announced in 1845, at the age of twenty, that she was going to marry a widower twice her age it had come as a shock. Charles had been against the match from the outset, but his daughter was besotted by the charm and good looks of the man she had met in the library, and would not listen to a word against him.

John Shiels was a corn trader from the Borders. After his first wife had died, he had farmed out his two young children to his family in Earlston and moved to Edinburgh. To make matters worse, Charles discovered only weeks before the wedding that John had been bankrupted twice and did not have the wherewithal to secure the lease on a flat. He had had no choice, then, but to invite them to live with him in Drummond Street, replacing his daughter's bed with a large four-poster as his wedding gift and installing them in what was already her room. Charles was away a good deal touring during that time, and when the couple's child, Lottie, was born, the disruption had hardly affected him.

Little Lottie had begun hauling herself to her feet and edging round the furniture by the time Charles retired from the stage, in 1848, after a career spanning more than forty years. The process of retiring had taken several weeks before packed Theatre Royal audiences. Murray had spoken a few kind words on the final night, presenting him with a rather lovely silver cup, and he had since begun to enjoy a calmer pace of life in Edinburgh. He had tolerated his son-in-law's presence, enjoyed the company of his daughter and begun to acquaint himself with his delightful little granddaughter. Now and then he would receive an invitation from Liverpool, Newcastle, or one of the provincial Scottish theatres, and he would pack a small bag and go there on the railway.

The sudden death of his son-in-law in 1850 had brought this brief season of semi-retirement to a devastating halt. His daughter took to her bed, inconsolable with grief, and would hardly leave her room. She soon became ill. Before long she seemed to lose the will to live, and never found it again. It took her a year to die, slipping and sliding quietly through his fingers like water. Now she was gone he hardly had the strength to look after himself anymore, let alone the child. At night a cold hand squeezed his heart, wringing out the last remaining drops of his energy along with his famous sense of humour.

Charles emerged from the quiet of the churchyard into the commotion of the Kirkgate, leaning more heavily than usual on his walking stick. Ambushed by the triple stink of ripe fish, stale ale and fresh horse dung he began to feel dizzy and looked about for somewhere to sit. Clattering hooves sliced sharply through the thick din of the crowded street and Charles was relieved to see a horse cab approaching. He flagged it down, paid his fare and clambered in, smoothing the back of his brown worsted frock coat beneath him and sitting with a grateful grunt, glad not to have been obliged to scramble to the upper deck.

He had barely sat down when the horses set off again at a brisk trot, causing him to bump shoulders with the gentleman sitting next to him and drop his stick to the floor. It skittered away and came to rest under the skirts of a lady whose substantial girth was spilling over two seats. She stared at Charles to see what he would do next, her chins wobbling like milk puddings with every jolt of the cab. He smiled politely.

'I am most dreadfully sorry to inconvenience you with my clumsiness, dear lady, but I wonder if I might borrow your umbrella to hook my stick out from under your seat?' She folded her arms and pursed her plump lips. Confident of winning her round with his charm Charles held his hand out for the umbrella. 'I should be most grateful if you would also oblige me by lifting your skirts *ever so slightly* so I can see where the darned stick has come to rest.' He arched a bushy eyebrow, and she handed him the umbrella. Then, with great dignity, she hitched her voluminous burgundy taffeta skirts an inch or two off the dusty floor, revealing surprisingly dainty black button boots and turning *ever so slightly* pink.

Once he had retrieved the stick he returned the umbrella and inclined his head to his fellow passengers, acknowledging a light smattering of applause. In the past he would have made more of such a moment, extracting all the humour from it like juice from a ripe orange, but his appetite for such shenanigans seemed to have abandoned him.

Out of the corner of his eye he noticed a young man whispering and nudging his friend. 'Oh, my conscience, it's the Bailie!'

A smile tickled the corner of his mouth. Charles was used to being recognised in public, but many grief-drenched days had passed since the last time it had happened. He placed his top hat on his lap and settled back into the squeaky, bouncing seat, his thumb stroking small circles in the hat's black felt nap.

Invitations had continued to arrive throughout his daughter's decline, and, for the most part, he had accepted them, always hoping she might revive. His most recent performance had been only six weeks ago, once again as the Bailie in *Rob Roy* at Edinburgh's Theatre Royal. A rapid decline in his daughter's condition later that night had made him cancel all further engagements. Since then, Charles had stayed within the confines of his home to be near her for the last weeks of her life, for her funeral, for a few quiet days of mourning. His heart was scoured and empty now, and he doubted he would ever perform again.

He stared out of the window and wondered how he had maintained his enthusiasm for the stage for so very long: the heat and glare of gas lights; the buffeting discomfort of long journeys; the squeeze and itch of new costumes, greasepaint and tight wigs; the challenges of fine-tuning his postures, inhabiting new characters; his head constantly spinning with stories and lines to learn; so many songs to sing, accents to craft, gestures and expressions to perfect. Row upon row of ever-changing audiences had jostled their way into packed theatres across the country night after night, year after year, decade after decade, challenging him to grab their attention, expecting him to delight and surprise them, to make them laugh and shout and clap and cheer – sometimes to make them cry. They had deserved his best and that was what he had given them. His best years.

His children had been cared for by his maids, for the most part, since Hector was born: first Dorothy, then her niece, Izzie, who had replaced her when she retired. Twice, in an attempt to be more fatherly, he had arranged for the children to come to the Theatre Royal to see him perform in some farce or pantomime, but Hector's behaviour afterwards had been so boisterous on both occasions that he had given up the idea.

The cab stopped for a few minutes at Pilrig Street to refresh the horses. The shouts of ostlers and clattering of buckets brought his attention back into the cab as sharply as a sudden battering on his dressing room door used to pull him out of an absorbing script. Someone stepped out onto the cobbles calling 'I think I'll walk the rest of the way' and Charles leaned forward to look out of the window, wondering for a moment whether to join him. But the cab began to move again before he could decide and he settled himself back in his seat.

His fame had continued to grow after Charlotte died, and he had thrown himself into his work, cutting his ties with the Theatre Royal and developing a show of monologues at the beginning of the 1840s, which he called *The Real Mackay*.

Murray had made an event out of it, speechifying at length about Charles's twenty-two years of honourable service at the theatre, telling the audience: *your approbation has placed him foremost in the foremost ranks of his profession, may every happiness and good fortune attend him wherever he goes!*

In his show he reprised all his most popular roles: Bailie Nicol Jarvie, Dominie Samson, Dumbiedykes, Meg Dodds and others, as well as his most well-known songs and skits and mimicry. He took week-long seasons wherever he was invited: Perth, Aberdeen, Dundee, Montrose, Glasgow, Greenock, Newcastle, Liverpool – Edinburgh, sometimes, too. Unscrupulous theatre managers sometimes went as far as to advertise him on their playbills when he had not been booked or even invited, in the hope of drawing bigger crowds, and an enterprising circus manager even developed an act starring himself as Bailie Nicol Jarvie on horseback. Newspapers as far away as Australia, New Zealand and America published reviews of his performances in British theatres. Occasionally he was sent clippings with letters urging him to come and tour in those countries. They were the only invitations he ever turned down. Charles was recognised wherever he went, paid more than ever before and awarded an honorary Doctor of Laws by Glasgow University for his personification of 'The Glasgow Bailie'. He was 'The Real Mackay', living everywhere and nowhere, belonging to everyone and no one.

He shifted in his seat and twiddled the silver ferrule at the top of his elegant Malacca walking stick, staring at the words engraved on it, turning it slowly: The Real Mackay.

And what is The Real Mackay supposed to do with himself now?

His son-in-law's catastrophic financial misfortunes had landed squarely on Charles's shoulders like a sack of coal in 1850, just as he had begun to adjust to a slower pace of life. Suddenly he was obliged to take to the stage again, for a full season in both

Edinburgh and Glasgow – where a terrible tragedy had occurred in the Theatre Royal the previous year with 65 people crushed to death in a desperate attempt to escape a fire in the gallery. It had been exhausting, especially with the worry of his daughter becoming so ill.

Patronising comments were bandied freely by the press about his 'pecuniary hardship', making his teeth ache, so when he was afforded the opportunity to give a speech in Edinburgh's Theatre Royal and explain his situation, he took it. The overwhelming support from his audience had been deeply moving. He turned some of his carefully chosen words over in his mind as the cab trotted up the long, familiar incline of Leith Walk.

'Ladies and gentlemen, when I quitted the stage, about two years since, with every prospect of enjoying comfort during what remains of my old age, I little dreamed that I should have, so soon, to return to it. I need not advert here the circumstances that have induced me to do so; your kindness shows that you sympathise with me.'

The mournful shriek of a child drew his attention and he saw, at the side of the road, a mother crouching, her skirts bunched around her in the dust, rubbing at the bloody knee of a little boy.

Lottie. He must think of *her* now, not himself. *That's the trick!* Charles knew his granddaughter needed him, but the urgency of her need frightened him, made him want to run.

He would not run, though. Not this time.

Five years old, with the loss of her parents freshly on her, the child had lost all her sparkle and zest. There was no avoiding the fact it had fallen to him to roll up his sleeves and dig her out of her despair, to see her shine again.

Charles combed through one of his fulsome grey sideburns with his knobbly fingers. He would have to develop the role of Jovial Grandfather – a role which, to his shame, he had hardly yet explored – just as he had studiously avoided the role of Widowed Father for so many years. He had spent such slender slices of time with his children, always wrapping himself in a multitude of excuses rather than facing their need of him. It had been so much easier to become someone else than to face life without his darling Charlotte. The two little ones had already attached themselves to Dorothy before their mother died, but the terrible grief in Charlie's eyes was a constant accusation. He could hardly bear to look at the child. Lottie had that same look now, and Charles felt woefully inadequate to help her.

The cab swept on up the hill towards the Adelphi Theatre. No doubt he and Lottie would learn to muddle along together somehow, but something would have to be done soon about their living arrangements. He would not be able to manage for much longer where they were, with only the help of Christine, the woefully inadequate maid who had replaced Izzie when she left to be married last year.

Charles began to roll the Jovial Grandfather idea around in his mind like a barley sugar, prodding at it tentatively until its sweetness seeped into him. The cab veered left onto Leith Street and he leaned back in his seat to balance, imagining himself telling stories to the children about his travels, his life on the stage, his famous friends.

He had four grandchildren, two girls, two boys, all less than ten years old. Gathered at his knee they would gaze up at him adoringly, pestering him for more. Perhaps not. Perhaps they would tell *him* stories, pull him by the hand to come and see this or that, or beg him to chase them, laughing at his hirpling gait as he failed to catch them. *An adventure, then, one way or another.*

He stepped out of the cab at the top of Leith Street and stood for a moment looking across the road at his old haunt. The London comedian who had taken on the management of the Theatre Royal when Murray had retired from his managerial role at Edinburgh's two main theatres the previous year was making a worthy effort, but events seemed to be conspiring against him and he was losing money hand over fist. Charles would not be surprised if he closed the theatre down for the remainder of his lease.

It was a big block of a building, topped by a stone pediment embellished with floral carvings, its tired façade hardly recognisable now as the grand neoclassical building of Charles's heyday. Although critics had called it the plainest public building in Edinburgh when it was first built, the simplicity of its design had always appealed to Charles. Three imposing statues used to grace its roof, heralding the drama on offer within: Shakespeare standing on the apex above the main entrance, flanked by the Muses of Tragedy and Comedy on the two lower pinnacles. All the statues had gone now; Shakespeare had been replaced by a chimney.

Thankfully, the old portico at the front of the theatre was still recognisable with its smooth Corinthian columns, but there was a new balcony on top of it now, with a chunky stone balustrade and six large, boxy gas lanterns.

Charles shook his head and smiled. *The remodelling of this grand old theatre under your supervision cannot be described as your finest hour, I'm afraid, my friend!* William Murray was a great actor, a prolific playwright, an inspired stage manager and a theatre manager of great genius – but he was no architect.

He wondered again what rage had possessed Murray to destroy all his diaries and every book he owned relating to the theatre when he retired, and why he had felt compelled to give away his entire stage wardrobe. It had been the talk of the green room. Above all, Charles reflected, he would never understand how Murray had married another young actress so soon after his lovely wife, Ann, had died – as if it were simply the normal ebb and flow of life to start again and make a whole new family. Ellen Gray was a young actress from London who had joined the company a few years before Ann's death. Following her predecessor's path, she soon gave up acting to look after their growing family.

He crossed the road and walked under the portico to inspect the playbill-plastered wall, scanning the display carefully, following it round the corner where it continued down the side of the building onto the North Bridge. His eyes ranged over all the notices until he saw what he was looking for, its torn edges flapping forlornly in the breeze:

The admirable National actor
MR MACKAY
Who is engaged for a Few Nights only
will make his First Appearance
On March 12th 1852
in his Original Character
Bailie Nicol Jarvie
in the National Opera of
ROB ROY MACGREGOR – or Auld Lang Syne

Would that performance really be his last? He was tempted, for a moment, to give in to the melancholy that was slipping an arm round his shoulders like an old friend, but he straightened his back and turned away. He would put his mind to the role of Grandfather, become an expert before the week was out. Lottie would be back to her sparkling self again before the summer. *Now that would be a worthwhile achievement!*

He crossed the North Bridge, the early spring sun warm on his face. Perhaps he would take a pot of tea and some buttered scones with Lottie when he arrived home, and a dollop of raspberry jam.

NINETEEN

Lottie was sitting on a silky cushion in the corner of the bedroom where she had slept with her mother for as long as she could remember. Until a few weeks ago. Her face was turned towards the bright morning sun streaming through the sash window. She was squeezing her eyes half closed, her flickering eyelashes breaking the bright light into moving patterns, hoping to catch sight of a fairy out of the corner of her eye. Even better, a trace of the ghost of her mother. If she saw either she promised herself she would stay very still and not frighten them away.

When her mammy grew poorly she had begged to be allowed to continue sleeping in the looming four-poster bed with her, curling round her every night to try and make her warm, singing magic spells quietly into her soft hair to make her better.

One night the nurse said enough was enough and her mammy must be left in peace from now on. Lottie was taken to the kitchen and told to share the box bed with Christina, the maid. Although she liked opening and closing the little wooden doors, Christina was not soft to cuddle and sometimes pushed her away with her bony elbows.

Her mammy's bedroom was Lottie's favourite place to go in the daytime, especially when the sun was shining. It was quiet and smelt of lavender. There was a hand glass on the table by the window, a silver brush and comb, and a bottle of lavender water that she sometimes opened when no one could see, putting a dab under her nose and rubbing it into her skin so she could smell her mammy all day.

When her mammy had died last week Izzie had come to help Christina with everything and Lottie had run to bury her face in the comfort of her apron. Lottie wished Izzie had not gone away. She had smiling eyes and was soft to cuddle. Now she had her own baby she only came on special days. Izzie had stroked her hair and explained they were going to wash her mammy's face and comb her hair so she would look her best. Then they would dress her in a pretty dress and lay flowers round her. When she was ready Izzie promised she would fetch Lottie to come and say goodbye.

Lottie had stared at her beautiful mammy, lying in the box of flowers, for a long time before she felt brave enough to touch her face. Her skin was so cold she pulled her hand away at once. Then a tall man with dark, curly hair had barged into the room talking in a loud voice. Her grandfather was following him, saying, 'Pipe down, for pity's sake, Hector, can you not show your sister some respect?' When the man saw Lottie he'd stopped and said, 'Well, hello little missy, I wondered when I'd be seeing you. I'm your long-lost uncle!'

He had come towards her, holding out his hand and smiling as if something was funny, and she had begun to scream. She could not stop screaming for a long time. Her throat still felt sore when she thought about that man.

Izzie and Christina bustled noisily into the room: short and soft, skinny and sharp, each dragging a packing case.

'Ah! I thought you'd be in here Lottie! Come and help me, we're to pack your mammy's things.' Izzie smiled, but Lottie folded her arms and looked away. 'Aww! Come now, lassie, it'll be fun!' Lottie put her hands over her ears and sat tight on her cushion. Something was very wrong. She squeezed her eyes shut to block out what was happening. Through her fingers she could hear the wardrobe door open and realised the maids had started taking out dresses. She could hear the silk whispering. She opened her eyes and stood up.

'Those dresses belong to my mammy. Why are you taking them out?'

'Dinna fret yersel' now, Lottie, it's for the best, you'll see.' Izzie put the blue sprigged cotton dress she was holding on top of the pink silk one already in the packing case, then came towards her, arms outstretched. Lottie was torn. She wanted very much to be gathered into Izzie's softness, but she wanted her to stop moving the dresses too. She stood her ground.

'I'm going to wear Mammy's dresses when I'm a lady, Izzie, so you must *leave* them in the wardrobe, till I grow big.'

'O' course you'll wear 'em pet! I'll keep 'em safe for you at mine till then! Christina told me there'll be nae room to store 'em where you're going, so I offered to keep 'em in my parlour where I do dressmaking for folk. For the time being at any rate. Mr Mackay was that pleased, I reckoned he'd've telt you, poppet!'

'What do you mean, there won't be room? Where am I going? I live here, in Drummond Street, with Grandfather.' Christina had started folding dresses again as if the world were not suddenly coming to an end.

'Oh, pet!' Izzie had brown eyes like roasted chestnuts and a sprinkle of freckles on her nose like brown sugar. Lottie unfolded her arms and allowed Izzie to hold her hand.

'Your mammy and I made some o' these dresses together you know, they're very pretty. I'll tak good care of 'em till you grow into a lady, you'll see.' Izzie picked up a pink shawl, covered in colourful swirling patterns, and looked at it with a sad face. Then she gently wrapped the pretty shawl round Lottie's shoulders.

'Here, you should have something to remember her by, Lottie.' The shawl felt warm against her neck. It smelt of her mammy's lavender. Lottie's eyes began to sting and she realised her nose was running, cold and wet, onto her upper lip. She sniffed. Izzie pulled a handkerchief from her apron pocket, wiped Lottie's face, and dried her eyes. Then she wiped her own eyes, and Lottie realised Izzie was crying too.

'Why did you say there won't be room where I'm going?'

'I think you should ask yer grandfather yersel', lassie. It's no' for me to say. He's in his study at his desk. Remember and knock before you go in now, won't you?'

TWENTY

His study was a restful room. He would miss its calmness. It had dark green walls, a red silk Turkey carpet, and a long window onto the street with a little wrought-iron balcony. He would not miss the tavern directly opposite, though, nor its raucous night noises and intrusive smells.

The elbow chair in which Charles sat was one of the few items he would be taking with him. Its brown padded leather seat was quite scuffed after so many years of use, but he was very fond of it. He was taking his mahogany desk as well. The rest of his furniture would be collected later that morning and sold at Lyon and Turnbull's auction rooms in George Street.

Something had been done regarding living arrangements for him and Lottie, but Charles was not convinced it was the *right* thing. Ten days ago he had lunched with Charlie at the Theatre Royal tavern in Shakespeare Square to discuss the situation over mutton pies and ale. Charlie worked nearby at the Inland Revenue office and they had lunched together at the tavern several times over the years.

The best solution, they agreed as coffee was served, would be to pool resources. Charlie and his family would leave their small flat in Barony Street, where the lease was coming to an end shortly anyway, and Charles would move out of Drummond Street with Lottie, foregoing the remaining two years of his lease. Together they would secure a lease on a larger property somewhere nearby where they could all live together.

Unfortunately, his son had taken the matter into his own hands since then and procured a lease on the very flat in Dublin Street where he had moved the family after Charlotte died. He had not consulted Charles, and now everything was happening too fast.

Charlie had sprung it on him without warning a few days ago. *The moment I heard the lease had come available I felt I had no choice but to act fast, Father. Moving back there together will surely be a great comfort to us all at this sad time, don't you think? Like going home!*

It certainly would *not* be like going home for Charles. Living at 23 Dublin Street again would stir up all manner of uncomfortable memories. However, the deed was done, so there was no point contesting it. Charlie was convinced he was doing the right thing and had moved in already with his wife Bella and their three children. Charles and Lottie were to join them in the morning.

He pushed himself wearily to his feet and walked over to a large oak bookcase filled with his extensive collection of books. Packing them properly into the wooden crates his son had procured for him would take time. He could not rush the process. His books were like old friends and must be treated with respect.

He selected an antiquarian book and held it fondly, stroking the weathered brown calfskin cover: Ramsay's *Tea-Table Miscellany*, the first book he had ever bought.

Another favourite was a second edition of George Thomson's *Select Songs of Scotland*. He wrapped the Ramsay in brown paper, placed it carefully into a crate, and selected the Thomson. Good old John Sinclair had shown Charles his copy of this when they were in the regiment together all those years ago. *It must be nearly fifty years!* The Burns song his friend had come across in the book had quickly become one of Sinclair's signature songs, eventually becoming a national favourite and finding its way into Pocock's *Rob Roy Macgregor – or Auld Lang Syne*.

Charles placed the Thomson in the crate beside the Ramsay and stood for a long moment, remembering all the times he had sung that song on-stage – *well over a thousand, surely, maybe as many as two*. He pulled out a green, cloth-bound copy of Alexander Whitelaw's *Book of Scottish Song* and it fell open at an old song Charles had discovered himself and made popular: 'Bide Ye Yet'. He had found the lively little song in an antiquarian book recommended to him by his neighbour. David Herd's *Ancient Scottish Songs and Heroic Ballads* was an unassuming, plain little volume, printed around the time his mother was born, but it was bursting with treasures and had quickly become Charles's favourite book. When Whitelaw acknowledged his find in print in 1843, it had made him feel he had, at last, contributed something to society that would outlast him – unlike his endless cavorting on-stage: *'Mr Mackay, the comedian, has been instrumental in rendering [this song] a general favourite.'*

Charles closed the Whitelaw, packed it with the other books, and took his precious copy of Herd from the shelf. He walked over to the window to make the most of the light and flicked carefully through its wafer-thin pages, delicate as the wings of a moth, enjoying the feel of them against his thumb, the tiny flutter of air.

'Grandfather?' She had crept into the room so quietly that Charles was taken by surprise.

'Aha! Pretty little Lottie, what what whattie?' He put the book on his desk and gave her his full attention. His improvisation, he knew, had been rather lame, and he could tell by her frown it had failed to hit the mark. She stood facing him, scrutinising him with clear blue eyes, hands perched where hips would one day be, in perfect imitation of Christina, her tone surprisingly imperious for one so young. *She is cross with me!* Her eyes were the same colour as her mother's, and sometimes they had a fiery energy her mother's had never had.

Charles raised innocent eyebrows, as if asking why she was so cross.

'*Why* did you tell Izzie to pack Mammy's dresses and take them away, Grandfather? She said there won't be room for them where we're going – where *are* we going? We live *here*!' Charles regarded Lottie's lifted chin, her defiant stance, and was unsure whether to laugh or cry. It dawned on him he had gone about everything in the wrong way. He should have unfolded the plan to her a few days ago, listened to her worries, reassured her – not left her to find out about the move from the maids. Such clumsiness. He would have to do better if this was going to work. He sat down and rested his hands on his knees.

'Well, little soldier, you and I are going to have to be very brave now your mammy has flown away to join your father with the angels, don't you think? Mmmm? Perhaps you could look after me here all by yourself when Christina goes to her new family tomorrow? What d'you think of that idea? Eh?' He hoped his teasing smile and throaty chuckle would charm her. It did not.

She shook her head, her shortbread ringlets bouncing charmingly.

'No, of course not. What was I thinking?' Charles clapped his palm to his forehead and pulled an exaggerated grimace. He thought he could detect the beginning of a smile, but it soon disappeared, like sunshine behind quick clouds. Lottie was right. This was no time for such nonsense. He leaned forward and took one of her hands, so small and white, in his great clumsy fist.

'In truth, Lottie my girl, although Christina is doing her best to look after us both I fear it is not a happy arrangement. Don't you agree?' The child delivered a solemn nod, accompanied by the slightest tremble of her lower lip. He would have to tread carefully.

'But, Grandfather, who will cook our supper if Christina leaves us? And where will I sleep?' Panic had pushed the defiance out of her eyes and her breath was growing shallow; a storm was brewing. Charles could feel his feet slipping and sliding beneath him and knew he had to find a firm footing again before she began to scream. More than anything he dreaded her screaming.

He pulled Lottie onto his knee.

'My dear girl, tomorrow we are going to move into a big flat in Dublin Street with Uncle Charles and Aunty Bella and all your cousins. Won't that be fun?' He turned her solemn, heart-shaped face gently towards him. 'We'll have a fine time there Lottie, my lovely, a fine time. I promise you.' A single tear was glistening on her pale cheek and he wiped it away with his thumb.

'We can visit Izzie sometimes, too. You like her, don't you?' Lottie nodded and snuggled into his lap, burrowing inside his grey frock coat, sniffing and snuffling, but thankfully not screaming. He let her rest against his brown tweed waistcoat for a while, until her breathing slowed. Then he extracted her slowly and sat her up, giving what he hoped was a reassuring smile and brushing her hair from her eyes. Carefully, slowly, he slid her onto her feet on the faded Turkey carpet.

'Off you pop now, Little Lottie Poppet. Go and help Christina and Izzie pack your pretty dresses and dolls so we can take them with us tomorrow.' He watched her walk to the door, and when she turned to say goodbye, he noticed her dress was covered in forget-me-nots that matched the blue of her eyes. He smiled back, lifting his hand in a wave. She was so like her grandmother, especially the way she sometimes held his gaze, her chin slightly lifted.

The next morning Charles was sitting at his desk staring out of the window at a grey day. All his packing was done and he was almost ready to leave, but he had received a letter which had shaken him to the core and he needed time to think. There was a soft knock on the door. Charles put the letter on his desk with a sigh and turned round to find Charlie had arrived.

'I have a cab waiting at the kerb, Father. I thought I could take Lottie down the road now, with the first of the luggage. That is, if you're quite ready for her to leave, of course.' Charlie's long, pale face was framed by sleek sideburns and his light brown hair, parted on the left, was combed flat. He was wearing a slim, black frock coat – impeccably tailored – and his shawl-collared waistcoat was made of dark green tartan. Quite the gentleman. Different from his raffish younger brother in every way.

'Ah yes, dear boy, what a good idea. Meanwhile, I have a letter I need to attend to, and I'm expecting the auctioneers' carter to arrive soon to collect my furniture. Tell Lottie I'll be there for lunch though, would you? I wouldn't want her to worry she's left me behind!'

'Of course, Father.' His son paused for a moment. 'I'll come back later this morning with a cart for your desk and chair, and your books and so on. Hopefully you'll be comfortable enough up front with me and the driver. It's not too cold today. Dry as well.'

'Thank you, dear boy.' Charles gave his most encouraging smile to try and dispel the awkwardness that always seemed to come between them.

'Bella has arranged a celebratory luncheon for us and the children are very excited to see you both.'

'Ah, how very good of her.' Charles began to wish his son would leave. What was he doing, dithering in the doorway? He wanted to read the letter again, to take in the awful news without being rushed.

'I hope you will find it a comfort staying in Dublin Street again, Father.' Charlie ventured. *Hardly!* Yet he had begun to wonder if there might be a certain inevitability about it. Perhaps life, after all, was more of a circle than a straight line. Charles nodded.

'I shall see you later this morning, Charlie. Goodbye!' He turned back to his desk, one hand raised in farewell.

'Goodbye, Father.'

When the door closed Charles let out a long sigh and felt his shoulders relax.

He picked up the letter.

William Murray had died suddenly in St Andrews. He had moved there from Edinburgh only a few months ago, after taking his final bow. Although Murray had not been in the best of health, it was a great shock to read he had simply died in his armchair at home two nights ago, after an evening spent with friends. There had been no warning whatsoever. *So much for enjoying your retirement, old friend!*

Charles pulled a fresh sheet of paper from his brown leather writing case. He was not at all sure what to write to Murray's poor widow. He flicked open the lid of his inkwell. There was to be a funeral in St Andrews in a few days and the thought of such an arduous journey, combined with the obligation to meet so many people from his past, was exhausting.

He sat for some time, thinking about William Murray. The man had played such a prominent role in his life for decades, yet Charles had never really understood him. Sometimes Murray was a friend, a fellow actor, a comedian. More often than not he was an employer who made sure he had what he wanted on his own terms. Always, he had seemed supremely in control. He had acquired the royal patent for the Theatre Royal when his sister retired in 1830, as well as the management of the Caledonian Theatre, which he had renamed the Adelphi. Charles had still been under contract with him at the Theatre Royal at the time, but Murray had given him leave to accept the multitude of invitations that were coming his way, allowing him to come and go as he pleased and eventually develop his own show, for which he was eternally grateful. Charles shook his head, thinking again how it was beyond his comprehension why Murray, a man whose whole life had been dedicated to the theatre, had so comprehensively obliterated all traces of it when he retired.

The low rumble of rolling barrels across the street brought Charles back to the matter in hand. He picked up his Waverley dipping pen, filled the nib with thick black ink and began to write.

TWENTY-ONE

Lottie had drawn the slippery, peach-coloured eiderdown up to her chin and was lying on her back, arms by her sides, eyes wide open in the dark. She was frightened to move in case she woke her cousin, Jane. After Aunty Bella had said good night to them all and blown out the candle Jane had whispered, *Remember this is my bed, Lottie – you mustn't take up too much room or wake me up with your wriggling*!

She turned the cover back carefully, slipped her bare feet onto the chilly floorboards and felt about for her shawl. Lottie was not afraid of the dark. She walked slowly towards where she remembered the door to be. The doorknob was smooth and cold under her fingers. A slight twist to the right, a click, and the door opened. In the hallway she slid her way along the wall, hand over hand, until she arrived at the kitchen, where a line of pale grey light was seeping under the door. She opened it and saw the moon, spreading silver over everything through unshuttered windows.

Lottie closed the door softly behind her and stood very still, looking round the moonlit kitchen for the black and white cat, wondering if she had gone out to roam in the city. The kitchen cat had allowed Lottie to stroke her on her lap for a long time in the afternoon when she had not been sure what else to do. She loved the feel of her silky fur, the vibrations of her quiet rumbling breath against her legs.

It was warmer in here than in the bedroom.

She tiptoed over to the box bed in the corner. It was not like Christina's bed in the Drummond Street kitchen. The pale wood of this bed was covered with carved patterns of flowers and cartwheels. Lottie ran her hand over the smooth shapes, prolonging the moment, unsure if she should disturb the maid and risk being sent back to bed.

She pulled the door open carefully and climbed in, closing it behind her. It was dark inside. Warm and safe. She burrowed under the blanket. Mary was soft to cuddle and did not push her away.

When Lottie woke in the morning she was back in Jane's bed, her pink shawl still wrapped around her shoulders.

TWENTY-TWO

'That's a fine waistcoat you have on today, Mr Mackay. That wee peck o' yellow in the pattern brings a braw light to your eyes, sir, so it does! Now let me tuck a fresh neckcloth under yer chin and we'll keep you dry and clean. Aye, that's grand. Lean back a wee bittie if you wouldnae mind. I'll be finished in nae time at a'.' Mr Cromby, the barber, was a big, beefy man with thick black hair, a pencil-thin moustache and nimble fingers that achieved magical results every time. He had been Charles's barber for over a decade and had removed more than one troublesome tooth for him during that time as well. Now that all Charles's friends seemed to be dying off, Mr Cromby probably knew him better than anyone.

'It's a particular favourite, Cromby, I must confess. I've had it for many years. I was hoping the playful nature of the design would help me rise above the dreich mood that settled on me the moment I opened my shutters on what I had hoped would be a fine May morning to discover nothing but thick fog.' Charles screwed his eyes closed as Cromby lathered his face. It was a relief to give himself up to the ministrations of an expert for a while. That morning, his first in Dublin Street, he had been in dire need of soothing. A good, close shave and a trim of his hair and whiskers were proving just the balm he needed.

The air was still damp when he emerged twenty minutes later, fresher of face and lighter of spirit. The High Street was alive with the raucous cries of hawkers and traders, yelling costermongers and rumbling cartwheels. He wove his way up the hill, glad of his walking stick in the crowded thoroughfare. Singsong shouts of 'Caller herring!' rose above the general commotion and his attention was drawn to a young fishwife in her bright red and yellow jacket and boldly striped skirts. A wheel of glittering silver herring winked at him from the wicker creel on her back and Charles was tempted. He slowed his pace for a moment, but the fishy smell reminded him how much he was enjoying the fresh lemon and bergamot tang of the barber's pomade, and he walked on empty-handed.

He strode down Dublin Street with the *Scotsman* newspaper rolled under his arm, the spring sun pleasantly warm on the newly smooth skin of his face and the taste of fresh coffee in his mouth after a pleasant half-hour in Mr Muir's Refreshment Rooms. Down the hill only the tops of the trees in Drummond Place Gardens poked their heads above the persistent haar still rolling in from the Forth like a wispy white sea.

He climbed the stone steps to his familiar front door and went inside. Light was pouring into the stairwell from the long window above him and a smell, sharp and damp like lye and wet sand, nipped at his nose. Charles climbed to the first floor, sliding his hand up the gracefully turned wooden banister, and stopped outside the door of their flat. He glanced up, wondering who else was living at No. 23 these days, then pushed the door open. He slipped his walking stick into the hall stand, hung his coat on the only vacant hook and took his hat with him into the room which now functioned as his bedroom and study. It was the same room he had used as a study years ago, which was both a good thing and rather unsettling.

He closed the door and put his hat on the console, making a mental note to buy a tabletop hatstand. There was only room for one hat on the stand in the hallway. The walls had been painted a deep red colour, and there was a large oak wardrobe. The bed was a cumbersome four-poster, swathed in drapes of fussy crimson and cream floral damask, piled high with at least five blankets and a generous scattering of pillows. Charles had arranged for a looking-glass to be hung near his washstand by the window, but his books were still packed in crates. He would have to look for a suitably large bookshelf, or perhaps have some shelves fitted to the wall.

Charles sank gratefully into his beloved elbow chair, still not quite believing the twist of fate that had brought him back here. *The last time I sat in this chair, at this desk, by this window must have been almost twenty years ago.* He picked up the newspaper, but memories were jostling and pushing for his attention, like an unruly crowd queuing for tickets at Mr Garbutt's box office. *Well then, so be it.* He put the unopened *Scotsman* back on his desk and sat back, folding his hands in his lap and allowing the reins of his mind to slip through his fingers. He was curious to see where his ungoverned thoughts might take him and wondered if it would be a rough ride.

A long-forgotten moment came to mind and Charles watched it unfold like a scene in a play. He saw his younger self pacing up and down in the Broughton Street parlour, extremely agitated. He was ranting at Dorothy, telling her to clear out everything that belonged to Charlotte, to give it all away to some worthy institution, to her own sisters, to anyone who would take it, so long as everything was gone by the time he came home that night. They were moving to Dublin Street in three days and he did not want to take any of Charlotte's things with him.

Dorothy had looked up at him defiantly, her round face red with indignation, her narrowed eyes flashing. She was cross and it had made her bold. *Lord above, Mr Mackay! How could ye?* She had flung open the doors of the huge wardrobe and he was engulfed by the smell of rosemary and lavender, dazzled by

Charlotte's gorgeous skirts and gowns and costumes, drenched by the onslaught of the memories they evoked. All her scarves and necklaces were hanging from their uneven hooks exactly as she had left them; the top shelf was still a tumble of colourful hats and feathers; Charles was transfixed. He stood in front of the wardrobe, inhaling the scent of her, his damp, sweating fingers opening and closing over the gold pendant in his left hand – the only thing of hers he was allowing himself to keep. *Just do it, Dorothy, and that's an order!* A flash of sunlight bounced off the wardrobe's internal looking-glass and he shut the doors quickly, afraid he might glimpse a reflection of his wife ordering him to come to his senses at once.

It was a sobering scene.

Charles leaned his elbows on the desk and pinched the bridge of his nose with his fingers, deeply ashamed of his behaviour all those years ago. Quite apart from his inexcusable rudeness to Dorothy, it struck him for the first time that depriving his children of all their mother's things had been an extremely selfish thing to do. He had not been thinking of them at all, of course, not for one second. When she was taken from him Charles could not bear to be near anything of hers. He had convinced himself he would not be able to think straight until it had all gone. Every last feather.

He pictured Lottie wrapping her pink Paisley shawl round her shoulders every morning, taking it to bed with her at night, and his selfishness stuck in his throat like a fishbone, making him cough and pull at his collar.

A door opened in the hall and he swivelled round in his chair when he heard children's voices, but it closed almost at once and quietness settled around him again. The parlour had been requisitioned for a schoolroom in the mornings, with Bella's younger sister, Maggie, acting as teacher. They had waited for Lottie to move in so all the children could start together. This was their first day. It would be interesting to hear how they had fared.

He turned back to his desk and resumed his train of thought.

After Charlotte's funeral Charles had spoken to Murray, so recently bereaved himself. He had explained his need for a complete change of scene and Murray had replied: *Take all the time you need, Mackay. You know you're welcome back on-stage at the Royal whenever you're ready.* The theatre had been about to undergo a massive rebuilding programme in any case and would have to be closed for at least one season, so it seemed as good a time as any for him to take some time off and travel. Charles put his affairs in order and sent letters to theatre managers across the country letting it be known he was available to perform anywhere and everywhere. Soon his fame presented him with a legitimate escape route as wide as the Champs-Élysées, and he took it.

By September Charles was playing the Bailie in the Liverpool Theatre Royal's production of *Rob Roy*, and shortly after that he had left the country altogether. He found himself ensconced in Paris in January 1829, writing a facetious letter to Sir Walter Scott about the infamous Burke and Hare trial that was causing such a stir in Edinburgh at the time. Hoping to distract his friend, who was suffering from increasingly poor health, he had referred to his offspring in an offhand way and signed himself 'Nicol Jarvie' – a game he often played with Sir Walter. It had occurred to him, as he signed with a flourish, that he had almost forgotten his own name for lack of using it. Then it struck him, with much more force, that he had almost forgotten his own children for lack of seeing them.

Ten days later he was back in Dublin Street, patting his offspring on their heads and telling them to behave nicely for Dorothy as he had an important dinner engagement.

In the quiet of his bedchamber Charles had changed into his best clothes. Striking a pose in front of the cheval, he had fingered the bit of yellow-patterned waistcoat showing above the low lapels of his knee-length damask coat, smoothed back his thick, dark hair and thought he would do well enough.

It was a cold night. Charles had wrapped a long black woollen cloak around his shoulders, picked up his top hat and the Malacca walking stick he had recently acquired, then shouted over his shoulder, 'Goodnight to one and all – have a merry time!' before closing the door behind him.

The second Theatrical Fund dinner in the Assembly Rooms in George Street was to be attended by almost four hundred of the most distinguished gentlemen in Scotland, with the exception of Sir Walter Scott, who was unable to come because of his poor health. Charles had been planning to give a speech that would have made him blush. It was a shame he would not hear it first-hand. Although Charles was used to speaking to audiences of thousands when acting, appearing as himself in front of such an illustrious gathering was a different kind of challenge altogether. His heart was ticking fast and shallow, like his gold pocket watch, as he approached the grand entrance to the Assembly Rooms.

'Well now, Mr Mackay, I see you are one o' the gentry tonight and I'm one of the servants!' His old friend Jones made a mock bow. Jones and several other members of the company were acting as stewards for the event.

'Och we're a' tapsalteerie th' nicht ma guid man!' Charles slapped him on the back, gave him a grin and handed over his cloak, hat and stick.

Once again, the large, elegant banquet room looked magnificent. Row upon row of long tables were set with white linen, gleaming silverware, exotic floral displays and an abundance of sumptuous food. Crystal glasses and decanters sparkled in the abundant light cascading from several huge chandeliers. Every table was crowded with gentlemen dressed in their finest, appetising aromas competed for attention in the warm air, and the room bounced with boisterous conversations.

Charles consumed rather more of the splendid dinner than he had planned, and when the time approached for him to make his speech he found himself feeling a little tight of button. The Lord Provost stood and prayed leave to propose a toast: 'To the Theatrical Fund of Edinburgh – long may it continue to prosper, and long may it continue to be supported by so respectable and intelligent a company as I see now before me.'

The respectable and intelligent company rose and raised their glasses enthusiastically, then took their seats again, scraping chairs on the polished floor and talking noisily amongst themselves. Charles remained standing, surveying the glittering scene, waiting for the lively assembly to realise he was about to speak.

When the hubbub settled, he began: 'My Lord and gentlemen, I rise on behalf of my brethren to return our thanks for the toast just given. I look back upon the first Scottish Theatrical Fund Dinner with a feeling of pleasure and pride. Who can ever forget the night when the immortal author of *Waverley* withdrew his mask, and stood revealed to his admiring countrymen? We, gentlemen, never will.' He paused for the inevitable cheers and applause, the stamping and clinking of glasses.

'On that night did the Shakespeare of our day confer on the actor a degree of imperishable honour. Amongst the many beneficial effects resulting from the universal perusal of the works of this great author, are we indebted for the wonderful revolution of opinion in this country in favour of *our art*.' Charles knew everyone would be expecting him to adopt the manner and voice of Bailie Nicol Jarvie now, to offer a little light relief and make them laugh, so he transformed himself into the pompous magistrate for a moment and gave them what they wanted.

'I have seen what *my worthy faither, the deacon, guid man, wadna ha' believed*.' Good-humoured heckling followed and he waited for it to simmer down before giving his audience something new to think about, something that brought his dear mother's voice to the front of his mind and a lump to the back of his throat.

'Yes, gentlemen, I have seen the aged Presbyterian *venture into the theatre*! I have looked upon his stern and rugged countenance – I have beheld his rigid features relax – his face become illuminated with a smile – his eye beam with joy, and his whole soul yield to *uncontrollable and clamorous delight*!' Charles paused for a sip of claret while people shouted their approval and banged on the tables, causing their plates and glasses to jump precariously. He brought his speech to a close by acknowledging the amiable foundress of the fund, Mrs Harriet Siddons, and her talented brother, Mr William Murray, then resumed his seat.

The scene was so vivid Charles almost forgot he was sitting in his elbow chair in Dublin Street in the late spring of 1852. He rubbed his face with his hands, pushed himself to his feet and walked over to the window. A handcart loaded with boxes was being pulled up the street by a boy of no more than ten, his shoulders tensed under his shirt, his round face red with exertion. A strange sensation crept over Charles, as though time had collapsed and he was his younger self watching the same scene from the same window. *How is it, Mackay, that you have washed up back here after all these years?*

He went back to his desk to look for a sheet of paper. It suddenly felt very important to remember the order of things. *Perhaps if I begin to write it out it will come back to me.* He sat down, picked up his pen, and discovered he did not have the inclination to write. He returned the pen to its holder, leaned back and closed his eyes again.

He had felt like a ship in the fog with no compass when Charlotte died. Utterly lost. On a whim he had taken a lease on 23 Dublin Street and moved the family there to get away from the scene of so much grief. Whether it had been the right thing or not he had never been quite sure. Dublin Street had seemed homely enough whenever he was there, thanks to Dorothy; the children well cared for too. He had used the flat more as a base than a home, though, allowing his work to take him away much of the time.

The lease had come to an end in 1836 and Charles had decided to move the family St James Square, almost opposite the Theatre Royal. Charlie was sixteen by then and working as an apprentice clerk. He refused to go with them and opted to move into digs instead, surprising Charles with the vehemence of his feelings: 'I've had more than enough of policing Hector in your absence, Father, I wash my hands of him.' The reprimand had stung and Charles had let him go. Hector was only ten but already roaming the streets and up to no good, according to Dorothy, who also gave her notice when they moved. She had been feeling her age and had suggested her young niece, Izzie, whom the children already knew, would make an ideal replacement. So Charles, Hector and fifteen-year-old Charlotte had moved to St James Square with their new maid, who was only seventeen but very capable, and sometimes Charlie turned up on Sundays for lunch.

Charles began touring round Scotland more extensively, drawing huge crowds wherever he went. His contract with Murray throughout the 1830s had been more like an open invitation to perform in the Theatre Royal whenever he was in town and had the inclination. On the rare occasions he spent time at home he saw that Izzie was making a fine fist of things. She seemed on good terms with his daughter and was not afraid to raise her voice to Hector, who always seemed to grow in his absence. He sometimes met Charlie for lunch in town. Charlie had become quite the young gentleman and kept his father at arm's length in the politest manner.

It had come as a surprise when Charlie announced his engagement to one of the Winters' brood, their neighbours in St James Square. All of a sudden the children seemed to have grown up without him noticing. Charlie and Bella were married in St Cuthbert's on January the 22nd, 1844, and set up home on the Southside. Charles had terminated his contract with Murray altogether by then and, freed from the obligation to live within calling distance of the theatre, had moved to the Southside as well. It would be nice for young Charlotte, then almost twenty, to be near her brother and his pretty young wife. Hector however, not yet eighteen, refused point-blank to go with them and ran away with a group of strolling players. Charles had no idea where his youngest son was until he turned up at Drummond Street for Hogmanay over two years later: 'Dreadful job finding you, Father, you seem to make a habit of moving house!'

Lord knows why we moved quite so many times! Was I running from something, perhaps? Looking for something? For someone? Charles and young Charlotte, along with Izzie, had not been in Drummond Street long when his daughter fell in love. Now here he was back in the flat he had taken after his wife died, as though life had revolved like a wheel since then and deposited him right back where he had started life without her.

He opened his eyes. His mind felt clearer now he had retraced his path. Outside, the morning mist had lifted and the day was brightening. Charles went to the window again.

Dublin Street was an elegant, wide street. He remembered how pleasant he used to think it was to have so much space between him and his neighbours across the road. He pulled up the sash window for some fresh air and cooking smells wafted in from a nearby kitchen. *Good Lord, it must be nearly lunchtime! Where has the time gone?* He fished his gold pocket watch out of his waistcoat and discovered it was almost o'clock. Good. Charles was feeling the need for company now. He was more than ready for some chatter from the children, too, after so much contemplation.

A seagull swooped down from the roof and grabbed a discarded crust from the cobbles in its orange beak. It was a great deal to swallow, all this self-knowledge. Especially when one had a fishbone stuck in one's throat.

TWENTY-THREE

Charles reached for his watch and squinted at it. The sun had drawn a white pencil line round his wooden shutters and there was just enough light for him to discover it was past nine o'clock. Ah well, he was an old man now and could be forgiven for sleeping so late.

He threw off the bedcovers, swung his feet to the floor and fished about under the bed for his embroidered slippers, careful not to kick the chanty, which he remembered was quite full. Then he shuffled to the window, scratching himself through his nightshirt, and threw the shutters open. Summer had arrived overnight and the sky was delightfully blue, with only a few wisps of white cloud.

Breakfast was well underway in the kitchen when Charles put his head round the door, washed and brushed and ready for whatever the day might bring.

'A very good morning to you all! Please forgive my tardiness!' He grinned broadly at his four grandchildren, nodded at his son and daughter-in-law, took his seat at the table and cut himself a thick slice of brown bread.

'Good morning, Grandfather,' Jane, the eldest child, replied politely. Her two brothers looked at him shyly, their mouths full and their tongues apparently tied. Lottie was sitting on a low stool by the cooking hearth, a small blob of jam on her cheek. The black and white kitchen cat was asleep on her lap and she was smoothing the silky fur behind its ears. Charles beamed mischievously at her, adding a wink as an afterthought, and she grinned briefly – a glimpse of sunshine between clouds. *She'll soon get to know her cousins and be easy with them – for now at least she has the cat!*

Bella poured Charles a cup of his favourite Earl Grey's tea.

'I trust you slept well, Charles?'

'I certainly did, Bella!' She smiled at him and turned to her husband.

'I think we're all beginning to settle in nicely now, don't you think Charlie?'

'I do believe we are, my dear. Good morning, Father.'

Charles nodded at his son, took a sip of the scalding tea and turned back to his delightful daughter-in-law.

'I think I slept rather *too* well, judging by the time I woke!' Bella was a treasure. His son was a lucky man to have such a wife. She had fine, straight hair the colour of cinnamon that she wore in a slippery chignon, and clear, pale skin that was prone to flare in the heat of the kitchen or at a harsh word. She was a calm woman, quick to smile, slow to anger, strong and steady with a pleasant, round face and pale-lashed hazel eyes. Bella was also a diplomat. She could sweep away uncomfortable undercurrents with the lightest touch before they made people feel ill at ease. Charles guessed that was why Lottie had been allowed to leave the table before her cousins.

He spread creamy butter generously on his bread, reached across the table to help himself to a kipper and squashed a portion of it onto his bread, releasing its deliciously salty, smoky aroma.

'Fish on a Saturday morning, Bella?'

'I know. Mary is so clever! Only yesterday she heard from

Maud upstairs that a Newhaven fishwife comes out of her way to stop in Queen Street early on a Saturday morning before going up to the High Street.' Mary emerged from the scullery at the sound of her name, drying her hands on her apron. A woman of middling years with a thickening middle, wrinkles and humour radiated from her dark button eyes and her hands were always busy.

'Aha! A most useful piece of information, Mary, well done to you! And full marks for rising at dawn to catch the wifey!' Charles toasted the maid with his teacup and Mary smiled, dipping him a mock curtsey. 'Who is "Maud Upstairs", by the bye?'

'Maud is Mr Calder's maid, sir, they're just above us.' Mary returned to the scullery and Charles turned to his son in disbelief, forcing him to look up with the intensity of his gaze. Bella began to fuss with their youngest son, Tommy, wiping his face, and spooning porridge into his mouth, humming a little song to him under her breath, and the three older children sat quietly, as though they had sensed a change in Charles's mood and were waiting to see what would happen next. *No matter, let them see!*

'Thomas Calder the ironmonger, is it Charlie? Is he still here after all these years?'

'Yes, Father.' Charlie was fiddling with his napkin. 'He was always very kind to the three of us when you were away. He used to help Dorothy with all manner of practical things … I kept in touch with him after you moved the family to James Square and I took lodgings. I used to come back here sometimes to visit him, have a bite of supper and a blether.' Charles kept his voice low, reigning in his irritation.

'That's beside the point, Charlie. Did you ask Mr Calder to let you know when this flat became available, for some bizarre reason best known to yourself?'

Charlie was inspecting the crumbs on his plate, scraping them into a straight line with his knife. He looked up with a flicker of defiance.

'He suggested the idea to me, Father, and I agreed it might be a good one.'

'Aha! So good old Calder is behind all this! That makes sense.' Charles was leaning towards his son now. 'So, tell me, Charlie, did you already have the lease secured before we even discussed the idea of moving in together?'

Another bashful nod.

Charles sat back abruptly, dropping his napkin on the table.

'Well! I think it would have been decent of you to let me in on your little ruse, don't you? I might even have agreed to it!'

'I'm sorry, Father. I thought it would be for the best. You were not quite yourself when my sister was so ill, and then, when we knew she was …'

'Alright, never mind, what's done is done. We're all here now, for better or worse.'

Charles addressed his next comment to his daughter-in-law in the hope that she might pour some oil on the troubled waters.

'And do we know who else is living in our stair, Bella?'

'Yes, Charles. There's a Mr Andrew Webster, a solicitor in the Supreme Court who has his two sisters with him. A very upstanding gentleman from what I've heard. And on the top floor there's a cabinet-maker.' She had brought the charged atmosphere off the boil with ease and Charles was grateful.

'How interesting. I must say, it is very nice to know with whom I share a front door and a common stair.' It was a pity to spoil a good breakfast with an argument. He took another bite of kipper, then dabbed his mouth with his napkin and laid his hands on the table, splaying his fingers wide in readiness to push himself to his feet.

'So, what is everyone doing today, Charlie?'

'I'm off to buy my newspaper shortly, Father. I plan to read it in the parlour for a few hours while Bella takes the children to her mother's. You're welcome to join me. Would you like me to buy a *Scotsman* for you?'

'That's very kind of you, Charlie, but I haven't yet decided what I shall do this morning. Will Lottie be joining you, Bella?' He looked over at Lottie, but she had turned her face away and was busying herself with the cat.

'She is welcome to join us if she likes, Charles. It'll be fun.' Bella's bright voice failed to evoke any response from Lottie. 'My mother still gathers her brood every Saturday, Charles, and cooks copious amounts of delicious food for us all. We go as often as we can, as do most of my brothers and sisters and their families.'

'It sounds like quite a gathering. I imagine you all pitch in?' Charles had found Mrs Winter warmly generous and hospitable the few times he had encountered her during their time in St James Square. He had been sorry when she lost her husband, so it was good to hear she still had the energy and inclination to gather her large family every week. He knew Bella's two youngest brothers were still at school and that she had three little nieces, so it would certainly be lively. Perhaps too lively for Lottie, though. She had hardly got to know her own cousins yet, never mind meeting theirs!

'Oh yes, we spend all day cooking and eating and gossiping while the children play in the square, if the weather's fair. I usually bring them home, tired and happy, just in time for bed.' Bella was beaming as she described her wonderful family and Charles was happy for her, glad for his son, too.

However, it was clear he would have to think of something else to occupy Lottie. Perhaps he should try out the Jovial Grandfather role he'd dreamed up the other day. *Yes, that's the answer!* He and Lottie would go for a little outing, just the two of them. He looked over at her. The cat stretched, then turned round twice and settled itself in her lap again, giving him an excellent idea.

Sunlight was winking playfully on the wet cobbles, after a short, sharp shower, and the Firth of Forth was looking bluer than the sky above it. Charles and Lottie walked down the hill together, her small hand soft and warm in his dry, calloused fingers, pink blossoms bobbing on the trees, her voice chirruping beside him like a little sparrow. His stick tapped the cobbles intermittently and there was a spring in his step.

'You and I, aye Lottie Lulu? Off on an adventure together!' He looked down at her trusting face and grinned his biggest grin. When she smiled back a rush of relief flooded his chest and he realised how anxious he had been about her. Charles began to swing her arm back and forth as though they were two schoolfriends, and the idea made him laugh out loud. Lottie joined in.

'Where are we going, Grandfather?' She skipped every few steps to keep up with his long stride.

'Well now, there's a good question if ever I heard one. If you are referring to this morning rather than life in general, which I'm guessing you are, we are going to try and discover what kind of creature is making that tremendous roaring noise – can you hear it?' He stopped suddenly and bent down, cupping a hand to his ear and making what he hoped might sound like a distant roar, without moving his lips. She giggled.

'Don't be silly Grandfather, it's *you* making that noise!'

'Ah, but Lottie, it *might* just as well be Wallace, don't you think?' He had her attention now and decided to have some fun. 'You know about Wallace the Lion who lives along the road from us, don't you?' She stared at him, her eyes and mouth open wide, and he knew the outing would be a great deal more entertaining than he had anticipated.

'A lion? Like the one in my picture book who lives in the jungle?' she squeaked.

'Exactly so, dear girl, exactly so.'

'Is there a jungle along the road?'

'Not a jungle, no, but there is another kind of place where lions live. It's called the Royal Edinburgh Zoological Gardens.'

A zoo had been opened over ten years ago in the gardens of Broughton Hall and, although Charles had never had the occasion to visit it, he had read numerous comments about it in the newspapers and considered himself well informed.

'Oh! Let's go to the zoo gardens, Grandfather! Can we? Pleeease!' Lottie started jumping up and down and suddenly her colour was quite high.

'We shall certainly go to the Zoological Gardens, my dear. But you must promise not to become too excited. Ha! Now there's an impossible challenge. Especially when you think of all the tigers and monkeys and leopards in there, as well as Morrichy the Military Mascot and the grizzly bears, not to mention the bald cockatoo! There may even be acrobats and a military band as well!'

They turned right at Drummond Place and walked along London Street.

'There it is, Lottie, across the road!' Charles pointed at the elaborate gates, delighted to find himself feeling rather excited for the first time in far too long.

TWENTY-FOUR

Lottie held her grandfather's hand tightly and stared up at a huge animal, the like of which she had never seen or imagined. Morrichy was as big as a building. She was standing right beside him and he was looking at her with wrinkly, friendly eyes. His skin was grey and baggy, as though it were too big for him, and his legs were like four knobbly tree trunks.

She watched in amazement when Morrichy's long, snaky nose picked up a large bundle of straw from the ground and showered it over the soldiers in their red jackets and tall hats who were standing nearby, playing merry tunes. The straw fell like snow and everyone laughed. The soldiers did not seem at all surprised and carried on playing, smiling at the animal as if he were a cheeky friend, shaking off the straw in between blowing their trumpets and banging their drums. A piece of straw found its way inside the neck of Lottie's green woollen cape. It was sharp and prickly on her skin. She pulled it out and dropped it on the ground.

'Roll up, roll up, children, time for the ride of your lives!' a man in a soldier's jacket called. Her grandfather bent over and whispered in her ear.

'Are you brave enough, Lottie, to ride an elephant like Queen

Victoria's little princes and princesses?' She looked at him quizzically. He was always joking and teasing. It was sometimes hard to understand what he meant. Then she noticed two rows of chairs tied to the back of the huge animal and her eyes grew wide again.

'Buy a ticket for her Grandad, why don't you?'

Grandfather winked at her and bought a ticket from the jolly soldier. Lottie waited to see what would happen next. The man waved a stick at the elephant and slowly, slowly, the great beast lowered his huge body onto the dusty ground and knelt in the straw, blinking his little piggy eyes.

'Come along now, don't be shy, children. Who's first?' A boy who was bigger than Lottie ran over to Morrichy and she watched the man show him how to climb onto the chairs. The boy looked very comfortable in his seat; very pleased with himself, too. Then two girls walked over, holding hands and whispering to each other. Lottie let go of her grandfather's hand and followed them.

There were almost as many children sitting on the elephant as she had fingers on both her hands if she left out her thumbs. When they were all sitting comfortably the man shouted at Morrichy to stand up and waved his stick again. The great creature began to rise to his feet, making everyone sway about. Lottie clung very tightly to her seat. One of the girls screamed and her sister put a hand over her mouth. Lottie clamped her own mouth shut to keep her scream inside. The scream wriggled around in her tummy, trying to get out, until the elephant was standing up and the chairs stopped swaying.

Lottie looked down at her grandfather and smiled. He looked so small! He waved at her and she called out, 'Look at me, Grandfather! I'm a princess!'

He lifted his top hat and called back, 'You certainly are, my dear girl, you certainly are!'

TWENTY-FIVE

Charles glanced out of the window. It was just past midday, the sun was shining jauntily from a clear sky, and a steady stream of people were walking up Dublin Street, decked out in their finest. A vast bronze statue of the Duke of Wellington had been erected in front of Register House and there was to be an inauguration ceremony that afternoon. Everyone would be there.

He could hear the family gathering in the hall and went to the looking-glass to straighten his Paisley silk cravat. He combed his hair back from his high forehead, tamed his eyebrows with a licked finger, picked up his hat and went to join them.

Jane and Lottie were tying straw bonnets under their chins with Bella's help and his eldest grandson – another Charles, who went by the name of Chas – was wrestling with the buttons on his jacket. Two-year-old Tommy was still having his morning nap and Mary was going to mind him.

'Here, young Chas, those look tricky – let me help you!' Charles frowned comically at the serious expression on the six-year-old's face as he bent over to button him up. Bella nodded her thanks.

To everyone's surprise and delight Charlie was joining them, even though it was a weekday. The Inland Revenue office was closed, as were all the banks and most of the public offices. No one would be able to work in Charlie's office in any case, with such a hullabaloo going on right outside the windows.

Bella fixed her bonnet at the hall glass then turned to her husband, who was standing by the front door surveying the scene, top hat in one hand, doorknob in the other.

'I think we're ready, now, darling!'

'Excellent! Come along then, everyone, and remember to stick together. We don't want to lose you in the crowds!'

The children skipped down the stairs in front of Bella. Charles put on his hat, took his stick from the hall stand and followed them, leaving his son to pull the door closed behind them.

Lottie slipped her hand into his as they set off up the hill together in the buttery morning sunshine. Jane was walking arm in arm with Bella, and Chas was running to catch up with his father. Soon all six of them had been swept into the crowd.

'Grandfather?' Lottie tugged at his hand, her face turned up towards his.

'Aha, Lottie Lulu! Do I sense a question poised on the tip of your tongue, preparing to leap at me like a puddock from a lily pad?' He gave her hand a squeeze.

'What's a puddock, Grandfather?'

'Why, it's a frog, of course – unless it's been kissed. Then it would be a prince, I suppose!' She giggled gratifyingly before allowing the puddock to leap from its lily pad.

'Is today Friday?'

'It certainly is, my dear, which means tomorrow will be Saturday!'

'Can I visit Izzie again tomorrow when the cousins are at Granny Winter's?' Her expression was full of longing and Charles guessed the little girl might be in need of cuddles.

'I don't see why not! In fact, I'll take you there myself.' He began to swing her arm back and forth and she skipped a few steps, her face brightening into a smile.

It was almost midsummer and the day had grown quite hot. All along George Street Hackney carriages and cabs were competing for space to set down their passengers, the drivers' shouts rising hoarsely above the din of hooves striking cobbles like flints on steel. St Andrew's Square was milling with fashionably elegant ladies in wide, swirling crinolines, twirling colourful parasols, arm in arm with fine, spruced-up gentlemen, all making their way cock-a-hoop towards Princes Street. Charles squinted up at Viscount Melville on top of his ridiculously tall column and chuckled, wondering what the 'Grand Manager of Scotland' would make of it all from his lofty viewpoint if he could speak.

'This way Little Lottie Poppet, come along, not far to go now.' Charles pulled Lottie's hand under his arm and she looked up from under her bonnet, smiling. '*Tuck yourself under my arm, Mattie, there's no disgrace in a bailie walking hand in arm with gentle blood.*' He laughed at her confused expression, patting her hand and promising himself he must read *Rob Roy* to his grandchildren soon. It was about time they were acquainted with the Bailie.

Charles and Lottie pushed on through the throng, keeping the others just in view, and turned left into Princes Street where they joined the huge assembly in front of Register House. People were hanging out of every window and sitting on all the rooftops, platforms constructed for the occasion were overflowing. Charles could not remember such crowds since the inauguration of Sir Walter's monumental monument almost six years ago – or perhaps since the visit of King George thirty years ago. It was hard to believe thirty-seven years, to the day, had passed since the famous victory at Waterloo. That memorable year, 1815, was also the year Charles felt his life had begun in earnest, the year he became an actor, the year he met Charlotte O'Keefe.

The Iron Duke himself would not be in attendance, being of an advanced age and not in the best of health. However, there was a large group of retired officers on the steps of Register House, all decked out in their uniforms and shining medals, some of them proudly sporting laurel sprigs in their bonnets to indicate they were veterans of Waterloo.

Charles noticed plenty of not so finely turned-out army pensioners among the milling throng too, many of them minus arms and legs. He steered Lottie towards the theatre, hoping she would not be distressed by the sight of the maimed soldiers. Black and red plumes could be seen bobbing above the heads of hundreds of people gathered on the North Bridge and Charles guessed a Highland regiment had been brought in to keep the peace. He was delighted to see a military band stationed right outside the theatre, even more delighted when it struck up a familiar tune as they approached.

Mr Horatio Lloyd, the Theatre Royal's current lessee, had invited Charles and his family to join his gathering on the balcony. There would be an excellent view of the proceedings from there, as well as seats for those with weary legs, and refreshments to keep them all going for the duration. It was still only just gone one o'clock, and the unveiling ceremony was not scheduled until three.

Young Arthur Lloyd soon opened the door to Charles's knock and they all stepped gratefully into the cool, dark lobby. Arthur was a cheeky-looking lad with a strong, wide face, a mop of dark hair and a snappy way of talking.

'Follow me, fellow thespians. Allow me to lead you through a magic portal onto our Balcony of Delights!' He scampered up the staircase and stopped on the first-floor landing beside the three long sash windows at the front of the building. The lower half of the central window had been pushed up as far as it would go and there was a low stool on the floor in front of it. Young Arthur gestured for everyone to step through the window and the children laughed and scrambled outside without a second thought. Charles, ever the gentleman, turned to Bella.

'After you my dear! I must confess I am curious to see how this unusual arrangement will work for a lady decked in skirts of such considerable volume!' Bella smiled broadly at him, as though eager to rise to his challenge. Then she gathered her bronze and coffee-striped hooped skirts in her left hand, took her husband's proffered hand in her right, dipped her head elegantly and was through the window at once with no trouble. Charlie followed her and Arthur turned to Charles, raising an eyebrow in perfect imitation of Charles's trademark expression.

'Well now, young Arthur,' Charles said with a chuckle, 'when I was about your age I used to stand outside this building and dream of scrambling up onto the roof of the portico to see which window an unfortunate sailor once called his 'porthole' and climbed through to evade the necessity of buying a ticket. Never did I dream I would be scrambling through that same porthole in my dotage! Ah well, needs must!' He passed his stick through the window to Lottie, who was watching anxiously, took the boy's hand in a firm grip, held onto the window frame with his other hand and hoisted himself onto the stool with a grunt. Then he bent his head, stepped through the 'porthole' and found himself standing on the broad balcony, blinking in the brightness of the sun and feeling mightily pleased with himself. Just as he had always imagined, the view was magnificent.

'Ah Mr Mackay, my good man! I was hoping you would come along and bring your delightful family with you!' Mr Lloyd shook Charles's hand enthusiastically with both of his, then clapped him on the back and ushered him towards a chair, pointing out the sweets and cakes and lemonade to Bella, winking at the children and saluting Charlie.

'Help yourselves now, everyone! Arthur will assist you should there be anything else you require, or young Robert here – won't ya boys!' He grabbed another son, not much older than Arthur, by his shirt sleeve, making faces at them both until they all burst out laughing. Charles sank into the proffered chair and gratefully accepted a cool lemonade. The band struck up another tune with a catchy drumbeat and he closed his eyes with a satisfied sigh.

Despite the misfortunes that had beset him since he'd taken on the lease of the Theatre Royal, Mr Lloyd still had the look of the successful comedian he had been, with his jolly, round face and a moustache like a brush. He never complained about his troubles; by all accounts, Charles reflected, his difficulties probably stemmed from over-enthusiasm, and a generous heart. There were only two months left on his lease now, as he kept telling his guests, *So I thought I might as well make use of the old place for a party!* Charles wondered if he would return to London, though he had lived and worked in Edinburgh for so many years now, perhaps it had become like home.

Arthur began to entertain the guests with impish impressions of various dignitaries strutting about on the platform below. Charles found the impudence of the lad's impersonations highly amusing, although perhaps his mockery of Major General Napier, who was sitting sedately on his horse beneath the portico, was taking things a little too far. The man had lost his arm at the Battle of Waterloo and was a hero. It was a loss that should be respected, not ridiculed. However, the lad was young and would soon learn. Arthur had his father's famous comic walk down to a fine art as well. Charles gave him a hearty cheer and clapped his hands.

'Well done, Arthur, good show!' The boy gave a theatrical bow then disappeared through the window to answer another thump on the door. Charles stood up and stretched his back, then ambled over to join his son at the balustrade.

'Well then, Charlie, here we are on top of the old portico with the finest view in town! Did you know this new statue is yet another triumph from young John Steell?'

'I heard as much, Father, yes – he seems to be a most prolific sculptor.'

'Quite so, Charlie, quite so. Did you also know he lived near us on Calton Hill, many years ago?' Charlie shook his head. 'I thought you'd be too young to remember the Steells. A very artistic family. A very *large* family! Hmm.' Charlie nodded. 'Have I ever told you about our other illustrious neighbour, Mrs Maclehose at No. 14 – or Clarinda, as Robert Burns used to address her in his love letters?' Charlie gave him a half smile.

'You certainly have, Father, many times!'

'Ah!' Charles smiled back ruefully, glad the slight frostiness that had remained between them about the flat seemed to be thawing.

'I met old Thomas Calder on the stair the other day by the way, Charlie. I meant to tell you before. Had a bit of a chat with him about his idea to bring us all back to our old flat. He seemed genuine enough about wanting the best for us.' Charles paused for a moment. 'I think I may have been a bit harsh on you about all that. Sorry old boy, I fear I was somewhat overwhelmed by the thought of facing all those memories. Not my favourite activity, dwelling on the past!' He smiled brightly and Charlie nodded again, this time with a broader smile. That was better. *Good to clear the air.*

There was a commotion at the window and Mr and Mrs Wyndham emerged with their little girl. Charles raised his glass to them.

'The Wyndhams are doing a fine job with the Adelphi, you know Charlie. I was so surprised at Murray's funeral when Wyndham asked me to perform there for a few nights, though. I do believe it's done me the power of good, getting back on the stage. I must admit I had begun to think it might never happen again.' He took another sip of his drink, smacking his lips and looking down at Lottie with wide eyes to make her laugh.

She had been stuck to his side like a little shadow all day. Charles wished she would run and play with her cousins. It was taking her much longer than he had expected to recover her confidence. All the other children on the balcony – most of whom seemed to belong to Mr Lloyd and his patient wife – were racing up and down in an excitable manner. Charles had heard sugar could have that effect on children and smiled to himself at the fun of it, looking round to see if his son would order his offspring to sit down quietly. Much to his surprise Charlie was still watching the comings and goings below and seemed oblivious of his children.

Charles went back to his chair and Mr Lloyd flopped into the chair beside him with a plateful of fancy cakes.

'I hear you have a son who fancies himself an actor, too, Mr Mackay. I'm not at all keen for Arthur to take to the stage, but he's a determined sort of chap, has quite a talent, too. I expect he will wear me down eventually and I'll give him a hand up of sorts. After all, his brother Fred is already acting, so it would hardly be fair of me to stop him. What about your son, Mr Mackay, Hector's his name isn't it?' His host took a bite of cake and looked at Charles, chewing expectantly.

'Well now, Mr Lloyd, since you ask, Hector has hankered after the stage – or should I say hankered after *attention* – ever since he could walk. Like yourself I've always been unhappy with the idea of him following in my footsteps and I must confess I haven't given him much encouragement.' Charles pushed his hair back from his forehead and ploughed on. 'Unlike yourself, though, I don't believe my son has much talent. In fact, it's been rather excruciating to hear of his recent exploits in Liverpool, where he introduced himself to Mr McKenzie, a dear friend of mine, without consulting me, in the hope of gaining an introduction at the Theatre Royal.' Charles felt uncomfortable with the direction the conversation was taking and began to cast about for a distraction. 'Aha! I do believe a procession is approaching!' He stood up, smiling politely at Mr Lloyd and wishing he had kept his thoughts about Hector to himself. He walked back over to the balustrade and looked down at the milling crowds. *That was some surprise McKenzie sprang on me though, must be all of fifteen years ago, although it seems more like five.*

He had visited Liverpool's Theatre Royal several times over the years, acting in various productions, and in 1837 he had been invited to supper on the last night by one of the theatre's main supporters, Mr McKenzie, at his home in Cable Street – just a few minutes' walk from the theatre. He had been anticipating a quiet supper with McKenzie and his dear lady wife, but the door had opened onto quite a gathering. As if that were not surprise enough, after supper McKenzie had called for quiet and drawn Charles's attention to a side table where a red velvet cloth was draped over something the shape of a small box. McKenzie withdrew the cloth with a flourish, to applause from the assembled friends, then presented a beautiful gold snuff box to Charles, indicating that he should open it at once. Inside was an inscription: 'Presented to CHARLES MACKAY, Esq, of the Theatre Royal, Edinburgh, by a few friends in Liverpool, admirers of his professional talents and private virtues.' It was one of his most treasured possessions.

Hundreds, if not thousands, of freemasons were marching down the Earthen Mound onto Princes Street in their white gloves and aprons, banners waving, colourful insignia on display. It was quite a spectacle. Lottie's little hand slipped into his and Charles hoisted her up to stand on his feet so she could see over the balustrade. The band below was playing again and all along Princes Street the crowds were parting, like the Red Sea, to let the Masons through. The front of the procession arrived at the canvas-draped statue and formed up while the Grand Master joined the other dignitaries on the platform.

There was a long prayer, followed by a masonic ritual involving a level, a square and a plummet, culminating in three bashes from a mallet. Charles watched his eldest grandson's face, smiling at the intense focus of his attention, then Lottie began to wriggle and he bent to whisper in her ear.

'D'you see that big green cloth down there?' She nodded. 'What do you think is hiding underneath it?' She shrugged her little shoulders and looked up at him, her head on one side. 'It's a *huge* statue of a duke on a beautiful horse, Lottie – a very special horse called Copenhagen.'

'Copenhagen,' she whispered back.

'Yes. Do you want to see him?' She nodded enthusiastically. 'Well now, if you can just wait for the important gentleman to finish his speech, I think he will pull the cloth off very soon and you will be able to see the lovely Copenhagen, and his rider too. What do you think of that?' She nodded again thoughtfully and stopped fidgeting.

The canvas was whisked off at last, revealing the horse rearing up on its hind legs in a miracle of gravity-defying engineering. The duke himself looked serenely in control, sitting astride his favourite steed, calmly directing his forces and pointing a finger directly at the theatre. The band began to play 'See, the Conquering Hero Comes!', and, from the vast sea of people stretching as far as the eye could see, huge waves of glorious singing rolled towards them.

There were three cheers for the talented sculptor, then a cannon was fired from the castle, and a volley of artillery replied from the direction of the Salisbury Crags. A peal of thunder broke over the castle and a few drops of rain began to fall the moment the cannons fell silent, as if perfectly choreographed by a grand theatrical manager. Charles silently saluted his old friend Murray, even now orchestrating from the heavens.

The applause and cheering continued unabated in the street below and Charles had a strange urge to take a bow from the balcony. He laughed at his foolishness, and when Lottie looked up at him he had an idea.

'Would you like to see inside the theatre, little one?'

TWENTY-SIX

Lottie held her grandfather's hand tightly in case she lost her way. They walked down a dim passage and through several doors, then brushed past a long curtain and arrived in an echoey room, lit only by a beam of light coming through a small window high up. It was too dim to see the walls or the ceiling, but she could tell it was enormous by the sound of her grandfather's voice and the ruffle of cool air on her neck. There was a dusty smell and the floorboards wobbled under her feet.

'We are standing on the stage, Lottie. In front of us are rows and rows of empty seats reaching right up to the ceiling! This is where I act in my plays, poppet, where I sing my songs and make people laugh.'

Lottie squeezed his hand and stayed quiet to see what would happen next. A lamp came on, high up, and she could see some seats beside it. Then another lamp was lit on the other side of the room.

'Good old Arthur – what a lad! I thought he'd play along with my game! Look Lottie, can you begin to see the size of the place?' Another lamp came on nearby and she could just make out all the seats stretching up to the roof, as her grandfather had described. Suddenly he let go of her hand, stepped forward and began to sing loudly:

'Fa la la la la!' The deep notes flew out of his mouth, growing bigger and louder until they seemed to bounce off the walls all around her.

'How did you do that, Grandfather?'

'Well now, little Lottie Lulu, I just took a deep breath and let my voice come out. The theatre did the rest. Do you want to try?' Another light flared brightly.

'Will that be that enough, Mr Mackay?' A voice came from somewhere very high. Lottie craned her neck to see if it was the boy who had helped them through the magic window.

'That's just grand, Arthur. Many thanks! We'll not be long – give us five more minutes, maybe, then come and douse them, if you would be so good!'

'Right you are, sir!' Her grandfather took her hand again.

'Let's sing together, shall we, Lottie?' She nodded. She really wanted to know what her voice would sound like in the huge theatre. *Will it fly up to the ceiling and swirl around like Grandfather's?*

'Ready? Let's sing fa la la la la. One, two three …' She opened her mouth. Nothing came out at first, but when she tried again she made a little squeak, followed by a smoother sound. Soon they were singing together, her piping voice flitting around his deep, rolling notes like a little bird fluttering around a great honking goose.

'Jolly well done, Lottie Lulu! Bravo!'

Suddenly she wanted to hear her voice on its own. She dropped his hand and heaved in a huge gulp of air. When she opened her mouth to sing it felt as though a bell were ringing in her throat. The sounds she made curled high up to the ceiling, the words loud and clear. She was completely amazed. It was the most wonderful feeling Lottie had ever felt and she never wanted to stop.

Her grandfather started to sing with her again, and Lottie wondered how he knew the special song her mammy had taught her:

'The bells rung,
And she sung
Ding, dong, dell,
It is well!'

TWENTY-SEVEN

Chants of 'Mackay! Mackay! Mackay!' flooded the theatre, along with the hearty thumps of stamping feet. Charles was attending the opening night of the Theatre Royal under its new management, and he had fondly imagined a seat in a box to one side of the auditorium would be discreet if he sat well back. Apparently not! Most of the audience had risen to their feet and were demanding that he acknowledge their tributes. Reluctantly, he pushed himself to his feet with both hands and stepped forward into the light, transforming himself into the jolly comedian they were all applauding. He gave three comical waves and an exaggerated bow, then considered it safe to resume his seat in the shadows, hoping they would turn their attention to someone else.

The packed audience had been amusing itself for some time now, recognising any well-known person in the house and bestowing lively tributes. The new managers of the theatre were a pair of young actors, and Charles wished them well. It was not an easy thing to manage a theatre and continue to act, as he well knew from his own bitter experience with Jones in Perth all those years ago.

The boxes, pit and galleries were full, though, the old place smart with fresh paint and full of light. Charles was surprised to find himself feeling quite emotional when the conductor walked on and was greeted by enthusiastic applause. When the orchestra struck up a lively rendition of the familiar overture to Auber's popular opera, *Masaniello,* he sat back, closed his eyes, and relaxed. The overture was followed, inevitably, by 'God Save The Queen', during which Charles spotted his old friend Emma Nicol amongst all the other actors on-stage. He decided to wait for her afterwards and find out how she was faring. She was one of the last of the old troupe from those early days in Edinburgh and was very good company. It had been too long since they'd met, apart from briefly at William Murray's funeral.

The music subsided and one of the young managers took it upon himself to give a tediously long speech. He was reasonably amusing, but Charles tired of him when he began to compare himself with his predecessors. The first play was a comedy about something and nothing. It was followed by dancing, then a farce. Charles was unimpressed. He slipped away at the end of *Binks the Bagman*, wondering if he would bother coming to the Theatre Royal again. Perhaps he should have gone to watch *The Merchant of Venice* at the Adelphi. The Wyndhams were doing a good job there.

Outside it was still light, the September air surprisingly balmy. He stood across the road from the theatre, leaning on his stick, nodding politely to people who tipped their hats and shouted greetings to him as they left the pit and gallery doors. The fine folk coming out of the box door did not notice him. They were only interested in being handed quickly into the hackney carriages jostling to line up nearby, horses facing west, an exasperated officer of police attempting to keep order.

Emma appeared suddenly, striding up the side of the theatre from the stage door, her maroon velvet cloak swinging open to reveal an emerald-green silk dress shimmering delightfully under the gas lights that blazed brightly from the portico. She saw him at once and raised an elegantly gloved hand, her strong, familiar features lighting up.

'Charles, my dear, what a pleasant surprise – it's been too long!' She was a tall, graceful woman, the same height as Charles, perhaps very slightly taller. She took his arm, planted a kiss on his cheek and he noticed her perfume – something exotic and spicy that he could not place. It was a pleasantly still evening and they walked companionably along Princes Street, arm in arm, talking and laughing about the evening's entertainments. After a while Charles began to look about for a cab.

'Are you still in the same old place on the Southside, my dear? I should like to see you home, if I may.'

'How very gallant of you, Charles! But I moved in with my aged aunts in North Union Place about six months ago. We can walk there in no time.' She smiled fondly at him and they turned into St Andrew Street, continuing in companionable silence as they skirted the wide square.

'I've moved recently as well – back to Dublin Street, for my sins, No. 23 again, as it turns out. It would appear we've been neighbours since May, Emma!' She laughed heartily and Charles noticed the lines laughter had carved on her face. He patted her hand affectionately, wondering about the lines that would have creased Charlotte's face by now, had she lived as long as her friend.

'The night is young, Emma. Perhaps we could partake of a wee dram together if you have such a thing? I've a mind for some reminiscing – what do you say?' They turned right into York Place and he tucked her arm under his, as he used to do on-stage when he was the Bailie and she was Mattie. Just round the corner from Picardy Place she stopped and fished a key out of her reticule.

No. 17 Union Place was not at all how Charles had imagined Emma's home would be. There was a musty smell inside the dark, chilly hallway and no rug on the flagstone floor. The bottle-green walls were lined with large, forbidding portraits interspersed with unlit sconces covered in drips of cold, grey wax. Emma led him up a flight of well-worn stone stairs to the first floor, where warm light was spilling extravagantly into the landing through an open door.

'Now then, come along in, Charles, and we shall have that dram. We have so much to talk about!'

Emma's parlour was a marvel. Gorgeously coloured glass lamps sat on little side tables and candles flickered brightly in silver holders on the overmantel. Deep red velvet curtains draped the tall windows and a fire was burning brightly in the grate. Her delightfully mysterious perfume filled the room – exotic and spicy. *Bergamot, perhaps – or maybe sandalwood, yes, that's it! Sandalwood!* The walls were painted the colour of peaches and, much to Charles's surprise, one of them was plastered with old playbills. Elaborately decorated costumes and colourful feather boas hung haphazardly on the back of the door and there was a jewellery stand on a large console, bedecked with dozens of necklaces and bangles. Several wide-brimmed hats were piled on top of one another on a shelf, their long, coloured feathers intertwined like the tail of an exotic bird.

'Ha! You should see your face, Charles! This is my little haven in a house full of elderly aunts from the previous century. The maid keeps it bright for me coming home. She knows it cheers me.' Emma removed an open book from a brown velvet chesterfield and plumped up a crimson silk cushion, indicating to Charles he should take his seat there, beside the fire.

'You'll have gathered I'm still signed to the Theatre Royal, Charles, and now I have these Young Turks as my managers! We shall have to see how they fare. Better than poor old Mr Lloyd, hopefully! My debut with them is to be on September the 18th. We're putting on *Waverley*. Wish me luck!' She was standing by a mahogany wall cupboard, taking out two crystal glasses and a decanter. 'But what of you? Tell me everything that's happened, Charles, since your terrible tragedy in the spring.' Emma smoothed her green silk skirts and sat on a lyre-back chair opposite Charles, placing the glasses and decanter on a low table and pouring the whisky.

'You're looking well, at least, which means there must be a few bright spots in your life. Have you been back on the stage again, Charles, or is it the grandchildren, perhaps?' She handed him a small glass with a generous measure and settled herself back in her chair, nursing her glass with a mischievous smile on her face.

'Wyndham managed to persuade me back on the stage once or twice at the end of May, but other than that there's been nothing since I stopped in March.'

She looked at him with sympathy for a moment, her head on one side, her beringed fingers wrapped round her glass. Then playfulness lit up her face again.

'I knew it! It's the grandchildren, isn't it! I understand children can have the most marvellous effect on melancholy.'

'Indeed they can, Emma, indeed they can!' Charles smiled at her fondly. 'You know, it's a great comfort sitting here with you, I must say.' Emma nodded thoughtfully. 'You meant a great deal to Charlotte. She missed you terribly when you went to London.' Charles took a sip of whisky and closed his eyes while it slipped down his throat like fire.

'Dear Charlotte. Such a beautiful, strong and talented woman. I miss her every day, even now. I still regret that I wasn't there for her when she was so terribly ill …'

'We must all follow our dreams, Emma. She always thought of you fondly, wished you well. But you came back when your mother died, and that was a great comfort to *me* – to us both, I hope.' He gave her a sheepish smile and she blushed slightly. Then she leaned forward and laid a soft hand on his, leaving it there for a moment.

'Exactly so, Charles, exactly so.' Her voice was deep and thick with emotion when she spoke again. 'You know everyone is still talking about you at the Royal? *Charles Mackay – undisputed star of the Theatre Royal.* They were good times.' After a pause she looked at him boldly and smiled. 'Indeed, I believe I shall drink to The Real Mackay!' Emma took a generous swig of her whisky, feigning surprise with lifted eyebrows until he laughed and proposed a toast in return, bursting into song with Thomas Moore's familiar lyrics.

'And here's to *The Last Rose of Summer, left blooming alone, all her lovely companions are faded and gone* … including me!'

'Leaving me, as old as the century, with all the Old Lady roles and a bunch of young actors who hardly know their craft!' She made herself look old – eyes narrowed to slits, mouth turned down, shoulders hunched – then sat up and changed the subject abruptly while he was still chuckling.

'So you've gone over to the Adelphi now, Charles?'

'Well, I wouldn't put it quite like that – I don't expect I shall perform there again, or anywhere else, for that matter.'

'The Caledonian, we used to call it, d'you remember – the Pantheon before that.'

'It was called Jones and Parker's Circus when I was a youngster, then the Equestrian Circus. Did you know that old Henry Johnston fell hopelessly in love with his wife there, when she was performing on horseback all those years ago? Neither of them were much more than children at the time.'

'I've heard that too! It was Corri's Concert Rooms when we first arrived here from London. I must have been about three years old.'

'Ha! It's always been a place for marvellously illegitimate theatre, hasn't it? Horses, lions, child prodigies, contortionists, dancers – clowns swinging from the ceiling! Used to be no holds barred for theatres without a royal patent, back in my heyday.'

'D'you remember how furious Murray was when they changed the law about ten years ago and made it a free-for-all?' Emma was smiling at the memory. 'He was livid that he still had eight years left on his patent and insisted he should be refunded – to no avail, of course. Maybe that's why he took on the Adelphi as well, to try and keep his monopoly in Edinburgh.'

'Very likely so. Ah well, we can't really control what happens in our lives, can we – especially the increasing speed of the passing years!' Charles pulled a wizened grimace to emphasise his own advancing age and they both hooted with laughter.

When Charles went home, much later, he felt greatly revived and a full moon accompanied him all the way to his front door.

Late the next morning Charles arrived home with the *Scotsman* under his arm and noticed a card had been left for him on the console in the hall. He turned it over and saw Mr Wyndham had called. Charles went straight to the kitchen to find out more. Bella was helping Mary set the table, her sleeves rolled up and her slippery cinnamon hair falling from its pins on one side. Little Tommy was tugging at his mother's apron, whining for attention.

'Ah, Bella, I thought I'd find you in here. Are the other children still at their studies in the parlour?'

She smiled wearily, pushing her stray hair behind her ear. 'They should be finished shortly, Charles. Maggie is staying for lunch today, maybe she's keeping them working a few minutes longer than usual. She's brought us a lovely ham from our brother's shop.' Charles had noticed the deliciously savoury smell the moment he came in the front door but had been distracted by the card from Wyndham.

'Of course, dear, how wonderful!' He held up the card. 'I was just wondering if you knew anything about this? Were you in when Mr Wyndham came to call this morning, by any chance?'

'Yes, I was, Charles. He said I was to ask you to come by the Adelphi later today, if you have the time. He has a proposal for you.'

'Right. Thank you, Bella. A proposal, you say?' Charles decided he would have to contain his curiosity until after lunch, Maggie's ham smelt far too delicious to miss.

It was a ten-minute walk to the theatre at the top of Leith Walk and Charles arrived at the stage door shortly after two o'clock. He was let in by the man in the watch-box and found Mr Wyndham in the green room. Wyndham was a tall, slender man with fashionably floppy dark hair, a long straight nose and fulsome sideburns that almost met under his chin. He had large brown eyes and was smartly turned out in a navy coat, white waistcoat and green Paisley silk cravat.

'Ah, Mr Mackay, I see you received my message! Thank you so much for coming. Would you care to join me in my office?' Mr and Mrs Wyndham had been managing the Adelphi since William Murray had retired from the management of both Edinburgh's main theatres. He had been a hard act to follow, but the Wyndhams seemed to be making more of a success of the Adelphi over the past nine months than poor old Horatio Lloyd had done with the Royal. Lloyd had gone bankrupt shortly after his midsummer balcony party and was currently languishing in Holyrood's debtors' sanctuary with his family, licking his wounds.

The Wyndhams, both actors, seemed to be full of energy and inspiration. Mrs Wyndham had a particular talent in training children to perform, and it occurred to Charles as he followed Wyndham up the stairs that Lottie might benefit from joining one of Mrs Wyndham's troupes of children for a pantomime at some stage – when she was older, of course. It was something to consider, at any rate, especially as she had enjoyed singing on the theatre stage so much. Her enthusiasm to recite lines from *Rob Roy* when he had read the play to the children recently had surprised him, and she had mastered a grand Scots brogue in no time.

Charles took a seat facing the desk, which was littered with letters, scripts and open books. 'I must confess you have me curious about this proposal of yours, Wyndham.'

'Yes, well – firstly, please forgive my muddle!' Wyndham laughed nervously and began sorting his papers into piles. Charles decided to put him at his ease.

'I would like to thank you, Mr Wyndham, Robert, for your kind invitation to take part in your excellent productions here last May. Despite my initial reluctance it turned out that treading the boards again was just the tonic I needed after my terrible loss. I must say, I have been feeling much more myself again since then.'

The young man smiled and leaned forward, steepling his fingers. 'I'm very glad to hear that, Mr Mackay, very glad indeed.' He cleared his throat and continued earnestly. 'You may be aware, Mr Mackay, that we are in the process of refurbishing this old place – yet again!' Charles nodded and they both chuckled. 'The grand reopening is to be on Saturday, November the 6th, and we were wondering – that is, Rosina and I were talking and we thought – well, to put it bluntly, we would be greatly honoured if you would consider taking to the stage again for the winter season with us here at the Adelphi Theatre.' Wyndham pulled a kerchief from his waistcoat pocket and mopped his glistening forehead, his eyes searching Charles's for a response.

'Well now, Robert, this is indeed a turn-up for the books! Not what I was expecting at all! Indeed, I had quite reconciled myself to a life beyond the stage since those few engagements here in the spring ...' Charles was prevaricating to give himself time to think. A look of disappointment appeared on the young man's face, and before he knew what he was doing, Charles found himself agreeing.

It turned out that Wyndham was hoping he would take the role of Sir Pertinax MacSycophant in the play *Man of the World* to begin the season. It was a role he had never played before, except short excerpts for the purpose of mimicry. He could still remember the first time he had seen the play, from the wings, less than a year after he and Charlotte had arrived in Edinburgh. Henry Johnston had played Sir Pertinax and Charlotte had played the nanny. Charles had three whole weeks to perfect the part, and he could hardly wait to begin.

'Now it's all agreed, Mr Mackay, I should very much like to announce your forthcoming season next week, if I may?' Charles nodded his agreement as he rose to take his leave.

A letter was waiting for him on the console in the front hall when he arrived home. He tore it open at once.

'Well, I'll be blowed! What in heaven's name is going on today?' Charles strode straight into the kitchen in search of an audience, his son being at work and the children at their schooling again in the parlour. 'Listen to this, Bella, you'll not believe it!' His daughter-in-law wiped her floury hands on her pinafore and pulled out a chair for him. Charles declined it with a brief shake of his head. He was far too agitated to sit down. So Bella sat on it herself, folding her hands in her lap and looking up at him expectantly.

'What an extraordinary day this has turned out to be, Bella! Not only have I been offered the whole winter season at the Adelphi, but I have in my hand a letter from Edmund Glover, manager of Glasgow's Theatre Royal!' Charles was pacing up and down the kitchen, which was not a great distance and took him only four strides in each direction. He paused for a response, one bushy eyebrow raised, eyes gleaming.

'Is it another invitation, by any chance?'

He resumed his pacing. 'Exactly so, Bella! He has invited me to join him next month! The plays are to be *Rob Roy* – of course! – *Guy Mannering* and *Heart of Mid-Lothian*!' He paused again for dramatic effect.

'Oh, Charles, that is all very wonderful! Although it does

sound rather overwhelming – possibly even a little too much for someone of your mature years. Do you really think you can work in both theatres at once?' Charles sat down at the table, his shoulders slumping a little.

'Ha! You're probably right, my dear! Indeed, you've put your finger on rather a sore point, Bella, I must confess, by mentioning my age. It has been bothering me recently. Although I'm aware my allotted three score years and ten will soon be completed, I'm not entirely sure *when* that will be.'

'What do you mean?'

'It may surprise you to learn, Bella, I've always been unsure of my precise age – our father never wrote anything down nor marked our birthdays in any way. I'm afraid dear William died without knowing his age – though he was far too young, I must say – and I fear Peter will too, wherever he's washed up these days. It's a dashed uncomfortable feeling, not knowing such a thing.'

'Oh Charles, I'm sorry to hear that. It must have been so hard for your father, looking after you all on his own.' Bella, picked up the cat and settled it on her knee, giving it long, firm strokes from the white patch on the back of its head to its sleek black rump. Charles watched her, narrowing his eyes slightly.

'Did Charlie ever tell you about my affidavit, by any chance, Bella?'

'No, I don't recall him mentioning anything like that.'

He drummed his fingers on the table for a moment.

'It was shortly after John Shiels died, leaving me all his debts and forcing me out of my rather enjoyable semi-retirement. The press resumed writing copious amounts of drivel and speculation about me, of course, all of them taking Lockart's *Life of Sir Walter Scott* as their source regarding my origins. It infuriated me. I didn't want the world to think I was born in Glasgow. In the words of King James, I'm a real Edinburgh gutter-bluid. So I decided to put a stop to it.' Bella poured some tea for him and the cat jumped to the floor at the disturbance, stalking out of the kitchen with its tail in the air.

'What did you do?'

He took a sip of tea and gathered himself for what amounted to a confession.

'I was in the office of John Stoddart, Justice of the Peace, putting a statement together for my affidavit – he's quite an intimidating man, you know. Well, he took me off guard by suddenly insisting we needed to include my date and place of birth, and the date I went to Glasgow. I can tell you, I broke into a sweat!'

'Oh my goodness, Charles, what on earth did you do?'

He spread out his fingers on the table and studied the back of his gnarly hand: swollen joints, mottled skin, blue veins.

'I stood there like a fool, Bella, frantically working backwards from the year I had joined the volunteers, which I think was 1805, imagining myself to have been about eighteen at the time. I blurted out that I was born on the north side of Edinburgh's High Street in October 1787, that we moved to Glasgow when I was about nine and I stayed there about five years, after which I was a wanderer in many lands, before settling back in Edinburgh in 1818.' Charles looked up into Bella's kind, familiar face and felt such a sense of relief he burst out laughing, slapping the flat of his hand on the wooden table. 'Ha! As if matters! I signed it, I agreed that copies should be sent to all the national papers, then I left the office and only began to do the arithmetic as I walked down the street! A fourteen-year-old boy wandering in many lands – what kind of a person is that? Not me, anyway! Never mind.'

'It hardly matters anymore though, does it Charles, life goes on, people forget.' He took a noisy slurp of tea and nodded thoughtfully. Then the letter from Glasgow caught his eye and he was just reaching across the table for it when Mary came in from the scullery, wiping her hands on her apron. He grinned a welcome and picked up the letter.

'Be that as it may, Bella, I'm going to accept both invitations, however old I am! I'll talk to the Wyndhams regarding the juggling of dates, and we have the railway these days, which will help us make it all work! I could stay with William's son, Lauchlan. He's a good sort. Been to see me a few times at the Glasgow Theatre Royal, writes to me now and then. He's making a good success of his printing business, by all accounts.' He stood up and began pacing the room again, turning to Mary with a flourish to declare, 'It seems The Real Mackay is back, Mary! Ha!' Charles was almost beside himself with excitement by this time and gratefully accepted Mary's offer of a hot brandy. After a sip and a pause for breath a new thought occurred to him and he grinned wider than a cat with a bowl of cream.

'I do believe the children should come and watch me on my opening night at the Adelphi!'

Three weeks later, on Saturday evening, Charles walked along to Picardy Place and stopped to gaze at the refurbished Adelphi. The theatre was lit up with such an abundance of beautiful lamps it looked like a castle on a hill, its elegant portico and front windows facing down the wide avenue of Leith Walk. It had already attracted a large crowd, with over an hour still to go before the doors were opened. Charles had no doubt the grand opening night would be a sell-out. *Good for them!* In two days' time he would be taking to the stage in there again himself, and his grandchildren would be sitting at the front, watching him act for the first time. Excitement surged up from the pit of his stomach and he laughed at himself, still so inspired to be stepping onto the stage and entertaining the crowds at his advanced age.

Charles wondered whether to see if Emma was at home, but instead he turned for home and an early night. In the distance a leerie was carrying his ladder from one streetlamp to the next, leaving little circles of misty light in his wake.

TWENTY-EIGHT

Lottie and her cousins gathered in the front hall on Monday evening, dressed in their finest. Aunty Maggie was there too, looking very pretty in her hooped gown of cream silk with sprigs of purple flowers all over it. She had a neat, pale green spencer around her shoulders and her dark hair was piled on top of her head. Lottie could tell her aunty was excited by the smile she was trying to hide.

'What's in your bag?' Chas asked her, pulling at the embroidered reticule dangling from Aunty Maggie's waist.

'Tickets and sweeties, and you'll get neither unless you're on your best behaviour for me tonight, young man!' She ruffled his head fondly with a gloved hand.

Even Tommy was coming, although it was already past his bedtime and he would probably fall asleep in the theatre. The entertainment was going to be three hours long, including intermissions, so it was likely they would all fall asleep before the end, according to Aunty Bella. Aunty Maggie was taking them as Uncle Charlie and Aunty Bella had another engagement they *simply could not miss.*

'Are you quite sure you'll be able to manage by yourself, Maggie?' Aunty Bella was tying Jane's pink bonnet under her chin and looking anxious. Lottie smoothed her hand over the soft blue velvet of her borrowed cape and did a half twirl to make her pink and lilac-striped dress swirl out below her knees. Jane had been so kind to her when she chose which outfit to borrow. Lottie decided she would sleep in her cousin's bed from now on. Mary had never once sent her away this past year, but every morning Lottie woke up in Jane's bed anyway, so she thought she might just as well sleep there all night, now they were good friends.

Grandfather had told them a few things about the silly man he would be acting so they could understand some of the story. He was quite a nasty man, with such a funny name that none of the children could say it without twisting their tongues into a muddle of giggling.

Once they were all wrapped warmly against the November chill they clattered down the stairs and walked to the Adelphi Theatre together, Aunty Maggie pushing Tommy in his perambulator. It was not very far from Dublin Street.

The theatre was all lit up. It looked so beautiful, they stopped and gazed at it for a moment before crossing the wide street.

'It's like fairyland!' Lottie cooed under her breath. Jane was holding her hand and gave it a squeeze.

They left the perambulator and their cloaks in the cloakroom and Aunty Maggie assured them they would be able to collect everything at the end. Special seats in the middle of the front row of the pit had been saved for them. When the curtain eventually rose, after the music had stopped, a room appeared on the stage with a lot of bookshelves painted onto the back wall. The audience was suddenly quiet. Then two servants appeared, talking to each other about letters and the postman. There was no sign of Grandfather yet. Lottie yawned.

'When will *Grandfather* appear?' Chas said suddenly, in his normal, loud voice. Lottie gasped and Aunty Maggie leaned over and put a hand over his mouth, whispering that he must not speak loudly like that, and trying not to laugh.

'Ganda! Ganda!' It was Tommy's turn to cause a disturbance next. Lottie could hear people whispering and tittering behind them and wondered if everyone in the audience was looking at them.

'But I thought Grandfather was acting in the play – where can he be?' Jane was as perplexed as her brothers and seemed equally unaware of how far her voice was carrying.

Lottie squirmed round in her chair to look at the audience and a gentleman nearby smiled at her. He had a pencil in his hand and was scribbling notes in a little book. She frowned at him and turned back, slumping down in her seat. There was still no sign of her grandfather, and she had no idea what the actors were talking about anymore.

Aunty Maggie passed a paper bag of boiled sweets to all the children. Lottie plunged her hand into the sugary bag and popped one in her mouth. She pushed it around with her tongue to pass the time, desperate for her grandfather to come on-stage.

'When will it be *Grandfather's* turn, Aunty Maggie? I'm getting bored.' Chas was trying to whisper, but his voice was loud enough to distract even the actors and raised a ripple of laughter in the audience again. Lottie nudged him.

'Shush, Chas – I'm sure it won't be long.'

The syrupy sweetness of the barley sugar made Lottie feel sleepy and her eyes were beginning to droop when her grandfather came striding onto the stage at last. The whole theatre was suddenly in uproar. Everyone jumped to their feet, clapping and shouting and stamping as loud as a thunderstorm. Lottie and her cousins turned round and watched the audience in amazement, mouths and eyes wide open.

'Oh my goodness – they really like Grandfather, don't they!' Jane shouted over the din. Lottie turned back and looked at him again, standing in the middle of the stage, not at all shy, with a silly expression on his face and a bright sparkle in his eyes. He caught her eye and, for a moment, she knew that sparkle was just for her. It filled her to the very brim with happiness.

When the applause tailed off and the audience began to sit down, her grandfather carried on with the play as if nothing at all unusual had happened. Lottie was soon swept along with the story and forgot she was in a theatre. All the children clapped whenever they felt like it and spoke out whenever they thought of something to say, hardly noticing the stifled laughter that followed their comments, or the scribbling of the pencil in the row behind.

'How like him – that's just him, isn't it!'

'Oh, look at Grandfather – he's angry now!'

'Hear how he swears – he doesn't do that at home, though!'

'Ah, that's Grandfather alright!'

'Yes – that's Grandfather, isn't it just!'

'Three, two, one – I'm coming to find you, ready or not! Ha!' Grandfather had been so jolly and full of fun since they watched him acting in the theatre. It was a shame he had to go to Glasgow on the train so often.

Lottie and her cousins were hiding and their grandfather was seeking. She could tell by the sound of his teasing voice that he was in the hall. It was dark and stuffy behind the thick crimson drapes in the parlour. Her dress was new and fitted her perfectly. She loved the wide red and yellow stripes and the soft, slippery feel of the material. Izzie had given it to her to wear for Christmas and Hogmanay when Lottie had visited her last Saturday, telling her it had been her mammy's when she was six, which made it extra special. Lottie was going to be six in a few weeks.

Her restless hands were smoothing the soft fabric again when the curtain was yanked back, making her blink in the brightness of the lamps.

'Boo!' Grandfather swept her off her feet and swung her round, his hands under her armpits. He put her down almost at once and leaned on the back of a chair, trying to catch his breath. 'Ha! Perhaps I'm a bit old for such hi-jinks these days – or perhaps you've grown a good deal, Lottie! Probably a bit of both! Come along then, I need to find the others before bedtime, so you must help me!' He offered her his arm. 'Lead on, Mattie, through the foul paths o' darkness!!' She slipped her hand under his arm and they marched off to the nursery together, singing their favourite verse from one of his silly songs:

> *'In favour o' Mattie a word let me say,*
> *Of Lunnun queans she's worth a dozen ...'*

TWENTY-NINE

Charles came out of his room much later than usual, pleased to have a day with nothing much planned. The night before had been his final performance before Christmas and he was very tired. The smell of oranges and cloves was wafting into the hall through the open kitchen door on a wave of excited chatter and he smiled to himself at the thought of sharing the festivities with all his grandchildren this year. He wondered if breakfast might still be a possibility and went to investigate.

The season had been a triumph. He had not only felt invigorated by his busy schedule but was delighted to be told he had delivered some of his best work at such a late stage in his life. The applause for his entrances as the Bailie in *Rob Roy* had often been more deafening than he had ever experienced, and the convulsive bursts of laughter peppering his performances were extremely gratifying. In the broadsheets and reviews he had been variously described as 'the veteran actor', 'this venerable artiste' and 'this old and distinguished favourite', but he was feeling younger and more alive, more himself again, than he had done for years. His Highland fling as the Bailie had more vigour in it than he could remember having for more than a decade.

The Adelphi Theatre had enjoyed full houses throughout November and December, although rain and hail had threatened to keep people away. Charles was already looking forward to his performances there in January. He was pleased for the Wyndhams. They were good people. Somehow, he had managed all his appearances in Glasgow as well, travelling by train and staying overnight with Lauchlan and his growing family. Mr Glover had been a delightful host at the Glasgow Theatre Royal and Glasgow audiences were as enthusiastic as the home crowds in Auld Reekie, if not more. There had been moments when Charles had looked up at the gallery and been overwhelmed by the thought of the disastrous crush of '49, which still seemed so very recent to him. Perhaps three years was a long time to enthusiastic theatre-goers, though. Long enough to forget what it was inconvenient to remember anyway.

The glowing reviews were so effusive that Charles had indulged himself by cutting the best of them out of the newspapers and keeping them in his desk drawer. He had shown some of them to Lottie one afternoon and her face had shone ('I'm going be an actor one day, Grandfather, and people will write things like this about me!'). Charles had dropped the cutting back in his drawer and slid it shut, smiling fondly at her. *What a silly, vain old man I've become, lapping all this up and putting ideas in her innocent little head!*

The reviewer for *The Courant* had singled out his opening night in the Adelphi, waxing lyrical about what a delight it was to see the grandchildren sitting in a row at the front of the pit, their little faces all lit up, their naïve comments delighting audience and actors alike. That performance, so the writer said, ranked among Charles's most remarkable impersonations 'for truth and finish'. Apparently, several scenes were so powerful they showed that, 'while Mr Mackay is the most natural of actors, he is also one of the most finished and artistic'.

One reviewer, however, had had the temerity to compare a recent performance of his with one of the long-deceased Henry Johnston's and it had irked him more than he would have expected: 'Johnston was a man of presence, tall, stout and handsome, but with Mackay we forget the figure of the man in the power and vigour of his acting.' It was a compliment, of course, but a sly one, with that old dig about his inadequate appearance, his lack of height cropping up yet again. Henry had undoubtedly been a brilliant, handsome actor in the old style, but he had also been an unsettling and unreliable character, and always seemed to make Charlotte uncomfortable. For that alone, Charles had disliked him.

'Halloo there, big brother! I hope your house is swept clean, your fireplaces are spic and span, and all your debts are paid!'

Charles was sitting by the fire in the parlour when Hector blew in through the front door, accompanied by a chilly gust of wind. His booming voice in the hall was raising the roof as usual and Charles beckoned Lottie to sit beside him. They would greet her Uncle Hector together and this time, hopefully, she would not feel the need to scream.

Charles listened to his youngest son stamping loudly on the mat, teasing Charlie about being back home at No. 23, then the door flew open and suddenly Hector was filling the spacious parlour with cold air and bombast, shaking snow and drops of water out of his mop of dark curls like a dog. He was wearing yellow breeks, knee-length leather boots and a broad-striped black and white waistcoat with a bright blue cravat, topped with a green velvet jacket and a grin almost as wide as his handsome, square face with its long, full sideburns. Hector surveyed the room, looking very pleased with himself, then blasted out a greeting.

'Happy Hogmanay to one and all! I have sweeties, come and get them, children!' The boys ran over to him at once to feel in his pockets and he shrugged his shoulders helplessly at no one in particular, as though apologising for his huge popularity. Supper and family had been awaiting Hector's arrival for well over an hour, though, so he was rather less popular with his host.

'Let me guess – the train was held up? You forgot your luggage? What could it have been this time I wonder?' Charlie had followed Hector into the parlour and closed the door behind him. There was a steely edge to his voice, his forced politeness barely disguising his irritation. Charles wondered if he should try and have a word with Hector on Charlie's behalf. It really was most thoughtless, the way he came and went as he pleased with little or no communication between times, hardly ever contributing anything but sarcasm and balderdash to the proceedings.

Hector turned to Charlie and, with a flourish, presented him with a lump of coal wrapped in a dark blue kerchief, giving an exaggerated bow and making the boys squeal with delight.

'A gift for a tall, dark, handsome man to take out on his first-footing adventures when the clock has chimed the midnight hour!' Hector pulled a ridiculous face at Charlie, then punched him on the arm. 'Come on, Charlie, I was but an hour or two late!' Charlie remained stony-faced and silent. 'Alright, I confess I missed my train because of my confused state of mind after a grand night of celebrations. But what is the point of life if we can't have fun now and then, tell me that, eh? On that note, I hope you're well supplied with the good stuff for tonight's festivities!' He rubbed his hands together and turned to smile at Bella and Jane, who were sitting by the window. 'Now then, where are my manners! I must greet everyone else!' He nodded amiably at Charles and Lottie and strode over to the window.

'Ladies, ladies, how delightful to see you both again, and looking so pretty with the bloom of youth about you, the both of you!' Jane was unable to hide her blushes when he took her hand and bestowed a kiss, but Bella was not at all enchanted. She pulled her hand away quickly and stood up.

'That's quite enough of your nonsense, Hector. Now go and greet your father and Lottie and we can take our seats at the dining table for supper, if it's not entirely ruined.'

'Yes, ma'am!' Hector saluted Bella and went over to see his father. Charles stood up, and Lottie leaned into his side quietly, looking at her feet, while Hector pumped his hand and wished them both a merry Christmas. She was still very shy of him, but Charles was thankful she no longer seemed terrified.

The grandchildren were going to perform a little scene for the adults after supper as a surprise. They had been talking about the idea since Charles had first read the script of *Rob Roy* to them in the autumn. They had begged him to read it again after watching him act on-stage, then Lottie had shyly asked if they could put on a scene together for the family. Preparations and rehearsals had been under way since Christmas Day, programmes secretly written and illustrated too, and all the children were in a state of high excitement about it.

The little acting troupe styled themselves 'Her Majesty's Servants of the Dublin Street Theatre' and they were going to perform the Snoring Scene from *Rob Roy Macgregor*. Also on the programme was the Burns song: 'Auld Lang Syne'. There was to be juggling with two oranges by Chas, a dance from Lottie and Jane – who had recently begun to take dancing classes with Mrs Wyndham – and last but by no means least, some impersonations by Grandfather Charles. It was an ambitious programme, which was why Charles had taken a long snooze after lunch.

The children were fit to burst throughout supper, itching to leave the table and begin the show. Jane, who was eight years old and very dependable, was going to give the introduction and play Mr Owen; seven-year-old Chas would be the hapless Frank; Lottie was going to play sweet Mattie, while Tommy, at very nearly three years old, had promised do his best to impersonate

St Mungo's Clock. His job was to bang the large copper dinner gong whenever his grandfather directed him. Charles would, of course, for well over the thousandth time, be reprising his famous role as Bailie Nicol Jarvie.

Three dining chairs were pulled away from the table and arranged in a half-circle facing the large bay window, which had been cleared of furniture. Jane placed colourful programmes on each chair. A few props had been gathered behind a decoupage screen in the corner earlier in the day, and that was also where the actors would be donning their little bits of costume.

The audience of three sat down, an expectant hush fell, and Jane proceeded to set the scene with great self-possession. Then Charles strode out from behind the screen:

Bailie Nicol Jarvie (Grandfather Charles): '*So, that Dougal creature was an agent of Rob's! I shouldn't wonder if he has one in every jail in Scotland! Well, I have done things this night that my father, the deacon, rest be with him, would not ha' believed! – but there's balm in Gilead. Mr Owen, I hope to see you at breakfast – Eh! Why the man's fast!*'

Mr Owen (Jane): (Lets out a loud snore.)

Frank (Chas): '*And the sooner we depart, and follow his example, sir, the better – it must be near midnight.*'

Bailie: '*Midnight! Well, Mattie shall light you home, but no tricks – none of your London – no, now I think again, I'll see you home myself.*'

Charles looked in horror at Chas, as though imagining what tricks he might get up to if left on his own with the innocent young Mattie late at night, and there was a pause for Chas's parents to laugh at the idea. Charles crept across the room, pretending to be invisible, and put the beater back into Tommy's floppy hand. The lad had almost dropped off to sleep sitting patiently beside the gong, but the chubby little fellow sat up at once and began to batter 'St Mungo's Clock' with great enthusiasm. Charles put a finger to his lips.

'Hush now, Tommy lad! Just one beat at a time, if you please.' His exaggerated stage whisper, complete with his exasperated grimace, made the other children laugh and Tommy quickly stopped banging. Instead, he waited meekly for his grandfather to point towards him and banged it only once each time. The play continued:

Frank: '*Hark! Hark! Now from St Mungo's tower the bell proclaims the midnight hour.*'

Tommy: BOME

Mattie: '*And thro' the city far and near, from spire and turret now I hear—*'

Tommy: BOME

Frank and Mattie: ''*Ere yet the first vibration dies, each iron tongue of time replies—*'

Tommy: BOME

Mr Owen: '*Augh!!!*' (Snoring.)

Bailie: '*Hark! Hark! From Mister Owen's nose, a cadence deep, a dying close—*'
Tommy: BOME

Mr Owen: '*Augh!!!*' (Snoring.)

Frank, Mattie and Bailie: ''*Ere yet the first vibration dies, his nasal organ quick replies—*'

Tommy: BOME

Mr Owen: '*Augh!!!*' (Snoring – then waking up.) '*Bless me! Every way I am undone, I did not dream of being here but snug in sweet Crane Alley, London, and stocks were up, and I— O dear!*'

ALL: '*Home, home we must no longer stay, for soon will peep the morning light, now let us haste come, come, away, fare well at once, at once good night.*'

After a whispered reminder the actors made a line, two on either side of their grandfather, and held hands. Charles lifted his hands, leading them in three deep bows, and Charlie and Bella clapped enthusiastically, while Hector gave three slow claps and a *Bravo*.

'Wonderful, my dears, well done to all of you!' Charlie called out, still clapping.

'Yes, children, and Grandfather too of course, you were all marvellous! How did you remember so many words, I wonder?' Bella held her arms out to Tommy as she spoke and he ran into them, clambering onto her lap and sticking his thumb in his mouth. His eyes were closed in seconds, and she stroked his face fondly, brushing a stray curl off his damp brow. The other three children stood waiting to see what would happen next; there were other items on the programme.

'Another triumph, Father! You absolutely shone, as always, of course!' Hector poured himself a large whisky and stood in front of the fire with a glint in his eye, rocking back and forth on his feet, projecting his voice more than necessary. 'Unlike your rather wooden little troupe of "Dublin Street Players". I think you did them a disservice, Father. They may be young, but you could have given them a few more hints, don't you think? Still, helping young would-be actors develop their skills never was your strong point, I suppose.' There was a moment of shocked silence, then Jane surprised everyone, especially herself.

'We are not wooden actors, Uncle Hector! That's a very unkind thing to say!' She turned quite red, her eyes glistening with unshed tears, then ran from the room sobbing pitifully, followed swiftly by her father. Chas and Lottie stayed where they were as though rooted to the spot.

Charles walked over to the fire, picked up the poker and jabbed the coals, causing sparks to fly and flames to leap up the chimney. Hector was looking insufferably pleased with himself.

'You can be such a child, sometimes, Hector. There's really no need to upset the children to provoke me, you know.'

Hector smirked. 'I see the instinct to defend with a poker hasn't left you yet, Father! May I suggest *the next time you fight, let it be with your sword and not like a wild Indian!*' He chuckled into his whisky, then took another swig.

'Oh, very droll, Hector. I'm glad to see you're so familiar with the script of *Rob Roy*. You never know your luck – one day you might be called upon to act in some real drama!' Bella stood up. Tommy was asleep in her arms, his head resting on her shoulder.

'Time for bed now children, come along.' Chas looked crestfallen as Bella carried Tommy off to bed, but Lottie walked over to Charles, stood on her tiptoes, and whispered something he could not quite hear. He bent forward, cupping his hand round his ear.

'What about my dance with Jane, Grandfather? And the song, and everything else on the programme?' Charles straightened up again, smiling what he hoped was a reassuring smile and taking both her little hands in his.

'Aha, Lottie Lulu – I'm afraid there has been a last-minute change to the programme. This sort of thing often happens in the world of theatre. Your dance, the song and the juggling will now be presented tomorrow afternoon to a new audience!'

Hector snorted into his whisky and Charles lifted one of Lottie's hands, twirling her round with his finger, making her dress flare out prettily. She smiled shyly, gave a deep curtsey, then bade them both good night – kissing Charles on his cheek and not quite catching her uncle's eye. Chas waited until she had gone, then produced two oranges from behind his back.

'It's alright, Grandfather, you don't need to put me on tomorrow's programme. I'm not very good at juggling anyway.' He gave the oranges to Charles with a rueful smile. 'Thank you very much for a nice evening. Goodnight, and a Happy New Year to you both.' He turned and left the room just as his father came back through the door.

Charles found himself standing at the fireside between his sons, holding an orange in each hand. For once he was lost for words. He put the oranges on the nearest side table, wiped his hands on his kerchief and winced as the inevitable bickering began.

'I hope you're satisfied with yourself for ruining our evening, Hector. There was absolutely no need for it! Jane is a very sensitive girl.'

'Well now, there's really no need to take on so, big brother! I was just having a little dig at our famous father. Someone needs to keep his feet on the ground, don't you think? Especially after all his recent posturing on the stage!' Hector turned to Charles. 'What's the plan, Father? Are you simply going to keep on delighting your devoted audiences until you drop dead in front of them, like poor old Mr Palmer?'

'Hector! How can you even …' It was kind of Charlie to jump to his defence, but Charles was tired of this now. He put a hand on Charlie's arm.

'It's alright Charlie, Hector is entitled to his opinions, and it's a reasonable question, I suppose.' He turned back to Hector. 'I believe the eminent actor to whom you refer had recently heard of the death of his second son, whom he loved dearly. When a fellow actor spoke the line *your children would have amused you in many a dreary hour*, Mr Palmer was so overcome by his feelings that he fell, lifeless, on the stage. So, Hector, let us hope for *your* sake that history is not repeated, shall we?'

Judging by his expression, Charles had caught Hector out, and it gave him a ridiculous sense of satisfaction.

'To answer your question, though, I am simply responding to invitations, as I have always done. And, for what it's worth, I'm enjoying myself immensely. I don't see that there's any harm in that. I'm feeling very well on it, too, since you seem so concerned for my health.' Charles sat down and stretched his legs out in front of the fire.

'Well, perhaps you should give it some thought, Father. After all, a man of your age …' Hector took another swig of his whisky, held his brother's gaze as though challenging him to contradict him, then made himself comfortable in the other wing chair opposite Charles, effectively dismissing his brother from his own hearthside. Charlie turned on his heel and left them to it without another word.

It was disappointing, ending the evening, or rather the year, like that, but Charles reminded himself it was ever thus between his boys. Hector had always chafed against his older brother, who was usually only trying to keep the peace or save him from some catastrophe. Lord knows what had gone on between the two of them during his absence. It must have been hard for them both.

Charles decided to take the opportunity to ask Hector a bit about himself, hoping peace could be made with Charlie in the morning when they all went to church. Hector himself, of course, would probably take off to the Red Lion later tonight, and the chances of him coming to St Cuthbert's tomorrow were almost none. He would turn up for supper again, most likely, or for afternoon tea at the earliest, by which time the children would have become fractious again, waiting so long to exchange gifts.

'I see you still have the Liverpool box, Father.' Hector was fingering the engraved gold snuffbox on the mantelpiece, opening and closing the lid as if trying to annoy him. 'You might be interested to know I've been doing rather well in Liverpool myself, recently. Mr McKenzie introduced me to the manager and I've acted in several productions there recently.'

Charles sat up straight. 'I'm well aware you went to visit Mr McKenzie without mentioning it to me, Hector. He wrote to me of it. I'm none too pleased, I must say, that you prevailed upon his goodwill towards *me* in order to advance your *own* career.' Hector's smile remained firmly in place, but his eyes became slits that were impossible to read. Charles thought how like Peter he looked, with his unruly dark hair and square face, and wondered again, for the hundredth time, where his brother had disappeared to, or if he was even still alive.

'I imagined you might be somewhat supportive of your son, Father, but it seems I was mistaken.' Hector refilled his glass and Charles wondered if he might have overreacted. *Surely no one would give him parts he is incapable of playing just because he's my son?* He took a long sip of his own whisky and decided to take a different approach.

'I certainly am interested to know if you've been offered any good parts, Hector.' Hector sat down again, arranging his long legs languidly as if trying too hard to give an impression of confidence.

'As a matter of fact, I shall be performing in the New Year pantomime, *Clari – The Maid of Milan* – at Liverpool's *Theatre Royal*.' Hector sat forward, the light back in his eyes. 'The new scenery is going to be spectacular, and the Brothers Lauri are guaranteed to be most entertaining, with their incredible acrobatic feats and famous clowning.'

Hints of the vulnerable little boy who used to plead with his father to stay at home and read him a story began to slip through the cracks of his bravado as he continued. 'I'm taking the Old Man part of Pantaloon, myself.'

Charles decided to humour his son, although New Year pantomimes had never been a dramatic high point in the year for him. 'Ah, very good, Hector – Pantaloon – that sly old man who always seems more foolish than he really is!'

'Exactly so, Father. And, as I have the perfect role model right here in front of me to study this week, I should be ready to make a great impression when I take to the stage!'

'Ha! *Touché*, Hector, *touché*!'

THIRTY

All over Edinburgh people were gathering in elegant town houses, crowded taverns, supper clubs and cosy rooms to toast the national bard, to celebrate the immeasurable contribution Robert Burns had made to Scotland's culture, with haggis and whisky, poetry and song, friendship and company and humour.

In the Adelphi Theatre everyone was busy preparing for another performance of the national play the people of Scotland had held dear for so many years – *Rob Roy Macgregor – or Auld Lang Syne*. Charles had played the Bailie to a most enthusiastic full house the previous week; tonight he was anticipating another. In his pocket, like a talisman, he carried a small, folded clipping that had unnerved him: *A greater treat could hardly be found anywhere within the walls of a theatre. Yet when we lose Mr Mackay (but may the time be far distant) we shall certainly lose one of the brilliant links that connect the past with the present generation.*

Charles was not planning to be lost quite yet; he was having far too much fun, and hoping 1853 would be as full of engagements as the past year had been.

In the green room Charles was dressed and ready to go, as inspired as he used to be when he'd first played the Bailie on the northern circuit. The Hostess walked past him to take her place behind the curtain, her red silk dress rustling, and Charles felt his heart contract.

The overture began.

The audience fell silent.

The play commenced.

When his moment arrived Charles strode onto the stage, buzzing with energy. He knew at once his acting was good, exceptional, even – perhaps one of his best performances. At the same time, he felt detached from it, as though watching himself from high in the gallery. Borne along effortlessly by his years of experience, he led the audience through the story as if in a dream. Before he knew it, the curtain dropped on the last scene and the audience stood as one, cheering, clapping, shouting and stamping – calling for the Bailie to come before the curtain and receive their thanks and admiration.

He returned to his adoring crowd and stood centre stage, feet planted wide, hands on hips, eyes ranging slowly over all the people in the upper and lower galleries, the boxes, the pit. He nodded and smiled in acknowledgement of their immense applause, bowed several times, stooped to pick up the flowers they threw at his feet, then raised his hand for quiet.

'Ladies and gentlemen, on this most auspicious night in the Scottish calendar, I thank you all most sincerely for the warm feelings you have always shown towards your "Auld Acquaintance", Bailie Nicol Jarvie! He is not forgot!' The audience erupted again, and Charles walked into the wings on air.

He lay awake for a long time that night, still feeling he was being swept along by a great tidal wave of energy, no longer knowing where it was taking him.

Charles opened his eyes, but only one eyelid lifted. Slightly. Just enough for him to see daylight. He could hear low voices humming like bees, but could not turn to see who was in the room. His head was pounding.

A face loomed over him.

After a moment of confusion, he realised it was Bella.

'Please don't be alarmed, Charles, but you seem to have had an episode of apoplexy during the night. I found you most unwell this morning and called Doctor Middleton. He is here now and will explain more.' She disappeared from his line of sight. He tried to thank her, but his lips would not move.

Another face came into view.

'Dear fellow. This is all most unfortunate, but, as a result of the quick thinking of your daughter-in-law, we have been able to let a little blood and stabilise your condition. I have every confidence you will make a good recovery, given time.' Charles wanted to ask how much time? He wanted to know if anyone had been to the theatre to tell Wyndham he would not be coming in today; he wanted to say he had a thumping headache. But he could not so much as grunt.

'Now then, Charles, try to rest. It will not help your recovery if you fight your paralysis.' His friend, John Middleton, was talking to him again. 'Rest is the key. Rest and good nursing to keep you fed and watered. Mrs Mackay has sent for a nurse, and it may give you some comfort to know she has also sent a message to Mr Wyndham at the Adelphi.' *Thank goodness for that!* Charles felt his body relax and sank into a doze. He could still hear the doctor's voice, but it sounded very far away.

'If all goes to plan and you are a *patient* patient, as it were, Charles, you should be out of bed and able to walk, to use your hands and so on, by the spring. Meanwhile, please allow yourself to be nursed, and let nature to take its course, dear fellow.'

Two days later Charles opened his good eye and blinked. Charlie was sitting beside his bed.

'How are you feeling today, Father? I hope you're rested and the nurse has made you comfortable.' Charles was able to make a slight grunting sound in response, nothing more. He could hear a newspaper rustling.

'I have here this morning's copy of *The Weekly Review and Dramatic Critic* – I should, perhaps, remind you that today is Friday, January the 28th, 1853, Father, in case you have lost track somewhat ... as a result of being indisposed.' *Indisposed! What a very polite word for my condition, Charlie, and how like you, dear boy, to select it.*

'I would like to read an article that concerns you, if you would be so kind as to indulge me.' *As if I have any choice in the matter! Still, best to know what people are saying about my calamity I suppose.* He grunted the most amenable grunt he could muster.

'It's entitled: *Illness of Mr Mackay.*' Charlie cleared his throat and began to read: '*The National Dramas of The Bride of Lammermoor and Rob Roy have formed the leading attraction at the Adelphi since our last – and certainly it is no ordinary treat to witness our venerable countryman, Mr Mackay, in the character of Caleb Balderstone (one of the most amusing, perhaps, of the "Great Unknown's" creations), or Bailie Nicol Jarvie.*'

Charlie stopped reading for a moment, fished out a handkerchief and blew his nose, then carried on.

'*It is deeply to be regretted, however, that his engagement has been suddenly broken up in consequence of severe illness, and although it is the universal hope that he may soon be restored to health, yet it is questionable whether he may be able again to delight the world with those inimitable delineations of Scottish character, of the olden time, which have made his name so celebrated.*'

There was another pause, and Charles wondered if he had heard a barely concealed sob. *Bless the dear boy, he was always such a sensitive lad.*

'Sorry, Father. Would you like me to continue?'

Charles blinked his eye and the reading continued: '*On Tuesday evening* (it was Burns Night, Father, if you recall) *he played the Bailie, in* Rob Roy, *with more animation than he did last season, and, as everyone remarked, with all the fascination of his younger years. At the close he was rapturously called before the curtain – and, in acknowledgement of the honour, begged to return his sincere thanks. His brief, but appropriate, address was loudly applauded.*'

Charlie blew his nose again. 'I am only sorry, Father, deeply, sorry, that I wasn't there to witness what may have been your last appearance on-stage. I will never forgive myself!' His voice caught, and Charles wished he could at least pat his son on the arm, tell him nothing mattered, he was here now and that was enough.

'Forgive me, Father, I am feeling rather overcome with emotion. I should very much like to finish reading the article though, if I may. Rest assured I shall keep it for you to read again yourself as soon as you are feeling better. Hhmmm: *Next morning the bills of the day announced* Redgauntlet, *with Peter Peebles to be performed by Mr Mackay – at night, the audience were astounded to learn that, in consequence of the sudden and severe indisposition of Mr Mackay, the first piece would be changed to* Masaniello. *Mr Wyndham intimated that he had seen Mr Mackay, and that he was glad to say that, although the attack under which he laboured was a severe one, yet there were hopes he would soon be able to resume his engagement.*'

Charles wanted to ask his son when Wyndham had been here, in his bedroom. He could not remember seeing him. Instead, he just lay quietly, like a stone on a riverbed, allowing Charlie's words to float past him like leaves on the surface of the water.

'*That this may be the case we sincerely hope. It is not to be wondered, however, that his friends feel alarmed. At an age so advanced as that of the venerable actor, illness is not easily shaken off. But let us anticipate the best. We have not been able to ascertain the precise nature of the ailment of Mr Mackay, but we believe it is justly attributed to over-exertion.*'

The night nurse was a sharp-eyed little woman with a pointed chin, thin grey hair scraped tightly into bun and strong bony arms. There was a smell of carbolic about her and she had very little conversation. Charles was relieved to know nothing about the person whose job it was to wash his body and clean his mess.

Every night she sat by the fire, keeping a few coals glowing in the grate, knitting by the light of a candle. If he stirred, she looked up; if he was distressed, she attended to him in whatever way was required. Each morning she fed, washed and shaved him, changed his sheets, dressed him in fresh nightclothes, and left without a word, carrying a bundle of stinking laundry.

THIRTY-ONE

More than a week had passed since her grandfather had been taken ill and still Lottie had not been allowed to see him. Whenever she asked if she could go into his room she was told he must rest. On Saturday, when everyone was sitting round the breakfast table eating and drinking and talking loudly, Lottie screwed up her courage to ask again.

'Aunty Bella, I really *must* see Grandfather today. Izzie gave me a nice rug to put on his bed to cheer him up, and I've drawn some pictures to show him. Please let me!' Her aunt put down her teacup and sat very still for a moment before replying.

'Perhaps you could spend an hour or so sitting at his desk this morning with your pencils and draw him another picture. Then he will see you if he opens his eyes.'

'Oh yes! Please let me do that, Aunty Bella! I will be very good – I'm six now, after all!' Uncle Charlie looked over at them and Lottie crossed her fingers under the table, hoping he would not forbid their plan.

'Do you think that's wise, Bella? Doctor Middleton has ordered complete rest.'

'I know, dear, but Charles takes a particular interest in Lottie and for all we know he may be worrying about her. I think we should give her a chance.' Aunty Bella took Lottie's hand under the table and Uncle Charlie looked at his pocket watch.

'Alright then. But only for an hour. Then I'll take her along to Izzie's, as usual. Once you've settled her with Father, Bella, perhaps you could take this noisy rabble over to your mother's and leave me in peace with my newspaper!'

'Thank you, Charlie.' Aunty Bella wiped Lottie's hands and face with a napkin and stood up. 'Come along Lottie, let's fetch your pictures and that rug and get you settled.'

It was very warm in her grandfather's bedroom. The shutters were open, flooding the room with white winter light; the fire had been built up high and was crackling and spitting. There was an odd smell that was not very nice.

Lottie stood by the door, looking at the still figure lying on the bed, no longer quite so sure of herself.

'Come and sit on Grandfather's chair, Lottie.' Aunty Bella led her to the desk and arranged her pencils and some sheets of paper on it. 'You can look round at him whenever you want. If he opens his eyes – well, it will probably be one eye because the other one is having a rest – then you can sit on the little stool by the bed and let him see you. You can talk to him, too. He will be able to hear you, but his voice is having a rest too.'

Aunty Bella stroked Lottie's hair and Lottie closed her eyes.

'I know you'll be good, darling. You love him so much, don't you!' Lottie nodded and bit her lip, not sure if she could speak without crying.

When Aunty Bella closed the door, the room felt different.

Lottie spread the green plaid on the bed, smoothing the corners carefully, then sat on the stool and peered at her grandfather's face. He looked very old. His skin had turned pale grey and was saggy around his eyes. Dozens of wrinkles had carved wiggly lines on his brow and beside his eyes. His mouth was open, and he was breathing through it with a raspy, scratchy sound. His teeth were yellow with brown stains on them, and the smell of his breath was very stale.

'Hello, Grandfather, I've come to visit you. I only have one hour, so you'd better wake up if you want to see me.' She waited to see if his breathing would change, if he would open one eye.

Nothing happened.

Lottie fished under the bedclothes to find his hand and he made a strange gulping sound and closed his mouth. She pulled his arm out and placed it on top of the covers so she could hold his large, bony hand with both of hers. She squeezed it gently. There were blotches of brown on it she had never noticed before.

'Can you hear me, Grandfather? I brought you a lovely rug. Izzie thought you'd like it.' No response.

'Jane's been helping me learn Mattie's words in *Rob Roy*.' Still no response.

'I'm going to be an actor, like you, when I grow up Grandfather! We could act together. I could be Mattie and tuck my arm under yours!' She stared at him, willing him to answer, trying not to cry.

'I *know* you can hear me! *Please* open your eyes!'

One of his eyes began to flicker. It opened a little way. He was looking at her! Lottie sighed with relief. She felt as if she had been holding her breath for more than a week.

She squeezed his hand again, very softly, and smiled her brightest smile.

'Hello Grandfather! I've missed you *so* much!'

THIRTY-TWO

It was unusual for the front door to be chapped on a Wednesday morning. Charles listened carefully to see if he could recognise the visitor's voice. He was sitting by his bedroom window in his new Bath chair, with Charlotte's familiar green woollen plaid tucked round his knees. He had no idea how it had suddenly turned up, but he was glad of its warmth and it was a great comfort.

Three months had passed since his unfortunate episode and he was feeling a good deal better, although he still tired easily and needed help with many of the practicalities of life. John Middleton had assured him his health would continue to improve if he continued to rest, so he had been trying his best to be a *patient* patient. It was very tedious.

There was a soft knock on his door and a dishevelled young man put his head round it.

'Mr Mackay, is it convenient for me to visit?'

'Wyndham! What brings you here this fine May morning?' Charles gave a lopsided smile and Robert Wyndham came in rather hesitantly, not looking his usual dapper self at all.

'I've come for your advice, Mr Mackay, if you have a moment. Have you heard about the fire?' Wyndham pulled up a chair to sit beside Charles at the bay window. There was a distinct whiff of smoke about him, and his dark brown eyes were flickering with anxiety.

'Good Lord, what fire, Wyndham? Your family? The theatre?' His lips still felt numb and he knew his speech was slurred, but Charles forgot his embarrassment in his concern for his young friend.

Wyndham pulled a kerchief from the pocket of his red waistcoat and mopped his brow.

'The Adelphi was completely destroyed by fire last night!'

'Good gracious, Wyndham, what a terrible shock!'

'No one died. Thanks be to God! But my dear Rose was up in the gallery with our son Fred – who's only a week old, for God's sake. What were we thinking? They had to be rescued and I was beside myself with worry!' Charles wondered if Wyndham might be about to cry, the poor man seemed so distraught. He lifted a stiff hand and leaned forward to pat his arm rather clumsily.

'You mustn't blame yourself, dear boy, these things happen. They're safe, and that's all that matters.'

'You're right, Mr Mackay. Thank you.'

'You know, it's very strange, Wyndham, but last night I had a veritable nightmare about that awful tragedy in Glasgow's Theatre Royal in '49. I wasn't there, myself, but the dream was so vivid: the smell of smoke, the yell of terrified people, the blind panic and the crush of the stampede. I woke drenched in sweat, feeling as though I was being crushed myself. I believe over sixty people died that night. Tragic. Mm.'

Wyndham nodded thoughtfully. 'Perhaps a whiff of smoke curled through your open window last night while you slept – it's possible, I suppose. You're not very far from the theatre here.'

'Ah, the mysteries of life continue to elude us, don't they Wyndham. Indeed, the older I become the more I realise how very little I know! Ha! Now tell me, are you insured?' Wyndham looked up with a sharper focus in his eyes.

'Yes I am. And I shall have a magnificent theatre built on the site as soon as it has been cleared. It will take several years, though, and I cannot afford to wait that long with nowhere to put on productions in the meantime.'

'I see what you mean. That's quite a predicament.'

'I've had an idea, though, and I would very much appreciate hearing your opinion on the matter.'

The door opened and Bella came in with coffee and cinnamon buns. Wyndham jumped to his feet, took the tray from her and put it down on the desk.

'Delicious! Though you shouldn't have gone to such trouble, Mrs Mackay!'

'You're very welcome, Mr Wyndham. It's the least I can do in the circumstances. I do hope your wife and children are alright and have the support they need. If there is anything I can do …'

'You're too kind, Mrs Mackay. We have excellent help, thank you, and I shan't stay away from them for long.' Bella nodded. Then she indicated the tray and coloured slightly.

'You may need to assist Charles somewhat with …'

'We shall manage splendidly, shan't we?' Charles nodded and Bella smiled and left the room. Charles was thankful yet again for the thoughtful discretion of his daughter-in-law.

Wyndham poured two coffees, added milk and sugar and stirred them both vigorously with a little silver teaspoon. He picked up a cinnamon bun and resumed his narrative while tearing off a small piece and handing it to Charles without the slightest embarrassment.

'I'm thinking of taking on the lease for the Theatre Royal, Mr Mackay. It's been lying empty since those youngsters gave up on it after their first season. What do you think?' Wyndham took a long sip of coffee and held Charles's gaze expectantly over the rim of his cup.

‘That sounds like an excellent plan, Wyndham. When can you have it?’

‘I aim to find out later this morning. At once, I hope, so I can open in a fortnight.’

‘Jolly good, Wyndham! And I certainly wish you the best of luck in your new enterprise.’ Wyndham held Charles’s cup to his mouth and allowed him to take a good sip, then set it down and handed him another morsel of bun. Charles went along with his visitor’s nonchalance. He was surprised by how comfortable he felt in the company of this enthusiastic and generous man who had so recently given him such a run of wonderful opportunities on-stage despite his advanced age.

And now the theatre in which he had taken his final bow had been razed to the ground. *How strange are the twists and turns of life!*

‘I hear you came to visit me after my calamity, Wyndham. Thank you for that. I also hear you’ve been putting it about you’re still hopeful of my return to the stage! Ha! No chance of that, I’m afraid’ Wyndham laughed and sat back in his chair, chewing another bite of his bun.

‘It’s true I may have said that to a few folk, but I’ve since conceded defeat and I promise I shan’t mention it again.’ He dabbed his mouth neatly with a napkin, his dark eyes twinkling. ‘I was developing a new production for you to star in, though, Mr Mackay. That’s why I held onto my hope of your return for as long as I did. I doubt the play will ever see the light of day now. The leading comic role was written for you, and no one comes close to being your equal in such characters.’ Charles perked up, his vanity flattered, his curiosity piqued.

‘Are you going to tell me about it, Wyndham, or do you plan to leave me dangling?’

Wyndham laughed and Charles wiped his mouth clumsily with a napkin, suddenly aware he had begun to dribble.

‘It was a play about the Reformation – as told in Scott’s *Tales of a Grandfather*. It seemed an appropriate link to you, being a grandfather yourself! It was to be called "Auld Reekie, or The Good Old Times". You were to have been the blustering Macer for a Supreme Judge, trying to keep order in his chaotic court. It was shaping up to be very amusing, with some bizarre insights into the tortures, burnings and witchcraft so relished in those "good old days of yore". I do believe it would have been a great success, Mr Mackay. However, it was not to be!' Wyndham sipped more coffee and Charles nodded thoughtfully.

'No, it was not to be … Let me tell you something I haven't mentioned to anyone else, Wyndham. Last Friday was the twenty-fifth anniversary of the death of my darling wife, Charlotte O'Keefe.'

'I'm sorry to hear that.'

'Thank you. She was a vibrant, beautiful and talented actress, but she never really had the opportunity to shine. Mostly because she was married to "The Real Mackay", as it turned out. I regret that. More than anything else in my life. William Murray never gave her a chance. I discovered too late that my success was all that mattered to him, filling the coffers of his theatre as it did, and making him a rich man.' Charles suddenly felt exhausted. He dabbed his damp mouth again and closed his eyes.

There was a knock on the door and Bella came in. Charles wondered, not for the first time, at her instinctive ability to anticipate his needs before he knew them himself. He was more than ready to be helped into bed for a snooze.

Mary opened Charles's shutters to a pale grey midsummer's morning a few weeks later and helped him take some porridge and tea, the night nurse having seen to his more personal needs an hour or so previously.

'Would you like anything else, Mr Mackay?'

'No thank you, Mary. I think I'll just lie here and rest while my breakfast wends its leisurely way through my body.' The maid closed the door behind her and Charles lay staring at the overcast sky, smoothing the green plaid with his gnarly fingers until he lost track of time.

There was a knock on the door and Bella came in.

'Good morning, Charles. How are you feeling today?' His daughter-in-law always smiled so brightly he could not help but smile back.

'Ready for some company my dear. I am heartily sick of my own!'

'Well, you're in luck. I shall be taking the children out soon for their Saturday visits and Charlie is looking forward to your company this morning.' She helped him swing his legs to the floor and sit on the edge of the bed, draping his green Paisley silk dressing gown round his shoulders and pulling his arms through the sleeves.

'Thank you kindly, dear. Tell me, what is that lovely fresh scent on my laundry, Bella? I've particularly noticed it this past week.' Bella turned slightly pink.

'Ah, yes, I hope you don't mind, Charles. I've taken the liberty of sprinkling lavender water on your sheets and pillowcases, your nightshirts as well. Charlie likes it when I push a sprig of rosemary in the bottle, so I thought … he says it reminds him of his … well, of his childhood.'

'Exactly so.' There was an awkward pause.

'Now then, where are your slippers, Charles?' Bella said rather too brightly as she crouched to fish under the bed for his red velvet moccasins. She slipped his stockinged feet inside them, put her hands under his arms and lifted him into his Bath chair. Charles had been surprised by her strength the first time she had lifted him, until he realised he no longer weighed much more than her children.

'Thank you my dear. You are too kind.' They were back on safe ground. Charles had found the scent of his wife on his sheets both comforting and disturbing, in addition to the mysterious appearance of the plaid. It was good to know the smell was not a figment of his imagination – that he was not, as yet, losing his mind. He would ask Bella about the plaid soon. Dorothy must have kept it. *What else did she keep?*

Bella wrapped the plaid round his legs, tucking it carefully over his cold hands, then removed his nightcap and gently combed back the unruly waves of his hair. Grey hairs had begun to appear since his illness, but it was still quite thick – though he had recently admitted to himself it was beginning to recede at the front.

'There! Handsome as ever! Shall we go and join the others?' Charles nodded and smiled to cover the indignity of his incapacities and she wheeled him through the hall into the kitchen.

'Here we are!' Bella trilled. The grandchildren all looked round and shouted greetings as they jumped down from the table to run over and kiss his sunken cheeks. He held Lottie's hand for a long moment with his weak fingers, smiling a lopsided smile just for her, which she rewarded by hugging him round his neck and giving him a kiss in the centre of his forehead.

'That's enough fussing, children, you'll tire your poor grandfather out! Come along now, coats on, time to go!' Bella and the children bustled noisily out of the kitchen, all waving goodbye and talking at once. Both men sat quietly for a moment, waiting for the front door to slam and silence to descend.

'Would you be so good as to pour me some tea, Charlie?' It was ridiculous to feel self-conscious in the company of his son, but Charles was annoyed his speech still sounded so slurred. There were a few things he wanted to say, and he was feeling on edge.

'It has occurred to me recently, Charlie, that I should make an amendment to my will. It's more than a year since your sister passed away and three of my trustees have already predeceased me. Now, with this blasted setback – well, I feel it would be tardy of me to leave it much longer.'

Charlie's expression brightened.

'I must say, Father, it comes as a relief to hear you say that. I've been wondering for some time how to mention the subject, but it always seemed so cavalier to bring it up.' Charlie began spreading butter onto his toasted bread energetically – back and forth, back and forth, crunch, crunch, crunch. Charles placed his hand on top of his son's, splaying his broad, square fingers to bring the frantic spreading to a halt, and noticing with surprise how mottled his skin was compared with Charlie's smooth, white hand.

'If you would be so good as to help me, dear boy. It would put my mind at rest.' Charles gathered himself. The next subject he wished to address was more tricky.

'Hmm, there is something else I wanted to say, Charlie.' His son flashed him a look of concern. 'You can rest assured, it's not bad news. I simply want to say how very much I have appreciated your generous, unstinting support these past weeks. I owe you and Bella a great debt for your tact and kindness towards me in my current predicament.' He took a slurp of tea and replaced the cup in its saucer with a trembling hand. *Go on, say it now!*

'Hmmm. I know I have not been much of a father to you over the years, Charlie, since your mother died. I'm not at all proud of myself in that regard.' Colour flushed his son's face and his eyes remained glued to the table.

'Not at all, Father. You've always done what you could over the years … even though at times it was … that is to say, it has been difficult …'

'Better to stop right there I think, before you run out of words entirely! I have been a self-absorbed and foolish fellow, and that's about the size of it!'

The comical sound of the words spraying from Charles's awkward, rubbery lips made them both laugh and Charlie looked up, smiling with relief. Charles had planned to say so much more – to apologise for so many things: for leaving his devastated eight-year-old son to deal with the grief of losing the mother he adored by himself; for his all-too-frequent absences throughout the long years of Charlie's childhood; for leaving him to manage his sister's and brother's emotions and struggles as they all grew up effectively parentless; for being so wrapped up in his fame, so caught up in all the characters he portrayed, that he sometimes forgot he even had children. That was how he saw it now.

Instead, Charles swept away the crumbs he had sprayed onto the table with his white linen napkin then wiped his hands slowly and carefully, enjoying the humour of the moment, the warmth of their shared smiles. He had made a start.

'One more thing, Charlie. I was wondering if you've heard from Hector. Have you managed to track him down and let him know about my calamity yet?'

'I received a letter from him just this week, Father. He sends his condolences and says he will try to come and visit. Although he will probably leave it until Hogmanay, as usual.'

'Aha!' *He has a letter from Hector!* Charles wondered why he had not received one himself. Perhaps Hector thought he was too incapacitated to read. The rapscallion had not been too far off the mark with his jest about Charles dying on-stage though, as it turned out.

'I've also had a letter from John Shiels' sister, Margaret, who sends her condolences and wishes you well. She's been writing to me occasionally since the funeral, Father, to ask after Lottie. In fact, I've sometimes wondered if it might be a good idea for Lottie to meet her relatives in Earlston, now she's a bit older. She has grandparents there, aunts and uncles, even a half-brother and sister, I believe. It might boost her confidence in some way, don't you think? She has lost so much.'

'Well, Charlie, that's quite a thought! It's true I have no right to keep her from her father's family just because John was such a pettifogging, double-dealing, unreliable charmer. I suppose his family may be quite different! Ha! In any case, Lottie may not have me with her for much longer; she will need their support as well as yours when I'm gone. Kind as you and Bella are to Lottie, she's not your child.'

'Please don't say such things, Father. I'm sure you still have years ahead of you!'

Charles looked his son squarely in the eye.

'Come now, we both know that isn't true.' He glanced at his hands and changed the subject. 'Lottie's formed quite an attachment to Izzie since her mother died – have you noticed? I'm not sure it's entirely appropriate, Charlie. So yes, it's about time she knew she has other family she can call her own.' An idea had occurred to Charles while he was speaking, and he smiled broadly. 'I know the very thing! The moment I'm well enough to see to myself again, to walk a few steps and so on, Lottie and I will go down to Earlston together on the train! Perhaps we could go and see if my portrait is still hanging at Abbotsford, too!'

Charlie shook his head and smiled fondly at him, raising his eyebrows as if to say *whatever next?*

'Now then, would you please take me back to my room, and help me onto my bed, dear boy. I'm suddenly very tired.'

THIRTY-THREE

Lottie loved Saturdays. The moment the door of Izzie's flat opened and her smiling, freckly face appeared, a delicious smell of freshly baked shortbread wafting out to greet her, Lottie felt a floaty feeling of happiness.

Izzie was teaching Lottie to sew. She was making a sampler with the letters of the alphabet and her name on it. It already had zigzag patterns round the edges, and she was going to add some flowers soon. She was very proud of it. When it was finished she would ask Aunty Bella to put it in a frame and then she would give it to Grandfather. Almost everything in Izzie's flat was about sewing. Apart from baby Molly, who was growing into a little girl now, and could stand up if she held onto a chair.

'Will you help me, please, Izzie?' Lottie was sitting by the window with her embroidery frame on her lap, squinting at the needle, trying to thread a new colour.

'I'm just changing Molly, poppet, why not ask Aunty Dorothy? Her beady eyes still work, even though her ears are not so good anymore!' Lottie was a tiny bit jealous of Molly, but preferred to share Izzie with her than not have Izzie at all. She took her sewing over to the old lady sitting by the fire and knelt on the floor beside her. There was a musty, sour smell about

Aunty Dorothy's brown woollen skirts and her faded blue apron was patched. She always wore an old-fashioned cap she called a mutch over her wispy grey hair and her mouth had collapsed because she had no teeth. Her leathery skin was covered with so many wrinkles you could never count them all. Aunty Dorothy was almost deaf, too, but her eyes were as bright and mischievous as a kitten's. She took the proffered needle and threaded it before Lottie could even ask, chuckling at her surprise as she handed it back.

'Aye, y're a canny wee lassie, for sure, Lottie. Ye mind me o' yer granny, so.' She mumbled her words through bare gums, her bottom lip constantly moving up and down as though she were chewing something. Lottie fetched a cushion and settled herself more comfortably at Aunty Dorothy's feet, hoping for a story about her granny. 'Are ye guid at keepin' secrets, lassie, eh?' Lottie nodded, making her eyes wide to show she was the best secret-keeper in the world. 'Weel noo, I've a wee secret I've kept in my pocket for mony's a year.' She slipped her bent and knobbly fingers into the wide pocket at the front of her apron and bent towards Lottie, grinning slyly. 'You'll mebbe be interested tae hear it, eh? *Izzie!*' Her voice was suddenly sharp and loud and Lottie jumped back, looking round at Izzie, wondering what was happening.

'Oh, Aunty, you rascal – you're wantin' tae let the cat oot the bag today, I'm thinkin'!' Izzie had put Molly in her truckle bed for a nap and was heating up chocolate drinks for them all. 'Aye, well, I'm thinkin' you're right, she's gey old enough tae know. Let's tak our wee meridian while you tell her the secret, Aunty, then I'll tak her through tae the sewing room and show her.' Lottie was beside herself with curiosity. She sat up to the table obediently for her hot chocolate and shortbread but kept her eyes fixed on Aunty Dorothy.

''Twas when yer granny died it happened. I was servant tae yer grandparents since afore yer Uncle Charlie was born – did ye ken that?' Lottie had had no idea Aunty Dorothy had been her grandfather's maid before Izzie. She sipped another silky-sweet mouthful of warm chocolate and waited for the delicious secret to unfold.

'So. Yer grandfaither was gey crabbit wi' his grief when yer granny died. He telt me one morning tae clear oot a' her things afore he came hame the nicht – he couldnae bear the sight o' them ony mair.' Aunty Dorothy nibbled and sucked her bit of shortbread with her toothless gums and Lottie tried to picture her grandfather being angry and shouting at his maid. It was hard to imagine. He must have been so sad he forgot his manners.

'He said tae gie it all away – tae the midden, tae the puir folk, tae my sisters – he didnae care, sae lang as it was gone frae his sight for ever. Puir man.'

'What did you do with it all?' Lottie was imagining a pile of colourful gorgeousness and longing to know where it all went.

'I left yer Uncle Charlie minding yer mammy, him a sensible laddie of eight and she a biddable wee treasure, just three. Then I tied Hector on ma hip wi' a plaid tae stop him runnin', and we went oot tae find a lad to tak a message and fetch ma sister Morag frae Leith. She was wi' us by noon wi' a few sacks, and brought her lass, Izzie, too!'

'Izzie met my mammy when they were little girls?' Dorothy chuckled at Lottie's amazement and slurped her hot chocolate, smacking her sunken lips together.

'Aye, she did. She's no' much older than yer Uncle Charlie! They two played thegither noo and then. We packed all they dresses an' shawls an' hats an' shoes an' beads an' chemises an' drawers an' – whit else – the green plaid, aprons, a muffler, stockings and a spencer – all o' it went intae the sacks. Yer wee mammy sat on the floor watchin' us wi' wide eyes, yer Uncle Charlie helpin' like a gentleman, Izzie foldin' like a proper wee washerwoman, and that young rascal Hector pullin' things oot aifter we'd put them in like the mischief he aye was! We had tae get a handcart for Morag and Izzie tae tak it a' hame.' Aunty Dorothy grinned toothlessly at the memory, dabbing her eyes on a kerchief, and Izzie poured more chocolate into Lottie's cup, wiping her mouth gently with a damp cloth. Aunty Dorothy cleared her throat with a deep burbling noise, then spat into her handkerchief.

'We decided, ma sister and me, that we'd keep they clathes and costumes and things in the room she shared wi' Izzie at hame, and that we'd use some o' they bonnie fabrics tae mak a few wee dresses for your mammy, seein' she'd lost her ain mammy and hadnae a thing tae remember her by.' Aunty Dorothy started coughing and Izzie ran over to help her, patting her back, fetching camphor to rub on her chest until the smell of it filled the room. Lottie wandered back over to the window and picked up her sewing, her mind reeling with the thought of the sisters stuffing sacks full of her granny's lovely clothes and costumes and taking them away to hide. *Where is it all now? Can I see it? Or were all the dresses cut up and made into new ones for Mammy?* Lottie wondered if she had worn one of them without knowing, maybe the red and yellow striped frock Izzie gave her to wear for Christmas which had belonged to her mother.

'Izzie?' Lottie could not keep her questions inside anymore. Aunty Dorothy had gone to sleep in her chair by then and Molly was snoozing in her cot, so Lottie had Izzie to herself at last.

'I ken what ye're thinkin', lass, and the answer is – we have it all here!'

'What? Here in your flat?' Lottie jumped down from her chair, dropping her sewing on the floor. 'Where is it?'

'We've all yer mammy's things frae Drummond Street as well! I'm lucky tae have a wee room for ma sewing, Lottie – till there are more weans! I've a muckle closet in there, stuffed full o' wonders! D'ye want tae see?' Lottie was lost for words and nodded excitedly.

'It's a secret, mind! Ye mustnae be lettin' on tae yer aunty or yer cousins – and never tell yer grandfather, or he'll gie me a row!' Izzie laughed and made a silly face and Lottie wondered if she would be able to keep such a huge secret buttoned up inside herself.

'Waverley Station! The perfect place for us to set off on our travels, don't you think, Bella? The new branch line to Melrose is called the Waverley Route as well – I feel the gods may be conspiring in our favour!' Lottie looked up at her grandfather's happy face, delighted he seemed almost back to normal.

'Let's hope so, Charles. It's quite an ambitious journey for someone in your delicate condition, you know,' Aunty Bella replied. Then she turned to Lottie. 'You'll look after him, won't you, dear? Remember, he mustn't carry any bags, and he *must* be helped on and off the railway carriage.' Lottie was thrilled to be addressed in such a grown-up way. She would be seven on her next birthday and was therefore quite capable of taking responsibility.

'Yes, Aunty Bella, of course.' Her grandfather gave her a sly wink. One side of his face was still a bit droopy, but his eyes were as sparkly as ever. They were standing beside a big, black railway engine which huffed out huge clouds of steam every few minutes. Suddenly it gave a loud toot and a man in a dark blue uniform blew a whistle.

'Quickly, now, Charles, Lottie, time to get on the train.' Aunty Bella held Lottie's hand as she stepped carefully over the wide gap from the platform onto the bottom step. Then she pulled herself up into the carriage, holding the rail tightly, and turned round see what would happen next. Their luggage was in a handcart on the platform and Aunty Bella gave some pennies to the porter to load it onto the train.

'Would you please help this gentleman into the carriage, first, young man.' The porter heaved her grandfather up the steps, then jumped back onto the platform to pick up the bags. The man with the whistle blew it again and the engine sent out another huge puff of steam, like the sigh of a dragon.

Inside the railway carriage the porter showed them to their seats, stowed their bags on the luggage rack, then returned to the platform.

Lottie knelt on her seat, smiling out of the window at Aunty Bella. When the train began to move, very slowly, she began to walk beside it, smiling and waving. Soon her aunt could no longer keep up and Lottie pressed her face against the window, clouding it with the steam of her breath, until she could no longer see even a smudge of her. Then she turned round and sat down properly, arranging her skirts and smoothing her hair.

'Off we go on our adventure, eh, Lottie! We'll soon be speeding along like a racehorse, just you wait and see!'

Before long the countryside was flicking past so fast Lottie felt dizzy, especially with the swaying of the carriage and the tickety-tackety clattering of the wheels on the track. Grandfather had closed his eyes, but she guessed he was still awake because she could see his fingers fidgeting with his kerchief in his lap.

Aunty Bella and Grandfather had talked to Lottie about her father's family a few weeks ago. It had turned her world upside down. Lottie had no memories of her father at all. It had never occurred to her that he might have a family, which would also be her family: the Shielses. She felt nervous and excited about meeting them all and hoped very much they would like her. Granny and Grandpa Shiels had an inn, and a farm, too. It would be so exciting if there were animals on the farm.

'Are you awake, Grandfather?' He opened one eye and grunted, then shuffled in his seat and sat up straighter, dabbing his mouth with his handkerchief.

'I certainly am, Lottie. Would you like to have a conversation?' She nodded. 'I have a question, Grandfather. What is the right thing to do when you are told a secret and the secret gets so big inside your head it wants to burst out of your mouth. Do you have to keep it inside?'

He looked at her for a long moment, his head on one side.

'Well now, Lottie, that is a good question. If it is a secret about something dangerous or unhappy or frightening, then you should tell it to someone grown-up who you know very well and trust.'

She nodded to show him she was listening carefully, then piped up again.

'And if it's about something that makes you feel happy, then what?'

'Ah!' He smiled widely. 'In that case, Lottie, you should probably talk to the person who gave it to you and explain your predicament. Does that help?'

'Hmm, a bit, I suppose.'

He closed his eyes again and Lottie thought about her secret. Izzie had shown her all the beautiful gowns that used to belong to her granny last Saturday, and some of the dresses they had made for her mammy, too. They were gorgeous: soft and slippery, shimmery and delicious; and they were a secret. Lottie hoped very much that one day they would not be.

'Hello there Lottie – I'm Grandpa Shiels! I've bin beside mysel' waitin' tae set eyes on you, lass!' A tall, thin man with a slight stoop and a green checked jacket was standing on the platform holding his arms out to her when she clambered down onto the platform behind her grandfather, who was managing very well with his stick. 'Come and gie yer ol' grandpa a hug, then!' Lottie allowed the man to hug her, although she felt very shy. He smelt of animals and pipe tobacco.

After a bumpy ride in his open cart they pulled up outside a low, white cottage. Grandpa Shiels climbed down and gave the horse's bridle to a tall, dark-haired boy who appeared from nowhere and smiled shyly at Lottie. Then he called out, 'That's us arrived, Christina!' and a woman came to the door at once, wiping her hands on a stripy brown apron. She was only a head taller than Lottie and looked like a round pumpkin in her full yellow skirts. Her cap was old-fashioned, like Aunty Dorothy's, and she had a jolly, pink face with two wobbling chins.

She took Lottie's face between her red hands and planted a kiss on her forehead. 'Let me see you, bonnie wee thing! Oh my, oh my, you mind me o' yer mammy, so you do!' Then Granny Shiels hugged her so tightly that Lottie's face almost disappeared into her squashy bosom. She smelt of fried onions. Lottie could hear her grandfather coughing behind her as if he were trying not to laugh.

'Come away in and make yersel's at hame! We've rooms ready for ye and hot water to wash.' Grandpa Shiels was so tall he had to stoop to go through the low door. He lifted Grandfather's heavy bag onto one shoulder without as much as a grunt, and slung Lottie's canvas bag over the other.

When Lottie stepped into the dimness of the inn she realised it was full of people. They all began to talk at once and she stood very still. A lady in a dark silk gown which somehow made her pale eyebrows seem even paler stepped forward and took her hand.

'Lottie, my darling, d'you remember meeting me in Edinburgh last year? I'm your Aunt Margaret?'

Two other ladies pushed her to one side before Lottie could reply. 'Hello Lottie! I'm your Aunty Anne – and this is Aunty Jemima.'

'We've baked you a cake!' They were much younger, giggling and pretty in their puff-sleeved cotton dresses and frilly white aprons.

'Will you shake my hand, Lottie? I'm your Uncle Alex, and this wee lad here is young James, yer cousin. Say hello, James!' A younger version of Grandpa Shiels was holding out his hand, a little boy peeping at her from behind his long legs. She felt a gentle hand on her arm and looked round.

'Dinnae mind all they folk. I'll tak you up tae yer room and we can tidy up together for dinner. I'm your sister, Helen, and that boy who took the horse earlier, he's yer brother, Jimmy.' Lottie put her hands to her cheeks.

Her own sister and brother! It almost took her breath away. Helen was so beautiful, with her large brown eyes and dark, curling hair tucked into a frilly white cap, a freshly starched apron over her lilac print dress. When she smiled and hooked her arm into Lottie's, Lottie felt as if she had known her all her life. *How very strange.*

'Thank you very much. I should like to put my things away and brush my hair, please.' She was too shy to say she was hungry, but it was good to know there would be dinner soon, and cake.

THIRTY-FOUR

Lottie blossomed like a cherry tree in Earlston.

There were moments when Charles felt a pang of jealousy, especially when her other grandfather made her laugh, or promised to take her to see the animals on his farm and gave her hand a squeeze. He was a good man, though, James Shiels. Hard-working. He ran a sizeable farm as well as the inn, and Charles discovered that his quick wit and booming voice made him a popular auctioneer at the local markets too. It was a comfort to know Lottie would have these good folk to care for her when he had gone.

A trip to Abbotsford was arranged for the third day of their stay, and Margaret Shiels decided to accompany them. Margaret was an excitable and enthusiastic woman and did not stop talking from the moment they climbed into the cart to the moment they arrived. When the cart rolled up the drive and came to a halt before the splendid grandeur of Abbotsford House, Charles felt the need for a little time on his own. He had never been here before, but he knew it had meant everything to Sir Walter and wanted time to reflect.

'Might I suggest, Margaret my dear, that you and Lottie avail yourselves of the opportunity to explore this wondrous place unencumbered by the limitations of my hirpling gait? I am content to sit here in the cart with young Jimmy – who has driven us here so splendidly by the way. These cushions you brought, Margaret, are very comfortable, and I have my woollen plaid on my knees. I'm sure Jimmy would be happy to hand me down when I'm sufficiently restored to attempt a little walk.' Charles beamed his biggest smile.

'A sensible idea, Mr Mackay. You have a nice rest, and we girls will go and look around, won't we, Lottie!' Lottie smiled up at him, content to leave the talking to her new aunt, who was already holding her hand.

'If you happen to find my portrait during your wanders, perhaps you would be so good as to come and fetch me, Margaret.'

'Of course we will, Mr Mackay! Now then, Lottie, off we go!'

The sun was shining and Charles was feeling pleasantly warm and drowsy. Margaret's trilling voice faded into the chirruping and chattering of the birds, and Jimmy went to fetch water for the horse. Charles allowed his mind to wander.

He gazed up at Sir Walter's glorious baronial mansion and its surrounds, imagining that genial host, dogs yapping and yelping and milling around his feet, tails a-wag, welcoming his guests as they swept up the drive in their barouches and landaus to join him for a few days at his country idyll. Charles had dipped into his set of Lockhart's *Memoirs* enough times to know Sir Walter sometimes took his guests up into the tower after a hearty dinner, to show them the magical moonlit vista. It looked very sturdy and castle-like, with its crenellated stone balustrade. *The view from there must be magnificent.*

Charles fingered the silver ferrule on his walking stick for the thousandth time, thinking of his old friend, Sir William Allen, who had one just like it. It was Allen who had painted the portrait he was hoping to see shortly: a good likeness of him as the Bailie, wielding the poker and looking anxious.

It had grown quite warm. Charles lifted the green plaid from his knee and put it on the seat beside him, then closed his eyes again, enjoying the sun on his face.

It had not taken him long to rumble Lottie's secret. The plaid had started him wondering what else Dorothy might have kept. When he had noticed Lottie using the London handkerchief on the train, he'd known he was right. Lottie's bright-eyed enthusiasm made him think she must have seen some of Charlotte's beautiful gowns, so he had teased her yesterday, describing the red gown with the embroidered bodice; the tartan gown Charlotte was wearing when he first set eyes on her; the mint-green muslin chemise she had worn to Murray's first wedding. Lottie's shocked expression had been most gratifying. Then it all came out in a gush. Charles had been rather taken aback to hear that some of Charlotte's other gowns had been used to make dresses for his daughter and granddaughter, that they had both worn them right under his nose, and he had never noticed.

He began to snooze. Sir Walter had always seemed a distant figure, in many ways, yet he had often referred to Charles as his friend, and the feeling had been mutual. Scott's stories had provided wonderful opportunities for Charles to develop as an actor over the years, and he liked to think the success of the stage plays had contributed something of value to Scott in return. He owed Sir Walter a very great deal and had said as much in his retirement speech: *Had he never written, I never should have been noticed as an actor; it is to the pen of the mighty dead I owe my theatrical reputation.*

The sound of yammering drew him back into the pleasantly warm afternoon. He opened his eyes. Margaret and Lottie were emerging from the front door, both talking at once. They waved at him and came hurrying over.

'You simply must accompany us to the Chinese Drawing Room, Mr Mackay, it is a room of great beauty and style!'

'The study's so full of books you can't even see the walls, Grandfather!' He held his hand up for silence, smiling fondly at them both.

'I'm delighted you've had such a marvellously diverting time, ladies, but I fear I must content myself with your descriptions for now. I will be pushing my legs to their absolute limit just to walk inside the front door of the old place! If you could hand me down, Jimmy, I should be most grateful.'

Jimmy looked so like a younger version of his father that Charles had to check himself when old resentments flared into frowns. He was a tall, good-looking lad with a mild manner, a shock of brown hair and a hint of fuzz on his chin. He was surprisingly strong as well. Charles leaned heavily on his arm and allowed himself to be lifted down.

'Thank you very much indeed, young man!' He straightened up and brushed the country dust from his coat, then took his stick in his right hand and held out his other arm to Lottie. 'If you would do me the honour of tucking yourself under my arm, Mattie dear, *there's no disgrace in a bailie walking hand in arm with gentle blood!* I may have to lean on you quite heavily though.'

Lottie stood on her tiptoes and reached up to adjust his cream neckerchief, replying in her best Scots brogue, '*Now, wrap this kerchief about your thrapple – there – leave a wee bit room for your mouth – ye must needs ha' a drap o' the cordial your faither, the deacon, was so fond of!*' They laughed at their private joke until he noticed the look of confusion on Margaret's face.

'Ah, Margaret, my dear. Forgive us! Mattie is a character in the play of *Rob Roy*. Lottie has been learning the part recently and we practise it together sometimes.'

'Oh, of course, I see!' Margaret smoothed her hair and patted it, smiling brightly.

'Shall we proceed?'

They entered the imposing front door and Charles stopped

to stare at the extraordinary collection of ancient weaponry covering the wood-panelled walls. Lottie, who had seen it already, tugged impatiently on his arm.

'The library is this way, Grandfather, you must come and see all the books! I wrote our names in a big visitor's book – and the date – isn't it all so exciting!'

'It certainly is, dearest. But may I ask, before I begin my perambulations, did you manage to locate the painting I described?'

'Of course we did! Come along, I'll show you. You're wearing the same neckerchief as the painting today, Grandfather, that's why I said the lines from the play!' His astute granddaughter had rumbled his little bit of vanity and he gave her a wry smile in acknowledgement.

It was an unsettling experience, standing before a likeness of his younger self as a confident, famous, strong young man. The three of them stood looking at it for a minute or so, Margaret and Lottie both quiet after their initial outbursts of excitement.

Then Charles turned abruptly.

'I should like to leave now.'

'Mr Mackay, I wonder if I might, perhaps, accompany you and Lottie back to Edinburgh for a few days. I must confess I have been so bold as to purchase a ticket already.' Margaret had waited until Lottie had gone to bed before broaching the subject. Although Charles was surprised, he could see no reason why not. They would surely be able to make room for her somewhere at 23 Dublin Street.

'What a fine idea, Margaret. I have no doubt Lottie would love to retain your charming company for as long as she possibly can.'

'Oh, thank you so much, Mr Mackay, thank you so much.' Margaret dabbed her perspiring upper lip with a small lacy handkerchief and proceeded to explain herself more fully.

'I simply cannot bear to part with our dear Lottie just yet. I am so sorry for her, Mr Mackay, not having her parents. I know there's nothing I can do to replace even the smallest aspect of her dear mother, but perhaps I can come and see her from time to time, take her for little outings and so forth?'

Margaret's very short marriage to a much older man had come too late in life for her to have her own children. Now she was a childless widow living at home with her family again. Charles could see that her maternal instincts had been roused by Lottie and decided to give her free rein. Besides, it would be nice for Lottie if her aunt started to visit and take her out on jaunts, she might be a good companion for the child when he was no longer able to fulfil that role himself.

THIRTY-FIVE

The sound of children yelping usually sent Charles in the opposite direction from its source. However, on a windy March morning in what had so far been a remarkably dry year, that of 1854, he detected a delicious note of excitement in the whooping that emanated from the kitchen very soon after breakfast. He decided to investigate. The children would normally be at their studies in the parlour by now, but fun and games appeared to be happening and he would hate to miss them.

'Grandfather, quick, come and see!' Little Tommy, now a lively and inquisitive four-year-old, grabbed his hand the moment he opened the kitchen door and pulled him towards the scullery, where the girls were crouching on the floor, cooing and laughing in delight. 'Their eyes are shut and they're all baldy and ugly and small as mouses, Grandfather! Look!' Tommy was pointing proudly at the cat basket in the corner, near the slop buckets.

Jane looked up. 'Kittens, Grandfather! Three of them!'

'We're not allowed to pick them up yet though, they're only born this morning!' Lottie was beside herself, her face shining with happiness. She had been a different child since their visit to Earlston. Margaret Shiels had been up to Edinburgh twice in the intervening months to visit her, taken her out to buy pretty fripperies, treated her to cakes and ices, made her feel special in a way he no longer could. Margaret was even planning to take her to Earlston for a fortnight's holiday in August, and Lottie could talk of little else.

Mary came in, wiping her hands on her apron. 'Good morning, Mr Mackay. I'll need to move the basket in by the fire as soon as I can get these children out of the way. It'll be too cold for them in the scullery.' Mary had a charming flush of excitement about her as well, her little button eyes gleaming with fun. 'Mrs Mackay doesnae know yet, mind. I only found them after breakfast when I was cleaning the plates. Mrs Mackay and Chas went straight from the table to answer the door to Miss Winter. They're in the parlour the now, by the sound of it, setting up the school room. I dinnae ken what she'll make of 'em!'

'Well, we'll just have to find out, won't we children? Come along girls, Tommy, we have a very important announcement to make in the parlour and we must give Mary a chance to bring our new arrivals into the warm and make them comfortable.' These children had quickly become such a joy to him. He could hardly bear to imagine the fun he had missed with his own.

'Aha, Bella! It would seem my days as the Bailie are not yet over!' Charles waved a letter he had just opened with a wicked gleam in his eye. Bella was clearing plates from the table with Mary after lunch. She put them down with a clatter, her face a picture of anxiety.

'Oh, no, Charles – you cannot go on-stage again – I thought we had all agreed!'

'My dear, I do not deserve your kindness, forgive me, I'm teasing! The letter arrived this morning. It's from a young

Glasgow artist, Daniel Macnee, who wants to paint my portrait. It's to be exhibited in the Royal Academy throughout the summer. I think I shall accept.' Charles pushed himself to his feet. He picked up the two walking sticks he now used and had left leaning against the table and continued with enthusiasm.

'I can go through to Glasgow by train. Perhaps I could go on a Saturday afternoon so Charlie can accompany me. Then I'll stay with my nephew Lauchlan at his comfortable house in Grafton Street for the duration, which will probably be most of May. I'm sure he and his lovely wife, Janet, will be delighted to have me and will look after me extremely well. I believe they have seven children, now, so we shall have some fun as well, no doubt.'

'No doubt you will, Charles, no doubt you will!'

The smell of oil paint was over-powering. The fumes, rather than the aches in his muscles, made Charles require frequent breaks during the sittings.

Macnee was an affable young man with a broad grin, thick wavy hair and generous sideburns, who smiled often and had a great fund of amusing stories with which to entertain his sitter. Charles had brought his red jacket – not the original, but one which had served him well for hundreds of performances – and the cream silk necktie he had bought for his last season in Glasgow. He had hardly worn the necktie since, except on his visit to Abbotsford. He had decided not to bring the hat. His grandchildren had recently appropriated it for their games and it was already somewhat the worse for wear.

They discussed the pose on the first morning.

'Dear fellow, d'you think I could slip my right hand mysteriously inside my jacket, as though I were about to pull out a paper and wave it around officiously? I am feeling the lack of a poker, yet I fear I would not have the strength to wield such a thing for hours on end at my advanced age!'

'Perhaps you could show me what you had in mind, sir?' Charles struck the pose and was greatly relieved when Macnee said he liked it. He did not like the whimsical expression on Charles's face, however, and insisted on something far more serious. Charles would have preferred to look affable or amusing but did as he was told to the best of his ability.

When the portrait was finished Macnee invited Charles to view it for the first time. He pushed himself up from his seat, picked up his walking sticks, and made his way slowly towards the canvas, feeling rather apprehensive. Macnee was grinning broadly, wiping his hands on his paint-smeared apron, clearly delighted with his work.

'Come along now, don't be shy, Mr Mackay! I think the portrait will make quite an impression, the look in your eye is most imperious!'

'Ah yes, a very creditable likeness, dear fellow.' The portrait came nowhere near to conveying the character of Bailie Nicol Jarvie, neither did it capture what he imagined to be his own personality. He was pleased to see his hair had been portrayed a little browner than it really was, a little thicker, too, but his sideburns had been painted well and truly grey, which was fair enough for a man of his vintage. Charles found his stern gaze rather unsettling, though, and wondered what on earth anyone else might make of it. *No doubt it will frighten the grandchildren, which would be entertaining!*

On a warm Saturday morning in early June, when the children had gone out for the day with Bella, Charles was finishing an extended breakfast in relative peace and quiet when his son presented him with a copy of *The Art Journal*, folded open.

'I think you'll find this quite amusing, Father.'

'What is it? A dreaded review?' Charles glanced at the page and saw at once the item to which his son was referring:

Charles Mackay, Esq., Theatre Royal, Edinburgh, as Bailie Nicol Jarvie exhibited by Daniel Macnee in the Royal Academy, 1854, No. 218. The features are dry but expressive of shrewdness and penetration. Although the impersonation would be, as a portrait, eccentric, yet it does not realise the famous Bailie.

He put the journal on the table.

'He's right. I'm intrigued to read such a perceptive review, Charlie. I fear the Bailie has finally eluded me! Yet, however shrewd and penetrating my expression may have looked to this writer, I can assure you it was not. I believe it flitted between utter boredom, ridiculous anxiety and extreme discomfort. No doubt the painting will find some wall on which to hang where my face can stare with dry, expressive features, shrewdness and penetration at some poor hapless soul day after day.' Charles took a sip of tea and beamed mischievously at his son, hoping to withdraw to his room shortly without further discussion.

Six weeks later he received some surprising news in a letter from his nephew.

Dear Uncle Charles,

I thought you should know I have just purchased the excellent portrait of you painted by Mr. Daniel Macnee R.S.A. and exhibited at the Royal Academy to great acclaim throughout this summer.

It is now hanging in pride of place in my drawing room, and very fine it looks too! Indeed, it has inspired me to sit for a portrait myself so we can glower at one another from either side of the fireplace!

I look forward to seeing you again 'ere long, Uncle,

Your nephew, godson, friend and most loyal admirer,

Lauchlan Mackay.

Charles put the letter on his desk and smiled. He could not have imagined a more satisfactory outcome for the painting, and the idea of his stern face glowering across the room at a portrait of Lauchlan was most amusing.

THIRTY-SIX

The doorbell at No. 17 Lutton Place jangled more harshly than the one in Dublin Street. Charles found it rather unsettling – *particularly when it heralds the arrival of one's boisterous youngest son!*

Robert Wyndham had surprised everyone by inviting Hector to perform as Bailie Nicol Jarvie in his latest production of *Rob Roy* at the Theatre Royal, which he was now managing. Hector had arranged to travel by train from London, where he had recently secured a contract at the Theatre Royal, Haymarket. He planned to stay with Charlie and Bella and all the family in their spacious new home on the Southside for the best part of a week. Rehearsals began in the morning and the performance was to be on Saturday evening.

'Bella! Father! I'm here! Where is everyone? Thank you, Mary.' Charles opened his bedroom door to find Hector handing his top hat and a fancy cane to Mary. A slightly flustered Bella appeared from the kitchen, Tommy peering out from behind her skirts. Her face had grown as round as the moon and she was glowing with good health. She smiled and wiped her hands on an apron that barely covered the mound of her belly.

'Ah, Hector! Welcome! Did you have a good journey? How nice that you've arrived so early! Maggie's just taken the children for a walk but they'll be back in an hour or so, then we can all have tea in the kitchen. Tommy and I are making scones.' Hector grinned at her and her cheeks turned slightly pink.

'My oh my, Bella, you're looking quite the goddess! Charlie must be very proud!'

'Och, don't be so daft!' she countered, wiping Tommy's flour-smeared face with a corner of her apron, as if to hide a smile. Charles intervened.

'Why not join me in the parlour while we wait, Hector.'

The large parlour was richly decorated in dark greens and reds, with china knick-knacks and glass lamps on every surface. They sat down on a pair of oxblood leather wing chairs either side of the marble fireplace. It was warm for May, so no fire had yet been lit.

'Well, Hector, I must say,' said Charles, 'I was quite taken aback when Wyndham told me what he was planning and asked me for your address. I believe tickets have almost sold out already!'

Hector never sat upright in a chair, he lounged – perhaps to give a fashionable impression of *ennui*. Charles had prepared a little speech and was determined not to be distracted by his son's faux display of languor.

'I should very much like to lend you my jacket for the part, Hector, if it fits you, of course.' Hector's eyebrows rose and he sat up. *Well, it has saved him asking me for it, at least!* 'I'm afraid the hat has come a cropper, though, since the children acquired it for their pirate games!'

'The Real Mackay's jacket, eh? What an honour!' Hector's attempt at humour failed to fool his father. *He's surprised, I think. Maybe somewhat delighted, even – though he would never let on!*

'On a different subject, I should like you to decide whether you want me to attend the performance or not, Hector. I don't want to provide an unwelcome distraction, but I should very much enjoy watching you take on the Bailie! Likewise with

Charlie and Bella and the children. We feel it is for you to say which of us you would like to attend.'

At first, Hector shrugged his shoulders, as if it were all the same to him. Then he lunged forward, sweeping his arms wide, and blurted out, 'I want you all to come, of course Father! It would be unbearably tragic if any of you missed such an historic performance!' Hector burst out laughing. Charles smiled broadly.

'Indeed it would, Hector, indeed it would! In that case I shall splash out a guinea and hire a private box. No doubt Wyndham will call attention to us Mackays and we shall have to take bows and wave at the crowds, but hopefully they'll settle down and allow us to enjoy watching you improve on your old father's delivery! I imagine there will be plenty of laughter when you deliver all the lines referring to your *faither, the deacon*.'

Charles had begun to slide sideways in the slippery armchair, as he often did. Although less mobile than he had been last summer, he was grateful not to be back in the Bath chair yet. He grasped the arm of the chair with his good hand and pushed himself up a little.

'Joking aside, Hector—'

'Oh dear, that sounds worrying, Father – you never put joking aside, and neither do I!'

'That's exactly my point, really, Hector. I've been giving a lot of thought to the past of late. My incapacities have provided plenty of time for such ruminations, as you can imagine. In any case, I feel I owe you an apology, dear boy, for more than I can adequately put into words – chiefly for my absence in your life in years gone by, I suppose.'

Hector began to pick at his fingernails. For once, he did not interrupt.

'I'm aware it was Dorothy who raised you, Hector, to all intents and purposes, with only poor old Charlie to back her up when you started running wild …'

'That's a bit extreme, isn't it?'

'I don't think it is, Hector. I think it's an understatement. Charlie has told me enough anecdotes – in response to my recent inquiries – to confirm what I have long suspected, so there's really no need to try and pull the wool over my eyes.' Charles held his hand up to silence any protest. 'Indulge me please, if you would be so kind, dear boy. I know I have only myself to blame for my lack of involvement in your life, Hector. I'm also fully aware that the time I have left is limited and I would very much like to clear the air between us before it's too late.' Charles held his son's gaze for a moment and was relieved when Hector nodded in agreement without feeling the need to mock.

They sat and talked until they were called through for tea half an hour later.

Charles was amazed to discover his son was still in touch with Dorothy and visited her at Izzie's house whenever he was in Edinburgh. Hector talked fondly of Izzie too, and of the bountiful Saturday lunches they all, including Izzie, used to enjoy at the Winters'. He was in the midst of a story about some mischief he and Bella had got up to as children – being the same age they had been thick as thieves for a few years – when she popped her head round the door.

'How are you two getting on?'

'Fine, my dear, we are fine!' Charles managed to smother his urge to laugh with a friendly smile at once, like the professional he was, but Hector clearly did not trust himself to speak.

'Having a very jolly time, it would seem! I came to tell you the children are home and Mary is serving tea in the kitchen, if you'd care to join us.'

'How delightful, my dear! Would you be so kind as to help me up, old boy, my legs have hardly any strength in them these days, but I much prefer an arm to my sticks.' Hector hooked an arm under his father's and Charles was surprised to find himself feeling overwhelmed by feelings of affection as they made their way slowly through to the kitchen together.

Hector tried on the red jacket after tea and paraded about in it all evening, reciting lines from *Rob Roy*, much to the delight of the children, who were very reluctant to leave the fun and go to bed. Even Lottie seemed charmed by her uncle's playacting. Charlie, however, pleaded weariness after a long day in the office and retired with Bella not long after the children.

Charles and Hector took their seats by the fire again, which had now been lit. This time each had a glass of whisky in their hands.

'You look very fine in that jacket, Hector. I thought it might be a little tight on you! Ha!'

'Why thank you, Father, for your barbed compliment. I shall treasure it!' They both smiled into their drinks, comfortable in each other's company now, listening to the crackle of the flames and the tick of the mantel clock.

'Fame is a strange and fickle friend, you know, Hector. You can chase after it for all you're worth, but if you catch it, it'll take over your life. Then, suddenly, it will drop you and you'll sink into oblivion like an old boot in a peat bog, wondering what it has all been about! A case in point – if you see the name Charles Mackay in the press these days it usually refers to that excellent young writer from Perth. Indeed, I have his book about extraordinary popular delusions myself, it's rather good! I assume you're still in hot pursuit of fame, though, Hector?'

'Well, when you put it like that it sounds rather futile. But I should very much like to succeed on the stage.' Hector's eyes took on a slightly feverish quality and he sat forward in his seat.

'You can have no idea what it's been like to grow up in the shadow of such a famous father.' The unexpected comment jabbed Charles like a darning needle. He braced himself for worse, wondering why he had let his guard down with this unpredictable son of his. 'I never knew my mother, of course, but I know from Dorothy that she was a very accomplished actress. I imagine it must have been hard for her, too, watching your fame grow so huge while she was obliged to remain on the sidelines, nursing her children and her dreams, knowing she could never match your success, however hard she tried.' Hector sat back and took a long sip of whisky. Charles held his gaze and decided not to defend himself.

'Well, Hector, I expect you've been building up to saying that for quite some time. It must have been hard to find the right moment. I admire your courage. And you've made some very fair points, too, not that anything can be done about them now.' He took a sip of whisky and a deep breath.

'I loved your mother more than my own life, Hector. She was an extraordinary woman. It is entirely possible that I failed to understand her in some way, that I let her down, even – but I want you to know that I always loved and admired her more than any other person on this earth.'

Hector stared into his glass.

'I have made many mistakes in my life, Hector, but I do hope we can be friends now. And I honestly wish you every success. I don't know if I wish you fame, though. As I have said, it's a strange, demanding thing. Once it has you in its grip there's no escaping its momentum. It rolls along relentlessly, taking you with it whether you like it or not, sometimes stealing from you what you hold most dear.'

Charles let out a long sigh and they both sat quietly for a while. 'I confess I still feel terribly guilty about your mother. I find it so very painful to talk about her that I never do. You were right to question me, though, she deserved better than I gave her.' Charles pushed himself to his feet with great effort, holding onto the chair, then the mantelpiece for balance.

'Are you off to bed already, Father? I was hoping for a few tips about the Bailie before we retire!'

'Of course! But there's something I should like to give you first.' Charles reached for the gold snuff box on the mantelpiece. 'Rather than leaving this to you in my will, I thought I should like to give it to you now, Hector – a token of my respect for your professional talents, which seem to be developing very nicely indeed.' Charles handed Hector the box and sat down again with a grunt.

Hector sat quite still, staring at the box, his eyes glistening in the flicker of the fire. Then he lifted the lid and stared at the inscription, for once entirely lost for words.

Hector's performance was 'far from bad', according to the critics. Charles thought his son had done extremely well, given the huge expectations of the audience and the notoriety of the shoes he was attempting to fill. The children had loved being the centre of attention of course, standing up with Charles several times to wave and receive applause. Charlie had been surprisingly swept up in the occasion too, giving his brother a decent compliment later that evening. Even Bella had attended to support Hector, though her time was precariously near. The following week she gave birth to a healthy girl whom they named Frances Charlotte.

THIRTY-SEVEN

Chas began attending the Royal High School in the autumn of 1855, and the girls started at a dame school. Twice a week Jane and Lottie took dancing lessons with Mrs Wyndham at the Theatre Royal, too. Maggie Winter, always such an unfailing support to her sister, arrived at the flat first thing every weekday morning and took the children to and fro, usually with five-year-old Tommy in tow, taking a cab in bad weather, leaving Bella to nurse her charmingly placid little daughter in peace.

Charles found the flat rather too quiet for his liking without the children, but soon developed a pleasant routine for himself. Every Monday morning Mr Cromby, the barber, came to Lutton Place to give him a close shave and a trim, the soothing of the grooming and gossip proving an excellent way to start the week. He spent most of the other mornings dipping into his precious collection of books or chatting with Mary and Bella in the kitchen. Occasionally there might be a visitor – Robert Wyndham, Emma Nicol, his doctor. Then, after lunch – which he took in the kitchen – he would have a snooze, venturing out later in the afternoon for a stroll in the company of one of the children, walking very slowly with his two walking sticks, being helped down the stairs and back up again by Mary.

The winter came on early and was particularly cold. It seemed to drag on longer than usual too, and Charles wondered if he felt it more than the others because of all his aches and pains. He hardly went out anymore.

Hogmanay was a subdued affair. Conflict in the Balkans was rumbling on interminably, often casting a long shadow over conversations in the evenings with news of casualties in the Scottish regiments. James Mackay was born on January the 19th, 1856, and the sound of his new grandchild's cries in the night went through Charles like a knife. He had never been troubled by the nocturnal cries of little Frances, sleeping soundly through whatever little snuffles of complaint she may have made. Perhaps it was because James was born in the depths of a fiercely cold winter, like Hector had been. Sometimes in the night Charles thought time had slipped by thirty years and wanted to rise from his bed and run to take the screaming child from his poor sick wife so she could rest.

When spring finally arrived with a burst of bright green buds on the trees and a bold blue sky, it acted on him like a tonic. The warmth in the sun brought welcome relief to his aching bones as he sat by the window, and he began to feel a keen desire to be outside. He resumed his little strolls, grateful that no one pointed out how much shorter and less frequent they were than they had been the previous year.

Throughout 1856 Charles made the best of things, but as autumn turned to winter again, his health declined rapidly. Unable to walk many steps even with his sticks, he confined his shuffling to the flat and his world shrank. The less he walked, the less he was able to walk. Before long he was back in his Bath chair being pushed around and feeling himself nothing but a burden on the family. Bella was with child again and her mother had recently died. He could not allow himself to add to her load.

He employed a nurse, who came to help him in the evenings and stayed with him at night, giving him back a modicum of control over his situation. She saw to his needs in the mornings, too, before she left, so he could present a respectable face to the family. He managed reasonably well during the day with the ministrations of Mary, but could hardly lift a spoon or cup anymore, let alone use the commode. It was a most undignified process, this slide into decrepitude.

Charles was lying on his back, wide awake in the middle of the night, his breathing ragged and painful, his mind rampaging uncomfortably through old memories. The nurse came and held his head up to give him a sip of tepid tea. She mopped his brow, squeezed out the cloth and hung it on the bed rail, then settled him back down and returned to the fireside to take up her knitting.

He began to doze. The buzzing rhythm of blood pumping round his body grew louder until it filled his head like the sound of angry waves thumping on a wooden bow. He was on a steamship in the grip of a raging storm, coming home from London to his wife and baby son. Charles tried in vain to hang onto the slippery handrail, terrified he would be washed overboard, but his useless hands could not grip properly. The deck was rocking wildly beneath him, his legs were like jelly and his stomach was roiling with the relentless motion. He leaned over the railing to be sick.

'Sit up, if you can, Mr Mackay. I've a bowl right here for ye.' The nurse hitched him up, her strong hands under his armpits. She held a white enamel bowl beneath his chin and the smell of lye made him retch.

'I've a mind you bin dreamin' for some time, sir, and now you've likely got a fever too.' He heaved into the bowl again, and, not for the first time, saw blood in his vomit.

Charles attempted to thank the nurse with his eyes before sinking back onto his pillow, his heavy eyelids drooping, the cool cloth on his brow lulling him back to sleep.

He was standing in the middle of the stage of the Theatre Royal feeling like a fool. It was a farce, that much he knew, but Charles had forgotten all his lines and was beginning to panic. Suddenly an orange hit him on the arm. There was a scuffle in one of the boxes and another orange came flying his way. He bent to pick them up, then called to the orange-seller with a basket over her arm, not to waste her wares in this madhouse. When she turned towards him it was his mam.

She looked at him with sad eyes.

'There were no oranges, Charlie – I told a wee white lie, for my sins!'

Oranges were flying all around his head now, his grandchildren were throwing them at each other and Chas was shouting: 'It's alright, Grandfather, I'm not very good at juggling.'

Charles had an orange in both his hands but could not find anywhere to put them down. The smell of citrus was overwhelming.

Suddenly the doctor was peering at him, his face far too close, his breath foul.

'I'm sorry to tell you, Mr Mackay, but I have found a growth inside her womb the size of an orange. It's just a matter of time.'

Charles roared and threw the fruit at Murray, who was standing in the middle of the stage in a ridiculous red wig, grinning at someone in the wings. Then Charlotte emerged, in her red gown, stepping onto the stage and smiling her glorious smile when she saw Charles.

'You always said we were two halves of an orange, Charles – and so we are, my dear, so we are. '

THIRTY-EIGHT

Every day for the past week, Lottie had been sitting with her grandfather for hours. She knew he was going to die. Soon. No one had told her, she just knew. Visiting for a few minutes after lunch was no longer enough. It was very important to her that he was not alone when he went to heaven. Lottie had dug in her heels at the weekend, insisting on the importance of her vigil, and Aunty Bella had given in surprisingly quickly.

Her aunt popped her head round the door from time to time to see how they were, to fetch Lottie for meals or tell her it was bedtime; occasionally she insisted Lottie came for a walk, but mostly she let her stay with her grandfather, unless the nurse needed to see to him.

Sometimes Lottie looked at a book, sometimes she embroidered her sampler – which she would now have to give to someone else when it was finished – and sometimes she just talked quietly to him, watching his face carefully for any response.

Occasionally he opened one eye just a flicker, but mostly he seemed to be asleep. Now and then he coughed and could not catch his breath and Lottie had to run and fetch Aunty Bella because she was afraid.

She put her book down and looked at his strong face: his long, straight nose, his grey, bushy eyebrows, his sharp cheekbones. He had a wide, full mouth, too, which had always been able to take on any shape, as though made of rubber. Now his lips were dry and papery and stiff because he was breathing through his mouth: in, out, in, out, each breath rasping and laboured, each pause between breaths a question mark.

All the last drops of energy had seeped out of him in these past few days. Now he just lay there, his chin growing bristly with white whiskers, his pale grey skin speckled with sweat, strands of damp hair stuck to his brow.

Lottie leaned forward to smooth his hair into place, remembering all the times she had watched him comb it back from his high forehead in front of the looking-glass. She took a clean cloth and dipped it in the glass of water at his bedside, squeezed it until it stopped dripping, then carefully dabbed his blistered lips.

'Lottie, dearest,' Aunty Bella had opened the door so quietly Lottie was unaware of her presence until she spoke. She cupped Lottie's chin affectionately with cool fingers and turned her face towards her.

'You don't have to stay with him now he's sleeping, my dear. I'm afraid he won't be waking up again.'

'I know, Aunty Bella. But I would like to stay with him until he has gone to heaven, if that's allowed. I think he wants me to keep him company. He knows I'm brave and not afraid of such things – after all, I'm nearly eleven years old now.'

'Well, if you're quite sure.' Her aunt sounded doubtful but did not forbid it. 'I'll send Mary in with a cup of tea for you, and some cake. Are you warm enough, dearest? I can ask her to build up the fire if you like.'

'I'm quite warm, thank you. I have Grandfather's rug on my knee, and I've been keeping the fire in with a few coals now and then. A cup of tea would be nice, but I'm not hungry, thank you.' Lottie smiled her most winning smile and hoped her aunt would leave soon so she could concentrate on her grandfather's breathing again. She had been imagining each breath as a step along the path and was beginning to worry she would have to run to catch up with him.

The door closed with a gentle click. Lottie blew her nose and wiped her eyes and sat up a little straighter. It was impossible to imagine her life without him in it.

The tea was hot and sweet but Lottie still felt cold. She was wondering whether to add more coals to the fire when his breathing changed. She knelt beside him and held his hand, stroking his feverish brow, whispering in his ear, 'I do believe you are nearly there now, Grandfather. I hope you're not afraid. You'll soon be in heaven with Granny Mackay and Mammy.'

Each shallow gasp had become a mighty, rasping struggle for him. Lottie hardly noticed the tears slipping down her cheeks. All she could think of was breathing with him, as though it might help in some way. When he paused, she paused, wondering if it would be his last breath. When he resumed, so did she. The day had grown dim and only the glowing coals of the fire lit the room. *Please, let no one disturb us now!*

At last, try as he might, he could no longer draw in air. Panic rose in Lottie's chest. She watched him try again and again, his neck straining with futile effort, then a small, surprised sound came from his mouth, his eyes flickered, and he let out a huge sigh.

His head sank back into the pillow.

He was completely still.

Oh! He has gone! Goodbye Grandfather! I shall miss you so terribly!

Lottie slipped her hand carefully out of his and sank back onto her heels. She dared not touch him anymore.

The curtains had been left open and the moon was full, its light creeping slowly across the floor and onto the bed covers.

She watched its progress, transfixed, until its beam was shining directly on his pale, familiar face. How he had loved the lights shining on him when he was on-stage, she thought. How he would have loved this moment.

She was not at all surprised when the door opened and Uncle Charlie came in.

'Look, Uncle, Grandfather is in heaven and the moon is shining on him!'

'Oh Lottie, are you alright, dear child? You've been very brave to stay with him. He would have been so proud of you.' He walked over and put a hand on her shoulder. 'You must come along now, though. Your aunt has drawn a bath for you in the kitchen. Then you must eat some supper by the fire until you are quite warm again.' She looked up at him, then back at her grandfather.

'I'll stay here with my father now, Lottie, don't worry, he won't be alone. The nurse will be here shortly, too. She and Mary will tend to him.'

Uncle Charlie pulled her to her feet and she put her arms around him, partly to steady herself because her legs had grown numb from kneeling, but also because she needed to be held, just for a moment.

Lottie was dressed and ready: hair parted in the middle and pulled back tightly in a low bun; hands clean and smelling of lavender soap; Granny Mackay's embroidered handkerchief safely secreted in her pocket, ready to wipe her tears. The girls had been told to join Chas and Tommy in the nursery, to stay clean and tidy and wait to be called, while Frances and James had been taken to a neighbour's house for the day.

She could hardly bear the idea of waiting in the nursery all morning, so she stood by the door, dithering for a moment, then tiptoed out of the room, through the hall and into the parlour. It was full of chairs and flowers. The smell of the lilies was very strong. It tickled her nose. Every single chair and footstool in the house was in there, placed around the walls. It felt very crowded, even without any people.

Lottie could hear raised voices in the kitchen and decided to go back to the nursery. She fetched a cushion and sat on it by the door, which she left slightly open.

The doorbell rang and Uncle Charlie appeared in the hall. It was Cousin Lauchlan, covered in snow and stamping his feet on the mat. She had met him once before and thought he was nice. He had spoken to her as though she was an interesting person, not just a child, and his warm, deep voice was full of the sound of smiling.

Almost immediately the door opened again and in came Aunty Bella's sisters – Aunty Maggie and Aunty Jane – and her two youngest brothers, who were almost men now. Then Aunt Margaret Shiels arrived with her new gentleman friend.

The hall stand was covered in dripping coats and cloaks by now. Lottie watched a puddle forming on the wooden floor and spreading onto the Turkey carpet and wondered if someone would mop it.

It must be quite crowded in the parlour now.

Cousin Lauchlan came out of her grandfather's room, wiping his eyes with a dark handkerchief and holding the door open for Aunt Margaret to go inside.

Then Mr and Mrs Wyndham arrived. Lottie had been taking singing lessons with Mrs Wyndham recently, as well as continuing her dancing lessons even though Jane had given them up. Lottie liked her very much. Mr Wyndham shook Uncle Charlie's hand and clapped him on the shoulder.

'He was a great man, Charlie, a true original. We shan't see his like again, I'm afraid. He will be sorely missed.'

Uncle Charlie nodded politely, but Mr Wyndham had not finished.

'On the quiet, Charlie, I've been warned by a friend in the Edinburgh Council they're going to slap a compulsory purchase order on the Theatre Royal fairly soon. Word is they plan to knock it down and build a grand new Post Office.' Lottie gave a little gasp and covered her mouth quickly. 'What d'you make of that, eh? End of an era in more ways than one! Good job my new theatre is nearly built, let's hope this one doesn't burn down like the last two! Ha!' Mr Wyndham gave Uncle Charlie back his hand and followed his wife into the crowded parlour.

The Theatre Royal was going to be knocked down! Grandfather would have been horrified! Perhaps it was for the best that he never knew.

The front door had been left open and Lottie could hear Aunty Dorothy huffing and puffing up the stairs. When she arrived in the front hall, leaning on her walking stick and hanging onto Izzie's arm, it was all Lottie could do not to run out and hug them both.

'Come here and gie yer old aunty a wee hug, Charlie. I've missed you sorely, so I have! Why d'ye never visit wi' me like yer brother does when he's in Auld Reekie?'

Uncle Hector visits Aunty Dorothy! Where is he, anyway? He should be here by now.

All was quiet for a few minutes, then the minister arrived and Aunty Bella came to fetch the children to come and join the visitors.

After the service there was a crush in the hallway while everyone looked for their coats and cloaks and pulled on their gloves and muffs and scarves, the ladies jostling for a look in the looking-glass to tie on their bonnets.

Lottie followed her aunt and cousins down the dim stairwell and out into the bright snowy white of the cold November morning, where a line of black carriages were parked all along the side of the road.

Uncle Charlie called out to everyone, waving his arms, 'There should be enough seats for you all. I thought it best we go by carriage – it's quite a step to the Calton Hill burial ground from here, and what with the snow …'

Uncle Charlie and Cousin Lauchlan climbed into the first carriage with the minister, Aunty Bella's two brothers, Mr Wyndham and a man Lottie had never seen before. She could see through the glass sides of the second carriage that Grandfather's black coffin was already inside it. It looked beautiful with all the flowers piled around it. The black paintwork of the carriage was covered in fancy silver and gold decorations, too. *Grandfather would have loved it!*

Lottie, Jane and Chas climbed into the third carriage with Aunty Bella and Aunt Margaret, who had to squash their hooped skirts rather comically in order to fit through the little door. Then the solemn procession clattered slowly down the road and across the North Bridge, turning into Regent Road, and coming to a halt just beyond the Theatre Royal.

Aunty Bella and Aunt Margaret were handed out onto the icy road by the coachman and Lottie, Jane, Chas and Tommy followed them gingerly. The road was very slippery. A man in a red military uniform was playing a drum that hung around his neck, and another military man was playing a merry tune on a little flute.

The musicians stood nearby while Uncle Charlie and the other men in his carriage hitched the heavy coffin onto their shoulders. Everyone else formed a procession behind them and the musicians led them slowly towards a great stone doorway in the high cemetery wall.

Uncle Hector suddenly appeared, all dapper and dressed in black, and strolled up to the front, where he nudged the youngest Winter boy out of the way and put his shoulder under the coffin behind Uncle Charlie. The boy ran to join his sisters, shrugging his shoulders, and Lottie wondered where Uncle Hector had been all this time.

She looked round to see if anyone else had joined their

procession and saw dozens of black-clad people walking towards them from Princes Street and Leith Street, some of them carrying flowers. A group of women, hurrying along together with large black feathers in their hats, heads bent against the cold, caught her eye. Lottie thought they looked like a flock of fluttering crows, their cloaks and shawls flapping in the wind like wings. It was exactly the sort of thing her grandfather would have whispered in her ear to make her chuckle.

Laughing would be absolutely the worst thing in the world, though. Everyone would think she hardly cared about her grandfather, yet it was precisely because she *did* care about him, and loved him very much, that she had such a terrible urge to giggle. She concentrated on the progress of her black-booted feet on the icy cobbles and dug her nails into the palms of her hands through the thin cotton of her gloves.

The procession came to a halt halfway up the hill, by a deep hole in the ground. Lottie knew about burials, but this was the first time she had seen an open grave. It was very deep. Panic assaulted her like a sharp smell. The idea of her grandfather being lowered into the cold, dark earth and having suffocating soil shovelled over him was too awful to imagine.

She closed her eyes and blocked out the sounds of the straining men as they let the coffin down on its red silk ropes, thinking instead of his smiling face, his warm hand squeezing hers as they walked along together.

When everyone began to sing Lottie looked up at the wide white sky. Voices were dipping and diving and soaring all around her in the cold, clear air, like a huge flock of birds. She pulled in a deep, icy breath and poured her voice out to join them, loud and sweet and strong.

Author's Note

I came across Charles Mackay when reading through my mother's family tree research in 2015. The following is an extract from a letter I found from her cousin, dated 1992.

Aunt Evelyn offhand remembers a story about a Charles MacKay, an actor. Apparently, there was a successful stage adaptation of Scott's novel 'Rob Roy'. It made a great hit in Edinburgh because of the performance of Charles MacKay. One evening he could not appear, and the capacity audience was so incensed that it put up a mighty roar of 'it's no the real Mackay!' This gave rise to the phrase.

I was fascinated and wanted to know more, but no one in the family had managed to work out how, exactly, he was related to us, or even which generation he was. So, I began my own research and, with the help of some other genealogists in the family, discovered he was my five-times great-uncle.

I didn't stop there. The more I researched his life the more information I found – hundreds of anecdotes, speeches, articles, documents and references. I began to wonder if I should write a book. Charles Mackay had been such a famous comedian in his time, so loved by the whole of Scotland and beyond for decades, yet he had been completely forgotten.

I began to sew my collected fragments into a story with the threads of my imagination, collecting more fascinating scraps as I went along. All the events described are based on research, all the quoted speeches, reviews and articles are real, while social interactions, emotions and motivations are mostly imagined. All the named people were real, except for Dorothy the maid and Cromby the barber. Izzie was real, but I've imagined a different life for her.

One of the most exciting discoveries I made was that the portrait on the front cover of this book was bought by my great-great-great-grandfather, Lauchlan Mackay. One of his daughters was my granny's granny, and she used to tell the story to her grandchildren with great enthusiasm. When I found out she had grown up with his portrait hanging in her home, and as a child may even have seen him act, it made sense of her passion to keep his story alive, and our connection to him as well.

I hope I have done justice to The Real Mackay with my storytelling, and would be delighted if this book went some way towards reinstating him as the national treasure he truly was.

Acknowledgements

I set out to write the story of my five-times great-uncle about seven years ago, embarking on the task with great optimism and very little idea of how I would achieve it. It has been quite a journey, and I want to thank all the people who have helped me – both those I met along the way and those I already knew. I could not have done it without them. Needless to say, all mistakes are mine.

The first to lend me their sharp minds were my incredible genealogist relatives, Christine, Alison and Nick, who all made invaluable contributions with their research and early reading of the manuscript. Military historian, Eamonn O'Keeffe, gave me some very helpful feedback and new information after reading the chapter on Charles Mackay's experience in the Argyll militia. I'm so grateful to them all. Others to thank for kindly reading early versions and sharing their thoughts are my daughter, Lizzie, and my aunt, Diana. I also want to thank Allan, a member of the Edinburgh Sir Walter Scott Club, who went through the manuscript particularly thoroughly and gave me hundreds of thoughtful insights, and my daughter, Anna who stayed the course and read three different versions – giving me so much encouragement and astute feedback every time. Thanks, too, to fellow authors Jon, Robyn and Kate from Jericho Writers for taking the time to give helpful feedback to someone they'd never met. Last but not least, huge thanks to my husband and son, Addy and Jamie, who both listened to endless chattering about different aspects of the story as it developed and wisely decided to wait for the published version before reading it.

I also want to thank everyone who helped me with my research. Their willingness to answer questions and send me information was fantastic: Zoe Gruber, Paul Quast, Julie Lawson, Alejandro Basterrechea and Jacqueline Austin, National Portrait Gallery; Tom Barclay, Carnegie Library, Ayr; Philippa Cardy, Catriona Perry and Fiona M. Neale, University of Glasgow Library; Mazie Bowen, University of Georgia Special Collections Libraries; Dr Colin McIlroy, Curator Archives & Manuscript Collections, National Library of Scotland; Kirsty Archer-Thompson, Collections and Interpretation Manager at Abbotsford; Matthew Lloyd, Arthur Lloyd website; Eric Melvin, historian, Edinburgh.

Huge thanks also go to editor Clare Coombes, who gave the manuscript such a thorough overhaul at an early stage of development with her in-depth assessment, and gave me the confidence and inspiration to rewrite the whole thing again in a new way, more than once! Massive thanks too, to editor Helen Bleck for her careful, detailed copyediting, her perceptive observations and encouragement, for making me feel safe by noticing so many little errors, and for helping me get the final draft of the book ready to pull over the line. Becca Westwood has been lovely to work with on ideas for the cover, as were designers Chloe Messinger and Chelsea Taylor. Finally, many thanks to Holly Porter and rest of the team at Troubador Publishing for helping to make this book a reality.

Selected Bibliography

Baird, George, *Edinburgh Theatres, Cinemas and Circuses 1820–1965*

Baynham, Walter, *The Glasgow Stage*

Brown, Ian, *Edinburgh Companion to Scottish Drama*

Dibdin, James C., *The Annals of the Edinburgh Stage, with an account of the rise and progress of dramatic writing in Scotland*

Fairbairn, Charlotte, *The Real Mackays*

Grant, James, *Cassell's Old and New Edinburgh*

Hamilton-Dalrymple, Hew, *Records of the Ayrshire Militia from 1802 to 1883*

Huie, James L., *Edinburgh Dramatic Review, vols 1–9*

Lawson, Robb, *The Story of the Scots Stage*

Leach, Robert, *An Illustrated History of British Theatre and Performance*

Lockhart, John Gibson, *Memoirs of the Life of Sir Walter Scott, Bart.*

Morris, James, *Recollections of Ayr Theatricals from 1809*

Mudie, Robert, *A Historical Account of His Majesty's Visit to Scotland*

O'Keeffe, John, *Recollections of the Life of John O' Keeffe, vol 1*
Pocock, Isaac, *Rob Roy MacGregor, or Auld Land Syne! A Musical drama, in three acts. Founded on the popular novel of 'Rob Roy'*
Rigney, Ann, *The Afterlives of Walter Scott: Memory on the Move*
Scobie, Captain I. H. Mackay, *An Old Highland Fencible Corps: The History of the Reay Fencible Highland Regiment of Foot, or Mackay's Highlanders, 1794–1802. With an account of its services in Ireland during the rebellion of 1798*
Whitelaw, Alexander, *The Book of Scottish Song*